Praise for

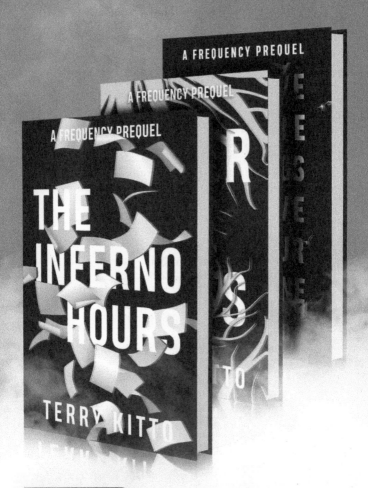

TERRY KITTO

I witness you!

T. Kitto

THE
FREQUENCY
THE IMPRINT QUINTET: BOOK ONE

PENNARD PRESS

Published by Pennard Press
www.pennardpress.co.uk

First published by Pennard Press in 2021.
Copyright © Terry Kitto, 2021.

Third Edition

Edited by Natalia Leigh of Enchanted Ink Publishing.
Proofread by Meredith Spears of Enchanted Ink Publishing.

Cover design and interior formatting by Pennard Press.

A CIP catalogue record for this book is available from the British Library.

Paperback ISBN: 978-1-8381815-0-5
eBook ISBN: 978-1-8381815-1-2

www.terrykitto.com

Reader Discretion Advised
*This work contains sensitive material not lt for all readers, including
depictions of murder, abuse, racism and homophobia. Please visit
www. terrykitto.com/the-frequency for sensitivity guidelines.*

Edith, Thomas, Eileen and Leonard.
Unconditionally, eternally.

Holly,
Faithful critique partner.

PART ONE

KEEP THE
LIGHTS ON

1

THE SHADOW WAS COMING.

Fifteen-year-old Rasha Abadi lay slumped against her headboard, the hem of her duvet clamped in her fists. She dreaded the shadow's return. For six nights it had come to poison her mind.

Rasha squinted through the nickel moonlight and scoured her bedroom for a sign of its arrival. It was the smallest room in caravan forty-five, and half-mended Oxfam charity electronics littered every available surface. Her clothes dryer aired the previous day's laundry beside her secondhand desk, which bowed under the weight of school textbooks she'd eagerly consumed. That was where the shadow would appear, just as it had every night the past week.

Her digital alarm clock on her bedside table blinked: 2:03 a.m.

It was time, again.

In the corner, tendrils of viscous darkness coiled into a silhouette not quite animal, not entirely human: a malformed head, a barrel chest, misshapen limbs, and a pinched stomach. It was black – an unearthly deep void unlike anything Rasha

1

had ever seen. The dark was hues of purple and brown in comparison.

The impossible shadow.

Rasha clamped her eyes shut, wishing it away – the shadow sometimes disappeared if she did. Only, with her eyes closed, she was plagued by memories of Syria.

Her bedroom's plasterboard walls crumbled, and in their place came rubble, fire, and ash: the remains of her family's apartment. Explosions shook the ground, screams filled her ears, and guilt gouged at her intestines. She reminded herself that she was in Cornwall – three thousand miles from her home city of Homs – and that she'd fled Syria four years earlier, even though her stomach knotted and her heart pounded as if it were happening at that very moment.

You're fine, she thought to herself, opening her eyes to the shadow. *It's just PTSD, that's what Dr Hewitt said. You're with Mum in Gorenn Holiday Park.*

The shadow grew so tall its waxen head would soon scrape the ceiling. It couldn't have been her PTSD; her mind only conjured Syria's decimation and their haphazard journey to Britain. Until that week, she'd never come across anything like it before. It was a shadow and so didn't have a body. If it only had a mind, then there was one thing it could be.

A ghost.

In their culture, they didn't have ghosts, for spirits didn't stay on Earth. The closest to that nature were demons called Shaytan, creatures with malicious intent.

Could that be it? Rasha asked herself. *Did she come back as a Shaytan to punish me?*

Rasha called her sister's name. 'Milana?'

The shadow stepped forward, and its chest heaved.

Rasha collapsed onto her bed, too scared to cry. Sweat

glued her untamable black hair to her face. The shadow didn't move closer; it didn't scream with agony or demand Rasha to atone. It did something impossibly worse: it stood rigidly and silently condemned her for what she had done.

'I'm sorry,' Rasha cried. 'I'm so sorry.'

Rasha wept and apologised, slumped against her headboard, as her mind plunged into memories of scorching fires, singed flesh and bloodcurdling cries.

2

A PANICKED SHRIEK.

Rasha sat upright in bed. The shadow was gone, and the room was awash with tepid morning light. Another cry. A flurry of white rushed past the window. Beating wings carried on the air. It was just a seagull telling the world to wake.

She put her head between her knees so that her racing heart would still. *Just a seagull . . . Just a seagull . . .*

Through the gap in her arms, her alarm clock read 6:20 a.m. Rasha wasn't too sure if she'd slept or fainted. Her adrenaline had waned, and in the shadow's presence she'd slipped into memories of Syria. Or were they nightmares? It was hard to distinguish the two. She dared not deliberate; it'd only induce another anxiety attack.

Her alarm clock blared at 6:30 a.m. Time to wake Haya. Since their family had been reduced to two, Haya had suffered extreme bouts of physically debilitating depression. It took her a long time to get going in the morning and longer still without Rasha's support.

She raised herself from bed. Her arms were weak, her chest ached — the aftereffects of another panic attack. A nettlelike sting smothered her body, as it always did when she encountered the shadow.

Rasha left her bedroom for the kitchen, her every other thought plagued by the shadow. She mulled between cupboard and sink to brew a green tea. *Its warped, melted body.* Own-brand bread sizzled beneath the grill. *Singed flesh.* The kettle whistled to a steady boil. *Milana, crumpled beneath rubble.*

Stop it, she thought.

Rasha grabbed a foil sertraline packet from the top shelf and poured a glass of water, assembled a bed tray, and moped to Haya's room. Rasha's mother was awake when she entered – it was unlikely she'd slept. Her face was gaunt, as to be expected for someone who had to be prompted to eat. Her thick black hair was neglected and speckled grey. Rasha lowered the tray onto her mother's side table and climbed into the bed beside her. Haya raised two heavy arms and cradled Rasha, who traced purple scars on her mother's arm with her hand. Haya had gained those marks by saving Rasha's life.

Only she and Haya had survived the explosion that fateful night in Homs. Haya had pulled her from the wreckage and burned her left forearm in a fire that shrouded the debris. Her father's and sister's bloodied remains eradicated all thought so Rasha remembered little of the following journey. They'd been crammed amongst crates in the back of a truck, hidden in a waterside town house in Calais, and sandwiched amongst other desperate asylum seekers in a shipping container. British border patrollers had cracked open the container and escorted them to a detention centre in Gatwick. Three months, two key workers, and an appeal later, they were granted 'leave to remain' and relocated to the village of Gorenn in South Cornwall. Since then, the duo had lived in a routine that Rasha tirelessly maintained to try to find some sort of normality.

'It's that time already?' Haya asked in Levantine, their mother tongue.

Their Syrian friends had often mused how Haya's daughters were mirror images of her, so when she looked at Rasha's plump face, warm beige skin, and wide green eyes with adoration and sadness, Rasha wondered whether she was a constant reminder of Milana.

She deliberated telling her mother about the shadow, but Haya barely had enough capacity for what was real.

'I don't know if I can do it today,' Haya uttered.

'It's a short day,' Rasha assured. 'Mr Keats said one deep clean, three stays. You'll be done by eleven. Then you can go back to bed.'

'There's laundry to do.'

'I've done it. Take your pill, drink your tea, and I'll get the sink ready.'

Rasha planted a kiss on Haya's forehead and left the bedroom. She arranged Haya's work clothes on the bathroom flasket and filled the sink with hot water. Haya held on for as long as she could before she rose to wash; the water would be at the perfect temperature by the time she did.

Rasha changed and avoided the corner where the shadow had been. Within twenty minutes she was in her patched school uniform, sat at the dining room table, munching on a pack of chocolate bourbon creams to suppress her appetite. Glucose, the perfect fuel for the sleep-deprived.

For someone haunted by shadows.

Haya stifled a yawn as she entered, acrylic tabard on, hair wound in a tight bun. With her was the cup of tea and plate of toast, which hadn't been touched. Haya was a far cry from the woman Rasha remembered in pre-war Syria when she'd worked as paralegal's secretary. Rasha supposed that Middle

Eastern qualifications meant nothing when she wasn't legally allowed to work under 'leave to remain.' It was why Rasha had begged the site owner, Mr Keats, to allow her mother to do cash-in-hand work – she craved a purpose as much as they needed the money.

Haya tutted playfully and offered her hand. Rasha reluctantly gave her the packet of bourbons.

'All this sugar,' Haya moaned. 'Your insides will rot, never mind your teeth.'

'Yes, Mama.'

'No sweets before lunch, you hear me?'

'No sweets before lunch.'

It was time for Rasha to leave, after all. She had four miles of country lanes to walk. She rose and hugged Haya.

'If I have to eat savoury, you have to eat *something*.'

Haya nodded.

'I promise,' she whispered.

'Unconditionally,' Rasha said.

'Unconditionally.'

Rasha squeezed her tightly, then donned her rucksack and stepped into the spearmint morning. She faltered on the bottom step and wrung the straps of her bag. She contemplated every lesson sat quietly, hoping to be left alone by teacher and student, every solitary break time spent in an empty classroom or toilet cubicle.

Get through it, she told herself. *Get through it and get back to the caravan.*

Not that solace was found during evenings spent in forty-five, the place she was meant to call home.

She took a deep breath and trudged on. Gorenn Holiday Park was compiled of caravans each within their own fenced ten-by-twenty-metre paddock, all arranged alongside a clean gravel path. Mr Keats's caravan was at the heart of the holiday rentals, adjacent to the maintenance shed and activities lodge. His family consisted of seven obese tabby cats that milled within their fenced enclosure. Rasha stopped a moment to itch one of their chins, taking in the sea as it frothed and rolled beyond the caravans, letting the cool salt air course through her nostrils and ease her lungs.

' 'ere, Rasha,' came Mr Keats's voice. 'What do you know about cats?'

The site manager, a thin man with a whisker-clad face and beady eyes, looked like an inquisitive otter walking on its hind legs. The morning wind threatened to rush under his bathrobe and Monroe him.

'They like fish, hate belly rubs,' she replied.

'They like fish.' He laughed. 'Well, 'parently mine dunt. They haven't touched a thing since yesterday. Gonna 'ave to take 'em to the vets, ain't I?'

'Best be on the safe side,' Rasha said. She nuzzled the head of an obese tabby.

'Speakin' of which, keep an eye out on yer walk. There's been some wrong un's loitering around here at night.'

'People?' Rasha returned. She always struggled with Mr Keats's thick accent.

'They ain't guests, I know that much. Probably lookin' to pinch gas bottles, so keep yer eyes peeled. Tell your mother, too.'

'Sure. See ya.'

School started in an hour, so Rasha continued on. Shadows at night, strange people who wandered the caravan site by day. Rasha's anxious mind couldn't help but put the two together. For a moment she deliberated taking the school bus but decided against it. She hadn't taken the school bus in months

– crammed into a metal box with no escape from bullies was far from appetising. Into the bending valley lanes Rasha went until the caravan park was a blip behind her. Despite the long walk in all varieties of Cornish weather, she enjoyed the momentary freedom from the concrete and plaster that caged her very existence, where benign livestock plodded along in the fields beside her.

Escaping her thoughts was another matter. The shadow plagued her mind. She didn't believe for a second that she'd imagined it. Its fathomless depths of black had absorbed all light in the room, whilst its silhouette could have been the decomposed carcass of an unearthly beast. Her imagination could not conjure such an image.

Not that it mattered. Rasha thought too much, and her lungs welded themselves to her diaphragm in anxiety's havoc.

Her neck prickled, just as it had when the shadow appeared.

Not here, not now. She circled, but the grassy verges either side of her were empty.

Could it be the shadow? No, the shade around her belonged to trees and power lines. Nothing unordinary in the lane. But in the neighbouring field, there was.

Over the hedge to her left, across the pasture by a dilapidated cow shed, Rasha spotted three figures. Hoods hid their faces. A woman and two men. The shortest man consulted a gadget in his hands. Mr Keats had spoken of strange people who skulked around the area. What's more, they looked straight her way. What else was there to see in the valley but fields and cattle?

They watched her.

Rasha ran as fast as her legs would carry her and never looked back.

3

A STAMPEDE OF STUDENTS thundered down Gorenn Comprehensive's poky corridors. Rasha dodged them as she went and glanced thrice at every turn. She couldn't be sure if the hooded people had followed her to school. What if they were people she already knew? Either way, she'd come to the conclusion that the shadow and the people were more than a coincidence.

Her train of thought was cut off as she thrust herself into dusty workshop 2B where her cohort chanted, 'Joel Tredethy tripped and broke his neck. Don't be weird or you'll be next.'

Rasha took a seat on the far back bench in the workshop, one that rendered her invisible amongst her peers. Mr Cridland, their gentle giant of a woodworks teacher, did all he could do to quell the teenagers' chorus. The song, as Rasha had learnt days into her start at Gorenn Comprehensive, was about a boy who tripped down a flight of stairs and snapped his neck in the nineties. Since then it had been used to ridicule unpopular classmates – people as strange or meek as Joel Tredethy had been. This day it was aimed at a boy named Gregory Dingle. An overweight and delicate kid, Gregory was hunched in his seat, his shrunken sports kit stretched across his rotund body. Their classmates ridiculed him whilst he looked at his bench, crimson face moments from tears. Girls to Rasha's right whispered that the class clown, Fred Parsons, had drenched Gregory's uniform in Lucozade, and he'd no choice but to wear his kit for the rest of the day.

Of course it was Fred Parsons, Rasha thought. Fred, his square face more acne than skin, perched on Gregory's bench and egged his peers on to guffaw at poor Gregory. He'd bullied Rasha too, in the first week she attended Gorenn. A brown-skinned girl who lived in a caravan with flawed English and an awkward disposition – how could he resist? A series of detentions waned his focus on Rasha, or perhaps he had gotten bored of her. She resisted the urge to retaliate and punch his pickled face, for she dared not bring trouble to her mother's door. Haya already had enough to contend with, as did Rasha; she had the shadow.

Rasha got out her portfolio and pencil case and pretended to busy herself with her work until Mr Cridland got the class to simmer. A man in his early sixties, he had taught in the school – in that department, in that very workshop – for nearly forty years. It showed. He spoke with a quiet monotone voice and often let an outdated PowerPoint guide the kids through projects with equipment the school no longer owned rather than lead the lesson himself. Rasha couldn't blame him; aside from her, none of her classmates showed the slightest bit of enthusiasm for design and technology. As Haya often used to recite, you can only lead a horse to water.

With the class settled into a hubbub of fervent gossip, social media, and coursework, Rasha slid from her bench and meandered to Cridland's desk with his fineliners in hand. He had let her borrow them to add to her portfolio, which

11

according to him was pointless because a quick assessment had her a predicted A* for the module. Nevertheless, Rasha wouldn't let it go if just one illustration wasn't rendered perfectly, and he had softened to Rasha because of that.

'You've even organised them by colour,' he exclaimed with an affectionate smirk. She passed them back to him with profuse thanks.

'It's quicker working warm to cool,' Rasha said.

Rasha was heading to the equipment cupboard right of Cridland's desk when someone called, 'Arse licker!'

She forgot herself and turned to the heckler; it was Fred, worst luck. His group of friends cackled, all eyes mean, hungry for a reaction.

She hung her head and hurried on.

'Joel Tredethy tripped and broke his neck . . .'

Rebel militia shouted from Homs's streets.

Chairs scraped, an outlandish bang.

The world upturned. Walls crumbled.

Rasha turned back. Gregory had thrown himself off his chair and dove at Fred, and they brawled. Their cohort egged them on whilst Cridland scrambled to get between them. There was no missile and no explosion, but it didn't matter.

Something was coming.

Breathe. Rasha's lungs could have been squeezed between a vice. She patted her trouser pockets for her inhaler, but it was in her bag, and a sea of brawling children lay between her and it.

Fluid swamped her lungs and windpipe. She bolted to the vacant store cupboard, doubled over, and retched. The brown sludge from her breakfast bourbons didn't come.

Clotted blood slopped out onto the floor.

Cobwebby static crawled along her skin, and a pressure

rippled through her cranium. She was no longer alone in the cupboard.

In the doorway was a boy – or something that had been once. His body was twisted, he walked on snapped shins, and his dainty arms flopped at right angles. Blood dribbled from his crooked mouth, frozen somewhere between a smile and a grimace. There was no doubt in her mind who he was: the boy whose name was used to taunt kids just like him.

Joel Tredethy.

Breathe.

The shadow, now Joel. It was confirmed: she was plagued by the dead.

Her lungs grew tighter, and the room spun around her.

4

RASHA FLED FROM THE WORKSHOP, sprinted across the Key Stage 3 playground, and locked herself in a toilet cubicle in the girls' bathroom. Her limbs shook, and her heart pounded, and in no time at all the bell chimed for morning break. Two periods had passed. Two hours of time, sat on a toilet seat lid, lost in anxiety's whirlwind.

Lost in thoughts of Joel Tredethy's pearly eyes and disjointed limbs.

She traced carvings on the cubicle wall with her hand. Love hearts declared fleeting romances. Petty playground propaganda stirred school gossip. The impermanent history of such little lives that existed between annual redecoration. What she would give to have an ordinary life, where her biggest worries were boys and grades and social media likes. She had all that and the dead too.

Joel Tredethy. The shadow.

The deceased, unresting.

Her mother once said, back when Haya had an optimistic outlook, 'You can only miss what you once had.'

Rasha couldn't disagree more. She missed a reality where

she wasn't riddled with PTSD and wished she wasn't in Cornwall, a place that could never be her home. Rasha longed to not turn to social invisibility as a coping mechanism, to only see those who were alive.

Ghosts, Rasha brought herself to think. *Call them by what they are; they are ghosts.* She was sure they were not a new symptom of PTSD. With PTSD, she only ever saw her deceased family as they lay in their final moments in the dust and rubble. The shadow and Joel Tredethy filled the space in which they appeared with a sense of being – an aura that they thought and felt independently. One came from her mind, and one did not. But she knew there was a way to confirm it.

In recent years, Gorenn Comprehensive – with its plummeting Ofsted results and poor reputation – had attempted to curry favour with the local community. From charity fundraisers to care home Christmas carolling – during all of which Rasha had found herself front and centre at all photo opportunities – their activities also included a public archive of all class photos way back from when the school first opened in the fifties. She was certain she had never seen a photo of Joel Tredethy before, so if she laid eyes on his face, she could determine if the boy was a figment of her imagination or was truly a ghost.

The bell chimed again. What was third period? IT with the stammering Mrs Stevens. Rasha crept from the toilet cubicle and did a round trip to Mr Cridland's vacant workshop. It wasn't the first time she'd fled with an anxiety attack, and – as he'd done countless times – Cridland had collected her bag and stowed it safely beneath his desk. She arrived in Mrs Stevens's computer suite in good time as the class unpacked their things. Rasha took to the corner, sitting behind a flip chart easel where she would go unnoticed. The computer blinked to life.

Logged in, Rasha navigated the school's website and located the archives, often swapping between windows as Mrs Stevens did her usual rounds of the classroom to confiscate students' smartphones. Eventually she found a list of each form group from every academic year. Halfway down the class register of 1996, she came across Joel Tredethy's name.

Front row, fourth from the left, the description read.

Sure enough, there Joel was, sat cross-legged on the gymnasium floor of the sun-washed photograph. Minus the milky eyes and shattered limbs, he was identical to his ghost in the DT workshop that morning: dark cowlicked hair, button nose, smile sucked in from an overbite. He had not been a figment of her imagination.

Unmistakably Joel, undeniably dead.

Anxiety froze her body.

Breathe. Her lungs became taut elastic bands.

Breathe. Fluid rose up her throat.

Breathe. Metallic blood oozed across her tongue.

The room chilled, but no one seemed to notice; her class watched the whiteboard with varied degrees of interest whilst Mrs Stevens marked their homework.

They didn't see Joel Tredethy's face amongst the flood of numbers.

He emerged from the wall as if it were a torrent of steam, his bright unblinking eyes fixed solely on Rasha. Blood foamed from his mouth and oozed across the whiteboard.

Bag in hand, Rasha kicked her chair back, stumbled between the rows of the computers, and raced outside.

5

RASHA TRUDGED THE FOOTPATH through Ratcliff Farm to shorten her journey home. Lack of sleep and nutrition had finally caught up with her; she may as well have waded through half-set cement. Pins and needles clawed her skin, so she knew the dead were nearby. Returning to the caravan had no appeal if the shadow might plague her again that night; any concept of another day at school was unbearable if Joel Tredethy chased her.

Caught between a ghost and a haunted place, she thought bitterly.

She'd eventually strayed from the footpath, for it ran snugly against the hedge. Instead she kept to the centre of the field so she'd be able to see the hooded people before they found her.

Beyond the wind's whistle came a motorised whir. An oblong shadow passed overhead – a drone, fifteen feet above ground. Various copper plates were fused across its belly, and multiple camera lenses glinted in the weak afternoon sunlight. One hooded figure from that morning had held a handset.

You're overthinking it, Rasha thought. The coastline was prone to aerial photographers, with the churning sea and

Wheal Gorenn Mine's engine chimney in the distance. She stood still to wait for the drone to pass on, thumbs squeezed between her fists, breath monitored.

The chuff of military helicopters swooping toward Homs.

The drone didn't leave. It hovered over Rasha, idling against the wind like a kestrel.

She was tired, oh Allah, was she tired of fending off monsters day and night, from one continent to the next. When would it end?

'Just leave me alone!' she roared.

She'd never outrun the drone. Stones were at the base of a crumbled hedge to her left. She darted over, grabbed one, took aim, and lunged. It scuffed the drone's underside. The machine wobbled. Realigned. She snatched up another rock as the drone turned, steadied her arm, and threw. It smacked a propeller. Sparks and smoke spat from its side. The craft veered into the sludge.

Rasha traipsed closer. Her frantic eyes sought clues as to who the hooded figures were. A serial number was printed on the drone's shell: *I-A-N-2493*. Beneath it was a symbol comprised of two interlocking circles.

The hooded people would come for the broken drone – Rasha couldn't fight off three grown adults. She scarpered through the mud, eyes fixed on the caravan site as it grew near.

She barged into her living area and slammed the door, forehead pressed against the cold glass, relieved to be inside.

'Rasha?' Haya called.

Her mother swanned into the kitchen, out of her work tabard and freshly washed.

Blood on her pallet. Joel Tredethy's twisted neck.

Panic must have shown on Rasha's face, for Haya squeezed her tightly. Beneath the Dove soap was the tang of bleach.

Despite that, Haya's hugs made her lighter.

'You're safe here, home with me,' Haya whispered.

Rasha wished she could tell her mother but knew it would do no good. With news of the shadow, Haya would charge her to a GP at dawn. The government would be less inclined to keep a refugee if she was declared medically insane. 'Leave to remain' only granted them a five-year citizenship, which would then have to be reviewed. They had to be no bother. The country – heck, even the caravan – was Haya's last chance of security. Rasha couldn't spoil that.

'You're covered in mud,' Haya mused. 'Was school too much?'

'Mm-hmm.' Rasha could only mumble in response.

'You'd better change,' Haya said. 'Before it gets all over the carpet.'

Rasha nodded, traipsed to her bedroom, and ignored the corner in which the shadow had materialised the night before.

Just in case.

She snatched some clothes from her Red Cross wardrobe and skulked to the utility cupboard. The Abadis couldn't afford to use the washing machine daily, so as the day transpired into evening, Rasha scrubbed her shoes and uniform with an old Brillo Pad found in Haya's cleaning basket. Once she'd had dinner and a quick lukewarm shower, it was nine o' clock.

Bedtime.

Rasha hugged Haya for as long as she could.

'Stop creeping, Ash,' her mother teased. 'I'm not mad. Take care of your things; we can't afford more. Unconditionally, remember?'

Little did Haya know that Rasha didn't creep. She took in her fill. She never knew if that night would be her last. It was a goodbye embrace.

'Unconditionally.'

As they departed the hug, Rasha studied Haya: the leaf-green eyes, just as hers, and the wrinkles that formed grief-stricken canyons around her eyes and mouth, which were the signature of the demons that Haya carried herself. She could barely confront the living, let alone the dead. Rasha would have to face it alone.

Rasha plodded to the bedroom. Her clammy hands grappled with the door handle. She didn't turn her lights on. What use was it when the shadow was more than the darkness? Her heart kicked inside her chest. She dove under the covers and wrenched the duvet to her chin.

Her exhausted body ached as if her very bones had been whittled from the inside out. Somewhere within her, deeper still, was her very own ghost, was it not? Perhaps that was what the shadow wanted – to strip her spirit away and take her body for itself. The Shaytan were known to possess people. If it was Milana, deep inside the empty void, then perhaps all she wanted was to take Rasha's place. After all, it was Rasha who should have died.

Silence.

Pure, unadulterated quiet. Rasha propped herself up on her elbows. Ears to the air, she hunted for her mother's snores, a seagull breaking into a neighbour's bin, even Mr Keats's TV turned to max volume in the caravan over. Not a sound but her rapid breath.

Static drummed on her skin like electric rain. She knew that past her ply wardrobe and the window with the broken curtain rail, the shadow would be in the far corner.

Come on then, she thought. Somewhere deep inside, she knew it heard her. *If you're going to kill me, get it over with.*

The impossible shadow unravelled in the corner.

Little Milana's body pulverised beneath stone.

Rasha buried herself beneath her sheets. Her heart kicked, and the shadow's chest expanded. Sweat saturated the mattress beneath her. The shadow's limbs lengthened and refined.

That's it, she thought. *It's eating my fear.* The quicker her pulse and the shakier her limbs, the larger it grew and the darker it became.

So Rasha forced her mind to other places – to happier times. Such memories never came easily for her, and they didn't that night.

Instead, she recalled her father in their Syrian living room. He'd yelled at her whilst Haya comforted young tearful Milana. Rasha had torn a letter to shreds, one that a neighbour's boy had given Milana before they'd fled the country. She'd been jealous – not that she'd have cared to admit it – but her father had seen right through that, as he'd had a knack of doing, and lectured her, saying, 'There's already a war outside. You'd do better than to bring it into our home.'

The darkness suffocated her. She needed light. Rasha punched her lamp's switch. The bulb managed a yellow flicker, then blew inside the shade. With stone-cold irony, a tongue of silver lightning licked the window. Rain pelted the roof –

Bullets shredded concrete.

The shadow's energy – a prickling static – washed over Rasha like the tide swallows the beach.

Her father, disembowelled and singed.

She couldn't move her body. This was not anxiety's doing. It was as if her nerves were wires in a parallel circuit.

Her vision shrunk as if binoculars had been pulled from her face. Absolute darkness pressed against her eyeballs.

Her heart beat to a new rhythm, and her lungs inhaled to a different pattern.

The shadow stole her body. Rasha was a stringless kite caught in a ferocious wind.

If I let go, she thought, *I will be a ghost too.*

At that very thought, she plummeted into depths of complete and utter nothingness.

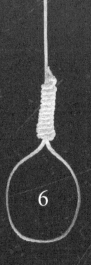

6

RASHA STUMBLED through an inferno that could only be hell.

A ravenous fire gnawed at debris to her left. It engulfed the charred ruins and poisoned the air with acrid smoke. She learnt how she was still alive: a steel girder had fallen against Rasha's bunk bed and sheltered her from the debris that was once her bedroom.

For rubble was all that remained of her family's Syrian apartment.

She'd been fighting with seven-year-old Milana over the letter she had torn when the missile struck. They were meant to have hidden underneath their bunk bed, but Rasha had stirred their argument again, and Milana had crawled out into the room when there was an explosion and the world upturned.

Milana, she thought.

In the rubble before her, amidst bent steel rods and hunks of sandstone, was a dusty hand.

'Milana!' Rasha cried, coughing through smoke as it clogged her windpipe. 'Milana, Milana . . .'

She shuffled forward, reached out with her bruised arm, and gripped Milana's hand. It was still warm. There was give: Milana could be pulled free. Rasha tugged. Rubble shifted, and fresh dust plumed against the flickering fire. Milana's arm ended where the shoulder should have begun.

Just blood and sinew, and it was all Rasha's fault.

Rasha dropped the limb, recoiled onto the ash-ridden floorboards, and retched. She brought up clotted blood, exactly as that day in workshop 2B.

Workshop 2B.

Rasha froze. *That's right*, she thought. *Joel Tredethy, Gorenn Holiday Park, and the shadow happened thousands of miles away in Cornwall.* The fire burned, smoke gushed, and Milana's corpse bled, but it wasn't truly happening.

It wasn't real. The shadow had put her there.

Rasha observed the scene. The edges of the firelight and the crumbled brickwork were licked by a crimson-and-cyan haze. Where there was movement came distortion. Flames pulsated in rhythm to her own heartbeat, and dust plumes echoed as if there were many layers of the same image. Beyond that, where Homs's remaining buildings should have loomed, was impenetrable blackness. Rasha deduced that this wasn't her memory, nor was it happening now.

It was somewhere new altogether. She had been fooled into thinking it was real. Perhaps the shadow was Milana after all, and she'd imprisoned Rasha in this place as punishment for killing her.

She was in hell.

Rasha stumbled through the ruins for a way home. There was a door intact, and she pushed it open only to find a tunnel. Deep underground, the air was warm and stagnant, and miners drove pickaxes into stone. Each lunge furthered a network of veins beneath the land. They coughed and spluttered; the work made them sick. Rasha's feet left the damp floor for metal walkways and clinical lights. Machines and formulas filled the caverns and voices carried on the air, all talking about ghosts.

Rasha raced blindly into the mouth of another tunnel only to find herself back in her decimated bedroom with Milana's detached arm.

A yell echoed across the heavens. It didn't seem to be part of the world in which Rasha's mind inhabited, but from the physical world where her body remained.

'Who are you?' Her mother's voice quavered.

'We're here to help your daughter, Mrs Abadi,' a woman replied gravely. Plastic fasteners clicked.

'Occupation, grade three imprint,' said a man with a smoker's husk.

'Let's engage,' the woman remarked.

Smoke stirred at the end of the decimated room. From the darkness came three cautious figures. Clad in various shades of black, hoods down, all that differentiated them in that moment was their hair: the woman had a bright lilac undercut do, the shorter man's was dirty blond and unkempt, and the taller man was a writer type with black curls galore. The men didn't come so clearly; their images were opaque and distorted, as if they stood behind frosted glass. There was no doubt in Rasha's mind: they were the hooded people from that morning.

'I'll engage with the imprint and . . .' The woman paused as if to ask herself what she could possibly do. 'I'll reason with it.'

Darkness took the men, and the woman approached.

'Rasha?' she asked and reached out a hand.

Rasha found that she could look into her. The name Shauna

came to her first, but that didn't sit right, and a different one found its way to her lips. 'You're Trish, aren't you?'

'Yes,' Trish said, eyes wide. 'Rasha, do you know what's happening?'

'I'm being possessed, aren't I? By a ghost?'

'Something like that. We don't have much time until it takes over your body. If you want to survive, you have to try everything I ask. Can you do that?'

Rasha didn't know where she was. What if this world was of the shadow's creation, to torture Rasha for eternity? Perhaps Trish was just another of those shadows that had stolen the woman's image to mock Rasha.

'What happens if I don't?' Rasha challenged.

Trish's leaf-green eyes glistened.

'Then you'll be lost here forever.'

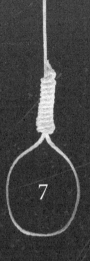

7

RASHA TOOK Trish's outstretched hand.

'Subject has been obtained,' Trish called out. 'Initiating extraction.'

They plunged through a door and into the apartment's hallway. The patterned rugs slipped beneath their feet, and the wall's plaster scraped under Rasha's fingertips. Solid, impossibly real. Yet it wasn't. The hallway was infinite, and every door they opened took them back to her ruined bedroom and Milana's bloodied remains.

'It's punishing me!' Rasha cried. 'I'm in hell, and it's punishing me!'

Trish squeezed Rasha's arms, her vernal green eyes wide with sympathy.

'There is no hell,' Trish informed her. 'There is only this place, the ombrederi. The imprint is feeding on your negative emotions. You need to be in control. See that door there? When we open it, we're going to see a time when you were happiest, yeah?'

Rasha nodded. The happiest she had ever been was before she'd had her father and sister ripped from her life. It hurt too much to go that far back. Trish wrenched the door open and led Rasha in. Their feet hit workshop 2B's chalky floor. Cridland stepped forward with an end-of-year certificate for best portfolio. Bullets obliterated him. Walls splintered and collapsed.

Rasha clambered from the rubble of her bedroom with Trish's support.

'There's got to be something else in you,' Trish pleaded. She was desperate now. Rasha sensed time was running out. Soon this would be permanent; Rasha would be trapped there, agonised by her wrongdoings for eternity.

'Trish.' The blond man's voice came from the outside – from the real world. 'Be careful. Don't allow yourself to be occupied, too.'

'Sam, I've got this!' Trish cried. She turned to Rasha. 'Do you have something?'

'I think so.'

They strode through an open door to their left, back inside the apartment's living room, only it wasn't war-torn and decimated. The hearth rug, the giadual sofas, the smell of Haya cooking a zesty tabbouleh – all was as it should be. Rasha, Haya, Milana, and their father played a game of charades. Despite the pop of gunfire outside, they mimed from cards and were riddled with laughter, the kind that helped her forget for a moment.

Always the simple things.

'Keep that memory, Rasha,' Trish instructed. 'Focus on the happy. Let it fill you up.'

Oh, it did. Her chest loosened, and her stomach lightened. If only it could last forever.

A door sprung up behind Rasha's father. She didn't want to go. If she stayed, if she could fend off the dark memories of the war, when the war seemed farther away in the southern districts, she would always be happy.

'This isn't real, Rasha,' Trish said gently, as if she knew what was going through Rasha's mind. 'Let's get you home to your mother.'

Haya. Of course. She couldn't let her mother be alone in the real world. Rasha let Trish guide her through the doorway.

They entered a boundless lighting shop, no walls in sight. Thousands of glass bulbs radiated light and warmth.

'Where is this?' Rasha asked.

'The ombrederi is a bridge between minds,' Trish explained. 'This is where my mind meets the ombrederi. A neutral place.'

At a counter stood a portly man, and Trish tiptoed to peck him on the cheek. They carried the same button nose and wide-set eyes; her father, Rasha presumed. He must have died, for Rasha sensed that anybody they saw in the ombrederi had departed the living. Trish turned to her.

'Now, you're going to be in darkness for a moment,' Trish said. 'Just a split second, but I promise you, keep your happy memory in your mind, and you'll come back to us.' She called to the outside. 'Prepare the EMP.'

From far off there was an electrical whine.

'Fire EMP.'

Static crackled. The lighting shop melted around Rasha and snatched Trish away. She was all alone. The heaviness of her body returned. Pain seared beneath her fingernails, and cramps rose from her limbs.

Rasha saw one last image of a wooden ship as it plummeted into a sea.

Then there was purple darkness.

8

'SHE LOOKED into my mind,' Rasha heard Trish mutter. 'She knew my name. She even knew who Shauna was.'

Rasha opened her eyes. She lay on the floor of her room in caravan forty-five, head in her mother's lap. Haya howled, and Rasha could only describe it as relief from a heartache well-known. Around them, Trish and her two accomplices consulted an array of gadgets. In the doorway, Sam flicked through the options of a touch screen monitor and showed it to his comrades.

'Imprint successfully expelled,' he confirmed.

Beneath Haya's cries and her saviour's babble, Rasha whispered questions as sensations returned to her body. 'Who are you? How did you find me?'

Stone-cold silence. Other times, she would get answers. 'Imprints, are they . . . ghosts?'

'Yes,' the curly-haired man said. He was called Will, except Rasha wasn't sure how she knew.

'Was the shadow an imprint?'

'We don't know,' Sam replied gravely.

Will crouched down beside Haya and Rasha.

'The Network has resolved your case. Rasha Abadi, we witness you.'

He began to rise, but Rasha grabbed his hand tightly. He had to know.

'The Vincent will fall,' she whispered.

Tiredness overwhelmed her, and the room spun violently.

'Mrs Abadi, she should come with us for a follow-up. We'll make sure she's okay,' Trish began. Her voice seemed far away now.

'She stay,' Haya growled in English, arms wrapped around Rasha.

Trish's face loomed in close, and she pressed her forehead against Rasha's clammy temple –

A winding lane surrounded by overgrown verges. A crumbling chimney stack.

Rasha had walked by it enough to know that this was Wheal Gorenn Mine.

'*Find us,*' Trish said impossibly, for she hadn't moved her lips. It had sprouted in Rasha's mind, so clear it could have been her own thought.

Haya pushed Trish away. Grogginess pulled Rasha's eyes closed. She feared the darkness.

'Keep the lights on,' Rasha pleaded, and sound and picture became one as she drifted into an undisturbed sleep.

9

RASHA WOKE SLOWLY. Her bedsheets, soaked in her own urine, were vacuum packed to her aching body. That was the least of her concerns. Deep scratches covered the plasterboard walls above her head. Her fingernails were bruised, cuticles bloodied. She remembered how her body had belonged to the shadow, her senses distant, heart beating to a new rhythm. Whilst she was possessed, in the world that Trish named the ombrederi, had her body defied physics and climbed her bedroom walls?

Her mind reeled with the prior night's events, and she couldn't pinpoint her first thought, but her most recurrent was, *I must find them.* The strangers in the night, unperturbed by the shadow as it tried to snatch Rasha's body.

She jumped from her sodden bed and tore the soiled sheets away, ignoring the pain in her fingers. The shadow had caused more carnage than she'd thought.

That had been the most frightening revelation. Her saviours had come prepared with cases of equipment and had spoken a language all their own – imprints and EMPs and extractions – yet with all their knowledge, when Rasha had asked what the shadow was, she'd been met with a grave, 'We don't know.'

With her soaked sheets bundled underarm, Rasha opened her bedroom door to hear Haya say in English, 'Rasha home. Rasha ill.'

She spoke on the pay-as-you-go Nokia that Mr Keats had handed down to them. That was school sorted. Rasha had no intention of going, of course. She tiptoed across the hall to the utility room, threw her sheets in the half-empty washing machine, turned it on, and sped into the bathroom to wash. No, she was skipping school to go to Wheal Gorenn.

The night before, Trish had put her forehead against Rasha's, and Rasha had seen the abandoned mining site, that was nestled on the edge of town. She wasn't mistaken; she walked past it twice daily, and even their drab uniforms had the engine house stitched within the yellow-and-black emblem. She didn't know how Trish had passed the message between their minds – if that happened at all – but she did know Trish and company wanted her to find them. Perhaps they could cure her.

Rasha was also desperate to reach Wheal Gorenn because, when the shadow had her contained within what Trish named the ombrederi, she had fought back. She'd also seen the mines, full of grimy workers hauling stone and cart, and how she presumed it was now, full of desks, gadgets, and clinically bright lights. The shadow had a connection to the mines that her saviours may not know.

Her father had always said that help is best returned. She could offer them information for saving her life.

Rasha quickly towelled herself dry and dressed in a mismatched outfit of Red Cross plaid. She tiptoed into the kitchen, swiped the half-empty packet of bourbons from the counter, and stowed them in her rucksack. She went to the front door and tried the handle: locked. She reached for the top of the doorframe where their caravan keys were usually kept, but all her fingers disturbed was dust.

'Stay inside,' Haya said in Levantine.

Rasha spun on the spot. Haya sat in the lounge area, merely a shadow against the drawn curtains. She staggered to her feet and walked closer to the kitchen light. Her eyes were bloodshot and her hair unkempt.

'Please, Mama,' Rasha said. She had contemplated lying, but Haya wasn't someone easily fooled; she'd worked in law, after all.

'You're going to look for those people, aren't you?' Haya asked. Rasha stammered for a response that didn't involve a partial lie. 'Aren't you?'

Haya's voice was shrill and broken – there was fear there. Rasha understood. The last time a member of Haya's family was in danger they'd been in the midst of a desolated city with death on their backs. The caravan was meant to be a sanctuary nestled at the edge of the world.

'You don't need to be scared of those people,' Rasha said. 'You heard how they understand ghosts, you saw the equipment they had. They can protect us.'

Rasha stepped toward her mother. Haya backed away towards the sofa.

'Mama,' Rasha said. 'It's just me.'

Haya fell onto the sofa and clutched at the cushion beneath her. Rasha realised that was the problem: it was just her. The girl who, the night before, had crawled along the walls, inhuman.

'Mama,' Rasha called. Warm tears spilled across her face. She edged towards her mother the way she'd approach a cowering dog. 'I'm not going to hurt you.'

Haya scooted back onto the sofa — any further and she'd be sat on the windowsill.

'Mama, don't be scared.'

She was just feet from Haya –

'Stay away!' Haya yelled. 'Rasha, just stay away, please.'

'I'm not a monster, Mama,' Rasha whined. 'I'm not . . .'

Am I? she concluded in her head.

By the wide, horrified stare that Haya gave her, her mother certainly thought so. If that was the case, she needed a cure more than ever.

Rasha turned on her heel and raced past the locked door into her bedroom. She raised the damp window, climbed onto the sill, and leapt to the gravel outside their caravan. Despite being eight thirty in the morning, the sun was beating down as if it were noon. Many caravan-dwellers were already sitting outside their abodes, relishing the beautiful start to their mornings after a stormy night.

Eyes to the ground, Rasha was hurrying to the site entrance when she heard someone call her name. It was Mr Keats, stood in his doorway. His tabbies mewed from cages stacked one on top of the other. She wouldn't have been in the mood to entertain Mr Keats – she had more pressing matters, after all – but he looked prepared to drive to the vet, and Wheal Gorenn was on the way.

'Need a hand?' she asked.

'Please.'

Rasha hauled the crates two at a time to his lemon-yellow Nissan Micra, and when she was done he asked, 'Need a lift?'

'Please.'

'School?' he asked as they climbed in.

'Wheal Gorenn,' she said and pulled the passenger door.

As she clicked her seat belt into place, she caught Mr Keats's cocked eyebrow. 'School trip,' she concluded.

The cats mewed and hissed from their travel cages. Rasha's nostrils itched with allergies as she elaborated on her lie – a mining history field trip, no less. Perhaps it was true – she didn't know what she would find there. Mr Keats pulled into Wheal Gorenn's drive and wished her fun, then the Micra disappeared in a flurry of dust and meows, and Rasha was alone on the narrow lane.

The road was moderately well-kept. The shrubbery either side was trimmed back, and its few potholes were patched with Tarmac. Tracks indented the gravel: it was frequented by vehicles. Rasha kept to its left side just in case a car sped along. Dense woodland smothered the road, and the sea's salty aroma came off the tail end of the howling wind. Through the leafy canopy, a stone chimney reared its head – the engine house, worn in comparison to its glorified illustration on her school jumper.

Gravel crackled under tyres. Rasha turned as a burgundy three-wheeled Reliant Robin trundled toward her. It slowed to a stop a metre away. Trish and Sam climbed from the front seats, and she heard Trish say, 'I told you she was coming, Bickle, and we were almost late.'

Trish, her hair now sky blue, approached first, face awash with concern.

'Help me,' Rasha begged.

10

RASHA WAS CHOKED with emotion; her saviours stood before her in reality's cold, hard light, two of three people she owed her life to.

'I'm a monster, and I need help,' she cried.

Trish stepped forward as if to hug her. She must have thought better of it and held her hands behind her back. Sam leant on the Reliant's bonnet, his face sour.

'Please,' Rasha muttered.

'We should take her to the Network,' Sam said to Trish. 'If James knows we've had unofficial contact, he'll have our heads. Think about the disciplinary.'

Trish looked at Rasha with sympathy.

'That can wait,' Trish said. 'Look at her; she needs some humanity. Take the Reliant. Meet us by the coal house.'

Sam huffed but didn't retort. He jumped into the Reliant and sped toward the engine house. Trish took Rasha by the hand, and they broke into the woodland to the right. Roots threatened to trip them, and crows cawed overhead. The trees thinned, and a wall of blue met them; the sea stretched from the cliff edge to the sky. To their left were crumbled foundations, the remnants of what Rasha presumed to be the coal house. Beyond that the ground was cratered from decades of mining and construction. The last intact engine house perched on the northwest fringe, just before a sharp decline into the raging sea below.

Nothing else was said between the pair until Sam approached them. He was quiet, in a world of his own, eyes tired, shoulders slumped. He perched on the remains of a slate wall as Rasha and Trish – 'Short for Trisha, but call me T' – walked the coastline. Trish seemed uncomfortable in the silence and filled it with proverbial nonsense. Rasha was grateful for her effort, for she wasn't accommodated in social circles often.

'How do you feel when you're near an imprint?' Trish asked.

'A ghost?' Rasha asked.

'Right.'

Rasha thought back to the blood that had oozed from her mouth when she'd seen Joel Tredethy, the shadow who infested her mind as if it were a weed leeching healthy soil of nutrients.

'It's like I'm becoming someone else. Becoming them.'

Trish nodded.

'That's engagement.' Trish reached out and pretended to knock on Rasha's forehead. 'We're not witnesses by chance. This noggin' of yours is complex and astounding. When you're born it's smooth – a pebble. Through experience it develops all of these ribbons and pathways. What do you know about the limbic system?'

'Is that a computer thing?'

'It's part of the brain,' Trish said in a sisterly fashion. 'Though you could say it's like the processor of a computer.

The limbic system develops differently person to person. Through extreme trauma it becomes sensitive to certain emotions, and how it develops affects how you process emotions. Take this cliff. It wasn't this way fifty years ago, and it won't be in the next fifty. It changes every day, the waves crashing into it, leaving their mark. Imprints are the same. Their energy transmits in waves, and it's the limbic system that catches it all.'

Rasha was lost in Trish's words and the lapping water. She recollected the labyrinth that her mind had been imprisoned in the previous night.

'Syria. My memories were used against me . . .'

'An imprint will latch on to familiar emotions. If it knows pain, it will find it. But don't look so downtrodden. Remember, the cliff is ever changing, and so are you.'

Rasha hoped so. She wanted to be old Rasha again, long before her mother had branded her monster and long before monsters had taken her family from her. Then again, had her family not perished – had she not led Milana to her death – she wouldn't have been a witness.

'I know who the shadow is.'

'The shadow?' Sam asked.

Sam hopped from the wall and neared the women.

'The one that . . . occupied me,' Rasha confirmed in an attempt to adopt their terminology. 'It was my sister, Milana. I did something terrible and – '

'The girl in the rubble who we saw in the ombrederi?' Trish asked. Rasha nodded, and the bright-haired woman continued. 'It takes the mind of a witness to become an imprint. If it were her, she would have come to you before now.'

Rasha sniffed to hold back tears. For once they would have been tears of relief. If Milana wasn't haunting her, as she had originally believed, then there was chance she had forgiven Rasha.

'I think I know where it came from,' Rasha said. 'When we were fighting it, there in the ombrederi, I saw into it. I saw the mines. Whatever the shadow is, it came from here.'

Perspiration dewed across Trish's and Sam's ashen faces.

11

THEY DARTED through the woodland. Branches tugged at their clothes as if to pull Rasha away from the strangers.

'Can imprints do that?' Rasha asked. 'Hide themselves?'

'There's one that has, yes,' Sam said.

He didn't care to expand. Rasha paused. She'd succumbed to their analogies and theories because they fed her appetite for answers. She was miles from civilisation with two people who could speak to the dead and ensured they told her as little as possible. A metre away was a chain-link fence. Beyond it, erected proud and strong, was the engine house. Around it were two angular warehouses whose windows seeped cold white light. People were there, and the duo avoided them. Sam had mentioned a disciplinary.

They have been fired, Rasha thought, *fired and AWOL, and I'm their bargaining chip, which is why they're telling me half-truths.*

'Who are you hiding from?' she challenged.

Trish and Sam stopped by the fence and turned to her.

'No one,' said Sam.

'It's complicated,' Trish said.

Rasha had heard the expression time and again from adults who excused her from conversation. *I was raised in a war zone, thank you.*

'I'll tell everyone about this place,' Rasha warned.

Trish and Sam turned to look at each other. Wide eyes and hand gestures communicated different views. Sam shook his head.

'We're facing a disciplinary because of what we did to you,' he said.

Rasha scowled.

'You saved me,' she said.

'It was our fault the imprint found you,' Trish said. She eased toward Rasha. 'It was an experiment. We're trying to understand how witnesses develop. We pushed it too far. It was a mistake.'

She was haunted at the same time each night – Rasha accepted that. They watched her walk to school in the morning and followed with a drone on her return. Mr Keats had warned of strange people who skulked about the caravan site.

'You did this to me,' Rasha growled. She shoved Sam with all her might. 'You made me like this!'

He held her wrists before she could strike him again.

'No, no,' Sam said. 'You were already capable. All we did was heighten your connection.'

'How did you find me?'

Sam gestured to Trish and said with a sly smile, 'The Hound herself.'

Trish glared at him.

'I can hear people, other witnesses mostly,' Trish told Rasha. 'Young'uns like you broadcast more than most. Last night was horrible, but there's a positive to it all. What you're capable of, we can help you control it. Are you with us?'

What quality of life would she have if she couldn't control engagement? Sleep-deprived, barely able to part real life from the dead – she'd never be granted permanent citizenship at that rate. If she couldn't control it, she'd lose Haya and Cornwall. Rasha nodded.

Sam led them at a sprint alongside the chain-link fence where a yellow hazard sign read, 'Danger, do not enter. Trespassers will be prosecuted.' They squeezed through a gap that probably trafficked foxes and badgers.

At a security door, Sam typed a code – which Rasha could have sworn was 1-3-6-6-6 – and they were inside. Stale warmth and sullen chatter met them as they trudged down a steady decline into the jaw of a mineshaft. Trish procured a band from her pocket, infused with many dull materials, and stretched it over her forehead. Rasha shot her a quizzical look.

'All these witnesses projecting their thoughts,' Trish told Rasha. 'Enough to drive anyone mad.'

Rasha supposed it dulled others' thoughts and noted how bitter Trish was about it. At the tunnel's end, two copper plaques were fixed to a wall. One read, 'The Imprint Activity Network is Funded by the Edward Penrose Trust,' and another was a memorial that listed names of deceased colleagues. Sam and Trish gestured to it as they passed.

'The river always finds the sea,' they chanted.

The shaft's throat was short and opened out into a large cavern lit by artificial lamps. Plasterboard offices were sprawled upon metal walkways. Sam and Trish whisked Rasha into another opening. She locked eyes with a stout frog-faced woman stood in the adjacent tunnel. The woman consulted a leather-bound notebook, smiled at Rasha, and scribbled amongst its pages. Rasha continued on with the two witnesses to the head of a ladder which descended into another tunnel. She hesitated.

'It's okay,' Trish said. 'It's safe. Like a tower block but underground.'

Tower blocks with little escape did not incite her with confidence.

A steel girder pulverised her father's body.

Rasha nodded, stepped onto the ladder, and descended into absolute blackness. Déjà vu amassed with each step as the shadow's memories ebbed and flowed into her consciousness. The pitter-patter of feet and hands on the metal rungs quickened. They found a winding tunnel which expanded into an ill-lit cavern. Its farthest, steepest wall was four storeys high. Many pillars, ranging in materials and sizes, supported the sloped ceiling. It gave the impression they stood under a gargantuan spider.

Sam and Trish raced over to the base of the wall where Will flitted between machinery with a clipboard in hand.

'We messaged Will ahead,' Sam said. 'He's going to help us.'

Trish beckoned Rasha closer. The wall was roughly hewn, its surface pitted like the faces of her acne-strewn classmates. Evenly spaced wires dangled from sockets along it, all embellished in tin. Trish crossed to a table and unwrapped a package from a sun-bleached cover. It was a helmet, crustaceous in appearance, riddled with kettle sockets that matched the plugs on the wall. Rasha had watched too many late-night sci-fi reruns on Channel Five to not be weary.

'What is going on?' she cried. Sam turned to look at her. Compassion glimmered in his sad eyes.

'Occupation is extremely rare,' Trish informed her. 'You could answer a lot of questions for us.'

Will and Sam looked at each other, eyebrows cocked. Will turned back to Rasha and gestured to the helmet that Trish connected to the wall via various wires.

'This is a receptor,' he explained. 'The wall is rich in tin ore; it has a compound that magnifies the frequency, strengthening your connection to imprints.'

'So when you wear the receptor,' Trish continued, 'you can extend your mind, your consciousness, into the ombrederi.'

'The frequency?'

'It's better if you experience it for yourself.'

'We want you to try and reach out for the shadow,' Sam said. Behind him, Trish muttered into Will's ear, probably to update him on what Rasha had told them. 'Can you do this for us?'

'You don't have to do anything you don't want to,' Trish said.

Will's stare pierced through her. Rasha played the ideas in her mind: the alternative possibilities, the consequences, percentages and fractions. Ultimately, there was only one answer. 'If I want to shut the imprints out of my mind, I'm going to have to learn to let them in when I want, aren't I?' she asked.

'Yes,' Sam said. 'It's all about controlling the threshold between the physical and the ombrederi.'

'We can control your connection manually,' Trish said. 'If you struggle, we can shut it out.'

'Is this the only way?' Rasha asked. She didn't want to admit that the machine scared her.

'The safest way,' Will confirmed. 'We all have guides, a particular imprint the we have a deep connection with. Until you establish that and train your mind, this is the best option.'

Rasha strode to an old chair beside the helmet Trish had

set up. She shuffled to find comfort on the hard seat. The trio waltzed around her.

'The helmet's heavy,' Trish warned.

With Sam's help, Trish carefully placed the helmet over Rasha's head. Attached to the bottom was a neck brace, which Rasha learnt was necessary when the weight of it pinched her shoulders. Sam latched them together whilst Trish placed electrodes at intervals on her forehead. She didn't expect the receptor to be heavy and claustrophobic.

Milana in rubble.

She looked out beyond the witnesses to the beams that could buckle at any moment, the only thing that stopped the cavern ceiling from crushing them.

A burning hellscape.

'Okay, Rasha,' Trish said. 'You need to clear your mind. I know, easier said than done. Focus on your breathing. In, out. In, out. As soon as you register any memories or thoughts – '

Her father's skull crumpled beneath stone.

'– cast them out, turn your mind back to your breathing.'

Rasha closed her eyes, then breathed in through her nose and slowly out of her mouth. In, out, in, out. She purposefully inhaled sharply through her nose when Syrian horrors invaded her memory. As she did, the metallic, oxidised air itched at her nostrils and lingered on her pallet like the taste of death.

Her father in the darkness, ash and dust turning his blood black.

In, out. The darkness of her eyelids conquered all.

'If your mind is clear,' Trish said, 'I want you to imagine a familiar place, a neutral or happy environment where you can bring yourself when entering the ombrederi. You know mine already.'

'The lighting shop,' Rasha said.

She recalled the warmth of it, and although it was cosy and familiar to Trish, Rasha needed an outside space. The week the Abadis moved to the caravan site, the friendlier locals held a fundraiser in their name to buy amenities and take a trip to the Lost Gardens of Heligan. It had been a beautiful spring day, just after a storm, and was the first time in months that Rasha surrounded herself with greenery. But it was no longer just a memory.

Rasha was in the ombrederi.

12

RASHA WAS ROOTED to a footpath amidst the botanical gardens. There was a soft colourful haze to the trees and plants: the ombrederi's atmosphere. Bushes teemed with acacias and brugmansias and bechsonarias, and amongst the leafy canopy came shrill birdsong.

'I'm here,' Rasha called out toward the treetops, to the real world.

'Great,' Trish's voice echoed back. 'We'll make the receptor live. You'll start to feel imprint energy all around us. Identify individual imprints. Plot them onto your neutral place. Right? Brilliant. Turning the receptor on in five. . . four. . . three. . .'

The click of a button. In her mind – the ombrederi – figures began to populate the gardens. Static energy crawled across her skin, and varied emotions – from heart-jumping elation to bowel-twisting sadness – whirled in her stomach.

'Do you feel that energy?'

'Yes.'

'Thoughts, memories, emotions, they all broadcast around us, through us. They tie us and imprints together. That is the frequency.'

The gardens burst with hundreds of imprints. Rasha understood: death wasn't an absolute end, but a further form of being. The ombrederi was another world, and the frequency energy connected the two.

'So,' Trish continued, 'if you feel ready, we want you to connect to the shadow. You have to find a mutual connection. Open your mind up to the memories you were thinking of the night you were occupied, the ones that drew the shadow to you. Remind yourself how that felt and call out to it.'

That was the easy part; the memories were always there.

Automatic rifles popped.

Bodies smouldered.

Milana's arm no longer attached to her body –

Heligan's trees uprooted themselves, and the undergrowth wilted. Rasha's feet hit the floor of a tunnel. She climbed to her feet, noting the tunnel's similarity to the ones she had passed to reach the tin ore wall. A colony of miners, their skin enveloped in soot, marched with pickaxes. At the centre of the shaft, a piston reached the height of the cavern. It was three times as wide as the men's waists. They climbed onto it to elevate their exhausted bodies to the surface.

An explosion rumbled. Torrents of rubble and dust shed over them. A metallic ping-ping-chink-ping, and the piston crashed down, cavern ceiling and all, and flattened the men beneath it.

13

RASHA OPENED her eyes to reality, heart thudding inside her chest.

The helmet's supports dug into her collarbone. She looked for Trish, Sam, and Will. The witnesses were there, but they were not alone. The miners were with them – they always had been. The heightened frequency energy coursed through her, and the imprints sharpened. Some were burnt or bloodied, others had lost arms and legs. A skeletal boy no older than Rasha was so close that she could see his brain throb inside his cracked cranium.

'Do you see them?' Rasha said.

'Often,' Will said. 'But only when we want to. You've got the receptor intensifying the signals, remember? They scare you, don't they? Have you ever walked past a dog and they bark and growl? They mean no harm, it's just a defence mechanism. Imprints are no different.'

The incomplete boy pointed to the back of the cavern. In the darkness behind Will loomed the silhouette of a window, its glass broken. Rasha's stomach knotted.

'I'm sorry, Will,' she said.

'For what?'

'Rasha,' Sam interrupted. 'Is it there? The shadow imprint?'

The miners' empty eye sockets demanded her attention. They ached for life and full bodies.

Chink, chink. A couple of miners hunched over a third whose arm was trapped beneath the fallen piston. They drew their pickaxes, raised them into the air, and hacked at his shoulder. The man screamed through a gag of torn cloth. Blood pooled around them and rose to her knees, her shoulders. Amidst the chaos was another man with dark features who strangled a woman with a slither of blue twine. The blood drowned them all, and it flooded into Rasha's mouth.

'Turn it off!' she screamed. 'Turn it off!'

At the flick of a switch, the energy dissipated. The miners and their blood dissolved until only Rasha and the witnesses remained.

'I'm sorry,' she muttered. Her face was wet. She wiped it – just tears. 'I couldn't, I – '

'So you found nothing?' Sam asked.

'Sam,' Will and Trish warned in unison.

'No, I did,' Rasha said. 'Does the name Michael mean anything to anyone?'

Sam and Will, their faces infinitely paler than before, turned to look at Trish, but she'd already fled the cavern.

PART TWO

THE WILTED,
THE WILD,
AND THE LOST

14

THE FREQUENCY WILL BE *the death of me*, Trisha Teagues decided.

She yawned, sat up straight in the driver's seat of the Reliant, and shook herself awake. Sam, slumped in the passenger's seat, absentmindedly scrolled through social media on his smartphone. In the back, Rasha gripped her seat belt and stared at the wilderness beyond her window. Their bodies were there, but their minds were elsewhere.

Trish eyed Rasha in the rearview mirror and wondered exactly where Rasha's mind had been in the caverns. She'd identified Michael – Trish's partner, or ex (that remained to be seen) – and recalled him strangling a woman. Trish knew it wasn't Michael's imprint; he was still very much alive, hidden at his mother's flat until the trial for Shauna's murder. Trish must have projected the image into Rasha's mind the night she'd been occupied, which Rasha had later regurgitated in the caverns. Either way, Trish had scarpered into an empty tunnel to let out the tears in private. She knew Rasha well enough to know the teenager would blame herself.

Trish blinked hard to snap back to reality. She shook off

the gut-churning feelings she'd inherited from Rasha – of being displaced and utterly alone, of being responsible for a horrendous crime. Fatigued and hungry, Trish's resistance to the frequency energy waned as though the barriers of her mind were failed harbour walls and emotional stimuli flooded in. She should have worn her dielectric band around people with turbulent minds, but when she wore it she felt like a muzzled dog, unable to make use of a vital body part.

Trish studied her smartphone as it slid across the dashboard with each sharp turn. It was the fifty-third time she had checked it that day, expecting for Hornes Solicitors to email with the outcome of her sister Shauna's trial, to tell her whether Michael had been sentenced and whether her life would become that little bit lonelier. She wanted to know, and she didn't. She craved justice, just not one where Michael was her sister's killer.

Haya cowered on the sofa in a dark caravan.

'You're not a monster, Rasha,' Trish said before she could stop herself.

'What?' Rasha asked from the back seat.

Sam reached over from the passenger seat and prodded Trish in the arm. He always disapproved when Trish slid into other people's minds – on purpose or not. He hid much himself.

'You can't compare yourself to rebels and militants,' Trish reiterated to Rasha.

Trish watched Rasha in the rearview mirror. Her eyes widened with realisation, and Rasha loosened her seat belt to lean forward.

'They're my thoughts,' she growled.

'I'm sorry,' Trish said. 'Won't happen again.'

'How do you do it?' Rasha asked. She settled back in

her seat, her intrigue overtaking her anger. Such unfiltered keenness for knowledge reminded Trish of her younger self.

'I dunno,' Trish said. 'Been able to do it since I was young.'

'Since your parents died? That was your dad in the ombrederi, wasn't it?'

Trish scratched a post-dye itch from her crown.

'Along with seeing imprints,' Trish confirmed.

'You can do it to anyone?'

'Just witnesses. Thoughts, emotions . . .' A craving – somewhere between hunger and thirst – tugged at Trish's jaw. She glanced at Sam. 'Addictions . . .' Sam raised his middle finger. 'It all broadcasts on the frequency.'

Ten minutes of painful silence followed until they reached the caravan park and climbed from the Reliant. The last time Trish and Sam had visited the Abadis' home, Rasha, occupied and lost in the ombrederi, had clung to the ceiling with her limbs bent at impossible angles. It had been Trish, Sam, and Will's first occupation, and they had almost killed her.

It wasn't meant to be that way. They'd monitored her from the stalls of an abandoned cow shed in the field over as part of a program to understand the development of adolescent witnesses. They had laced the caravan park with electromagnetic beacons, gadgets that drew in imprints as a magnet would pull metal shavings, until an imprint took her.

The shadow that no one could identify.

Rasha could have been dead – or worse yet, occupied for good. *It was all we had,* Trish told herself, not that she completely believed it. Opportunities to conduct isolated research with little to no bias was rare. Nevertheless, guilt lodged itself in Trish's chest and remained there.

The lights were on in caravan forty-five. Rasha had just reached the front door when it was thrust outwards. A tearful

Haya leapt out and collapsed on her. Words of Levantine passed between them – scolding and loving, the way fearful mothers mustered. Haya let go of Rasha and glared at Sam and Trish. Sam took a hesitant step backward; he never got on well with mothers.

'Rasha better?' Haya growled.

'Not as such,' Trish said. 'A little more time with us and she will be.'

'No,' Haya spat. 'No more.'

Haya ushered Rasha into the caravan.

'She's not ill, Mrs Abadi. She's gifted.'

'See her again, I call police,' Haya warned.

Rasha's face sunk. Haya slammed her door so hard the whole caravan rocked. With an exaggerated sigh, Sam sidled over to Trish, duffel bag slung on one shoulder.

'You're filling her with false hope,' he said.

'Didn't you need that at her age?'

Trish followed Sam to the neighbouring caravan. A myriad of tabbies hissed at them from its roof. He lowered himself to the ground and crept beneath it.

'It's still false,' Sam said. There was a click, and Sam clambered back out with an EMP. They were palm-sized contraptions able to create or destroy an electronic force field. He opened his duffel bag.

'Wait,' Trish said. 'Let's leave them here. Put them on deflect. She won't be coming to the collieries anytime soon. Any defence is better than none.'

Sam nodded and changed a few settings on the analogue control panel. The three LEDs on its side flicked from green to blue. A small electronic pulse popped around them, and the air freshened, filtered of frequency energy. He fixed it back into place underneath the caravan, and they moved on to the maintenance shed.

'I'm going to help her,' Trish said. She couldn't let it go; Rasha could've died, after all. 'Give her the support we never had.'

She meant every word. Rasha was in too deep to return to life before the occupation. Desperate for answers, engrossed in their responses, she'd tumbled down the rabbit hole. Sam's disinterest made her blood boil.

'Want to talk about the elephant in the room?' Trish pried. They reached the maintenance shed, which sat outside a sparse play area. Trish stepped onto a wooden bench, reached to its roof, and located the EMP they'd planted the week before Rasha's occupation.

'What elephant in which room?' Sam retorted.

A line of white powder upon a black coffee table flashed before Trish's eyes. When she turned back to Sam, she knew there were other things on his mind.

'The shadow,' Trish prompted.

'Oh, that,' Sam replied. He fondled the scar on his arm. 'She's young, inexperienced. She can't interpret what's happening. Juvenile babble.'

'I saw it, too,' Trish said as she changed the settings on the EMP. 'It's not like any other imprint.'

EMP back in place, Trish hopped from the bench.

'It was devoid of emotions,' she continued, 'of memory, of life – even the dead have life, Sam.'

'Not the first time an imprint has hidden their identity,' Sam said. Trish couldn't argue with that. Guides, the highest form of imprint, could lock themselves from engagement. Each witness learnt their skills with a guide. Trish and Sam shared theirs with Will and Network director James: a girl by the name of Abidemi. She'd been undetectable in recent

59

weeks.

Trish's mobile buzzed. She withdrew her phone from her pocket and was relieved to see that Will had texted.

'Is it Hornes?' Sam asked.

Trish shook her head. She opened Will's text and read it to herself just in case it wasn't for Sam's ears. They fought a lot, and Trish dared not reignite any smouldered fires. The message was safe to read, but it was also an urgent one.

'It's from Will,' Trish said.

'Great, can't even text his own boyfriend,' Sam sneered. Trish decided not to lecture him for that.

'I've been visited by an imprint,' Trish read aloud. 'Laboratory 2C. I think it's Abidemi.'

15

THE NETWORK'S DIRECTOR, James McKay, with his ice-blue eyes and weathered features, had one of the most expressive eyebrows; she knew they were in trouble without removing her dielectric band.

The indoor car park was a repurposed warehouse to maintain the illusion the site was abandoned. James fixed a 'baby on board' sign to the rear window of his people carrier when they arrived in the Reliant. He and his wife recently celebrated bringing his third daughter into the world, and he was rarely seen without milk stains on his shirt collar or wet wipes stuck to the soles of his shoes. Without a word, he beckoned them into the mineshaft. Sam echoed Trish's thoughts as they followed him into the activity centre.

'He was waiting for us,' he hissed.

Their shoes clanged on the iron walkway as they meandered between the many desks in the activity centre. Witnesses hustled to and fro to tend to duties. James's office was nestled at the centre of the cavern: a glass-and-steel cubicle. 'The birdcage,' as witnesses often mused, and James was their canary, who always anticipated danger.

Sam closed the door, and the office absolved the hubbub from outside. James stood behind his desk. He was not a canary of beauty; his scoliosis rendered him five feet four, five feet two after a long day. His piercing stare bored into the depths of their own imprints. Trish, Sam, and Will were the youngest in the Network – thirty-three, twenty-nine, and thirty-one, respectively – and they were often undermined; James was their formidable headmaster.

'The board has come to an agreement, and I'm relieved to say they've overturned your suspension,' he began. 'Which is a miracle considering the amount of policies and procedures you threw out of the window.'

He paused for a response, and Trish hated silence.

'Don't you want to know how we did it?' she blurted. James leant on the back of his chair, eyebrows arched.

'We are intrigued, as it happens,' James said. 'You've been invited to host a seminar tomorrow afternoon. I highly recommend you accept. It will do you favours when we come to an agreement.'

'An agreement on what?' Sam queried.

'Considering the Abadi incident, we'll be taking the adolescent program off your hands.'

'You can't,' Trish said. 'We created it from the ground up. The program supports young and vulnerable witnesses – '

'Which is why it shouldn't have resulted in a near death,' James retorted. 'It'll be passed on to someone capable.'

'Who?'

'Vanessa.'

'And what about us?' Sam hollered. Fists balled, face magenta, he must have anticipated James's answer.

'Sam, you're needed out on the field,' their manager responded. 'No, please don't interrupt me. You have a great instinct with lesser grades of imprint, and with the rise of activity we need the numbers.'

Sam kicked the chair before him. Trish thought he'd vault over the desk and throttle James, but he yanked the door open and bolted for the nearest ladder. Trish turned back to James.

'You know how much this means to him, to us,' Trish said. 'We needed it when we were Rasha's age. If that doesn't make us the most qualified . . .' She only had to imply her own instability or Sam's various ailments; it was rare for a witness to not be mentally disturbed with an addictive personality. They could see the dead, after all.

'The last thing you needed at that age was your well-being threatened,' James said coolly. 'Trish, you've procured outstanding results with the sonar project. I want you to focus on that. Give it the attention it deserves.'

Trish couldn't respond. Her throat ached from the tears she held back. *I haven't found Shauna*, Trish thought. *It's a failure.*

'I think it's best you prepare for the seminar tomorrow,' James said with a tone that drew the conversation to a close. 'There's a lot riding on it.'

Trish nodded and fled the birdcage without a word, darting through the activity centre, head down to avoid judgmental stares. She took the ladder down into the confines of the claustrophobic third level. The usual silence found there was punctured by Sam's yells from the laboratories ahead.

'How dare he take a witness from a priority investigation and put him out on the field with the beginners?'

Sam would have said 'with the incapable and inexperienced' had he not been speaking with Will. Trish passed a cluster of stalagmites. The laboratory's glass walls loomed into view, its mechanised door open to ventilate the humid space. Will sat at a metal bench outside the ECG rooms and patiently saw out Sam's tantrum.

'I'm not sure what you want me to say, Sammy,' Will said as Trish entered.

'Agree? That'd be a nice start.'

'It's not a casual shuffle of staff now is it?' Will replied. 'You're being demoted, purposefully, after the board communed and we agreed that what you did was – '

'How did you vote?' Sam asked.

'I defended you the best I could, but there was no denying – '

'You voted to demote us?' Sam cried. He mouthed, Fuck.

'Yes,' Will said plainly, confident in his morals.

'You've done the right thing,' Trish said as she crossed into the room. 'But Christ, Vanessa? The program will be closed by the end of the year, mark my words.'

'She opposed the project to begin with, yes,' Will said, 'but since the severity of the Abadi occupation she acknowledges how important it is and how imperative it is to do it right.'

Trish couldn't argue with that. Despite her reluctance toward Vanessa, the co-director was also matron of the Refinery, their private mental hospital. It ran smooth as butter for the decade Trish was a witness, so there was no doubting her expertise.

Will pulled Sam in and pecked him on the lips. Sam encompassed Will with his gangly arms. Trish hadn't seen them do that for a while. On the bench was a myriad of files and touch screen tablets. Will spent more time in the Network than anywhere else: a home bird in work, his nest a dishevelled mess of reports.

'You need a shower,' Will muttered at Sam. 'It's onion grade.'

'Maybe you could join me,' Sam said. He smirked as Trish screwed her face.

'I can't. Too much to get through,' Will said.

'Thought it was an offer that couldn't possibly be refused,' Sam said, and he let Will go. Trish filled the awkward silence.

'Abidemi visited you?'

Will gestured to the workbench.

'You know what it's like down here – the frequency energy is pretty meek. There was a flood of it. Whoever it was pushed my files to the floor.'

'But Abi?' Sam asked. 'She hasn't shown herself in weeks.'

'That's why,' Will said. 'I couldn't grasp a sense of their identity. Sam, maybe we should head to Pendeen this week, see if we can contact Abidemi. If she'll respond to anyone, it'll be you. At least we can get some answers about the shadow imprint.'

Trish nodded. Pendeen was situated on a ley line – a scrap of old occultist myth that was later proved true by the Network. Abidemi was often found there. Rumour had it she'd died on-site; imprints often remained where their bodies died, locked to a localised variant of the frequency.

Trish's phone buzzed in her pocket. Everyone who would contact her was in the collieries. She withdrew, and an email notification flashed across her lock screen from Hornes Solicitors.

Trish reached out and gripped the cuff of Sam's jacket.

'It's Hornes,' Trish gasped.

'Open it,' Sam urged. 'See if the bastard's been sentenced.'

'I can't,' Trish said. Her bowels contorted; had she remembered to eat that day, she would have been sick.

'Want me to?' Will asked.

'Please.'

She passed the phone to Will. He shared her want for justice, as did Sam, and had even gone as far as to say that Michael was guilty. He swiped her lock screen away, loaded the email, and exhaled a shaky breath. His eyes flitted back and forth. Face lit by the smartphone, it appeared gaunt and wilted, his heavy brow further pronounced. He grimaced.

'Guilty,' Will said. 'He plead guilty.'

Trish held back the urge to swear. She crouched, knees to her chest, a hand on the steel bench. A tsunami of emotion rushed through her: sad elation for Shauna having found legal justice, only to be swallowed by a riptide of indignation – Trish didn't believe Michael had killed Shauna. Hornes had no doubt told him to plead guilty to curry favour with the jury and have his sentence shortened. If that was the case, then Shauna's true killer would still be at-large. They'd never be found.

Sam squeezed her shoulder, but that only worsened matters. A guttural moan escaped her lips as she tried to hold her tears back. She'd been torn in two.

A haywire compass, unsure which direction her loyalties lay.

16

THE SEVENTY-FOOT narrow boat was propped up on two hay bale trailers. Swirled calligraphy, peeled by age, spelled *Calypso* on its left side. Sleep, a stout retiree who leant on a walking stick far too short for him, turned to Trish with a grin.

'Waddya thinkin', T?' he asked.

'Looks like home.'

Far better than the Reliant and collieries in which she had slept for the best part of a year; and a vast improvement to the overpriced, squalid flat she'd shared with Michael before that.

Michael, convicted of her sister's murder. Michael, connected to the rogue shadow imprint.

Trish followed Sleep across the farmyard as night encroached. They passed carcasses of abandoned machinery: a throng of wheelless ice cream vans, a rusted dump truck, Calypso, bound in a county with no canals. Sleep was a collector of lost things.

'You can move in tonight,' he said.

'I don't have any rent money right now.'

'Nonsense, I don't want nuffin',' he said. They strode to his cottage. Behind the grimy windows were piles of junk:

cardboard boxes, broken gadgets, and damp furniture stacked to the ceiling. Trish'd known Sleep since childhood, and he'd never entertained the notion of settling with someone. The rooms seemed less empty when full of junk.

'I could clean for you,' Trish offered.

'No need. It's all spares for repairs. Never know when it's needed. Besides, what friend of your father's would I be if I let his only daughter go homeless?'

Calypso certainly was better than sleeping on back seats and under desks. Trish hugged Sleep and crossed to the Reliant.

'How's she keepin'?' he asked, nodding to her trusted steel steed.

'Really great.'

'One of my best finds,' he said. 'Good thing about Reliants. She'll take you where you need to go.'

A scuff was visible in the paintwork. Trish purposefully stood before it.

'A wheel bearing might be on the way out,' she said.

'Don't worry, I've got one somewhere. See? Spares for repairs. Right, better get yourself sorted. The solar panels are in. No plumbing, though, and 'elp yourself to the kitchen anytime. Door's always open.'

'Good night, and thanks again!'

'Night, me lover.'

He waved and staggered into his cottage. Her stare lingered on him. Would her parents have aged so rapidly if they hadn't taken their lives? Trish wouldn't have been a witness; Shauna would have gone to university and not met her end in Penzance. Michael wouldn't be in Dartmoor Prison, as Hornes's email detailed. A domino effect where choices had little to do with fate.

Trish took the three bags-for-life of clothes from her boot and trudged up steps made of metal crates into Calypso. Despite being able to reach out and touch both walls, the narrow boat squeezed in a kitchen, saloon, bathroom, and two bedrooms. Every wooden surface, from the cupboard to the ceiling, was painted in duck-egg blue. Larger than the Reliant; small enough to not feel lonely.

A rummage through assorted cupboards and closets found relics left by its previous owner: cutlery, AA batteries, a socket set, and a bundle of Christmas decorations. Once she packed her clothes away in the farthest cabin, she went to the saloon and draped the set of multicoloured fairy lights over the furnishings. She plugged them in, and the interior became speckled with primary colours. Through squinted eyes it resembled the lighting shop.

'Teagues,' her father would often repeat, 'the name you can trust!'

Shelter wasn't the only reason for accepting Sleep's offer. The remaining farmland in his name – for the rest he'd sold or gambled away – was devoid of humans and cattle. There was no Wi-Fi or cable TV, and the nearest string of transmission towers was a few fields over. Little interference with frequency energy was perfect for accessing the ombrederi.

She sat cross-legged on the elm floorboards. Natural frequency energy crept over her skin, infiltrating her pores, her mind. She firmly thought of the shadow imprint and willed her foresight to play. She was determined to find Shauna, even if that was deemed impossible; she hadn't been a witness when she was alive, so she couldn't be a guiding imprint in death. Calypso's twinkling interior blurred to her family's lighting shop, then dispelled her into the ombrederi.

17

TRISH AMBLED across a freshly mown garden under the ombrederi's magnetic black sky.

Fen violet and pink bell heather burst from the flower beds. Autumnal leaves swept into the air to rejoin branches of the arthritic willows hunched on the border. And a body. Will, unconscious, nestled in the compost upon a bed of dew drops. Fennel sprouted from his eye sockets, and thistles shot from his open mouth.

The mouth of a tunnel opened up before him. Trish edged inside and found an ill-lit cavern. Sam lay on a soiled mattress in the centre of the room, his skin grey and eyes vacant. A mound of white powder rocked a set of weighted scales. Rocks cascaded and tore his comatose body apart.

Fire engulfed the scene, and there James raced to a blaze on a never-ending highway. Rasha, grabbed at by many hands, was bound by blue twine. The shadow, faceless, emotionless, stood amidst a fiery desert and offered its congealed hand –

18

TRISH WOKE. Orange sun leaked through windows she didn't recognise. *Oh, that's right. Calypso.* She rose, back stiff from a night on the saloon floor. Her phone was on the table. Battery: *12 percent.* Reminders: *seminar.*

Trish raised herself from the floor, skulked to the narrow bathroom, and washed her face with the bucket of cold water Sleep had provided. Sleep – had she slept? She couldn't tell if her lucid dreams were more. If her visions were foresight, she'd surely have no one left.

Loneliness impending.

The whiteboard projector blinded Trish and threw the fourteen board members before her into oily shadows. Trish was certain they'd oppose her hypothesis, Will included. Upon his advice, Trish didn't mention the shadow; he'd said it would only invalidate any claims she'd make. They faced a disciplinary, after all.

'Through occupation, my foresight was stronger than ever.

Even now, I can slip into her mind as if it's my own. Remotely.'

The PowerPoint presentation froze on the previous slide. She fumbled with the tablet – the spinning pinwheel of death.

'We hear what you're saying, but this hardly breaks new ground,' Vanessa said, her tone sympathetic. 'When the board trials an imprint, we share the same space in the ombrederi. That's over fourteen witnesses connected at once.'

Trish adjusted the dielectric band. She couldn't argue against Vanessa's statement; when an imprint was trialled over a misdemeanour, the board all convened into the ombrederi where they could examine the imprint's memories. A cocktail of anxiety and foresight led Trish to entertain several outcomes for the seminar; she had prepared for arguments. Trish continued in her customer service voice.

'On the contrary, I think it's the tip of an iceberg. Occupation and telepathy are one and the same, a connection between imprints, using the frequency in much the same way.'

James leant forward on the table to part himself from the board.

'We do not contest your findings – the opposite, in fact,' he said. Beside him, Will smiled supportively. 'What we do contest is your approach to the investigation, which should not have breached an occupation. Yes, Sam as well, we don't expect you to take full responsibility.'

'We were negligent, and we accept any repercussions the board sees fit,' Trish admitted. Barely true; she'd fight before accepting punishment. 'Occupations are rare but are imminent nonetheless; when they happen, results are usually disastrous. I am the only witness in the Network's existence to successfully expel an imprint from a host – one of the few with foresight. That must mean something. So I implore you – if I'm removed from the adolescent program, move me to the occupations unit where I can better explore my hypothesis.'

A shudder rippled through the board members; whether horror at the idea or awe at her bravery, Trish could not tell. Will stared hard at his notebook. Vanessa reclined in her chair, eyebrows arched, and James leant toward Trish, so much so that he would soon be sprawled on the tabletop.

'Your successful expulsion was not down to a tried-and-tested method,' he hissed. 'It was on a whim, and it is that whim that allows you to be here leading a seminar rather than being tried in a disciplinary.'

Vanessa tugged at James's shirt. He retreated back into his chair, took a deep breath, and continued.

'You will not be placed on the occupations unit,' he said, 'nor one that involves direct contact with the public for the next twelve months. At that point, your involvement with anything beyond sonar will be reconsidered.'

Blood rushed to Trish's face, and sweat soaked her jumper's collar. James raised his eyebrows to provoke a response. Trish could not find her voice; it had fled, as her body wanted to. She had to be careful. The Network was all she had now. She couldn't lose it.

'If it isn't too much work, I'd like a summary of all activity ran under the adolescent program,' Vanessa said softly. 'Submit it to the archives whenever is best for you.'

Trish smiled without thanks, for words could no longer break through the barrier of rage and embarrassment. She paced from the glass boardroom with as much restraint as she could.

As far as Trish was concerned, the board had lured her into the seminar under false pretences, emptied her of wisdom, and stripped her of privileges. Trish's hypothesis was completely new to her and Sam; the board considered it dated information. She descended the levels of the mineshafts, glad that she, Will, and Sam had not told the board about the shadow. Perhaps finding its true identity would give her argument more validity.

Trish arrived in Will's usual haunt. He'd be down at any moment. It was cool there. The frequency energy tickled her nape, and the darkness seemed less vacant. The usual trickle of water couldn't be heard from the adjacent waterlogged cavern. There would be the hum of the machinery and the rattle of the air conditioning unit that was overdue an inspection. It was as if she had crossed into a vacuum.

The shadow was there. Did it haunt her? The static energy was familiar and strange in the same breath. Certainly not Abidemi, as Will suspected.

The groan of the mechanised door announced Will's arrival. Trish broke her engagement to the imprint.

'Are you okay?' he asked as he hugged her.

'Not really.'

'That was harsher than I anticipated. I'm sorry.'

'Not that,' Trish said. 'It was here.'

'What, the shadow imprint?'

'Yes,' she said. 'I feel like I know it.'

'That's how I felt,' Will said. He closed his eyes, and his lids fluttered. Engagement unsuccessful, he opened his eyes. 'It's gone.'

Dark bags hung under his eyes. He wore the same button-down cardigan from the day before. Uncharacteristic stubble sprouted across his narrow jaw. He worked long hours, though that was nothing unusual. He crossed to the bench with a series of electromagnetic beacons – which Trish often teased reminded her of a swingball pole – and plugged them into an adapter to charge.

'What's going on?' she asked.

'Some of the lab's ketamine has gone. Hasn't been signed off for experiments. Go figure.'

The previous night while taking Rasha home, Trish hadn't worn her dielectric band. She'd seen lines of white powder on a coffee table; Sam's thoughts had been more than a craving. He'd used again.

'Oh bugger,' Trish exclaimed.

Dissociative drugs were commonplace in witnesses' practices to ease connection with the ombrederi. Two winters ago, Trish and Will had petitioned to remove them; a marginal proportion of their colleagues abused substances during their lifetime. They'd done it for Sam most of all, to eradicate temptations that lay in his path. The board had been unanimous in voting against the ban, and Trish couldn't help but think it had less to do with scientific integrity and more about the witnesses' own weaknesses.

'But Sam's sobriety?'

'Gone out of the window, along with his things, and him too if he even tries to deny it to me.'

'He could get help at the Refinery,' Trish said. She hated mentioning the Network's private facility. Though neither had been, they'd reason to fear it: it was the final home for aged witnesses once a lifetime of imprints had finally killed their nerve. Even though psychiatric help was given there, it wasn't somewhere witnesses ever wanted to go.

'The Refinery,' Will scoffed. He ran his fingers through his locks. 'Sam'd be worse than he is now. It's my fault. No, it is, I've neglected him.'

'That's all on him,' Trish said, squeezing his shoulders. 'It's his choice to take it, and it's his choice to seek help. Talk to him. It's all you can do.'

Trish held him and planted a purposefully moist kiss on his forehead. He sniggered and wiped his forehead with his sleeve. She sympathised with Will, but she needed answers.

'So, occupation,' she said. 'What's that about?'

Anxiety bled across Will's face.

'I know you know something, and Sam too. I don't need foresight – I saw how you looked at each other yesterday.'

Will shook his head, leant against his workbench, and stared up at the strobe lights for a moment. Then he said, 'Rose Bickle.'

'Sam's mum? She's in the Refinery.'

'Yes, but do you know why?'

'Witnessing drove her to insanity,' Trish said. Will shuffled his feet. 'You don't believe that?'

'Not since all this Abadi business.'

'What is access to the Refinery like at the moment?'

'Restricted. There was an energy spike. It broke through all the dampeners. Mayhem. You're not thinking of going? Bless her, but Rose won't be able to help you; she's more dead than she is living. You won't get answers from her. Not even Sam could.'

She nodded. It was clear why Sam wanted to numb the pain with laboratory grade dissociative drugs. She'd made equally reckless decisions in her search for Shauna. Rasha Abadi could be worth another visit. Just a courteous act of get-well-soons. *Or tell me what you know for a shed load of chocolate bourbons.*

'Speaking of occupation,' Will said. He lowered his voice. 'I think your hypothesis has legs, quite a few.'

'Thanks for sharing that with the board,' Trish quipped.

'I didn't say anything because I don't think the occupations unit is the best place to explore your theory. I think you have the right program already, and I didn't want it to be taken away from you.'

'Sonar?'

'Think about it. Everything we are, everything we do, it's all because of the frequency. Sonar makes imprints' memories become yours. All branches of the same tree.'

'Sonar's a borderline failure. I haven't been able to collate one solid memory.'

'Maybe it's not enough to have knowledge of an event. Perhaps you have to be emotionally invested?'

Trish nodded. Will spoke of Shauna, of closure, the one thing most witnesses desperately sought. She hugged him one last time and dashed to the storage warehouse.

She had contemplated using sonar to find Shauna before but always adhered to the Network's one fundamental rule when it came to equipment: not to be used for personal reasons. Of course, Sam flouted that every time he stole ketamine from the Network's stores. Will had recently planted deflectors at Sam's flat to cure his own imprint-induced insomnia. Desperate times meant disobeying guidelines.

The only entrance point to the storage warehouse was a coded gate. She punched in a number, relieved her access had not been restricted since the mishap with Rasha. The automatic lights cast insect-like shadows onto the walls from the witnessing paraphernalia that lay in wire display cases. If the activity centre was the erratic heartbeat of the collieries, then the stores were the nervous system containing countless gadgets in various states of disrepair. Trish took the receptor from its stand. This version was mobile, its shell bulbous to accommodate the battery and riddled with welding marks where the device was regularly adjusted and trialled. As it said on the tin – puns were Sam's territory, but Trish was secretly partial – it allowed for better reception to weaker imprint activity, those that absorbed and emitted memories without will. The target for the sonar program: using such memories to rebuild moments lost in time. It was hers, not officially and not with permission, but there were some things more important than abiding by the rules.

She had Shauna's killer to find and Michael's name to clear.

19

SHAUNA HAD TAKEN her last breaths in Penzance in an alleyway that intersected Market Jew Street and New Town Lane.

Trish traipsed down its cobbles and checked her watch: four in the morning. The old fishing port was otherworldly at night without the milling locals and squabbling seagulls. The metallic moonlight contorted the buildings either side of her into a Burton-scape of crooked lines and precarious structures. Trish took the receptor from her duffel bag and fixed it onto her head. She caught her smoky reflection amongst the cuts of meat in the butcher's window. Her eyes were bloodshot, her cheeks drawn; she looked halfway to death.

Receptor secured, Trish stood between a ramshackle garage and the side of a Cornwall Hospice. The receptor's motor hummed, and its weight caused her neck and shoulders to ache. Trish pulled a perfume bottle from her pocket. *Glam*, flogged by a reality television star. God knows who, but it had been Shauna's favourite, to the point where the expensive-to-the-pound-cheap-to-the-nose odour was Shauna. Every relic and every memory. Trish splashed a little onto her forefinger and drew lines with it across her neck. 'Stale rosé,' Trish often mocked. Shauna wouldn't disagree; she had been bought it for Christmas by her partner, Josh, and his family. They had thought a lot of Shauna – Trish too – but Trish lost them when she had chosen to defend Michael against amounting allegations.

After all, the evidence could not be disputed. That night, Michael was last seen leaving The Puffin and Hare with Shauna. He'd brawled with a teenager over a game of darts and was thrown out by the doorman. Later forensics found his DNA on all her clothes, as hers was on his. His actions after her death divided many. He'd been the one to call 999, and when the police arrived they tore him from Shauna's body where he knelt, sobbing into her stomach. Many, Shauna's in-laws included, put that down to guilt. Trish knew that Michael, who rarely kept on the good side of the law, would scarper if he'd committed such an act.

Trish pocketed Shauna's perfume, closed her eyes, and reached for the world that lingered just beyond her basic senses. Her mind fled into the ombrederi.

20

PENZANCE'S OMBREDERI was ablaze with the town's history.

A rabid pub fire tore through the roof of The Puffin and Hare. November floods rushed down Market Jew Street and took locals' rubbish bins with it.

Trish focused hard as Glam swamped her nostrils. The fire and the floods sunk away as paint wafts from a brush soaked in turpentine. A figure moulded itself from the shadows ahead of her. Trish's heart plummeted. *Not the shadow*, she prayed. *Not here.*

It wasn't the shadow imprint at all but a lanky woman who staggered forward and brandished a knife. She lunged and cut through another drunken woman. Trish took hold of the energy around the memory and forced the ground to swallow the imprints.

Trish needed a stronger memory. What was Shauna, above all else?

Teagues' Lighting Shop unravelled from the darkness. That night Trish had hid from social services. Shauna had coaxed her out from between the aisles of energy-saving LEDs, eyes anywhere but the counter. Their parents' bodies lay there. Shauna's face, just a teenager herself, came to Trish as vivid as it had been that night: gnome-esque with warm chestnut eyes. Those freckled cheeks creased with heartbreak.

No matter how many times Trish replayed the memory in her head, let her chest heave with the horror of her parents' death, the ombrederi never changed. Trish let the memory flutter away.

She didn't want to, but Trish thought of the act: murder. Her mind wouldn't let her put the act and Shauna's beautiful face together. It was unfair; it was disgusting.

It was life, she'd learnt, always closely followed by death.

Coarse blue twine. That had been in the coroner's report. It left a deep purple indent in the flesh of her neck, and her rounded face had become blue and bloated.

Trish breathed sharply. Cheap perfume.

Shauna materialised from the frequency energy and ambled up the alleyway as fast as her drunken legs would carry her. Tears turned her mascara to sludge across her cheeks. Her high heels clattered on the cobbles, hand on the wall of the Cornwall Hospice for support.

'I'm sorry, Trish,' she cried. 'Trish, Trish . . .'

'I'm here!' Trish called, but that was then, and Trish was now, and Shauna wouldn't be able to hear.

In fact, neither could Trish. Shauna's cries dissolved. The darkest shadows in the butcher's shop door rippled, and from them staggered a body on irregular limbs, awkward and splayfooted. What could be described as its head had no features; it was just a bulbous waxen facade.

The shadow imprint.

Trish shrunk in its aura. Despite its awkward posture and inadequate biology, the shadow imprint filled the air with a sense of superiority. Colour and shape disintegrated around its edges as if it were a humanoid eclipse.

21

WITH A WHIMPER, Trish lost the connection to the ombrederi and slammed onto the cobbles of Market Jew Street. The receptor slipped from her head and clanged to the ground. Had shock broken her connection to the ombrederi, or had the shadow cast her out?

Trish scrambled to her feet and rubbed the knees of her leggings, now torn and mottled with blood. She'd hit the ground hard, more than enough to rip her away from the ombrederi. Her hands shook as she scooped the receptor up in her arms. She hadn't imagined the shadow – that much she knew. It was as much part of the memory as Shauna or the buildings were.

It had been there the night Shauna died.

PART THREE

UNTETHERED

22

SAMUEL BICKLE wanted to investigate Pendeen alone.

The peninsula's cliff tops were barren in the a.m. and allowed Sam to indulge in habits that many would scold him for. As ever, it didn't turn out that way. Cavern fever set in, and Will was adamant he'd go with Sam – after all, eighteen hours in semidarkness and artificial lights was no good for anyone's mental health, let alone a witness's. Ten minutes after their arrival, Trish rang Sam. He spent the next thirty minutes listening to her recount the recent sonar trial in Penzance over loudspeaker.

Will kept in earshot as he stabbed EMP beacons into the earth. Trish's frantic words washed over Sam. He soaked up the waves as they rolled, silver in the moonlight. Sam adored Trish – she was often the glue that kept him and Will together. However, her one defining flaw was that she struggled to let go of things she couldn't possibly change.

'Are you sure you weren't just projecting onto the memory?' Sam asked again. 'You've been thinking about it a lot.'

'For the twentieth time, Bickle,' Trish groaned. 'It felt – how can I describe it – sentient. It had an aura, and when it appeared all sound and colour – '

An 8-bit chime informed Sam that Trish had lost connection.

'There goes her 5 percent battery,' he said.

'She might be under a lot of stress, but she has foresight,' Will said. 'If anyone will find something plausible with sonar, it's Trish.'

'Under a lot of stress, exactly,' Sam remarked. 'The last thing you should have done was suggest sonar.'

'I thought she could do with a distraction,' Will said. 'At least I'm trying to help.'

Sam dared not retort to Will's jibe. Yes, he had been indisposed when Trish had led the seminar and hadn't been there to support her. But she'd had Will, and that was better.

Will flitted between the probes to check readings for frequency energy. Behind them, the lighthouse loomed over Pendeen. It marked one of the most active ley lines in the county, mostly because frequency energy latched to tin ore. The Network hadn't taken to Wheal Gorenn or Pendeen on a whim, after all. Ley lines were often nicknamed 'anchor points' by witnesses, for imprints tended to gravitate toward the power sources; Pendeen was Abidemi's. They'd find her there or not at all.

Abidemi, the guide that had abandoned them, just as Sam suspected everyone would. For Sam, the strength of the anchor point wouldn't be enough. He withdrew a baggie of ketamine from his jacket.

Will snatched the plastic wallet from Sam's hand and scrutinised the ivory pills within; Will had to make his point. Sam abandoned the Network equipment and sprung at Will. He kept his eyes on the ketamine just in case Will flung them into the toiling sea below.

'You promised,' Will growled.

'Well, I can't withdraw without it,' Sam said. 'Abidemi's gone. She's being blamed for everything the shadow imprint has done. Needs must.'

Will threw the ziplock bag at him. He turned back to their equipment, plucked a probe from a bag, and thrust it into the soil where it stood upright.

Sam went back to his bags and took out a ridged square box: an amplifier. It gradually enhanced natural frequency energy and was far safer and more effective than an EMP. Used in tangent with a hallucinogenic substance, better still.

'When was the last time you withdrew?' Will asked.

'Successfully? Not since rehab.'

'You want to go back there? Worse yet, the Refinery?'

'I'm not going to get addicted.'

'You always will be,' Will scoffed. 'But that's not what I meant. If you protract at the height of a frequency spike, you might not come back.'

Sam ignored him, wrenched the last beacon from its container, and jabbed it into the dirt.

'Wouldn't you be so lucky,' he said under his breath in purposeful earshot of Will.

The probes beeped in unison with every twenty hertz of frequency energy. There were beeps forty seconds apart, but in no time at all it accelerated to every ten seconds, then every five.

'Nearly at the height of a spike,' Will said.

Sam ripped the baggie open, put a few pills on a closed hard case, and crushed it with the corner of a remote handset.

'For fuck's sake, really?' Will griped.

'It's quicker this way.'

Sam rolled the card flap of a cigarette packet, put it to his nose, and snorted. The ketamine stung his nostrils beautifully. As he stood upright, the effects were already upon him. The outlines of Will, the probes, and their cases became hazy, and colours bled into one another.

'The amplifier is live.' Will's voice reverberated. Sam's skin crawled. Abstract thoughts, neither his nor induced by ketamine, swam through the fog in his brain. 'Frequency energy is consistent.'

Eyes closed, Sam let his imprint succumb to the movement of the frequency energy as it lapped and rolled around him. The wind on his neck numbed, and the ache in his joints eased. His imprint shed the bone and sinew and post-winter fat behind like dough scraped from a proofing bowl.

Just his imprint.

Outside of his body, he looked back on himself, his face vacant atop the cliffs. Hair grey and face lined, he looked older than his reflection in mirrors suggested. Will hung back, lost in the motion of everything. Grass fluttered, waves hurtled, a barn owl swooped, and tears poured from Will's eyes.

It was all inconsequential.

To reach Abidemi, he had to think of the shame that bound them both together. The scar on his right arm was as painful as the day he was branded it.

Sam recalled that day in Keast Family Bakery – the unbearable heat from the many ovens, a poorly ventilated kitchen at the height of summer. Yeasty bread and vanilla buttercream wafted through the bakery, congealed with the cigarette smoke and sweat that clung to the bakers' whites. It had been Sam's first job since his mother's incarceration, living between bedsits, each more meagre than the last. He had refused the Network's helping hand, certain he could build a normal life. There never was a normal for Sam.

The previous night, Sam and his colleagues had embarked on an end of season pub and club crawl through Newquay's town centre. He thought of his mother often, of the occultist nutjobs that scuttled beneath Wheal Gorenn, and each time he did he necked a shot of vodka. Every time he saw an imprint entwined in the disco lights or loitering in empty hallways, he took a triple of tequila, until person and imprint had become one indistinguishable blur. During his intoxicated daze, he had kissed the kitchen supervisor, Tim, and later learnt the alcohol he had consumed clouded what little judgment he had.

The next morning, Tim and his kitchen assistants pounced on Sam. They dragged him to one of the ovens. Tim found an iron cutout in the shape of a carrot. He held it with tongs, opened an oven door, and pressed it against the bottom of the oven. When the cutout was warped from heat, Tim withdrew it and pressed it into Sam's forearm. The pain was excruciating; the shame was worse. It scarred his skin – marked his imprint. Only Abidemi had come close to experiencing a similar tragedy. Abidemi, who had still not come.

Abidemi who, much like Will, had given up on him.

Will.

His face swam into view. Horrified. Bloodied. Bruised. He fell through a sky of diamonds. Rasha was bound in rope and grabbed at by many hands. Trish was crushed in an iron fist —

Sam came back to his body. It was heavy as though he'd risen from a bath. Clouds had since cleared the evening sky, and stars swirled with Gogh-esque velocity.

He rose steadily, his hands numbed to the grass beneath him; he could have been wearing oven mitts. With the equipment and flashlight in hand, Will charged to James' people carrier, which they borrowed from their manager.

He never looked back to see if Sam would follow.

23

EYES. EYES EVERYWHERE. They watched Sam, and they judged him. In the activity centre, Vanessa peered from her desk when they passed. Will's pained expression as they sat at the table in the biology lab. Trish's scowl as she joined them amongst the glass walls. Even the Network's logo peered at him like owlish eyes. Embellished on equipment, ID badges, and push-pull doors, the logo comprised of two circles interlocked at an angle. Left to interpretation, Sam was certain it depicted engagement, the moment in which the frontal lobe latched to the energy of an imprint. He was also sure they scathed him for breaking his sobriety. For breaking Will.

Will ensured he took the available seat farthest away from Sam so that Trish sat between them. She was often the mediator between the pair, whether the issue was work or mothers or, as ever, drugs. That day she was preoccupied.

'I know what I saw,' she said. 'It was the shadow imprint. Speaking of which, did you find Abidemi?'

'No,' Sam said. 'Her signature wasn't on any emotional tethers.'

'The ketamine worked out for you,' Will sneered.

'I couldn't clear my mind,' Sam said. The haunting images of Will and Trish came back to him. 'Everything going on, with the disciplinary and with the Abadi girl – '

'Rasha,' Trish reminded him.

'Yep. I wasn't in the right headspace. This doesn't mean Abidemi is guilty.'

'Doesn't make her innocent, either,' Trish jibed. 'An imprint is incognito, haunts people to the point of occupation, as a guiding imprint goes AWOL.'

'Abidemi wouldn't break imprint code,' Sam said. He had always been surer of her than himself. 'I think it's more a coincidence that all of this stuff is happening since frequency spikes have escalated.'

Trish and Will sat upright and stared at him.

'A fifteen-year-old girl draws enough imprint activity for our systems to detect it,' Sam continued. 'When we do intervene, we only raise the frequency energy in the caravan site minutely, yet her susceptibility to it increases tenfold.'

'It's more than coincidental,' Will said. He spun on the stool, his tablet in hand. 'Look at these readings from Pendeen.'

He turned the tablet screen to them. A simple line graph depicted frequency waves in a forty-eight-hour period. The peaks ebbed and flowed in exact eight-hour cycles.

'It's like clockwork,' Trish observed. 'Only man-made interference could do that.'

'There's another spike incoming,' Will said.

Frequency energy tingled upon Sam's skin. Most of the tunnel and cavern walls in the Network were lined with a honeycomb pattern of deflectors, but for investigative purposes the laboratories weren't. Still coming down from his high, Sam was more exposed than most.

'Brace yourselves,' he said.

Energy shot through the glass room and penetrated his skull. The labs were swiped from Sam's view –

Wheal Gorenn unfolded around them in a time-lapse. At the epicentre of it all stood a girl with dirty-blond hair and a snapped neck: Abidemi. The shadow imprint joined her, with a gait neither human nor animal. Sam tried to reach out to Abidemi. The shadow would consume her. Instead, it stood by her side in solidarity. A torrent of water cascaded into the cavern –

The cold iron walkway. Sam climbed to his feet and helped Trish to hers. Will refused his help. Sam leant in and kissed him. It was a quick emotionless peck, a formality that sustained their relationship. It lingered, not with romance or emotional support, but with distrust. Sam had many bad habits, and disappointing people was one of them.

Sam wasn't going to mention the vision he had, but Will said, 'I saw Abidemi. I saw Abidemi and the shadow imprint.'

'Me too,' Trish puffed. 'Like they'd both been there, from the beginning, for all this time.'

24

SAM'S EXHAUSTED EYES reflected back at him from the Reliant's windows. Behind it, the entanglement of farm buildings and woodland passed by in a plum blur. Trish drove in silence; Will punched words into his iPad. No one was spirited enough to talk.

The Network was on high alert from increased frequency spikes. James had sent specialist teams to all of their seven high-frequency sites including Pendeen. Sam and Trish remained uninvited; being demoted had its perks. Despite his protests, Will was overworked and had been refused participation. Off-put by what he had experienced – and not fond of the idea of staying in the collieries completely alone – Will reluctantly went home with Sam.

After twenty minutes of dispirited silence, they reached Tresillian, and the Reliant's headlights caught the red brick of Sam and Will's apartment building. Once a priory in the 1700s, their building had passed through the hands of the rich and the fortunate until it was renovated into a handful of flats in the noughties. Weeds sprouted in the grouting, its west side stained where it took the brunt of wet weather. As they climbed out, Will turned back to Trish.

'We should keep what we saw to ourselves,' he said. 'James finds out we withheld information, we can say goodbye to the Network.'

Sam dared not respond that he wanted little to do with the Network; he'd only receive scathing retorts.

'Yeah,' Trish responded, tone sullen. 'Bye, Beaker. Bye, Bickle.'

The men murmured their byes back, and slammed the car doors shut. Trish reversed onto the deserted main road, tooted her horn, and sped toward Bugle.

The main lights in the Old Priory were broken, so Sam and Will had to ascend the stairs in the putrid green glow of the emergency exit signs. The night they met was much the same. They'd snuck into Sam's bedsit at night, careful not to wake his neighbours. That had been Sam's seventh day into his Network induction. After an hour of lovemaking, they'd lain awake into the early hours and declared their deepest darkest secrets, hopes, and aspirations. They'd spent every night together since, but that had ended two months ago. Sex rarely happened. Soul-bearing conversations were nonexistent. How much could someone change in two months? Were they strangers to each other?

Stale food, towers of dirty crockery, and soiled laundry bombarded their noses when they entered the downtrodden flat. Will went straight to the bin, emptied it, and left without another word. Sam placed his satchel on the counter and took out the plastic wallet of ketamine. If they weren't all used during withdrawal trials, it was compulsory to return them to the laboratories. Witnesses rarely did. He took a pill from the bag and held it between his thumb and forefinger. What abstinence could there truly be from a dependency that pivoted on the very fact one was abnormal? Ketamine did not cure him of his witnessing capabilities, nor did it allow him to forget them. It did numb the intensity of seeing the dead whilst the normality of the world became surreal. The two polar realities Sam struggled to live between merged into one cascade of colour and sound.

Sam skulked to the coffee table, crushed the remaining pills with a cast-iron ornament, and snorted them with a rolled five-pound note. He fell back onto the sofa. To his right were the balcony doors, and in front was the chimney breast. Light bent and refracted. The ceiling fan sparked with motion. Will was back. He spoke, but Sam couldn't process his words. Will pointed from the coffee table to Sam, and he yelled and accused. Sam began to talk back. He didn't know what; his mind was on the world that rotated around him. He felt every spinning particle and torrenting tide, every orbit as the Earth veered around the sun. Sam may as well have been occupied. In some ways he was, possessed by ketamine.

Will didn't see the tongues of fire lick the wall around the chimney breast – his mind was more resilient to frequency energy than Sam's. Imprints of priests darted forward, buckets in hand. The fire engulfed a cross on the mantle and gorged on a shelf of freshly printed testaments. The priests tossed water onto the flames, daring to be burnt. Anything to quell the destruction of their holy articles.

All in faith.

Will was beyond any notion of salvaging precious things. He had been for a long time. The cavalry of his shouts and tears were desperate last pleas; Will wanted to feel loved, but he was broken and tired, on the precipice of giving up.

Lost in the many delayed echoes of himself, Will gathered clothes and possessions and thrust them into bags as the fire dwindled to ash. The front door opened, and every lagging frame of Will's movement dissipated until he was gone.

Good, Sam thought. Will was free of him, his addictions, and his afflictions. It was better that Will thought it was his choice. He'd move on from Sam. He'd start his life again and be free in ways Sam could never be.

By the fireplace, the priests came together and observed the damage that had been done. Sam slipped into a world that existed between the ombrederi and sleep.

25

AT FIRST SAM thought it was his own reflection on the shower door. He wiped away the steam, his hand making a gull-like squeak on the glass, to find Abidemi's body above the toilet, her neck gripped by a noose, pirouetting in an absent breeze. Her eyes were open and hollow. Abidemi only came to Sam in her rawest form when she had a warning to deliver. Considering her absence from the Network, her message must have been urgent.

Sam lumbered from the bathtub and wrapped a towel around himself – misplaced dignity, as the dead did not care for modesty. Abidemi's projection shifted as he moved, sometimes a child and sometimes a woman; six hundred years of death could teach one more about life than living could.

He hadn't been aware of her arrival. The scalding water numbed the static that drummed on his skin. Sam closed his eyes. The underside of his eyelids burst with colour until Abidemi's aura – which radiated heartbreak and forbidden love – dissipated along with the ombrederi.

Sam opened his eyes to the loneliness of the flat once more. Beyond the steady drip of the leaky showerhead, the flat was silent. He tiptoed into the hall, taking care not to slip on the linoleum. Recollections of the previous night were jumbled with fire and urgent priests. He had been on the sofa, and Will had pointed and cried at the ketamine dust on the coffee table that was still there. Will wasn't. Sam's sins always remained with him.

His name was screamed, far off, miles away. No, it wasn't human or organic, but a car, the toot of its horn, and it was just outside the balcony doors. Sam whipped them open. The morning sunlight overwhelmed his eyes. The Reliant Robin was parked in the potholed car park. Trish impatiently tooted its horn and mouthed through the window, *Code red!*

He darted to the bedroom that was now just his. Still damp in places, he clothed himself and raced down the shadowy staircase before his shoelaces were properly tied. Inside the Reliant, Trish sped away from the apartment block and toward Gorenn. She didn't know what the code red was. It didn't deter her from prying. 'Do you need to go to the Refinery? Talk to James, he'll understand.'

Sam hadn't even mentioned the night before. Will had surely texted her. Either that or her foresight. He pulled the passenger visor down and inspected himself in its mirror. His skin was grey, eyes bloodshot.

'The Refinery is a load of bollocks,' Sam said. 'James knows it, the whole board knows it. He'd send me there and keep me there as punishment for everything we've done.'

'Sounds like you've given up, like you don't care about your sobriety.'

Everyone else – his friends, the Network, Will's family – cared for his sobriety more than he did. His afflictions were firmly on the outside for all to see, so everyone felt entitled to comment. How could he care for his sobriety? There was no true cure to seeing the dead day in and day out. Other witnesses had found peace with it. Sam knew it manifested in other, by no means healthier, ways. Consider Trish, who used her witnessing abilities to reconnect with Shauna using stolen Network technology.

'I don't want to be sober. The problem isn't me – it's everyone else.'

Trish slammed the brakes. The rear of the Reliant kicked out, and the car came to a stop along the width of the lane. A queasiness – from Trish's driving, the comedown, both – tugged at his intestines. Trish's voice rang loudly, and she thumped the steering wheel with every word.

'It's-a-problem-because-they-love-you. You-don't-hurt-the-people-you-love, you-just-don't.'

The dustcover on the back seat slipped, uncovering the receptor. Another unsuccessful night hunting Shauna and finding the shadow imprint, Sam presumed. *Grief is selfish.* Sam had always thought that.

'Code red,' Sam prompted. He wouldn't make promises he couldn't keep.

Trish revved the Reliant back to life, and the rest of the twenty-minute journey to the collieries passed in a quiet tension. The activity centre was in a grave silence when they arrived, as though everyone was in mourning. Trish was quick to confirm his suspicions.

'I think someone's died.'

A ripple of whispers coursed through their colleagues as they crossed the cavern to the birdcage. Vanessa, with an agility that defied the physics bound to her overweight body, dove inside and beckoned James out. He walked to them with a stoic purpose.

'I think it's the Abadi girl,' Sam whispered through the

corner of his mouth.

'It isn't,' Trish said. James was too close for Sam to question her.

'I tried to call,' James said. 'Let's go to my office.'

Considering the uneven ground on which their working relationship stood, Sam and Trish knew better than to question James and so followed him inside. Trish bowed her head as they went. All eyes were on them. All except Will's. He was probably metres underground in the laboratories. James closed the office door.

No. Will would be in the activity centre during a red alert. He'd demand to be given tasks, to fulfil his duty in a time of need.

Sam couldn't sit down, his feet rooted to the floor. He squeezed the back of the wooden chair. There seemed to be a malignant force nestled in the furniture, for as soon as Trish sat, she buried her face in her hands. James reclined into his, face wrinkled into a grief-stricken mosaic. He said through tears, 'Will is dead. I'm sorry.'

26

EYES, SO MANY EYES. Witnesses peered in through the glass from the activity centre. Trish's were pained and glistening, James's wide and waiting. So why did Sam smile?

It was ridiculous. It was Friday, and Sam would make up with Will, promise sobriety – another trip to the Refinery if he had to – and cook a chili for them. He'd apologise for his behaviour with a bottle of Will's favourite red, a cordial for himself. On Saturday they'd watch the local cricket match, then saunter to a nearby beer garden for the evening. Sunday would be a slow sweaty morning where their only activities involved their bed. To Will's parents' for a midday roast, tiptoeing through family politics and local gossip. Will couldn't have died when Sam's whole existence needed Will in it for it to mean anything at all.

'Sam, say something,' James pleaded.

Trish sobbed with sharp intakes of breath. Sam's face was dry. He stood and waited for a tide of sadness to slam against him. All that came was agitation.

'How do you mean, died?' he growled.

'What we know is limited,' James said carefully. 'The

police got there first.'

'You knew there was an issue?'

'There was a frequency spike in Rosenannon. Imprint activity was detected at his parents' property.'

'An imprint?' Sam was sceptical.

'Potentially.'

'So an accident,' Trish thought out loud. 'An engagement went wrong. He always said an imprint haunted that cottage.'

'Everything is speculation at this point,' James said. It bothered Sam how quickly this news became an investigation, peeling off any personal ties to the event. To Will. 'We dispatched the occupations unit there. They found a signature outside the house.'

'Who?' Sam couldn't have said it sharper if he'd tried.

James eyed him wearily, and maintained eye contact with Sam as he said, 'The signature was a noose. Abidemi.'

James continued to relay facts and figures, stuff strictly business that had no place in that moment. Imprints left signatures, an image or emotion, in their wake to tell witnesses they'd been there. Guilt niggled in the pit of Sam's stomach. Abidemi had met him just before Will's death, perhaps after – Sam could not pinpoint events to hours over the last couple of days. She only ever met him to warn him. Perhaps she'd tried to alert him of Will's death.

'This is a mistake,' Sam uttered. James and Trish didn't hear over their fraught voices. So Sam shouted, 'He can't be dead!'

James's and Trish's babble was cut off quicker than a guillotine to the necks of the guilty. James approached Sam, hands out as if to embrace him.

'I know this is hard – '

'I need to see. I need to see the house.'

Sam strode from the desk before a response was given and fled from the birdcage. James's and Trish's footsteps clunked as they chased after him through the myriad of desks. Trish called for him to come back. It was no good; he was adamant. His only concern was to prove that they were severely misinformed.

'Let him go!' James yelled. 'He's grieving!'

Wrong on both counts. Sam couldn't possibly grieve because no one had died. Of course Trish wouldn't let him go alone.

'Take me to Marge's and Phil's,' Sam barked at Trish as he ascended the main ladder to the northern exit. He dared not call it Will's; he belonged back at the priory with Sam.

Trish stumbled behind him. She sniffled and coughed as she went.

'I'm not in the right state of mind.'

'Then give me your keys.'

Sam reached the indoor car park, blinded by the sun as it filtered through the warehouse skylights. Sam turned to face Trish, a dishevelled mess. He held out his hand.

'You're in no fit state yourself,' Trish remarked.

'This can't wait,' Sam said. 'I need to know, Trish. Don't you understand? I need to know!'

'Okay, okay,' Trish said. She crossed to the Reliant, fumbling with her keys. 'But I'm driving slow.'

'Just get me there,' Sam said. He climbed into the Reliant.

The journey through the winding sun-washed B-roads was the longest forty minutes of Sam's life. He glanced at the clock on the Reliant's dashboard, then to his phone's lock screen, as if time had been bottled in gelatin. All he could picture was Will's face, bearing that defeatist smile he often wore when accepting Sam's apology. Sam would say sorry profusely.

He'd never give Will a reason to run to his parents again, and he would tell him that. But with every sluggish minute, the thought of Will taking Sam back seemed slimmer. When Trish turned into the Reeves' driveway, the concept of seeing Will's face was snatched away.

The Reeves' refurbished cottage wore slate and granite like armour. Will hated it, for it had been an imprint magnet during his adolescence. Sam detested it because it was the home of Margaret and Phil. Ex-owners of the local cricket club, Phil had become somewhat withdrawn in his later years and left Marge to spit her venom whilst he tinkered away undisturbed in the workshop. It had lost its aura with recent events. The window to Will's old bedroom, situated on the farthest side of the first floor, was shattered, and where glass should have been was a ripple of yellow police tape. Two emergency police cars and a van were parked on the gravel, around which loitered a medley of cops as forensics shed their bodysuits. All of them turned as the Reliant pulled up. At least ten pairs of eyes, all assuming, all questioning. That was when he thought, *What if they think I did it?*

He leapt from the Reliant before Trish had pulled it to a stop. He stumbled on the gravel, righted himself, and raced toward the cottage, sure to keep a wide berth of the police in case they were to hold him back.

'Sam!' Trish yelled. 'Sam, don't go in!'

The flower beds beneath the kitchen window were flattened where something heavy had fallen, cordoned off by more police tape. Glass dewed the gravel path.

Sam turned the corner to the side of the house and staggered into the two people he wanted to see least: Phil and Margaret. Margaret let out a hoarse gasp and Phil, who Sam noted was unsteady on his legs, managed to grab him by the arms.

'Sam, my lover,' he said, his eyes watery blue pools. Will's eyes. 'I'm sorry. Will – '

Sam fought his way out of Phil's grip. He pushed past them.

'Sam!'

Sam paid no attention. He barged through the side door into the reception-come-kitchen, skated across the kitchen tiles, and crossed into the low-ceilinged hallway. The main stairs to the first floor were steep and creaked under his weight. There it was: Will's bright blue door at the head of the stairs. More bile-yellow police tape was strung diagonally across the doorway.

There was no hesitation. He needed to know.

Sam threw the door open. It scuffed the carpet; one of the hinges had shattered. What was once a wardrobe and bedside table had been reduced to splintered fragments. The vintage floor lamp that Will had tried to steal for their flat was in a twisted heap by the window. The window was now just an empty orifice framing the summer day outside. Will had fallen to his death. Splatters of blood left an erratic spiral along the carpet, walls, and ceiling. His blood, adamant to remain on the Earth.

Sam's knees buckled.

Will's blood.

Trish arrived outside the door. She sobbed and panted, trying to catch her breath. She didn't dare enter the bedroom. What she could see was enough to make her cry.

Sam dared not look her way. He didn't want her to see his dry face. So he did his best to absorb the room, in the dishevelled mess it was, to make himself believe the unavoidable.

This is real, he thought. *This is real, so cry. Why aren't you crying?*

Only the bed frame seemed intact, whilst the shelves and photo frames had been obliterated. Even The Vincent, a print of a painting of the nineteenth century ship, was smashed and torn on the stained carpet. Will had hated it but kept it up to appease Margaret.

'Sam,' Trish gasped.

He picked the print up in his unsteady hands. The canvas had been torn. Someone had mentioned it so uncertainly that it had been dismissed on the very spot. That was it. The Abadi girl. It seemed the most important thing in the world. He repeated it to make sure it sounded right on his tongue, and it did.

'The Vincent will fall.'

INTERLUDE I

EWELLA RUNS because they called her strange. *Foles*, the village children cried in Kernewek. They wouldn't stop, so Ewella runs through wild woodlands and across fields of crisp mud. The summer sun scorches her shoulders, but at least the emotions she feels are her own. Two summers past, in a raid that pre-empted the Battle of Lostwithiel of 1644, Britons butchered her father and many other villagers. Since that night, her mind conjures the queerest of imagery. Memories not her own. Lust and greed and hatred surpass anything she encountered in her small years. The people she sees, who no longer walk the earth.

She reaches the cliff edge. There is a rocky descent to the ferocious waters below. The salty air cleanses her senses and dulls the world beyond her own mind. Back to herself. Back to Ewella.

She dares toe the cliff edge. A child of the wild country – the daughter of a fisherman, at that – and yet she cannot swim. A twisted spine and a lopsided pelvis leave her unable to float in the calmest waters. Ewella, the hunched maiden who converses with the empty air. Anything but powerful, as her name suggests. *Foles*, indeed.

As the waves beneath her, pictures roll into her mind and swirl against her skull. Goodness, what she sees. Desert plains dry because of a forever summer. Beasts with long teeth, longer noses, and impossible necks. Unbearable sadness punches her gullet. For a family torn apart. A family with ebony skin.

Giddiness overcomes her. She falls to her knees. Before her, a league out at sea, merely shadows against the glittering ocean, vessels float. Four, maybe five. Their sails are jagged as the rocks around her; it is not of British design. Perhaps that's where the memories come from.

Ewella picks herself up, unruffles her fraying dress, and races back to the village. Will anyone heed her? Chances are slight. Her brother, Arthek, burdened with their father's duties, will push her aside with embarrassment. Her mother will smack her for making up such tales. She'll also be smacked for fleeing.

The terrain flattens into meadows, and she spots the silvery leaves of catmint. That will be her excuse: flowers for her father's grave. The overgrown verge ruffles. It's a stifling summer day, for there is no wind. Something moves purposefully unseen. Wide hunting eyes glint amongst the leaves. Ebony men of large stature emerge with dirtied vests and trousers. Fear rids Ewella of her voice; a scream catches in her stomach as though tied with a fisherman's knot.

Hands grab at her and wrap coarse twine around her wrists and ankles. A stale slither of fabric is thrust into her mouth. She kicks hard and catches their pelvises with her heels. Fights with Arthek taught her men's weak spots. They slap her and drag her across the sunbaked earth. Her feet, which once ran so desperately away from her village, scrape across the rocky incline to the water's edge where she is cast into a dingy. Her five captors settle into the boat and drive it out to sea with their paddles.

Despite the terror at the captors who tower over her and the swell of alien imagery in her mind, Ewella cannot take her eyes away from her wild country as it shrinks from view.

PART FOUR

WHEN THE DEAD
COME KNOCKING

27

RASHA ENSURED she made her tie loose when she changed for school.

For the five nights since she'd last been at the collieries, she'd dreamt of being strangled by the man that Sam and Trish named Michael. Then he'd let go, and Rasha would fall for an eternity. Will often fell with her, bloodied and bruised, and shards of glass would hail past them.

Since her occupation, Rasha had heard nothing from the Network. Not that she needed to; Will's death was indisputable knowledge, as the sky is blue or how blood runs red. They were concerned with greater things.

Rasha just didn't know how she knew.

After a kerfuffle finding matching socks, Rasha floated into the kitchen. Haya brewed a green tea at the kitchen counter. Skin ashen and hair tangled, she probably hadn't slept. Since the occupation, Haya got herself from bed and took her medication without Rasha's assistance. She avoided being within proximity of Rasha. Fear was all her mother needed to regain her independence.

'Morning,' Rasha said in Levantine with feigned

sprightliness, hoping a positive attitude would entice her mother to come out of her shell.

'Yep,' Haya retorted. Her back remained to Rasha as she poured her tea, eyes fixed on the lifeless park beyond the window.

Their relationship had been sustained by transactional utterances of 'dinner' or 'bed.' Haya hadn't looked at Rasha once, at least not whilst Rasha looked her way. Haya denied her very existence, and it irked Rasha. After all, it was she who was occupied.

If only I could ignore it, Rasha thought.

Rasha feigned ignorance. 'Breakfast' was interpreted as 'morning, did you sleep well?' whilst 'bed' became the conclusion of a doting conversation about boys and coursework. She did things to please Haya. Rice Pops at breakfast, for example. Terribly bland crisp cardboard nuggets, nothing on bourbons. She poured a bowl and munched with her mouth open in the hope Haya would tell her off for poor table manners, to give some indication that they were still mother and daughter.

'We're learning about wavelengths in school,' Rasha said. 'They teach it like they're robots.'

Haya stayed silent. Her tea must have been scalding because she took short regulated sips and stared forward, focused on nothing in particular.

'Coding in IT. It's its own language.'

Sip.

'They say a fifth of us will be software engineers, that's where the industry is heading. Well, the ones who go university anyway. If we're allowed to stay in Britain, I want to go to uni.'

Sip.

Rasha glared at her mother. The grey unkempt hair. The jewellery that slipped over her thin knuckles. A shell of her former self. There was that saying – like father, like son – and Rasha fretted whether it could be applied to mothers and daughters. She wanted more from her life than perpetual fear and uncertainty.

Rasha rose from the table, her cereal half-eaten. She strode straight to the sink, elbow to elbow with Haya as she scraped the sodden remains of her Rice Pops down the drain and rinsed it with cold water. Haya snatched up her tea and sertraline and moved to the sofa. She plonked herself onto the cushions, body turned toward the large bay window.

There would be no hope that day.

She grabbed her rucksack from the coat peg and burst out into the damp morning. No goodbye – vacant words were worse than silence.

By the time Rasha had paced the length of the caravan park she was already soaked through and so was somewhat relieved to be under the cover of the trees in the narrow lane. She made a mental note to keep her raincoat hung by her rucksack for the mornings she would storm out of the caravan.

Not that she would be out in the open for long.

A mechanical hum followed Rasha for the best part of a minute before she realised that it wasn't a tractor in the neighbouring field. Behind her dawdled a beaten Land Rover. The backroads of Gorenn were frequented by cautious drivers who avoided overtaking pedestrians and cyclists in the narrows. Rasha backed into the verge to let them pass. The vehicle didn't speed up.

'Well come on, then,' she muttered. She'd be soaked to her underwear before long. The Rover crawled forward, and Rasha recognised the face behind the windscreen. It had stared at her, wide-eyed, in the collieries, much as it did now: the short, frog-faced woman with the leather journal.

The Rover was level with Rasha when it stopped. The woman reached over to the passenger door and cranked the window down.

'Rasha, isn't it?' she asked.

Rasha nodded, unsure how to respond. What if she misplaced the face? She couldn't risk mentioning the Network or Wheal Gorenn. Allah knew the repercussions.

The woman seemed aware of Rasha's discomfort and smiled toothily.

'I saw you at the collieries,' she prompted. 'I'm Vanessa. Hopefully that means you'll be joining us?'

'I'm allowed?' Rasha asked. Rushed into Wheal Gorenn and beckoned through deserted mineshafts, she'd been an unwanted secret.

'That's what it's there for,' Vanessa chortled. 'The Network is a haven for people like you and me.'

With a broad smile, Vanessa leant across the front seat and opened the passenger door.

'You're not going to walk to school in this, are you?'

Had she heard from Trish and friends, she would have declined, but as seemed to be the case since her arrival to Britain, Rasha had been abandoned by them that week. Rasha nodded, leapt into the Rover, and pulled the door closed. Vanessa trundled on up the lane. Her Land Rover was certainly a working farm vehicle: mud encrusted the foot wells, and the back seat brimmed with supplies from mismatched Wellingtons to a horse saddle. Vanessa herself, short and stout with a speckle of rosacea across the bridge of her nose, fitted the archetypal farmer's wife.

'Tell me, Rasha,' Vanessa said. 'What do you think

engagement is?'

Trish had asked a similar question the day Rasha first entered Wheal Gorenn. Since then she'd built upon her original response.

'There are walls around us. Engagement tears them down.'

Vanessa nodded. In the meek stormy light, she held a smile somewhere between satisfaction and, dare Rasha think it, concern.

'When the Network cures me,' Rasha continued, 'I will be able to keep the walls up for good?'

Vanessa glanced at her, face stony.

'Is that what they told you?' she asked. 'Sam and Trish?'

'More or less,' Rasha said.

'What you have isn't an affliction,' Vanessa said. 'It's a gift.'

Rasha pondered over the various hauntings, from the crooked shadow to the miners drowned in a sea of blood to Joel Tredethy with his limbs snapped at various angles.

'It's no gift,' she said. 'The stuff I see.'

'When you can control engagement, you'll bypass all of that,' Vanessa said. 'If you'll have me, I want to assist you. You don't need curing; you need nurturing.'

'You say it like it's a superpower,' Rasha said, not caring that she sounded scornful. Constantly seeing imprints' gruesome deaths was a disadvantage in her eyes.

'No,' Vanessa said with a smile. 'It's more than human.'

The Land Rover reached the school gate. Rasha unbuckled her seat belt and then looked at Vanessa. She still didn't quite understand what Vanessa wanted, but her offer tempted Rasha all the same. Trish and Sam had approached Rasha with so much caution and uncertainty. Haya glanced at her with horrified eyes. Rasha was tired of being held at arm's length. Vanessa promised to embrace what Rasha had been forced to bottle up.

'You're not much of a talker, are you?' Vanessa chortled. 'School finishes at three thirty? Well, I'll come back then. If you don't want me to mentor you, just walk right by my Landy. I'll get the message loud and clear.'

Rasha nodded, gathered up her rucksack, and hopped out into the car park alongside the school gymnasium. The canteen was opposite, and the smell of deep-fat fryers and powdered custard stirred her Rice Pop–laden stomach. Rasha walked away, stopped, and turned back.

'What happened to that man?' she asked. 'To Will?'

'If you're as special as I think you are, then you already know.'

Will plummets in a storm of glass.

Her stomach writhed. Rasha pelted as fast as she could to the nearest toilet.

28

VANESSA'S OFFER became more tempting as Rasha's day continued.

As Vanessa had driven her to school, Rasha had arrived forty minutes early. The only unlocked toilets were the staff's, where she'd idled for forty minutes, rocking back and forth until the panic attack loosened its grip on her lungs. Certain she could keep further attacks at bay, she headed to Cridland's workshop just as the bell for first period tolled. It was rare for Rasha to turn up to class on time.

Unperturbed by the laggard schoolchildren in the halls, Rasha walked with her head bowed as she deliberated over the cause of the anxiety attack, which was usually a recipe for another because guilt pumped around her body like a poison. She'd known Will would die – or at the very least that a terrible event would soon pass. Two voices sparred in her head.

You couldn't possibly have known that would happen.

I should have kept going to the collieries. Persuaded them to have me. Every night. I should have learnt and learnt until I knew. I could have saved him.

What sobered her as she crossed the playground to

workshop 2B was that she had Vanessa's offer on the table.

Rasha wouldn't have to make the same mistake twice.

Rasha arrived at the workshop to learn that the class had to work on their portfolios. Cridland had an assessment with the head of Design Technology to find their work was subpar at best. Rasha hid away in the back row in her usual spot. She unpacked her portfolio as the door opened and closed behind her, and Fred Parsons sat down at her table two seats over.

Rasha's body froze with anxiety-induced rigor mortis, as it always did around Fred and his friends. Rasha focused on the whiteboard before them as Cridland blundered through YouTube's menus for a video he had added to his watch-later playlist. She barely blinked until a rendering tutorial flashed up on screen. The illustrator resembled Haya before the decimation of Homs. She spoke with animated hands, produced puns about vectors, and often flicked her silky black hair from her face. Rasha wondered, if Syria's war hadn't happened, whether Haya would be as joyous. Perhaps Rasha would act the same. Confident and carefree, that was what Rasha craved. *Impossible,* she thought, *when the dead come knocking.*

Frequency energy itched her skin. Her mind slipped from her skull, on the verge of the ombrederi, much like it had that morning in the collieries. Rasha turned her head slowly, disguising her search for the imprint as an absentminded gaze out of the window. That was when she found Joel.

He stood bowlegged, and cartilage burst from his kneecaps. His misty eyes sharpened. With his twisted arm, Joel pointed through the window at Cridland.

Something struck her temple. A paper ball rolled to a stop on the desk. The window was vacant, and Joel was gone. Rasha unfurled the note to find wierdo sprawled across it. The *i* was incorrectly before the *e*: Fred's handiwork. She caught his gaze. She saw it in his eyes as they narrowed.

He knew she was abnormal.

Another frequency wave surged over Rasha and whisked her mind to the ombrederi.

29

RASHA WAS in the very same workshop, although it didn't
seem so old; the extractor fan by the window had a new shine
to it, and the wooden benches were free of graffiti and paint
stains. Hunched over his desk was Cridland. Wrinkle free and
with a full head of hair, Rasha presumed that he was at least
thirty years younger. That would mean it was the nineties.

Fred showed her a memory from within the ombrederi.

In walked Joel, his bones unbroken and his neck not yet
twisted, but he was peculiar in other ways. He dared not make
eye contact with Cridland and chose to look at the floor or an
empty corner. His trousers, hitched up high above his waist,
displayed his bare ankles. The laces on his leather shoes were
untied, trailing on the workshop floor.

Joel walked in just as Cridland unlocked a money box.
The teacher took out the wads of cash and coins and thrust
them quickly into the inner pockets of his workshop coat. The
label on the box read: Exeter School Trip.

'That's stealing!' Joel blurted, eyes fixed to the floor.

Cridland jumped, slammed the tin shut, and spun to meet Joel.

'No, no,' Cridland said, cogs turning behind his eyes. 'Joel,

I'm taking it to the bank.'

'I don't think so,' Joel said nervously. 'When Mummy takes money to the bank, she counts it and puts it into plastic bags. Banks won't take it otherwise, Mummy says.'

'Yes, I'm taking it home to do that,' Cridland stuttered.

'I don't think so,' Joel said. He shook his head, eyes now fixed on a fly that zigzagged around the strip light. 'I don't think so. I'm telling.'

Joel turned. He stumbled on his laces, recovered, and vaulted through the fire exit. Cridland rifled through his pockets, returned the money to the tin, locked it, and raced after Joel.

The workshop spun, colours bled into one another, and when the chaos stilled, Rasha's feet touched the stairwell that headed to the maths floor. Joel stumbled up the steps, Cridland on his heels. Outside the windows, both students and teachers lounged in the playground under the stifling sun.

'I'm telling Mrs Bligh!' Joel cried. 'Stealing is bad, stealing is wrong!'

'I wasn't stealing,' Cridland huffed.

They reached the third floor landing to the maths department. Cridland caught up with Joel and grabbed him by the wrist.

'You're right,' Cridland said, his voice empty. 'It was wrong. A bad mistake. How about this? I'll put it back, and no one will have to know.'

Rasha drew closer. Cridland gripped Joel's wrist tighter.

'I'm still telling,' Joel stuttered.

Joel's comment seemed to hit a nerve with Cridland, for he let go of Joel's wrist. Frozen with fear, Joel kept his arm suspended in the air.

Cridland stood upright, rolled his shoulders, flexed his

neck, and pushed Joel. The schoolboy teetered on the edge of the stairs. He went to step forward to maintain his balance, but he couldn't – his right foot was stood on his left's laces. Joel tumbled backward. His head cracked against a cement stair. Immediately dead. His limp body rolled and flailed down the two flights, joints snapping as he went, until his body came to a twisted heap in the hallway below. Cridland crept to the banister to peek at Joel's battered little body. The teacher and murderer wrapped his coat around himself and strode through the maths department, headed toward the adjacent stairwell.

Joel's body was left for someone else to find.

30

THE FIRST THING Rasha registered when she came back to the physical and pried herself from her desk was Fred's laughter. A couple of her cohort spun in their seats to face her. Fred mimicked what she must have looked like: mouth agape, frantic eyes watching the air.

'Quiet,' Cridland barked. 'Face the whiteboard.'

Her classmates did in an instant, but Rasha found that she couldn't look in that direction. At a murderer. The face of a monster.

The class simmered down and practiced rendering 3D objects on scraps of copy paper. Rasha's mind was far from gradients and shading. She was conflicted. Cridland had shown her more kindness than most, letting her borrow the department's equipment. He knew she used it to better her life at home and catch up with schoolwork. If they weren't acts of kindness, what was it in aid of? She stared at the blank page and waited for poor Joel Tredethy to come back and show her more.

'Psst,' Fred hissed to her left. 'Oi.'

Joel's falling body became disjointed and broken. Milana's arm severed from her body.

Fred prodded her arm. She looked at him without a care that tears cascaded down her face.

He whistled the tune of the Joel Tredethy song. It took on a new meaning and no longer filled Rasha with shame or anger but a fearful nausea.

The drone of speeding planes.

A shadow fell over their table, and Fred quietened. Cridland towered over them. A face that Rasha had once regarded as sympathetic and dishevelled, with its wrinkles and heavy eyes, now seemed angular and full of malice. He looked at Rasha's empty sheet of copy paper and to Fred's, which had a wispy oblong circle sketched onto its surface. Cridland's eyes, now sharp as a jigsaw blade, rested on Rasha. She wasn't sure if they expressed disappointment or something more venomous.

'If you don't have at least one shape rendered by the end of the period, it'll be a detention,' he said. 'For you both.'

Cridland's young face, watching blankly through the bannisters at Joel's squinched, lifeless body.

'Piss off,' Rasha snarled.

She quickly collected her things and threw them into her bag. Cridland stepped back, fists clenched but silent. To Rasha's left, Fred continued to snicker, although now it wasn't aimed at her but their teacher, unprepared as to handle the situation with his favourite student.

The class ignored the tutorials of the Haya-like woman and watched Rasha sprint from the classroom.

31

RASHA HAD BROKEN a singular promise to herself, one she had made during the journey from Calais to Britain. Crammed in a container upon a ferry, sea sickness passed through the asylum seekers. Vomit, urine, and Allah knew what else sloshed on the floor amongst the many feet and crates. The burns on Haya's arms, the very same she'd gained from pulling Rasha out of their apartment, oozed with infection. The makeshift bandages were black with blood and worse.

That journey was a breather from a constant onslaught of military and border patrol. And so, in the near-blackness, people whispered prayers for the dead. Between names they chanted, 'Verily we belong to Allah, and truly to Him shall we return.'

Rasha didn't indulge as Haya shared their family's names to a god who'd snatched them from their lives. She stood, rigid and silent, as if one fewer body swayed in the cramped container. Rasha promised herself she'd never heed evil again; fear wouldn't control her life.

Sat in an immaculate staff toilet cubicle, she realised she'd done just that. Not only had she let bullies and imprints instil fear in her, she'd befriended a murderer. She could set that straight.

She'd take up Vanessa's offer.

Usually, if she had hidden in the toilets for more than a period, the school counsellor, Mrs Retallick, would come find her and coax her from the cubicle. It seemed that they didn't bother to check the staff toilets. Either that or Cridland had reported Rasha's potty-mouthed behaviour, and she had graduated from a troubled refugee to a troublesome teen.

The last hours dragged until the final bell tolled. A torrent of footsteps echoed in the halls, so Rasha gathered her things and slipped from the bathroom into the crowd. Head down, she made sure to blend into the sea of black-and-yellow uniforms. She fled outside, crossed the Key Stage 3 playground, and scarpered to the parking lot alongside the gym. Vanessa returned in her Land Rover as she'd promised.

Rasha raced to the passenger door without hesitation and hopped into the cabin. Vanessa grinned toothily.

'I'm really glad to see you,' the woman said. 'We'll stop by the caravan site first and let your mother know.'

'No, don't,' Rasha interjected. 'She'll only worry. Can I borrow your phone?'

'Sure,' Vanessa said. She passed Rasha an Android mobile. 'Passcode is 1-8-3-7.'

'Thanks.'

Rasha typed in the passcode, opened the messaging app, changed Vanessa's keyboard to Arabic (Levant), typed in Haya's mobile number, and hammered out a text.

> It's Rasha, borrowed Mrs Branning's phone.
> Doing after-school art club. Back later tonight.

She clicked send, locked the phone, and passed it back. Vanessa had reached the main road and would be at the collieries in five minutes.

'What are we going to do?' Rasha said.

'The best way to control your connection with the frequency is to practice engagement with an imprint,' Vanessa explained. 'We'll head to the collieries and use a receptor to source a guide.'

'Will mentioned that,' Rasha said, her heart still heavy when she thought of him. 'An imprint I'm connected to. That I can train with.'

'The frequency, it binds us together,' Vanessa continued, far more enthusiastic than any teacher at Gorenn Comprehensive. 'It means that two people could be centuries apart, but if they experienced similar things in their lifetimes, they can use those emotions to find each other in the ombrederi. Unfortunately, this means it's usually the most traumatic experiences. It seems to be a fundamental flaw in the human condition that we are emotionally stained by negative events. . .'

Vanessa trailed off. Rasha imaged that for Vanessa to be a witness, she must have experienced a horrendous tragedy of her own. Her words made perfect sense. Rasha thought back over the imprints she had seen: the miners, bloodied and limbless, trapped in a crumbling tunnel beneath Wheal Gorenn; Joel, who'd been alienated by his classmates and met a fatal end at the hands of a monster, just as Milana had. They were imprints who could fathom what Rasha had experienced that night in Syria.

'There's one at school,' Rasha said.

32

VANESSA CONTINUED to Wheal Gorenn to get equipment for Rasha's training. Halfway there, a terrible thought struck Rasha and made her stomach sink.

'Everything that happened in Syria,' she said, careful not to say anything wrong; Vanessa showed a lot of pride for witnessing culture, more so than Sam or Trish. 'Imprints will draw it out of me. I'll never escape it.'

Vanessa turned in her seat, looking dismayed.

'Not at all,' the woman said. 'You have to build your tolerance to certain emotions. No, you've got potential for more than just engagement.'

'More?'

'Beyond, into new possibilities. You met Sam and Trish. Trish has foresight, and she's leading sonar, a program that allows one to collect memories from various imprints and rebuild moments in time.'

'Like crime scene investigation?'

'If ever there was a future when the Network and the Ministry of Defence could work together, sure,' Vanessa chortled. 'Then there's Sam. He can withdraw his imprint from his body, and in doing so can reach imprints that many witnesses wouldn't be able to detect.'

Vanessa admired her fellow witnesses.

'What about you?' Rasha said. 'Can you do any of that?'

The Land Rover shuddered as it tore onto the gravel of the collieries' yard. Vanessa parked in the warehouse and helped Rasha from the car. They descended into a mineshaft Rasha knew all too well. They reached the two plaques bolted to the stone wall outside the activity centre.

'Edward Penrose,' Rasha read. 'Was he a witness?'

'One of the best the Network ever knew,' Vanessa replied as they strode into the activity centre. 'We're indebted. If it wasn't for him, we wouldn't be here now.'

The horde of late-night workers peered at them – more so Rasha – from their desks as they passed between the chipboard partitions. Rasha slowed when she spotted Trish amongst the faces. Bleary eyed, Trish did not look well. When she spotted Vanessa leading Rasha through the cavern, she raised a hand in hello.

Rasha wondered whether she had been blamed for Will's death. Trish's stare didn't incite her with positivity. Rasha wanted to impart her sympathy to both Trish and Sam but supposed it wasn't the time or place. She gave a tender smile in return, hoping that it would signal she meant well.

Vanessa led Rasha to what she had known to be called the birdcage, then ducked inside to confer with James. The manager's office, a cylindrical glass room right at the centre of the hubbub, looked just as it had in the shadow's memories. Perhaps the shadow lurked in the darkness on the outer edges of the cavern, unable to get past the tin dampeners bolted to the stalactites above. Perhaps it prowled the ombrederi, waiting for Rasha to engage.

Her train of thought was derailed when Vanessa walked out with James in tow. A short, slightly hunched man, James was someone Rasha guessed was younger than he looked, and just as grief had chipped away at Haya, she imagined that was the case for him.

'Rasha,' he said, extending a hand. 'I haven't had the privilege of saying hello.'

Rasha shook it. She'd never shaken a man's hand before; it certainly wouldn't have been allowed in Syria. She'd not met anyone in Cornwall who was either that polite or formal.

'Hi,' she eventually said.

'We'll get the equipment together and then head out,' Vanessa informed him.

'Good night,' he bid them.

Vanessa led Rasha to a tunnel behind James's office. A meagre warmth swelled over them, and after a short but steady descent the tunnel opened out into a cavern with many entrances. Rasha recognised one: the receptor cavern. They trudged upward into a room in a ground floor warehouse. A variety of gadgets were stacked behind locked wire cabinets. Rasha could barely imagine how much it would cost to produce such equipment.

'Does the Edward Penrose Trust keep all this going?' she asked.

Vanessa continued to pluck equipment from the stores and put them into a hiking bag.

'All of our equipment, site maintenance, witnesses' living expenses,' Vanessa said. 'As much as people try, once you see imprints, once you learn about the world beyond ours, the ombrederi, the frequency, there is no going back to a regular life, to normal jobs.'

Rasha was downhearted; after the government had granted

'leave to remain,' all that kept her going was the prospect of university and a postgraduate job that paid enough to own her own place. Pure independence, total security.

'Witnesses are stuck here?'

Vanessa spun around, eyes sharp.

'You don't get stuck at home,' she said with grit. 'Think of it as a nest. People come and go. After all, if the Network was all we knew, we wouldn't have these gadgets or our scientific understanding. Right, that's it.'

Vanessa zipped up her hiking bag and slung it onto her back. They continued up a low-ceilinged mineshaft that Rasha knew would take them back toward the indoor car park.

'Tell me about this imprint,' Vanessa said. 'What has it shown you?'

'He was called Joel Tredethy. Well, I suppose he still is,' Rasha mumbled. 'He died at the school. That's what he showed me. He was killed because he was trying to do the right thing.'

'And what do you think the link is between you?'

Rasha thought a moment. Joel's life had been taken from him by someone that had a duty of care, and Rasha's family had been ripped away from her by militants fighting for her country's freedom. They'd both been wronged by those who were meant to protect them.

'We were betrayed,' she concluded. Ahead, the lights of the indoor car park glistened.

'Then that, Rasha Abadi,' Vanessa huffed, adjusting the straps of her bag where they slipped from her shoulders, 'is the key to greater things.'

33

NIGHTFALL TRANSFORMED Gorenn Comprehensive into a building barren and soulless, and Rasha detested it.

Settled in the courtyard between the DT and English buildings, Vanessa first defused an EMP, which she promised would wipe out the CCTV cameras. 'Like candles in the wind.'

The turn of phrase seemed strange coming from a woman so young, but Rasha let it go. She tried to make herself comfortable, which was hard when the school was a source of discomfort by day and even more so by night when it resembled the streets of Homs. Around them, Vanessa erected Rubik's-esque tin boxes at three points of a triangle. She didn't bother to explain what they were, nor did she need to. A fresh shock of frequency energy gnawed at Rasha's skin. Rasha presumed they would draw Joel in. Vanessa straightened up the last box.

'I'm quite fond of an allegory,' she said. 'Consider yourself a key. You were made to only fit certain locks. That's the first step in engagement. Understand how you are similar; how you fit together. There's nothing stronger than knowing what you want.'

What Rasha wanted was pretty simple: she wanted to be normal – to control the threshold between herself and the ombrederi. It consumed her every day to the point that her thoughts became default when she wasn't worried about imprints, schoolwork, or her relationship with Haya. She also had to find out what Joel wanted.

'I'm ready to engage,' Rasha said.

Vanessa nodded, her eyes wide with enthusiasm. She took her phone from her pocket and swiped her screen. The frequency energy around Rasha fizzed to new heights. She watched as her mentor took her leather journal from the rucksack and flipped to one of the last pages in the aged volume.

'Does journaling work?' Rasha asked. 'My school counsellor said I should try it.'

Vanessa looked confused at first, caught Rasha's eyes on her journal, then laughed and waved it in the air.

'Oh, when you get as old as I am, memories escape you,' she chortled. 'Especially when your attention is divided between here and the ombrederi.'

Movement ahead stole Rasha's focus. At the end of the courtyard were Cridland's workshop windows. The heads of the jigsaws could be seen, as if a row of students were still sat on the back benches. Amongst which, so white he seemed wrapped in moonlight, was Joel Tredethy.

'He's here,' Rasha uttered.

'That's it, engage,' Vanessa urged. 'Don't be scared.'

Rasha was far from scared. Joel felt like an old friend. She'd seen the worst he'd experienced, and through that learnt how Cridland was the one to beware.

Rasha recollected the night in Homs, the evening before the explosion, and the arguments her parents had. Their valuables were gathered in a chest under their bed, to barter safe passage across Europe. Their father slipped out under the cloak of night and returned to Haya to have long conversations. As they spoke – sometimes shouted, sometimes cried – they pointed to a map sprawled out between them in the light of their kerosene lamp. The plans were in place. Her father spoke with confidence that a friend of his, a double agent for the Syrian armed forces, predicted an artillery attack a week from then.

So why haven't we left? Rasha had thought. *What's holding us back?*

She'd never found out. The bombs dropped the following night and tore their family in half. Rasha had once supposed her father's informant was mistaken, for Homs was one of many sieges across Syria. Time passed, and Rasha saw more of the world, and she wondered whether her father had been purposefully misled. After all, the civil war had many sides. A true comrade would be hard to find in a sea of enemies.

Then Rasha was sucked into the ombrederi.

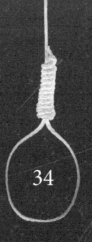

34

THE OMBREDERI first came as blackness imbued with a multicoloured sheen like an oil slick caught in sunlight. Amongst it stood Joel Tredethy, his hand outstretched. Rasha took it.

A room built itself up brick by brick, floorboard by floorboard, and on the single bed lay Joel, arms wrapped around his shins. There was Joel, body lamented by his death, stood beside Rasha, and there was another Joel, curled up on the bed, just a memory. Past-Joel's knuckles were bloodied and bruised. The window opposite looked over a garden where a shirtless muscle-bound man, body sweat-sheened, thumped a punching bag hung from a recycled swing set. Rasha presumed it was Joel's father. Past-Joel winced as each right hook landed.

Imprint-Joel motioned for Rasha to trudge on. As they did, Joel's bedroom folded away to reveal Gorenn Comprehensive's Key Stage 3 playground. Past-Joel yelled at a group of kids that sneered at him. 'You said I could play.'

A snooty blond-haired girl broke from the crowd and said, 'We did, and now we've decided you can't.'

A ginger kid tore past-Joel's satchel from his shoulder and threw it to the group of children.

'Give it back!' Joel yelled. He dared not look at the children or his satchel as its contents cascaded across the puddle-strewn courtyard. Instead, he stood rigid, eyes fixed on his untied laces, fists balled, until his emptied satchel was thrown to his feet and the school children raced off at the sound of the school bell.

The scene dissolved, and the courtyard came back. The sky above warbled with cyan light and cast the playground into an underwater twilight. Rasha wanted to ask why he hadn't fought back, why he hadn't fled to teachers for help. But she knew the answer: retaliating at school would bring trouble to a home that didn't need more, and schoolteachers were just as dismissive of him as his peers were. There was one thing that could satisfy them both.

'Get your own back,' Rasha said. 'Get revenge. It's what they deserve. What they all deserve.'

In a blink, they were within Cridland's workshop. Refracted violet and green light cast the benches and equipment into a haze. Rasha soaked in Joel's distorted imprint and looked beyond his broken bones and lacerations. A lack of confidence put his shoulders into a permanent stoop, his eyes fixed to anything but a human face. It wasn't within the boy's nature, certainly not in life, nor in death. She wished it for him. The world deserved malice after what the boy was given.

Then it happened.

White-hot agony fired through her limbs. The right side of her body was doused in cold, and in her mind came Joel's thoughts, just as clearly as her own.

Mr Cridland is a mean man, Joel thought.

Panic seared through Rasha's stomach. She had let herself

be occupied. Joel Tredethy had her body.

No. Her heart rattled inside her chest, and the night air rushed between her fingers. Her imprint, there in the ombrederi, was still connected to her body in the physical. Rasha stepped toward the workshop's fire exit to search for a way out of the ombrederi, and Joel sidestepped too. She reached for the door handle, as did he. She paused, hand suspended in the air, and Joel mirrored her: a pitiful, mutated reflection.

Joel didn't occupy her.

Rasha occupied him.

35

RASHA OPENED her eyes to the bleak night that hung over the drab playground. Vanessa wrung her hands as she waited.

Rasha became doused in Joel's aura: her kneecaps in splinters, her neck taut. She'd been overcome by his shy posture, his distrust for people, his fear of Cridland – a kind of horror only found in the living.

'What are you experiencing, Rasha?' Vanessa asked. 'Talk to me.'

'I can feel him,' Rasha stuttered in an attempt to make sense of the sensations coursing through her body. 'Everything I do, he does too.'

Rasha turned to get a better view of Cridland's workshop, and as she did Joel righted himself behind the glass, his misted eyes fixed on her.

'It's like I'm a TV remote,' Rasha said. 'He'll do what I want.'

Vanessa scribbled into her aged journal with a Biro.

'Push the connection, Rasha,' Vanessa said. She didn't seem at all surprised by what Rasha claimed to do, but she did seem eager to test it to its full extent.

Cridland's workshop window was between Rasha and Joel. Rasha dreaded the lesson she'd have there the following day; being in Cridland's company was a terrible thought. Perhaps she didn't have to be. She raised a fist in the air, and Joel did too. She swung it forward, punching into the empty space before her. Joel's swept through the glass. It shattered with a stupendous crash, spilling fragments across the playground.

Rasha jumped. Joel's aura faded from her body, and realisation dawned on her for what she had just done.

'I didn't . . . I didn't mean . . .'

Vanessa disregarded the broken window, grabbed Rasha's hand, and examined it in the near darkness. A laceration ran across the back of it, and warm blood trickled across her forearm. It oozed between Vanessa's fingers, but she didn't mind.

'I . . .' Rasha stuttered. 'The glass . . .'

The window had shattered outward thirty feet from where they stood. No glass projectiles made it to them. Joel stood in the empty window, nursing his right hand. Through Joel, Rasha had gained an injury.

'What does it mean?' Rasha asked.

Vanessa looked at her, eyes white in the beam of her upturned flashlight. They were frantic – not with worry or concern, but sheer excitement.

'You tore down the walls.'

36

RASHA HAD BECOME more than her body.

The morning after her stint with Vanessa, Rasha washed at the bathroom sink and took care with the stinging wound on her hand. Nausea came and went, which Vanessa had told her was a by-product of prolonged engagement. Exactly what Rasha had achieved was still shrouded in cryptic words. Before she'd forced Joel to break the workshop window, she had just been a passive spectator in an imprint's memories. It was as if she had become Joel. As Vanessa had said, she'd broken the walls of her mind. Rasha presumed that if she had become free of her own mind, then she'd broken into Joel's.

Her presence caused utmost horror for Haya. Dried, changed, and with her schoolbag packed, Rasha once again ate Rice Pops at the kitchen table. Haya sat in the living room and stared out of the window. She held a cup of tea in her hands but hadn't taken one sip. She was thinner again, her eyes sunken in their sockets. With a pang of guilt, Rasha realised that she hadn't been present enough the last week to ensure that Haya was well nourished. Not that she'd take food from her.

Nausea swam in her stomach. Rasha nudged her cereal around the bowl. She talked at Haya, muttering a long-winded and poorly constructed lie about where she had been the night before and how she had come to cut her hand.

'I was using a palette knife to sculpt this face from clay,' she fibbed. 'I had the face mounted on a wooden stick, and the palette knife slipped. Luckily, Mr Reed is a first-aider.'

Come on, she thought. *I texted to say I was with Mrs Branning. Catch me out, tell me off.*

Haya nodded slightly. Her hands shook, her wedding band chiming against the cup. Rasha scared Haya. She wondered what their dynamic would be if her mother knew of her abilities. Would fear push them further apart, or would it bring Haya closer?

'Some people gravitate toward power,' Vanessa had said as they drove back to the holiday park the night before. Perhaps Haya would run to Rasha for protection, run to Rasha for all the wrong reasons, and not because they were the last of their family surviving in a foreign country together. She didn't want to be considered other – she just wanted to be a daughter.

Rasha swiped her bowl to the floor. It shattered on the lino, and soggy cereal splattered on the cupboard doors. Haya flinched and spilt tea over her clean tabard. Her eyes met Rasha's, wide and horrified.

Rasha leapt up, grabbed her bag and waterproofs from the coatrack, and burst out into the misty morning. It said a lot that she was wanted by a group of imprint-wielding mine dwellers over her own mother.

She walked hard, ignoring Mr Keats's mewing tabbies. When she reached the coiling lanes she didn't bother to move out of the way for oncoming traffic. Drivers honked at her more than once, but she soldiered on with the rain on her back and the world on her shoulders.

Her morning at Gorenn Comprehensive passed in much the same way. Classmates' snickers and teachers' voices washed over her. Each exercise book she pulled from her rucksack remained unopened; she hadn't once taken the cap off her Biro. From maths to English to drama, Rasha became increasingly withdrawn, and after a lunchtime spent in the staff toilets once more, it was time for the last period of the day: DT.

With Cridland's rear window broken, the class was squeezed into the smaller adjoining workshop. Mr Cridland treated Rasha as any of her cohort: with disinterest and a quick temper. She couldn't tell if it was because of her outburst or because his workshop window had been shattered in the night. Cridland scathed the students with lack of progress on their current projects. He directed a group at the jigsaws to finish the base of their wooden lamps, which naturally included Fred and his band of bullies. Not wanting to be on the receiving on Cridland's temper, in fear of finding her end the same way Joel Tredethy had, Rasha took to the benches opposite the jigsaw machines to solder her main components to her circuit board.

It was simple work, just a parallel circuit with multiple LED outputs – nothing compared to the kitchen radios and vintage game consoles she'd fixed – which was good because every time Cridland swooped past her to check up on Fred and company's progress, a cold shiver shot through her body and her hands faltered with the soldering iron. Soon not only chills cascaded down her spine, but static pinched her skin and itched the cut on her hand.

Joel returned.

Cridland disappeared to check on the maintenance team

that was repairing his window, so Rasha turned on her stool. Fred and friends traded porn video links and cigarettes at the saws, and beyond that Joel loitered beyond the glass. His body was turned at an angle so that his face – contorted on his twisted neck – could stare right in Rasha's direction. Her blood ran ice-cold as though she had been injected with liquid nitrogen: an invite to leave the flesh-and-bone world.

Rasha presumed that, after showing her his death, Joel had achieved what he wanted. Her short time with the Network had taught her that the dead continued to live without bodies, sometimes in the ombrederi and sometimes in the physical world. The idea of imprints with unfinished business seemed redundant in witnessing lore.

Yet Joel continued to pester her.

Cridland reemerged, and Joel's pasty face revolved on his neck as he tracked the teacher's movements. Her classmates' chortles threw Rasha back to the workshop. Fred and company mimicked her with vacant faces and agape mouths. Her fear entertained them.

Cridland laid the equipment he'd gathered onto his desk and crossed the room to the jigsaws.

'Sit the right way and finish your stands or it's detention,' he hissed.

Fred and friends turned on their stools, still snickering at Rasha, and whispered the Joel Tredethy song under their breath. 'Don't be weird or you'll be next.'

Cridland bounded between the jigsaw cutters and Rasha's bench. He scathed them for their lack of work and threatened detentions. 'You waste my time, and I'll waste yours.'

All the while Joel limped ever closer to the jigsaws, arms flopping where they were ripped from his sockets. He stopped before Fred, leant across the saw, and pressed his frosted nose to Fred's. Those cloudy unblinking eyes.

Rasha leapt to her feet and skirted away from the jigsaws. Their blades whirred beside many hands.

Fred cackled harder. Cridland floundered around him and yelled, but it didn't make a difference; Fred had heard it all before, and it hadn't made him a better person.

Rasha hated Fred's pubescent chirp and the vile things he sputtered. He'd be better silent. She couldn't stand the fact that Cridland committed a murder and would never face repercussions. Rasha's skull fizzed with frequency energy. She seethed with venom for all Cridland and Fred had done.

It was then she knew she wasn't just Rasha. Her walls had gone.

She put her hand out before her and grabbed at the dusty air. Joel thrust forward and pinned Fred's hand next to his jigsaw.

Fred's laughter depleted. He struggled but couldn't break free. Rasha swung her hand, and Joel forced Fred's knuckles across the jolting blade. The machine shrieked as it punctured bone and cartilage. Blood flicked across the workshop and showered Rasha's cohort. The class screamed and fled to the farthest end of the room. The metallic tang of Fred's blood lingered in the dusty air.

Milana's dismembered arm.

Joel dissipated into the light of the window. Cridland slammed the emergency stop valve above Rasha's head. The saws halted. He grabbed at Fred with blind panic and roared for a first-aider. Jets of blood squirted from the stump where Fred's fingers used to be, and the boy, discoloured like old milk, slipped from his stool to the hard stone floor.

Rasha fled, leaving everything behind, and sprinted out of the school grounds.

Her father impaled by a steel girder.

She kicked her feet harder every time she was compelled to cry.

Haya's weeping arms and distraught face as she pulled Rasha from the wreckage.

Rasha stumbled on the collieries' gravel lane before she slowed. Lactic acid burned her shins, and her lungs no longer retained air. She was under the shadow of Wheal Gorenn's engine house chimney, a stone giant reminding her that there was no escape from the frequency.

No escape from what she had just done.

'Rasha?' Trish called.

Rasha caught sight of Trish as the woman raced toward her.

'I could hear you,' Trish said. She wasn't wearing her dielectric band. 'You were projecting.'

Close enough to see Rasha's tears, Trish's face washed with concern.

'Rasha?'

'I didn't mean to do it,' Rasha said. 'If I'd known.'

'Rasha, you're scaring me.'

'There's a boy at school. I set an imprint on him. I hurt him real bad.'

Perspiration dewed across Trish's forehead.

PART FIVE

ABSOLUTE CHAOTIC NOTHINGNESS

37

TRISH NEEDED her dielectric band to be around Rasha.

The teenager's mind blasted across the collieries' yard, blocking out all thought and sound. It was as if Trish had thrust her head against a blearing subwoofer.

I'm a monster. Worse than Joel and Cridland combined. What has Vanessa done to me?

Able to get Rasha to a state of calm, Trish asked Rasha to wait whilst she grabbed her dielectric band from the Reliant. Certain that taking her into the collieries would magnify Rasha's hysteria, Trish walked her along Gorenn Mount, the same trail she and Sam had led her along when first explaining the frequency. Just one week had passed since then, yet it seemed that an entire lifetime had unfolded.

'I was Joel, and he was me,' Rasha stuttered. 'Anything I did, he'd copy.'

They stopped where a fallen tree blocked their path. Face wet, Rasha looked out onto the babbling sea. Her tears quelled, and her breathing slowed. The sea could often do that; a silver lining to the Network being located in the collieries.

Trish trusted in Rasha's account of her classmate's

delimbing as much as she trusted in her description of the shadow imprint and believed, to some degree, that Rasha had predicted Will's death.

'I thought Vanessa was going to help me,' Rasha uttered. 'I'm worse than I was before.'

'Getting a grip on your witnessing capabilities is an emotionally turbulent time,' Trish said, speaking from her own experience. 'Lots of highs and lows.'

'I need to make it right.'

'What's worse than one mistake is making another,' Trish said. 'You need more training – '

'What if he's disabled now? What if he gets an infection and – '

'Hey, hey,' Trish said gently, and she pulled the teenager into a one-armed hug. 'You don't know that. We'll take it as it comes. We have to focus on doing good.'

'Are you going to tell anyone?'

'I'll have to the let the board know,' Trish said. 'So yes. Yes I will.' Trish took a breath, put some space between herself and Rasha, and asked, 'Have you seen the shadow imprint since?'

'Just Joel Tredethy. I know why you're asking me. Will. I'm sorry.'

'You've nothing to be sorry for.'

'I should have said something.'

'In all honesty, Rasha, we wouldn't have believed you if you did.'

Rasha sniggered and wiped her tears away. Trish continued.

'You saw The Vincent?'

'And a broken window. I suppose that . . .'

Trish was thankful Rasha didn't finish the sentence; she'd replayed Will's demise too many times in her head, and each revision was as painful as the last.

'Yes,' Trish said. 'The shadow imprint must have been planning Will's death. Did you catch its motive? A sense of who it is, anything at all?'

Rasha shook her head.

'I'm sorry,' she whispered. 'How's Sam?'

Trish pondered a moment. No texts, no phone calls; Trish had only caught minutes with Sam at a time as he raided the Network's drug stores every other day. She doubted Sam had been fully in reality since the day he'd discovered Will died – unwashed and, judging by the heady fumes wafting off of him, living on a diet of vodka.

'Struggling,' she answered. 'As we all are, struggling on. But what matters is that we keep on going. You too.'

'I don't think Mum can,' Rasha said. 'She won't look at me. She sees the girl climbing on the ceiling . . .'

'It won't last. Ever changing, remember?'

'Cliff and sea,' Rasha retorted.

Trish decided to speak to the board before taking Rasha home. When they got down to the activity centre, a hectic ruckus distracted her; the occupations unit gathered around the birdcage and dispensed equipment. Inside the birdcage, Vanessa and James argued. Whilst he stayed in his chair, Vanessa leant over him, hands on his desk. Trish led Rasha to her desk, told her to wait, and joined her colleagues.

Trish didn't know the occupations unit well, but she recognised Leri. A twiglet with a Lego-helmet haircut, Leri usually kept to herself in the laboratories.

'Everything okay?' she asked.

Leri's eyes widened. She faltered with her words, fumbling with the zip of her jacket.

'It's been a stressful day, to say the least. Just drove back from Lanhydrock.'

There was a cold atmosphere to the room. People skirted a particular subject, and Trish wished she didn't wear the dielectric band. She'd have pestered Leri further, but Vanessa and James exited the birdcage.

'We're classifying this as code red,' she informed the occupations unit. 'We'll monitor the situation daily until we can extract the occupying imprint.'

'There was an occupation?' Trish asked. Vanessa and James turned sharply, unaware she was there at all.

'With all due respect, it doesn't concern you, Trish,' James said.

Vanessa purposefully turned away from Trish to the occupations unit. 'We'll go down to test cavern 3C and use the terminal to try and consult guiding imprints on the matter.'

The unit meandered into the shaft beyond the birdcage. Vanessa pulled James in, muttered under her breath, and followed her colleagues.

'James, a word,' Trish said.

'Can it wait?' His was mind was clearly on other matters.

'Not unless you want Rasha Abadi to dismember another innocent child,' Trish retorted.

Mouth agape, James gestured for her to follow into the birdcage. They closed the door, shutting off the ruckus in the activity centre. Trish couldn't sit, restless with anxiety, so she paced back and forth in front of James's desk whilst she relayed Rasha's story.

'It was a mistake to train Rasha so soon,' Trish concluded.

'Without wanting to sound petty,' James retorted, 'comparing Vanessa's actions with your own, hers had far less impact on Rasha's well-being.'

'How can you sit there and compare a successful extraction

to an adolescent witness sawing people's fingers off?' Trish asked. 'Next you'll be saying Vanessa has her reasons.'

'Well – '

'Don't want to hear it,' Trish interjected. She took a deep breath and swallowed back thoughts of Will's bloodied room, Sam's grey skin and bloodshot eyes, Rasha splayed on her bedroom ceiling, Shauna's swollen purple neck. 'Rasha isn't emotionally stable. She needs someone she is comfortable with, a friend.'

'If you're implying yourself – '

'I'm as good as. Let me assist Vanessa.'

James pushed himself back into his chair and rolled his rounded shoulders. He turned away, stared hard at his computer monitor, then looked back to Trish.

'On one condition,' he said. 'Tell your friend to go home and stop stealing ketamine.'

38

TRISH DOUBTED she'd convince Sam toward sobriety. Will hadn't had much luck when he was alive.

In his office, James swivelled his computer monitor to face her; one in four of the CCTV grids framed the store's hand-cranked rolling shelves. Sam perused their dissociative drugs, the half-light casting a Gollum-esque silhouette over him. Trish faintly promised James to lecture Sam.

'And Trish,' James said as she exited the birdcage. 'If he doesn't listen, tell him the Refinery won't, either.'

Rasha had promised to stay put in the activity centre, so Trish traversed the various shafts and tunnels to the stores. Her mind would not stray from Shauna – Rasha, rather. She'd been overlooked and failed by every adult she came across. It was too reminiscent of Trish's own childhood, dragged from care home to foster family to psychiatrist, her witnessing abilities amounting to unprecedented and dangerous levels. What could Rasha become if she already controlled imprints?

What was Vanessa thinking, pushing the teenager so far so soon?

The laboratory's lights were on. Sam lacked tact in hiding

his drug abuse. Many, James included, would pass it off as a careless druggy craving a fix. Trish knew it was a desperate man's cry for help.

She found Sam whilst he wound the shelves closed and grabbed his wrist before he could plunge the pills into a pocket. Hand suspended in the close air, she felt his veins varicosed beneath his ashen skin. The bags under his eyes were so dark a stranger could mistake them for ebbing bruises.

'Rough day?' she asked.

'Rough life.'

Trish pried the baggy from his hands, surprised that he let her.

'You had an audience.' Trish jerked her head to the CCTV camera blinking above them. Sam sought the camera lens and shrunk in its presence.

'It's all very well having Big Brother judging me but not doing anything.'

'James threatened the Refinery, Sam.'

Sam stuttered, pushed Trish aside, and strode toward the lab's exit.

'It's a Bickle tradition by this point,' he muttered.

As Shauna had been on Trish's mind, Rose was never far from Sam's.

'I know we can't help Rose,' Trish said, 'but we can keep Rasha safe. That's got to mean something.'

She chased Sam as his pace quickened through the laboratories. As they went, the lights switched off and the darkness bit at their heels.

'They're very different cases.'

'Yeah?'

'Rasha was occupied. Mum wasn't.'

'You know that for sure?'

Sam stopped. He didn't turn to look at Trish. She suspected that his cheeks would shine with tears if he did.

'What does it matter? Doesn't give me my childhood back.'

'Will said – ' Trish stopped herself.

'He tried to tell me, too,' Sam explained. 'Back when Mum was sent to the Refinery, they were still called possessions; there was only exorcism. When did they turn out well for anyone?'

Trish couldn't fault Sam's logic. Before the turn of the century, before new witnessing science rebranded possessions as occupations and the group moved away from religion, the rare phenomena hadn't once been successfully treated in the UK.

'Was evidence ever submitted to the archives?'

Sam shrugged. 'I was a kid.' He arrived at the ladder to the southern exit. 'Heading home, or . . . ?'

'Going in that direction,' Trish said. 'Taking Rasha home.'

'She's here?'

Without another word, he bolted up the ladder two rungs at a time. Trish raced after him, but she wasn't quick enough. Before she reached the top, Sam's voice boomed through sublevel one. 'Rasha! Rasha!'

Trish bounded through the activity centre to her desk, where Sam towered over Rasha.

'You knew he'd die!' he hollered. 'You knew, you knew!'

What dwindling witnesses remained hurtled through the chipboard partitions. Vanessa and James erupted from the birdcage. James pulled Sam back whilst Vanessa hugged a shaken Rasha.

'What did it?' Sam yelled. 'What was it?'

'That's enough,' James growled in Sam's ear.

Vanessa helped Rasha from Trish's seat.

'Come with me,' she muttered. 'We'll get you home.'

When Vanessa and Rasha were out of sight into the northern tunnel that led to the car park, James released Sam and spun him around so that they were eye to eye.

'I know you're grieving,' James said. 'Will hasn't crossed from the frequency, so we haven't got answers. I'm giving you compassionate leave, and you better take it and not come back to the collieries. Listen, if I see you in the stores again, it won't just be the Refinery for you, it'll be dismissal.'

James cradled Sam's nape.

'We can't lose you, too,' James finished.

Sam's eyes watered, but no tears fell. He nodded, let his body relax, and allowed James to escort him toward the southern tunnel.

'I'll take you back to Tresillian,' Trish heard James say.

The remaining witnesses dithered back to their desks; they eyed one another but dared not say a word with Trish amongst them. Trish was the last to move. It seemed that details of Rose's incarceration had been kept from Sam. Perhaps they bore a connection to Rasha's occupation.

After all, everyone became entangled in the shadow imprint's web.

39

THE ARCHIVES were the only place in the collieries that Trish could take off her dielectric band, and it was for that reason she was anxious.

She descended to subzero two, past the mouths of the test caverns, and up the series of northern ladders to subzero one. The tunnel funnelled out before a breeze-block wall and, set within it, the vault's oxidised steel door shone in Trish's phone light.

Trish withdrew her keycard from her pocket, avoiding her outdated acne-ridden ID photo, and swiped it against the scanner left of the door. Metallic clicks and groans punctured the quiet, and the door swung ajar. Thankfully, her access hadn't been restricted since the disciplinary. Floodlights illuminated the space as Trish crossed the threshold, its off-white floors and walls chiselled to modernistic perfection.

Spaced at six even points across the cavern were round tin pedestals, electromagnets, and tethered to each was an imprint: the archivists. The six imprints had once been guides and were able to retain memories, so rather than risk printed documents and off-line servers falling into civilians' hands, witnesses transferred important memories into the archivists. It was a strand of the same science that later inspired Trish's sonar project.

Trish's heart drummed faster, but she dared not look at the archivists' forms, for there was little left. The archivists were inhibited with other people's memories; the more they retained, the less of themselves was left. Over time their forms degraded to skeletal acid-washed projections. Here and there features were distinct. As Trish passed the one closest to the vault door, a cataract eye followed her. On another, a hand with gnarled talons flexed and tensed. Trish dared not look as she stood on the centre dais between all six archivists. There were three kinds of deaths, as far as witnesses were concerned: existing as an imprint, dissolving into the frequency, and being reduced to an empty shell that roamed the Earth. The latter concept haunted Trish the most; an existence without memories was surely worse than an infinite end.

Trish reached the centre dais and, with trembling hands, removed the dielectric band. The six archivists' auras straddled against her mind. They did not shed memories or emotions – cold and empty, much as Rasha had described the shadow imprint. Yes, the shadow imprint. The reason she was there at all.

She closed her eyes and filled her mind with images of the mutant imprint. The ombrederi consumed her.

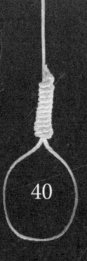

40

AN IMPENETRABLE FOG swamped Trish. In the ombrederi, her feet crunched on the gravel of the collieries' drive, and the engine house chimney loomed into view as she walked. This was the archives, the nerve centre of the Network, stowed safely within the frequency's wavelengths. The place where, if she looked well enough, Trish would find answers.

Shadows, she thought. *Shadows and emptiness.*

The fog condensed into solid shapes, and various rooms materialised across the collieries' yard as if she'd strode onto a theatre set. A middle-aged couple shivered beneath upturned sheets in their master bedroom, an occupied teenage boy writhed and squirmed in a poster-ridden room, and twin sisters scarpered from a dark forest. All were drenched in thick shadows – the most generic results for Trish's request.

Trish recalled what she had sensed of the shadow imprint, the gangly insect limbs that had staggered beneath a molten body, its skin neither flesh nor fluid but both, with a depth of absolute chaotic nothingness.

The fog didn't stir.

The shadow imprint, the shadow imprint.

Wind pelted through the whitewashed yard and slammed into Trish. She was thrust backward by invisible fists. The six mutated archivists tried to eject Trish from the archives. She dug her heels into the gravel and kept her mind on the imprint. For the archivists to do that only confirmed her suspicions: a secret lay buried deep within the frequency. If that was the case, such information wouldn't be obtained from the archives as easily. She needed a visceral memory.

Trish had memorised the date of Rose's incarceration: 14 January 2001, the turn of the new century and an abrupt kick into adulthood for sixteen-year-old Sam. She remembered some photos that Sam had stolen from retired witness Steph Blake. Steph had tried to extract – or then exorcise – Rose. The blurred Polaroids showed a crazed Rose with unblinking eyes and a skeletal self-abused body.

The archive's white mist moulded itself into the living room of a bungalow. Nauseating pastel wallpaper, earwax-orange settees, and diamond-patterned threadbare carpet were remnants of a bygone decade. Steph Blake, a woman with thinning ironed hair and thick-rimmed glasses, watched as Rose, bruised and brittle, repeatedly threw herself against the floor.

'7:29 p.m.,' Steph uttered into her tape recorder, fists shaking. 'Rose is – Christ. She is moving rabidly. It's not . . . not human.'

Steph paused, closed her eyes, and consulted with the air to her right. Trish rightly confirmed that Steph spoke to her guiding imprint, for the retired witness said, 'Are you sure, Percy? But what is that?' She stopped a moment, took a deep breath, and spoke again into the recorder. 'It's here again. The faceless one. Percy says it has a name – '

Before Steph finished her sentence, Rose clambered to her feet and leapt upon one of the sofas. She thrashed and hissed at Steph. The flickering wall lights illuminated a dripping mural smeared on the wall with faeces: a malformed body, pairs of wry arms and legs, and two bleeding eyes torn from the floral wallpaper.

The shadow imprint.

41

TRISH CEASED CONNECTION with the archivists and opened her eyes to the dim vault. She dared not spend unnecessary time in the archives considering what she had uncovered: the archivists kept a catalogue of all searches a witness made. Incognito mode didn't exist between minds. It wouldn't have been a problem, but Trish was certain the shadow imprint wasn't meant to be found.

The floodlights diminished behind her as she proceeded to the vault door. She recognised Steph Blake's guide, Percy Shilson, from the memorial at the collieries' entrance.

With her dielectric band fixed back into place, Trish raced through the rocky oesophagus to the terminal room. Guilt choked her. Had she told the board about the shadow imprint after Rasha's occupation, they could have consulted the archives for Rose's occupation. If she had been as transparent as witnesses were entrusted to be, Will's life could have been spared. If only she trusted the board.

The terminal room was vacant when Trish arrived. She raced straight to the one and only oval glass desk. The device was an evolution of the ouija board and had copper circles imbedded into its glass surface, making a QWERTY keyboard. Most imprints were too weak to project a physical form or communicate telepathically, and so instead they could spell out short answers to simple questions. Their energy would touch a copper key and create a closed electrical circuit that would then register on the adjacent monitor — hence how inherited the name 'terminal'. She flicked a few switches on the device's control panel. A motor purred, and the monitor blinked beside it, a blank word processing document upon its screen. A cursor pulsed, waiting for the dead to converse: the only way Trish could contact imprints whilst wearing her dielectric band.

'Percy Shilson,' she called. 'Percy Shilson, you are being beckoned.'

A torrent of frequency energy swelled around her. An imprint arrived. After her splurge in the archives, Trish was happy that her dielectric band blocked his form from her mind. It was rumoured that his afterlife began with the end of a shotgun.

Trish ensured that her questions were short and to the point. She needed specific answers quickly.

'You were present the night Rose Bickle was occupied?'

At the bottom of the keyboard were two separate keys for yes and no. Yes lit up and registered on the monitor.

'Were one of the imprints faceless?'

The cursor blinked.

'Did the shadow imprint occupy her?'

'Yes.' The terminal's keyboard lit up as a word was spelled out: G-Y-W-A. Trish consulted the monitor as the word came together.

'Gywandras,' Trish read. 'Does the Network know this?'

A few seconds passed, then –

'Yes.'

Trish deleted the file from the Anascribe program and turned the terminal off. She was thrust into darkness. The Network had been her home for the majority of her twenties.

It also swarmed with lies.

42

GYWANDRAS.

Trish had a name, one that meant no more than the very fact that it existed. Which, in a world where she would be dismissed at the very mention of it, became the driving force to find out more. The name, however, didn't help to establish the gywandras's motivations. Fear made her heart skip a beat when she thought, *That's if it has a motivation at all.*

As Trish meandered to ground level, Will's words echoed in her head.

'Maybe it's not enough to have knowledge of an event. Perhaps you have to be emotionally invested.'

Trish knew that if she hoped to learn about the gywandras, she'd need to learn more about Shauna's death and why it had been there. To do it, she'd need to accept one of the amounting visitation requests to Her Majesty's Prison, Dartmoor and look Michael dead in the eyes. She'd figure out how Rasha had seen Michael in the ombrederi and why the gywandras had watched Shauna die.

Trish skulked through the busy activity centre to avoid attention; working unsociable hours wouldn't be good for her disciplinary. She scuttled through the winding tunnel toward the storeroom. Sweat soaked her fringe by the time she finished her ascent, and when she wiped it away from her forehead a teal smudge was on the back of her hand. Last night's hair dye ran. She dove into the storeroom and swiped the receptor from its display case in the corner.

Clustered at the northern edge of Princetown, HMP Dartmoor was secluded within two rings of steep granite walls. A dense mist rode the tail end of a passing storm and gave the illusion it rode on the back of a cloud. There was nothing fantastical about it; it was the most sobering place in the world.

Once she was in the visitor's car park, Trish quadruple-checked her doors were locked and whisked through the gate into the main yard. She clutched her unlocked phone as to provide permission of her visit at a second's notice and patted the pocket of her denim jacket; her driver's license was in reach. Not that it would help – she was brunette in her photograph. Her hair had been dyed more the last eight years than she'd had a full night's sleep.

She ground her teeth along her walk across the car park. There was no way she could get away with wearing the dielectric band, which meant that her mind was open to the chaos and the dead that surely lurked inside the prison.

Trish slowed her pace when she neared the visitor's entrance to gradually acclimatise to the mounting frequency energy. From the mist loomed the outlines of imprints, misshapen and hollow, and they dispersed as quickly as they'd appeared. The prison, towering over her, made Trish's stomach whirl with guilt. That was the problem with foresight: emotions plagued her for events that had not come to pass. After checking her email and driver's license – her faded teal hair was not once questioned – the guard at the double doors let her through into the visitors' centre. Each guard she met was a cookie-cutter of the last as she was patted down, probed with a metal detector, and told to sign her details into the guest book, and when she was feet from each one she heard their thoughts.

Nice bit of kit we've got here.

Wonder if Mandy's doing pie for dinner.

That Pascoe kid, he'd be better off hanging himself.

More guards nodded and pointed her on down the hallways, in company of thoughts they believed only they could hear. The visitation room was a wide space, the size and smell of a school gymnasium, crammed with cheap plastic tables and chairs, and a children's play area in the corner. The officer led her to a table, where she repositioned her chair a few times. A double door opened, and a wave of inmates sidled in one by one. Brothers-by-broken-law, they were as identical to one another as the guards were. Grey tracksuits – modified to a degree – grade one haircuts, stoic expressions, robotic shuffles: the men looked tough. Trish knew that, when night fell, they were far from it.

I'm not going to make it another week, came one frantic voice. *Not another night.*

So what if I robbed the Londis? The big fat cats won't notice the difference. My kids were starving.

From the crowd walked Michael. He was barely recognisable at first, a doppelgänger of the others. When he saw Trish, he slowed. Perhaps he had given up on the idea of seeing her; perhaps he'd expected someone else. Trish didn't rise to greet him. A guard took him to the seat opposite her, where he reclined into his chair, cuffed hands on the table between them. There was drawn out silence when neither party wanted to talk. Lips quivered and throats were cleared. It was lucky that, throughout their relationship, Trish had built up a resilience to Michael's thoughts: his cravings for drugs, reminiscing of fights he'd been in, the girls he ogled at, or worst yet, sometimes hooked up with behind Trish's back.

'Your hair's green,' Michael finally commented.

'It's teal,' Trish said.

Michael grunted indignantly.

'Weird vibes this mornin',' he said. 'A Polish guy hung himself in the cell next to mine.'

Michael tired of small talk quickly, always had, but Trish wondered whether recounting prison fables helped him ignore his own bleak reality.

'No?' She sounded far from earnest. 'That's rough.'

'Nah, he was a kid fiddler. He knew the boys would get him, only a matter of time. If you don't get done by someone else, you do it yourself, or you get fucked up on spice.'

'There's that in here?'

'Everything gets in 'cause most of us ain't ever getting out.'

That's your own fault, Trish thought, and the floodgates opened.

'Guilty? Fucking guilty.'

'It was Hornes's idea,' Michael whispered, eyes on a guard who filled a paper cup at the nearby water dispenser. 'Get the shortest sentence possible. The odds were stacked aga inst me – '

'The evidence was stacked against you,' Trish hissed.

'On a technicality, that her DNA was on my clothing – '

'I read the court notes.'

She had, so many times that the visuals she'd gotten from it were branded in her mind, permeating every nightmare.

'Look,' Michael began, fists clenched. A guard flitted past their table toward commotion in the corner of the visitation room. He relaxed his posture and unclenched his fists. 'What I said in court was the whole truth. I swore on my mother's life. Shauna was in The Puffin and Hare after the rugby match. Said hello, gave her a hug, in-law politics, checking she was with her friends. I got thrown out, and the next thing I know, I find her lying in the alleyway, strangled – '

'I've read the notes.'

A young lad behind Michael yelled. Two guards flanked him, telling to remain calm or his visitation would end early. He pleaded with his dishevelled parents on the other side of his table. 'She's my daughter,' he sobbed. 'I've got a right to see her.'

He wore an Arsenal Football shirt; if a prisoner was compliant they earned back personal items. He had kept his head down and all to see his daughter again, Trish bet. Michael only had his drab granite-grey tracksuit. Trish hadn't meant to glare at him, but he caught it all the same.

'You think I did it,' he stated.

'I don't know what I think.'

'I think you do,' Michael growled. 'Hornes contacted you. A character reference, they said, from the victim's sister, could have done a world of good. I wouldn't have had to plead guilty. I could have had a chance.'

Trish snorted and turned her head from him.

'And write what? That you were faithful? Dependable? That you weren't going to and from Birmingham for dope?'

'I did what I did to keep a roof over our heads.'

'You could have done that if you'd stayed put in the milking parlours,' Trish retorted. 'Don't make it out that it was for me.

I was the last thing on your mind. I always was.'

She had accepted a long time ago that Michael was many things, and selfless was not one of them. Michael sat back in his chair and leered at her the way he would a stranger.

'I'm bored of you now.'

'I'm boring you?'

'Yeah, all this talking, goin' nowhere. Bored.'

Trish faltered. How could she mention the shadow imprint without sounding mad? Michael tended to hallucinate when abusing drugs, and the night Shauna died he'd had a cocktail of them. In such states, the things he envisioned were not drug-derived images, for Trish saw them too. He had a reception to the frequency, albeit limited. Were he capable of that whilst sober, he could have been a witness himself.

'What were you on that night, then?' Michael had never been one to shy away from his excursions. 'Craig said you'd blacked out a few times that night.'

'I was proper paralytic,' Michael said. 'A bit of Mandy, some blow. I could barely walk, let alone . . . It was a bad trip, truth be told. The shadows . . .'

Trish nearly slipped from her chair.

'The shadows?' she asked.

'Had lives of their own,' Michael continued. 'There were two of them.'

'What did they do?'

Michael leant back in his chair, brow wrinkled. He had Trish's vested interest for the first time, and so he spoke slowly.

'They followed me. The bar, the bog. Kept seeing them, wherever I went.'

Trish saw it emanating from Michael's mind. Two of the gywandras, waxen and malformed, were poised amongst the unsuspecting punters. And behind them, nailed to the bloodred wall, was a scuffed oil painting: The Vincent.

'The paintings on the walls, well, they moved, some Harry Potter shit,' Michael continued. 'An old ship, and it was sinking – '

Trish scrambled from her chair, Michael's shouts white noise as she fled the visitation room with a guard in tow.

Article: 39

Due to the research outlined in soruch 7A*, it is prohibited for anyone under the age of 18 to practice witnessing. 7A provides irrefragable evideence that a minor's frontal lobe is still in development: prolonged connection to imprints, and frequency energy at large, increased the risk of mental illness occurring in adulthood. The only exception to this rule is if said minor's quality of life is severely impacted by their connection to imprint activity.

*7A: Penrose, J. (2011). Witnesses and Mental Health Conditions. Cornwall: Imprint Activity Network, pp.1-30.

PART SIX

WHITHER WE
ARE GOING

43

SAM'S COMEDOWN was a bitter last hurrah.

Padstow's harbour swirled and pulsated around him. Frequency energy coursed beneath each stone building, swaying boat, and lapping tide. Now the Network's stores were inaccessible. Sam had gutted every drawer, container, and book nook of their flat – his flat, as he often reminded himself – for any remnants of alcohol and drugs. He dared not use what little money the Network's trust gave him on so-so street drugs before he went cold turkey. *For now*, he decided, *I'll only be plagued by the dead.*

He'd eloped to Padstow to watch the morning sun blister the sky. His grief was relentless. Sam hadn't slept well since the night James escorted him from the collieries and enforced compassionate leave on Sam. His cravings escalated in the absence of a hectic witnessing schedule. One half of his mind was occupied with Will. He had, in their six-year relationship, become half of Sam, it seemed. The other thought of narcotics, and he was intent on changing that.

Sam was a rare witness: he'd never encountered death in his twenty-nine years – the dead he had, but not death. His grandfather, on his mother's side, had passed when Sam was small. He was five then and only remembered the stories Rose told. No one had prepared him for it. Gut-punching sadness stole him in the quiet moments; he'd turn to talk to Will only to find the sofa to the left of him empty, or to check his phone to realise that Will would never text him again. Grief, a life sentence of spiralling depressive thoughts with no hope for a retrial.

A greying council maintenance worker picked up litter on Strand Street, a permanent stoop in his posture from a long working life of manual labour. On the high street, retirees mulled to the social club for another day of liver damage. They had all experienced grief, surely, and yet their lives went on. Life went on . . . until it didn't. Trish rarely called him nowadays, but when she did it was the same hopeful witnessing spiel: that Will wasn't truly dead, not for them. She cried over her predicament between her loyalty for Shauna and Michael. Trish had caught Sam on the toilet, where he had been for a while; he found himself taking longer to do most activities these days as trains of thought trundled through counties of alternate possibilities and scoured past fields of regret and towns of what-ifs.

A cluster of imprints at the farthest edge of the harbour wall – sailors when they were alive – prepared a merchant's boat. They passed supply crates between themselves, tightening ropes, plotting a course over a map. Enacting the day-to-day routines of lives they'd once had, invisible to the warm-bodied, the warm-bodied invisible to them. The drunkards, the maintenance worker, strung to their routines so inherently that what lay ahead of them in death, if they weren't fortunate enough to disperse into the frequency forever, was to continue their routines unaware they were dead at all. Sam favoured death's death itself: a dignified and absolute end. He'd hoped that for Will, deep down in his innermost thoughts, out of reach from Trish.

An influx of locals amassed in the harbour. Dressed in white clothing, their outfits were licked with red or blue from handkerchiefs and headscarves. A drum roll rumbled, and accordions wheezed. The swarm amassed along the high street: the 'Obby 'Oss festival. Since Will's death to that very moment, Sam had somehow exchanged a week of his life. He'd stared at walls and ogled at perfectly average people and found himself on the first of May. Not so dissimilar to imprints, after all. Sam slunk from the bench and wandered to the outskirts of the raucous.

The crowd converged outside of the Golden Lion Inn, and a song rose.

> 'Unite and unite and let us all unite,
> For summer is acome unto day,
> And whither we are going we will all unite,
> In the merry morning of May . . .'

The Teaser – a gangly man in black rags – lumbered forward and knocked on the door of the inn. A man burst from it, wearing a garish black-and-red cape strung to a wide hoop around his shoulders: the 'Obby 'Oss. He manoeuvred to the centre of the crowd, swirling between the merrymakers and the teasers, and swooped and glided in pretence of capturing one of the maids in blue.

> 'And bright is your bride that lies by your side,
> In the merry morning of May.'

The lyrics brimmed with hope and wonderment, and they excluded Sam. The tossing 'Obby 'Oss, with its insatiable appetite, mocked the hunger for life that he suppressed, or maybe his grief did; he couldn't be sure. It celebrated life, it welcomed change, summer's fast approach, and Sam could no longer stand being isolated in suspended existence –

Buzzing erupted in Sam's pocket. He withdrew his phone to see that Trish called him. Her foresight was impeccable. He raced to the edge of the crowd and answered.

'Sam, we have to – where the hell are you?' Her voice wavered.

'I'm Attenborough-ing a right old piss up,' Sam replied.

The gleeful May Day celebrations registered with Trish.

'Christ. Don't cause trouble. I'm coming to get you, and we're going to Marge's house.'

'Marge's house,' Sam repeated with distaste.

'It's all connected, Sam. I don't know how, but it is.'

Trish pulled up outside the band barriers on Quay Street ten minutes later. Sam noticed a cracked side-view mirror and a fresh dent in the passenger wing before he climbed into the Reliant; her mind had been on many things on the drive over, but it hadn't been on the road.

He gave her a pinch-punch-first-of-the-month-no-returning as they sped away, knowing it was childish in light of everything. Luckily, he said no more and listened to Trish recount the last three days without him.

'Percy Shilson called it the gywandras,' Trish concluded. 'Shauna, Rose, Will, and Rasha. It's all connected.'

'And you think the Network knows about this?'

'It's in the archives. Buried, but it's there.'

'You realise you're saying,' Sam grumbled, 'that it's been around for fourteen years. Maybe longer.'

'I know, I know. We might learn something at Will's house. We'll have to be careful. Keep our stories straight about work.'

The trio had spun an intricate web of lies about a start-up company, Shore Utilities. Will and Trish were both in HR, and Sam was an engineer. Margaret and Phil believed them, to their surprise; Will's mind would be wasted chasing employees for time sheets, whilst Sam could barely change a fuse in their Ikea floor lamp. A start-up company that struggled to find its feet. *Like many things*, Sam thought with distaste.

'How much time do you think we can get?' Trish asked.

'We need to get through the door first.' Trish blasted him a foul look. 'Eyes on the road, Teagues. He went to stay with them because of me. He would have told them. Marge would have coaxed it out of him.'

Over a cream tea, no doubt. Her scones were black magic.

'Plus the day you forced your way into their house,' Trish snapped. Old Phil, struggling on his bad hip, had to wrench Sam out of the cottage. Margaret cried in hysterics at them both. A shed-load of ketamine had been needed that night. As if she'd read Sam's mind, Trish said, 'And if they mention drugs? I'm not Scarlet Johansson-ing with your Hulk in there, not in front of his parents, not at the scene of the crime.'

'Scene of the crime,' Sam echoed through pursed lips. Trish prodded him hard in the ribs. 'Yes, all right, I will behave, I promise. Crime? You think someone did it?'

'What else?' Trish said. 'You're not thinking . . . ? But that's absurd.'

Get out of my head, Teagues, he thought bitterly, then continued vocally, 'He was stressed. Our relationship was basically extinct – buried, excavated, and put into a museum. I drove him from our home.'

'He wouldn't!' Trish demanded it to be true. It wasn't just

Sam she tried to persuade. 'He just wouldn't.'

They skirted around a word, one considered blasphemy amongst witnesses: suicide. A majority of them – Trish included – had close brushes with death's illicit companion. As witnesses, the odds they would come back as imprints were invariably in their favour. The concept of suicide lost any appeal to the desperate when their woes would follow them into death, just an unruly extension of a life so sour.

'Abidemi's signature was there.'

'She might have been there for a number of reasons. To warn him. To help him. As Will would have said, a closed mind – '

'Isn't open to answers,' Trish concluded. 'I miss him.'

'Me too.'

44

WILL'S PARENTS ambled out of their front door as the Reliant pulled into their drive. Their Maldivian holidays, excess drinking, and sports had caught up with them; skin ashen and eyes tired, both swayed on their feet.

Sam rose from the Reliant's passenger door. He was surprised to find they looked relieved, and as Phil limped forward, Sam learnt why.

'We thought you were police again,' Phil said, and Sam was reminded how Will sounded like him. Sam's stomach fell. 'They've been coming and going, all this talkin' but not sayin' anythin'.'

'Good to know our tax is being put to good use,' Sam retorted, taking Phil's hand. His could-have-been-father-in-law smiled. There was yearning in his eyes too, in the way that someone desperately wanted to talk to a person but their situation did not allow for it. In that case, Margaret didn't.

'We exist, then,' she hissed.

'Marge,' Phil cautioned.

'No Philip, no, goddamn it. You barge in on the day it happened, we have to throw you out. No calls, no texts. You wouldn't have thought Will had a partner.' Partner, far more ambiguous than boyfriend. 'I mean, were you even together in the end? He didn't say either way when he came home.'

Margaret's opening itinerary for Sam's recent visits. She implied he was a lousy boyfriend – correction, partner. *Check*. Lied that Will hadn't divulged all about their relationship over some proper home cooking. *Check*.

Margaret was a hopeless cause, so Sam sought for solidarity with Phil.

'I couldn't talk to you both over the phone. I wanted to come here, but coming back to where . . .'

Phil nodded but Margaret replied, 'That's not bloody good enough. We have to live here, day and night, sleeping down the hallway from it. We can't escape. We can't just bury our heads in the sand.'

An invite to go inside may not have appeared if it hadn't started to rain. Phil took Trish by the shoulder and led her in first. Trish gave her apologies for their loss, which softened Margaret a little. Having no daughters herself, she had always been fond of Trish.

Sam took up the rear. Will's parents lumbered into the kitchen. Phil's limp was worse; his left hip needed a replacement. Margaret was unsteady too, her busybody pace gone, inching across the kitchen tiles to tend to the kettle. Maybe they'd aged in the months he'd rarely visited. Maybe Will's death had gotten to their cores, rotting them from the inside out.

Phil settled into a chair padded out with cushions and invited Sam and Trish to the table.

'No parent should have to bury their child,' Phil said. Behind him, Margaret slammed cups and chinked teaspoons to drown out the noise. Sam wondered how many times she'd heard Philip repeat himself. 'You don't realise what a rigmarole it is. It's not the money I mind; can't take that with you, can you? They haven't released him yet. Coroner said something doesn't add up. Then you need certificates and have to send them everywhere. There's the funeral itself, of course – '

'I'll help,' Sam said. 'I can pay for everything.'

'We can't expect you to do that.' Phil sounded hurt. Sam knew he'd toed the line. He felt useless, and he hated it. 'But we do need help. Did he want to be buried? Cremated? Music? Flowers? Don't think even he knew. When you're that young, you're too concerned about living to think about what follows.'

If only Phil knew. It was those moments that Sam resented the Network. It forced them to live a lie. Will's family barely knew him. Like Will, Sam's adolescence had been burdened by his suppressed sexuality, a heaviness he hadn't known he carried until it was finally let go. Being a witness was very much the same; Sam hated the idea of keeping a secret rather than the secret itself.

Phil stared into the fruit bowl where only a melon sat, its skin warped with late signs of decay. Its flesh would be mulch. Margaret passed them three cups of tea in various shades of tan, a rarity in her compliant hospitality.

'He'll need clothes,' Margaret said. 'A suit. The funeral directors will make him look smart. There's stuff upstairs, the clothes he brought. And work documents, all in a box up there. We'll need to contact HR at your work, let them know officially.'

'I've told them. I can get you the details. Shall I – '

'Yes, you know where the bedroom is.'

Sam rose from the table and grimaced at Trish. He abandoned his tea – too milky for his liking – and skulked down the hallway. He took his time climbing the stairs to Will's room. Sam stopped on the landing and closed his eyes to skirt the edges of the ombrederi. Will had been constantly haunted in his adolescence. The imprint had often come as he slept and shrieked with a soul-tearing burden. He'd been too young to truly read its identity back then. Her imprint wasn't there now. It meant everything and nothing.

Sam stalled, completely on purpose. He pushed the door forward; it had since been repaired and no longer hung from broken hinges. The room was cleared of debris. A sun-bleached square of wall suggested the wardrobe had been there; Will's clothes were stowed in plastic storage boxes. The window was boarded up with plywood, but one thing that couldn't be removed was the splatter of crimson on the carpet, walls, and ceiling. Nose-burning bleach hung in the air; despite Marge's best efforts, Will's blood could not be scrubbed away.

Giddiness overcame him, and he put a hand against the nearest wall to stabilize himself. An unbearable heat swarmed across his body, dissipating just as quickly as it had come. In the farthest corner, a bright light crackled in Sam's periphery: a burning noose swaying from a crooked ceiling beam. Abidemi had been there, just as James said. Sam, overwhelmed by the reality of Will's mortal death, hadn't registered Abidemi's aura that day he barged into the room. The noose swung in circles as if it lured Sam to the ombrederi. Beneath the noose was Will's desk, the only item of furniture still intact, and atop it was a grey folder file. The night he died, Will would have, just as he had so diligently in the months prior, worked on his file – a file only the Network's board was allowed to discuss. Sam grabbed the folder file, sped from the room, and yanked the door shut.

His legs only took him to the end of the landing. He

collapsed at the top of the stairs. The thought of joining the others was not attractive, so he opened the box folder. Inside were sheaths of paper, unordered, furiously scribbled upon. Notes, ones that meant little to Sam, were marked against placeholders for paragraph and pages. That was, until he turned a torn sheet over and read: *Gywandras > transcendence.*

A silhouette appeared at the bottom of the stairs. Sam dropped the papers. There were no symptoms of engagement; it was Margaret, face impossibly ancient in the half-light of the hallway.

'We'll do Will proud,' Sam said, and he meant it. 'The funeral, together. Really celebrate his life.'

'Should have done that while he was living it,' Margaret hissed. 'He always thought he could fix people. He thought that's how love worked. And maybe it is, but you couldn't be mended, and that broke him.'

'Unfortunately, that's not how addictions work.'

'Then you should have let him go. You know what he said to me the night he came back, barely legible through tears? He said you took those drugs – no, I don't know what they are, drugs are drugs to me and Phil – he said you took those drugs so you could be in a world of your own. A different world to him.'

'That's not how it was.'

'It doesn't matter how it was; he *felt* that way, and it's how he felt that made him throw himself . . . I've had to grieve for my son twice. First when he came out, and now that he's . . . You'll never understand how that feels.'

'You can't blame me.'

'Who else do I have to blame?'

Sam's mouth gaped, unable to answer, so he closed it. Grief taught him to think before he spoke.

'I think you should go now,' Margaret said.

Sam could do no more than gulp back a retort, rise from the stairs, and descend past Margaret. After an abrupt goodbye, during which Sam dodged Phil's attempts to have them stay, Trish and Sam jumped into the Reliant and drove god knows where. Trish clipped a horse box at a T-junction.

'The gywandras could be connected to his death,' Trish pondered. 'And Abidemi was definitely there.'

'We saw them together, remember?' Sam prompted, thinking back to the frequency spike at the collieries. Will had been alive then.

'A premonition can mean a thousand things,' Trish said. She tapped the steering wheel, took a deep breath, and blurted, 'Will knew about the gywandras. He knew it existed.'

Sam flipped through the pages on his lap. He didn't want to confirm Trish's thoughts. Then he found another intriguing sentence.

'The body is nothing more than a cage inhibiting imprints from true transcendence,' he read.

'Transcendence of what?' Trish said.

Sam gripped the passenger side door handle as she veered the Reliant Robin from the dual carriageway onto rain-soaked backroads.

'I know James warned us off seeing Rasha again,' Sam said, 'but she's the only person alive who is connected to the gywandras.'

'I've been thinking the same thing,' Trish said. 'Coincidences don't just happen. Her powers are strong. She engaged with an imprint at her school and forced it onto someone. I'm starting to think that Will's death wasn't so straightforward.' Sam noted the sharp pang in his diaphragm whenever someone else said 'Will's death.' 'Rasha's occupation was rare in so many ways. Maybe Will's death was an occupation.'

Sharp pang.

'It's still a leap,' he retorted.

'Still more probable than suicide, on all counts,' Trish said. 'Perhaps . . . perhaps there is a way to lure the gywandras in, just as we did before.'

Sam was puzzled a moment, for the only time they had done that – inadvertently so – had been Rasha's accidental occupation.

'Hell no,' he barked. 'I won't allow it.'

'Hear me out, please. It'll be different this time. Rasha has already made the appropriate engagement – '

'Answer me this. If that girl – if Rasha – lost her mind, would you visit her week upon week in that shithole we call the Refinery and look into her eyes and tell her everything is okay and that she's safe there even though she doesn't know where "here" is?'

His mum's eyes, softly hazel, the skin around them further sagged and lined week after week. The real kind of horror that only the most unfortunate of children could ever know. Sam chewed his fingernails. He just wanted to move on. Something Trish couldn't – rather, wouldn't – do. It wasn't in her DNA.

Sam's phone vibrated in receipt of a call. He whipped it out of the cup holder.

'It's James,' Sam said, reading the caller ID.

'Just let it ring out,' Trish said.

'Last time we did that, someone died,' Sam reminded her. He swiped to answer and put the phone to his ear.

'Sam,' came James's panicked voice. 'I know you're on compassionate leave, but I'm gonna need you and Trish to come down. I presume she's with you. You're the only people who can help us. We've got a code red. It's another occupation.'

45

SAM NEVER THOUGHT he'd step foot in Angove Lodge again. To accommodate the ageing population, the one-storey care home had various extensions added over the years, each uglier than the last. Trish rolled the Reliant up before the home's garage doors as the sun set. Patinated windows brimmed with nests, beneath which sat a rusting minibus speckled in seagull faeces. *An absolute death is better than this shit*, Sam thought. He knew it to be true; his grandfather had spent the remainder of his days there. Rose often recounted that, whilst the carers were well-meaning, the workforce was spread thin amongst forty residents. At his end, his grandfather would have been better off at home with Sam and Rose, or even in his own downtrodden flat.

Sam and Trish climbed from the Reliant and unpacked the equipment James had asked them to collect when he pulled up in his people carrier. He hopped out and tottered over to them. He patted the square of Sam's back and hugged Trish.

'How are you both keeping?' James asked.

Sam and Trish looked between themselves. On the way over they'd agreed not to mention the gywandras.

'Turns out funeral plans make for great bonding with the in-laws,' Sam drawled. Trish scowled at him, passed bags to both men, and led the way to the front of the home.

'Where is the occupations unit?' she asked.

'Temporarily engaged.'

'The occupation in Bodmin?'

James did a double take at Trish; she wasn't wearing her dielectric band. Secrets were no more.

'Still ongoing,' James exclaimed.

'So the ban from public relations no longer applies?' Sam sneered.

'Temporarily lifted,' James said.

'What has the care home been told about us?' Trish asked.

'Private healthcare,' James replied, slightly hesitant. 'Sent by the patient's family. The woman I spoke to is an agency worker. Sounded desperate on the call, didn't ask many questions.'

'What do you know so far?' Sam asked.

'Ted Lower, eighty-six, MS, dysphagia, bedbound. The nurse on the phone said he's been experiencing unwarranted neurotic behaviour this last week. Ever since the frequency spikes escalated in Pendeen, as it happens.'

They reached a key-coded door. James pressed the buzzer.

A bedraggled shift worker arrived from the adjacent corridor. She slammed her key fob against the sensor. There was a meek beep, and the door flung outward. She raised her pencilled eyebrows as if to ask who they were.

'Doctor Peter Wright, Pink Cross,' James said before gesturing to Sam and Trish. 'My two juniors. All we can do at short notice. I spoke to Jill?'

'That's me. Christ, no, no, thank god you've come,' Jill said. She ushered them inside and shut the door quickly – a shrivelled raisin of a man scuttled toward it in an attempt for freedom. Jill led them down the corridor she'd come from. 'Don't bother signing in, can't leave him alone, not for a minute. I'm not trained for this, hell, I'm not paid well enough for this – '

I feel you, sister, Sam thought.

'It was a good job his son called when he did, I'd never have known he had private healthcare. Don't tell us agency nothin'.'

Sam raised his eyebrows, certain that James had feigned his London accent during the phone call.

'He's out of his mind,' Jill continued. 'Well, most are, but in a different way entirely. The GP put it down to a UTI, but I've seen plenty, and they've never caused . . . this.'

They stopped before a door. Sam noted a photograph on the door labelled 'Ted.' It was a picture of a confused man gazing up from his wheelchair with pearly eyes. Jill turned and put an arm across the doorway to stop them. Her nicotine-licked teeth chattered.

'I don't know if you know, but it's important before you see him,' she said. 'He hasn't walked in years. Not spoken for the same time. He's been blind since his sixties. My god . . .'

Jill sunk against the wall. James headed the party and pushed the door open. Inside, Ted stood with the posture of a healthy twenty-year-old. Blood raced across his forearms, eyes clear, and a toppled side lamp cast him into a half-light. Piss – the stale apricot kind – crept over Sam's nostrils: a catheter bag had emptied onto the frayed carpet by the hospital bed. Ted turned at the sound of their arrival, his bloodied nightgown hitched around his disjointed hips. Blood dripped from his flaccid penis where the catheter tube had been torn out.

James turned to close the door.

'We'll just get some privacy,' he whispered to Jill. 'Try to calm him down.'

He closed the door. It was four of them, alone in the room.

'We should try to speak to it first,' Trish said. 'Establish the degree of the occupation. Sam, I need a reading.'

'Sure,' Sam said. He fumbled with the equipment bag.

Trish approached Ted.

'Ted, can you hear me?' she asked. 'Can you see me, Ted?'

The old man cocked his head, birdlike, inquisitive.

'What's your name?' Trish asked, and the reply was higher pitched than Sam had expected, with a Russian accent.

'Nika.'

What followed was a torrent of angry words. They streamed from the old man's mouth faster than the man previously had capacity for. Ted, or rather Nika, paused, cocked their head, and awaited a response. When none came, another flurry of Russian was spat, harsher than before. Sam, the spectrophotometer in hand, fumbled to power up the gadget.

'Well,' Trish said, 'I take it no one knows Russian.'

'No, but I've got a reading,' Sam said. James looked over his shoulder at the screen. Ted's body appeared in a navy-blue silhouette. Inside him thrashed two wispy silhouettes: one green, which sunk from his body, whilst the second was red and thwarted the first. 'The imprint is dominant. We're losing him.'

Relief swamped Sam's chest: at least it wasn't the gywandras.

'Right, we're going to have to work to get it back,' Trish said.

Sam sighed. There was a sense of the forbidden, the kind where lust became warped and destructive, and it pulled Sam in.

'I'll engage,' he began. He didn't have time to close his eyes. Ted lumbered forward on his swollen legs. Bleeding where various tubes had been torn, Ted gestured to his penis, a useless tool in light of the man's ill health. He jerked his arms, and blood peppered parallel lines across the carpet. Ted stumbled against a cabinet, scattering photographs of his family. He rose with a disposable razor in hand: the tumble had been calculated. With one sharp motion, he sliced through his foreskin. A second swipe. A third. The bereft penis hit the carpet.

'Sam, engage for fuck's sake!' Trish screamed.

Sam closed his eyes and plunged into the ombrederi.

46

SAM'S NEUTRAL space – the sprawling ancient trees of Cardinham Woods – never came.

He was thrust into a meek treatment room. A thin bare woman was sat on a hospital bed. She only had one breast, its companion replaced by a scar that oozed with infection. Sam hazarded a guess that this was Nika, and as she conferred with her doctor he discovered it was cancer, or pak, the doctor often said in Russian, and he was old and wizened and leered above her as he recited that she was cured.

Sam saw into Nika's mind and found that she wasn't relieved. The doctor had touched Nika in places he never asked to, did things unrelated to her treatment, and through rape stole more and more of her soul. A parasitic man, worse than cancer. She'd survived one disease and would outlive another.

The doctor pinned her to the hospital bed and unzipped his trousers. She reached down, as if to hold the bed frame for the onslaught that would follow. Nika found the side table ladled with instruments. Her hand clamped around an object, smaller than she'd hoped – but alas, it was sharp. She whipped her hand up and jabbed a needle into the doctor's eye. Opaque fluid squirted from his eyeball, and his erection depleted quicker than a popped balloon. She reached out again, brought up a scalpel, and drove it through the doctor's temple. The life fell right out of his body, and his body fell to the floor.

'Anything?' Trish's voice reverberated from the physical.

Sam processed through the following memories: tense police enquiries, a media driven court case, and a miserable life sentence in a grungy prison. 'All because a man took what wasn't his,' Nika hissed from within the ombrederi.

'I can't find the taken,' Sam said to the physical.

'Think context,' Trish barked. 'You need to hurry.'

Nika was, above all else, emptied of any power or self-worth. To have connected to Nika, Ted must have empathised with her, for Sam had to connect to them both.

The scene whirled like water down a sink drain. The doctor rose from the hospital floor. But he was now a woman, matronesque with a wild Scottish mane. There was Ted, little Ted, aged seven, and little Ted loved Spitfires. He had countless drawings, and his daddy had made a model from matchsticks, and it really was the cat's pyjamas. The woman was called Josie, and little Ted sat on Josie's lap before the crackling fire whilst his mummy and daddy went out to dance with their friends. They had lots of friends and lots of dances, and per Friday night routine, Ted showed Josie all of his drawings since their last encounter. He concentrated on the drawings, absorbed in each detail and every feature of each plane, because Josie did the thing he really didn't enjoy. She had to do it; she said that if she didn't, and Mummy and Daddy found out, there would be no more Spitfires. The warmth of the hearth stung Teddy's eyes, but he dared not blink, not until it was over, and then when it was, he crossed to Daddy's armchair that smelt of tobacco and shoe polish. He played with the Spitfire and pretended to fly, away from Josie and the fire, up toward the sky to somewhere brilliant and new.

Sam superimposed himself into the memory, into the warmth of the living room, back turned away from Josie, whose form warped and bled.

'I can't find Ted,' Sam called into the real.

'Focus,' Trish said. 'Find some positive memories and bring him – '

Before she could finish the sentence, the memory changed again. Ted was married now, and he was tall and bearded and an engineer in the air force. His wife had untameable red hair. So did his three daughters, who leapt on him with thankful hugs and kisses on Christmas morning. Then he was fifty, his house in disrepair. His wife yelled at him because he was a drunk now – a workless, worthless drunk – and they didn't have sex anymore, and her hair was grey.

The memories continued to fall and twist and bend over themselves; in the destruction of one came another, a phoenix of red hair from the ashes of a fireplace. The poison of Ted's childhood seeped into them all.

'I'm struggling to get a grip,' Sam said in the physical.

A pain erupted in Sam's groin, in Ted's, and it was faint. Nika had resurfaced. A sharp pain tore across his testicles.

'Sam,' came James's urgent voice, 'get out. Come back to us. Now.'

47

SAM'S EYES jerked open to find a tide of blood on the carpet.

Old Ted fell to his knees, skin slate grey. Trish and James were shrunk against the back wall. Ted, under Nika's control, cut at the scrotum with the razor.

'Fuck this,' Sam said, then bent to his duffel bag, bringing out an EMP.

'Sam,' James warned.

'Article fifty-seven: expel both the imprint and the taken if the occupied is being inflicted a pain so severe that – '

'Death is the only resolution,' Trish concluded.

Sam switched the EMP on and flung it. The contraption scuttled across the carpet and landed at Ted's knees. It beeped once, twice, three times, then popped. White light flashed across the room. Ted collapsed to the floor. His physical life was over, as was his chance to become an imprint. At least the pain had ended.

Better to have an absolute death.

Sam stood rooted to the blood-soaked carpet. James and Trish pulled him to the bedroom window, equipment bags strung to their backs. Sam hesitated on the windowsill and looked back at photographs of Ted's happy family, now in a heap on the floor.

Trish pulled him through the window onto the gravel. They skirted the perimeter of the home back to their vehicles, ducking under windowsills as they went. The home's lights popped on and off: the aftereffects of the EMP.

Back in the Reliant, Trish and Sam followed James in his people carrier. They got purposefully lost in the tangle of backroads until they were out of sight of motorways and houses. The journey in Trish's car was alight with argument. James pulled over into the gateway of a nondescript field. Trish brought her car up beside his, and they piled out.

'We let a man die, and we fucked off,' Sam shrieked. 'What the actual hell?'

'We had to protect the Network,' James said.

Sam thumped the carrier's roof.

'To hell with the Network,' he cried.

'The carer, she saw our faces,' Trish said. 'If there was CCTV –'

'There wasn't,' James assured her. 'We'll lay low for a while, at the collieries, until we sort this.'

'How can we sort it?' Trish said. She pulled at her hair. It was lilac now. 'He's dead. The fourth occupation in two weeks.'

Sam couldn't stop her in time. He watched on as the information registered with James.

'Three occupations,' James said slowly. He glanced between his associates.

'Trish has a theory that Will was occupied too,' Sam said.

'Tonight just proves that. Doesn't it, Sam? Doesn't it?' Trish beckoned.

'Yes,' Sam said. It was beyond a coincidence now. 'We need the Abadi kid. We need Rasha. I don't give a rat's tail about her age; she's the only person to have survived an occupation. We need to know how.'

James leant against his boot. His eyes washed over the stickers in the rear window.

'We might find out how to confront the occupations when they come, emphasis on might, but it doesn't help us prevent them from happening,' he said.

James took a deep breath, turned to them, and said, 'We'll head to the collieries. She's already there. Vanessa's going to have her take the Long Walk.'

INTERLUDE II

A DYING MAN joins Ewella in the hold.

From what the maiden gathers, he ranks low and is forgotten by his crew members. He lies opposite the wall where Ewella is chained. A gash ladders from his left armpit to his right hip. Long forgotten by the crew, his wound is untended and grows greyer and greyer with rot. The deeper the fever runs, the more he sleeps. The more he sleeps, and the closer he edges toward death, the more Ewella sees.

On the first night she saw a burning village. The heat of the spitting fires was relentless as the sun above. The locals to this Nigerian village ran and shrieked. A wretched memory to infest the girl's mind, and a recurrent one at that. Another showed the ill man being dragged to the ship that he tried so desperately to escape. She learnt his name, too: Ebok.

There is no doubt in her mind that Ebok's memories are what led her to the shore. Thoughts cycle through his mind, and so her mind too. At first the words were alien to her, a language beyond Kernewek. She has become accustomed to the language, as if her mind is a book in which Ebok pens his words and their definitions.

My life is home. But there is no home. This boat is my life. But my life is home.

Ewella knows all too well. She pines to be back amongst her villagers – even those who taunt her. Ebok is unlikely to return home, for leagues of relentless sea lie between them. She finds strength knowing that hers is close by.

At the beginning of summer, Ewella failed to find paying work amongst the villagers. Her mother would often repeat to her unwilling ears that opportunity comes in the unlikeliest of forms. Ewella's comes in the shape of a boy her age, darker than the rest of the ship's crew. His torso is bare, and his ribs protrude. It isn't the boy's skeletal form that grabs her attention. He is the first crew member to tend to Ebok.

The scrawny boy kneels before Ebok, ladles salt water from a bucket, and washes the gash on the ill man's chest. Pain shudders through Ebok's body. Ewella knows he is beyond saving. The boy acts with tenderness; he knows, too. He still cleanses the wound. Ebok's twitches lessen as he drifts from the living once more. A tsunami of colour bombards Ewella's skull, and the wood of her prison floods away –

In its place is a stage erected in a dusty courtyard surrounded by market stalls. Merchants and keepers, as diverse as their products, haggle and barter. A crowd with square jaws, fair skin, and dark features gathers alongside the platform. Eager, excitable. Ewella catches a word, unsure if it is a title for man or place: Arab. Women, chained wrist to wrist and ankle to ankle, are lined before the crowd. Tears fall silently across the maids' unwashed faces. Hands rise amongst Arabians whilst a Nigerian yells numbers. These numbers are prices. The women are products.

Ewella's warm tears throw her back to the bowels of the ship. The vision gives way to the shadows of night. Her tears do not alarm her; grunts of pain do. She meets the boy's hollow gaze. Four of the crew members hold his limbs to the floor as a fifth lies on top of him and thrusts into his buttocks. The notion of two men in the heat of passion is plausible enough to Ewella. The fact one cannot give consent, merely a boy himself, is not. A few quick, hard thrusts. The man lies astride the boy for a heartbeat. He rises, tucks his member into his leggings, and clambers up the ladder, his four accomplices in tow.

The boy lies there for a moment. He blinks, then flexes his wrists and ankles where they had been pressed to the floor. He climbs to his knees and gathers his torn garments. A milky substance drips across his inner thigh. With his ripped clothes now just rags, he mops the fluid up. He scrubs his thighs, and the scrubbing becomes punches. Ewella shouts. The boy recoils toward the nearest wall, and shame burns across his face: he forgot he is in company. She is with him, and Ewella knows she must continue to be – through the rape and beatings and hunger.

Those poor protruding ribs. Ewella lunges into the corner of the cabin and searches blindly in the darkness. She returns with a dried fig; it weeps with age but is sustenance nonetheless. Most nights the men fight for food; naturally, the older and stronger are fruitful. She is guaranteed meals, dried figs mostly. She knows why now: she is a product to be haggled over at market.

Ewella stumbles forward and offers the fig to the scrawny boy. He watches her through his fingers as if he searches for an ulterior motive. He approaches and reaches out, and his fingertips meet hers. The fig exchanges hands. He sits and eats the whole fig as Ewella looks on. When he is done, he gives her a smile, and his brilliant white teeth glow in the darkness. A hopeful smile.

PART SEVEN

NO CHANCE AT
FORGIVENESS

48

RASHA MIGHT AS WELL have been a criminal.

Vanessa barely spoke to her on the drive over from the holiday park to the collieries, and the first thing she said when they descended into the intoxicating black mineshaft was, 'You've got us into trouble.'

Fred's delimbing. Trish had told the board.

'I didn't mean to,' Rasha said as she treaded down the sharp tunnel. 'I couldn't close the connection, and this boy, Fred, was being – '

'Enough,' Vanessa hissed. She stopped ahead of Rasha but didn't turn to face her. 'We're compromised.'

Vanessa stalked forward, and Rasha ran to keep up.

'Why don't you want people to know about my training?'

'Because there are people who'd want to stop it.'

'So what we're doing is bad?'

'It's beyond anything they can comprehend.'

They stopped at an intersection where paths went west and east. A shock of frequency energy chewed Rasha's skin. Vanessa nodded east.

'The Long Walk,' she announced.

'What is it?' Rasha asked, relieved that the darkness hid most of Vanessa's face.

'Correctional treatment for troubled witnesses,' Vanessa spat. 'And by witnessing protocols – outdated protocols, but mandatory nonetheless – you are troubled.'

'Correctional . . .' Rasha thought out loud. She considered Vanessa's sentiment when she forced engagement with Joel at school that night. She'd said Rasha's experiences in Syria, and her subsequent state of mind, was what made her a witness. It seemed her darker thoughts were no longer accepted.

'You're going to be tested,' Vanessa said. 'Four imprints, four extreme points of emotional experience. To continue with us, the board wants to bring you to a neutral place. To tempt you from darkness.'

'To make me good.'

'No, to make you subservient,' Vanessa said, disdained.

'Are they good imprints?' Rasha asked. 'The four?'

'They'll never go against Network protocol,' Vanessa returned. That didn't instil Rasha with confidence. She wanted to be back in the caravan with Haya, back in Syria before the bomb fell. To a time where she wasn't scolded for being a refugee or a witness haunted by her past.

A notification pinged. Vanessa withdrew her phone and read a message from the lock screen.

'The four are waiting,' she said, then gestured to the tunnel.

Rasha reached instinctively for Vanessa's flashlight. She jerked her hand away.

'You won't need it,' she said. 'Not where you're going.'

Rasha breathed in, out, in, out.

Rasha traipsed east and clung to a rope handrail tacked to the stone wall. With each footstep, a storm of frequency energy swelled around her. She wouldn't be the same after the Long Walk. Perhaps, if she found an instinct to engage with neutral imprints, she'd hone skills that kept evil at bay, to protect herself from the likes of Cridland, Fred, and the shadow imprint. To protect herself. In doing so, maybe she would win back the Network's trust. In doing so, maybe Haya would talk to her again.

For a moment she thought that Vanessa and company had joined her. Four people strode alongside her. No, they were imprints. They forced themselves against her mind, and brought themselves into her, and her into them.

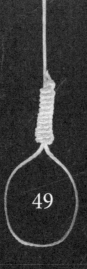

49

HEADS OF WHEAT grazed her hands, and roots crunched underfoot; before she knew it, Rasha had crossed into the ombrederi.

Ahead, the meadow flattened where shrubbery was reaped, and a wooden frame stood surrounded by workmen. They all had dirty-blond hair, dark eyes, and large ears: brothers, sons, and cousins, Rasha assumed. A gangly man with a concave chest stood amidst the pillars.

Patrick, he whispered in Rasha's mind.

He cackled at a dirty joke his boy had learnt from an American. He threw his head back and surveyed the work done so far. The beginning of his family home. He pictured his wife as she baked pasties and scones in the kitchen on Saturdays, the garden path his grandchildren would play upon.

World War II was far enough in the past as to not corrode such happier times. That month, in which the groundwork had been laid for Patrick's house, had been the most harmonious he'd ever known. The quiet after the storm. Of course, the peace wouldn't last, but the house would, and that was

Patrick's intention. It would outlive all who built it: a humble man's monument.

A breeze sauntered through the structure. Rasha understood what this imprint was meant to do: have her succumb to his tranquillity. The young men chatted as they pushed wheelbarrows of cement, while their fathers reminisced about their own parents. Were the men happy? Wartime blues must have festered beneath their skin. All at peace, all at once. An impossible feat for the human condition.

A hopeless wail echoed in the distance. Rasha treaded through another wheat field to a wild woman with weary eyes and sore cracked lips. *Macaid,* the tribeswoman whispered. She had travelled far across the rough terrain with her tribe. The night after the solstice, their map, drawn up on dried cow's hide, went up in flames by the campfire. They navigated by the coastal lines toward a seaside sanctuary they intended to call home. It was slow. The cliffs were devoid of clean water sources. Five days since the tribe drank. Minds hallucinated. Man and horse collapsed, dead before they hit the ground.

Macaid was considering throwing herself from the cliff tops, admitting defeat, when she heard a trickle. She stopped the convoy. Water gurgled. Ahead, a stream was visible, and upon its banks a herd of dead sheep rotted. Empowered with a surge of newfound need, Macaid and her tribe galloped upstream, past the green fly-infested dead. They found a lake. Every human dismounted and bolted into the water. They drank, washed, and rejoiced to a god many men had rejected. Macaid laughed and savoured her people's elation. She leapt from her horse and joined her folk in the water. Her shire wouldn't follow. Many of the horses didn't. They sniffed the water with distrust and dug their hooves into the dirt.

A worried yell. Commotion filled the air, and her people

waded out of the lake. Macaid understood why: there was a white tint to the water.

Days passed, and the convoy hadn't moved from the waterside. Within hours, those who'd drunk became sick as the poison overtook their malnourished bodies. At sunrise the death toll was in the twenties; the next night Macaid nursed the last of her men before death took him.

Macaid was alone among a hundred dead bodies, and the same again in starved horses. What was a chieftain without a tribe? She walked into the water, cupped her hands, and drank deep and true. It was bitter, as death should be. She lay back and let herself float on the water. Her weak eyes filled with the sun. It had beat down on them all thirty-seven days of their hopeless migration. It won, and it didn't matter.

Rasha rose from the chalky water, as she had risen from the rubble of her Syrian home, and she walked on. If she were the chieftain she would have picked herself up. She'd always search for her home. Rasha walked until she ran.

Max ran, too. He'd learnt to run fast. Less chance of being grazed by his dad's fist. Well, not his real dad; Kenneth was the fourth boyfriend Max had known his mum to have. Mum sure loved him and told Max to call him dad. It was all kept hush-hush, though, because of Benny Fits, whoever he was. He'd learnt to hide well. The key was to be quiet. Beside the boiler in the airing cupboard had become Max's safe space. As soon as Kenneth began to drink, Max would go the cupboard with a few select toys, a flashlight, and his overdue Tracey Beaker book. He couldn't return it to the school library; Max wasn't allowed to go school if he wore visible bruises. The teachers were nosy, Kenneth said, and they looked down at them. It was okay, though; he loved the book and wanted to keep it. He liked how the kids found doting new mums and dads.

His mum's screams grew louder and more desperate as the destruction of the kitchen sounded below Max. It quietened. Heavy footsteps creaked on the stairs. Kenneth staggered up them. A feathering of plastic told Max the blind had been ripped from the landing window again. Max buried himself as far as he could go into the corner of the closet and pulled sheets over his head from the shelf above. He wanted the darkness to gobble him up.

Milana hid in the dark. Rasha didn't mean to impose her own memories. This was how Max would persuade her, she was sure. Milana reached out to Rasha from beneath the crumpled bed. Rasha took her hand and squeezed it. She couldn't endorse the fear any longer. She'd experienced much, much worse than an abusive drunk in her time, and she could hurt people in terrible ways herself.

But perhaps not as much as Stephen.

Stephen Cardy's meaty knuckles gripped the steering wheel as his van hurtled through narrow village streets. This was the only thing he had control of – not his adulterous wife, nor his naughty kids, nor his closefisted boss. No. The vehicle he did. The TV sets he should have delivered were in smithereens, so glass and hardware swashed back and forth across the floor. He wanted to break things.

The first victim was an elderly woman. Her brittle bones turned to powdered sugar as she struck the bonnet. In the passenger's seat, Rasha gripped the door handle. She knew this was a memory. She couldn't get hurt. *So why does it feel real?* she thought.

The van turned onto the high street, amongst the midmorning bustle, and claimed a mother pushing a rickety pram. Skulls cracked the windshield. A dusty baker crossing from the Spar with a fresh pack of cigarettes had his jaw torn away by the wheel arch.

The van mounted a pavement, teetered to one side, and then rolled across Penryn high street. The cabin spun. Person and vehicle crunched underneath Rasha before the van came to a stop. Stephen wasn't done. He was angrier – he needed longer. It hadn't been enough hurt. He scrambled out of the broken driver's side window and dove toward terrified onlookers. Rasha followed. The road behind them was in carnage; twisted bodies and blood tracks painted the tarmac. Penryn or Homs?

Shrieks filled the air. She'd seen into Stephen, a victim of fraud. His wife had slept with the vicar, and his manager had threatened him with suspension. The horror he imparted did not counteract the things he endured, Rasha knew that. But she understood each death relieved his hurt, and in quick succession more so. It numbed Stephen's pain.

The pedestrians scarpered. It was only a memory. She couldn't hurt anyone, not really. What would it matter if she took her anger out on a bypasser? Stephen did, and it was real for him.

Patrick had reminded her of a purer way to live. He pointed at the incomplete house, more perfect than he envisioned. His family built it, and they were content. Their troubles wouldn't last forever; the family cottage could. They'd cherish the summer's memories until their dying days.

Except, Macaid's roars, heartbroken and bitter, said different. A pain that couldn't be ignored. Happiness could not be chosen; tell it to the tribespeople who floated facedown in the misty water. Tell it to Macaid who took her own life because she knew she had been inbound for lifelong grief.

Max was beaten that night. Kenneth dragged him from his closet. He was struck and struck until his heart gave up.

His mind went first as his imprint detached from his battered little body. No remorse. War wasn't remorseful either. The Western world kept calm and carried on as the East continued to collapse and burn. Max would have wanted revenge if he hadn't been so fearful, if he hadn't been so weak.

Stephen was satisfied. He swiped a bug-like man into a wooden bench.

Before she knew it, Rasha strode toward an estate agent who was welded to the cobbles by fear. She thought of President Bashar al-Assad causing the revolt in Syria, Fred's taunts of her being a terrorist, Joel Tredethy perpetually haunting her, Haya pretending she didn't exist. The estate agent embodied them all.

She raised a fist.

50

RASHA SNAPPED from the ombrederi and fell to the tunnel floor.

Her arms unsteady, she rose to her feet. If she'd remained in the ombrederi, Allah knows what she would have done, where Stephen would have taken her next.

'Vanessa?' she called. 'Vanessa?'

She tripped on the uneven ground, staggered a few feet, and managed to save herself. She was alone. Vanessa had abandoned her, and she was metres underground, in the dark, with no way out. Imprints skirted around her subconscious, wanting to engage with her or worse: for Stephen to draw her in to his violent ways.

Milana crushed by debris.

Light wavered through the inkwell of darkness ahead. Voices resonated down the tunnel toward Rasha.

'Her reception to the ombrederi is beyond her age,' Vanessa said. 'She wasn't occupied by any old guiding imprint.'

'So they lied to us, or they don't know,' came a woman's flowery voice. 'You think it was the gywandras?'

'She's shown signs of being a coercer. There isn't anyone

like it in the UK, let alone the Network.'

'She'd be perfect for the initiative, in time.'

Rasha was certain she was the topic of conversation. She paused so they wouldn't hear her approach.

'I think she could transcend,' Vanessa said. 'Even now, with little training.'

Rasha kicked a stone, and it clattered across the tunnel floor. Vanessa called her name.

'Coming,' Rasha replied, acting as nonchalantly as she could. As she traipsed to the exit, she tried to remove the look of accusation from her face. Her suspicions were proven true: her witnessing training fed an ulterior purpose. One that, she realised, confirmed the Network's knowledge of the shadow imprint.

The gywandras.

The opening up ahead leaked early morning light. The sea crashed against the cliff wall, and gulls squawked to declare a new day. The Long Walk, indeed. Rasha exited the mouth of the tunnel. The turbulent wind and infinite Celtic Sea overwhelmed her after the near silence and darkness of the Long Walk.

'Who did you connect with?' Vanessa said as she prompted Rasha up a footpath that snaked to the top of the cliff.

'Stephen.'

Vanessa gripped Rasha's hand – the one that was injured the night she'd engaged with Joel.

'You didn't even try,' Vanessa scathed.

'I did, I did, I'm just tired,' Rasha said, and that was also true. 'With school and this.'

'Vanessa . . .' Leri warned.

Vanessa released Rasha's hand. Rasha barged past the women to the cliff top. From there was a clear view between the trees and chain-link fence to the collieries' yard. Two vehicles veered onto the gravel, one being Trish's Reliant. Trish. Rasha sprinted down the slope toward them.

Trish, Sam, and James slammed their car doors and shouted amongst themselves. Vanessa and Leri huffed and puffed behind Rasha, but try as they might, they couldn't catch up with her.

'Trish!' Rasha called as she reached them. The trio turned to her, every face riddled with worry.

'Rasha,' Trish exclaimed. 'Are you okay?'

Vanessa and Leri joined them.

'What in the frequency is all this commotion?' Vanessa asked, breathless.

Rasha studied Trish's and Sam's faces. They were crestfallen, eyes red. Sam was agitated, unable to keep his body still. The iron door to the collieries buzzed open, but no one dared enter.

'Tonight's code red was a death,' James informed them. 'Elderly patient at Angove Lodge, Wadebridge. The taken couldn't be reinstated. We had no choice but to invoke article fifty-seven. The nurse saw our faces, but we gave aliases. No CCTV in the immediate area.'

'I'll have Gregory scan police records,' Vanessa said. 'Find some doppelgängers. It'll be best for you all to lay low.'

Rasha realised they plotted to frame petty criminals for their misdeeds. How powerful could the Network be if they infiltrated police records? How could they, as an organisation, preach a moral compass when they did so many bad things?

'And the imprint?' Leri asked.

'A Russian guide by the name of Nika,' James said. 'We didn't find any logs of her on Anascribe.'

Sam locked eyes with Rasha as if trying to communicate

another version of the truth. She noted how drawn his cheeks were, how pronounced his brow had become.

'I'll check with the archivists,' Leri continued.

'I want to go home,' Rasha interrupted.

'We can take her,' Sam said, his hand on her shoulder. 'If we're laying low, our homes will be best. I haven't had visitors since Theresa May was elected. Hope that isn't an omen or something.'

'I'll take her,' Vanessa said.

'It's on the way to the priory,' Sam said matter-of-factly.

Vanessa took a long hard look at Sam.

'Take her straight home,' she said, relentless.

'Aye,' Sam retorted.

'Come on, Rasha,' Trish said. Rasha dared not look back at Vanessa, eyes on the Reliant.

The trio hopped into Trish's iron steed and trundled along the wooded lane. Rasha leant toward the driver's seat to ask Sam and Trish, 'What do you know about the gywandras?'

51

FAR OFF the beaten path, Trish drove Sam and Rasha to a disused farmyard. Rasha learnt Trish's family friend owned it. In the low morning sun, the scrap metal and farmyard machines could have been the excavated remnants of a prehistoric graveyard. Dragged from pillar to post herself, Rasha knew that it took a pitiful set of circumstances for someone to live that way.

They raced from the Reliant to the canal boat. Trish promised them that Calypso had the perfect conditions to practice engagement. When they were inside the cabin under multicoloured fairy lights, they shed their coats and jackets. Trish brought Rasha up to speed on the gywandras.

'It's plagued all of us,' she concluded. 'You, my sister, Sam's mum.'

'And Will?' Rasha asked before she could stop herself.

'It seems that way,' Sam croaked, eyes to the floor.

'We don't know what it is,' Trish said, 'or what it wants.'

Rasha's stomach knotted; an unknown entity with no clear agenda was a new kind of horror. *What if it just wants to cause pain?* Rasha wondered. *Pain and suffering to all.*

'You want me to try and engage with it, don't you?' she asked, hesitant.

'Much like you did that day with the receptor,' Trish said. She procured one from beneath a sun-bleached dustcover. 'This one is mobile. It's not connected, so it isn't as powerful, but neither do we have the tools to cut engagement for you.'

What she'd overheard after the Long Walk stayed with her. She didn't want to invest faith into mere strangers.

'Vanessa said I was a coercer,' Rasha explained, 'and they wanted me to transcend.'

'We don't know what that is.'

'Then how can I trust you?' Rasha said.

She was surprised that Sam answered before Trish.

'Because we want bad things to stop happening to good people,' Sam said.

Rasha was certain he referred to Will's demise, his mother stowed away in a place that witnesses seemed to fear. His actions, careless drug use, and introverted demeanour were certainly misjudged, but he meant well. All Rasha had to do was look into his sad hazel eyes to know that.

'What do I do?' Rasha asked and settled onto a bench in the saloon.

'We need to recreate the conditions of the last time,' Trish said. 'Get yourself back into the headspace, thinking and feeling everything you were then.'

Milana crushed beneath stone, her father disembowelled.

Well, that's the easy part, Rasha thought.

Trish's lip curled slightly, and Rasha was sure she'd heard her thoughts. Trish brought the receptor over and placed it on Rasha's head as Sam adjusted the neck brace beneath it.

'This one's a lot heavier,' Rasha said.

'It's the battery,' Sam explained. He knelt down, eye to eye with Rasha. 'You're sure about this? You don't – '

'Let's get it over with.'

Trish switched the receptor on, and Sam navigated the spectrometer's interface.

'Ready when you are,' Sam said. He glanced at Rasha, then his eyes moved back to the spectro's screen.

Rasha nodded, took a deep breath, filled her tight lungs with damp air, and let Syria erupt into her consciousness.

Oh Allah, had Rasha howled, hunched over the remains of Milana's body. Her throat stung at the very thought. A fire spat to her left and spewed acrid smoke across the debris. All Rasha ascertained was how she hurt Milana, and there was no chance to make amends. No chance at forgiveness.

'Rasha!' a voice croaked. Haya had erupted from the smoke and tugged Rasha from the wreckage. Away from Milana.

'No, Mama . . .' Rasha cried.

'I know,' Haya said. She wrapped her arms around Rasha. 'We have to go. If we want to live, we have to go.'

'I don't want to,' Rasha had cried. She didn't want to go; she didn't want to live.

'Rasha,' Haya pleaded. She pulled her only daughter to her feet.

An explosion thrust them against the wall. They rebounded and hit the rubble. Haya's arm burst into flames, and fire devoured her shrug. Rasha clambered to her feet, grabbed what had once been the living room curtain, and smothered Haya's arm until the heat simmered and the smell of singed hair dissipated. Haya nodded thankfully. Rasha threw the curtain aside. A wound wept and bled on her mother's forearm. It'd need a doctor; they had to leave.

Rasha offered her free hand and helped Haya to her feet. She gained her bearings: they were on the first floor. They'd fallen an entire storey. They stumbled in the darkness, unable to find the staircase to the ground floor. The precarious floorboards creaked with the weight of the debris. Rasha and Haya treaded toward the sill of a decimated window. The apartment's wall had fallen into the alleyway and provided a ledge of sorts to climb down upon. They fled through the ruined streets. Gunfire tore through the air, and explosions rumbled on the horizon.

An impenetrable silence. Rasha opened her eyes at Calypso's innards. The gywandras came. It stooped to fit inside the saloon, its irregular legs bowed to accommodate its bulbous torso. Its oily skin was a liquid mirror, reflecting the Calypso's gloomy interior and their horrified faces. She saw into it – through it – as though there wasn't skin or flesh or even a skeleton for that matter, but instead a void so expansive that if she stared any longer Rasha would plummet into it and never stop.

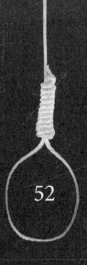

52

RASHA FOUND HERSELF in a study-come-library. Printer paper, tacked upon every inch of available wall, rustled in a polite wind. Across them were scribbles – formulas of many words and numbers beyond comprehension.

On the pine floorboards lay a girl. No. Her body hovered inches from the ground, and her shaggy blond hair and Powerpuff Girls bathrobe billowed around her. A minute middle-aged woman knelt beside her, urging her to stop, to be well, to 'Be my Kasey!'

53

RASHA AWOKE on the Calypso's saloon floor. The lights were out, and for a moment she thought the other two had disappeared.

'It's gone,' Sam said.

She sat up, and hot pain shot across her back. She rolled her shoulders; she hadn't felt the fall when it happened, only when she woke from the ombrederi.

'What happened to the lights?' she asked.

'They blew,' Trish said. She raised the blinds to let in sunlight. 'There was an immense surge of frequency energy. What did you see?'

'I don't think I saw anything.'

Sam sighed.

'I mean, I wasn't just shown something. I was taken there.'

'Taken? Taken where?'

'There was a girl. Kasey. She was floating, actually floating, above the floor. Her mum was so upset. It was an occupation.'

Trish unpacked her phone, likely to check their Anascribe database.

'What other occupations have there been?' Sam asked.

'There's no need. You won't find it,' Rasha said. 'It's happening now.'

54

'I OVERHEARD LERI talking the day you were . . . helping yourself to supplies,' Trish said to Sam as the Reliant bombed down the A39. Rasha sat in the back, seat belt clamped in her hands. Her stomach churned at the prospect of what they headed toward and the speed at which they did so. 'The occupation was in Lanhydrock. I don't know where, specifically, but the Network has been tending to it.'

'Could you find it with the receptor?' Sam asked.

'I can try.'

'What do we do when we get there?' Rasha faltered.

'We're gonna save her, Rasha,' Sam said.

'And that old man?' Rasha asked. 'You said he died. What about him?'

'We didn't have you with us.'

Rasha sat back, unsure of what Sam thought his comment would achieve. The thought of being responsible for another's life made her chest clamp with anxiety.

Lanhydrock was new to Rasha. It took twenty-five minutes to get there, by which time the sun glared in the sky. A rugged stretch of countryside whirled past the windows, interspersed with reams of farmland and throngs of transmission towers. Trish pulled up beside a sign that read, 'Trebyan,' and gave up the driver's seat to Sam.

'You can drive?' Rasha asked him with trepidation.

'Not legally,' Sam retorted.

Trish joined Rasha in the back of the Reliant as Sam pushed the car forward. The clutch thunked.

'Easy!' Trish said.

She unravelled the receptor from its dusty bag and placed the precarious device around her head and shoulders. Rasha helped her with the buckles and straps now that she was more than accustomed to the contraption.

'Thanks, bird,' Trish said, then winked. 'Watch how a pro does it.'

Trish closed her eyes and leant back on the seat, and she crossed to the ombrederi. Her eyelids fluttered as her eyes rolled beneath them.

So that's how it looks, Rasha thought. She understood why her classmates ridiculed her for it. *She seems to enjoy it.*

'We need to head north,' Trish said. 'Back through the farm, past the school.'

'On it,' Sam said. He made a haphazard three-point turn and raced back toward the main road.

'What do you see, Trish?' Rasha asked.

'The girl,' Trish said. 'Kasey, she's lost and alone and running. Running from the gywandras.'

Sam accelerated. Once they'd passed the small elementary school, Trish instructed them around Lanhydrock House and Gardens, a left turn, and two right turns. They trundled through a well-kept parish dotted with expensive detached houses that Rasha could hardly fathom living in.

'Stop!' Trish said. Her eyes snapped open. 'Here, she's here.'

They'd pulled up at a gated cottage. The building had been renovated with accents of steel and glass, separating itself from the rest of the traditionally kept parish houses. Sam parked in a gateway opposite.

Trish fled the car first, her bag of equipment in hand, and Rasha and Sam took the rear. The group paused at the gate whilst Sam pressed the intercom to its right. He hopped from one foot to the other, the way a runner would before a marathon. A nervous voice came through the static on the intercom.

'We're not having guests tonight.'

A shrill scream sounded twice: once from the house and a millisecond later from the intercom.

'We can help your daughter,' Sam responded.

'I told you lot not to come back.'

'We're specialists from the Network,' Sam somewhat lied. 'We've cured people in similar conditions.'

The intercom went off. A breeze rustled through the trees overhead, indifferent from the roar of the sea. *Buzz.* The gate teetered inward. The group hurtled across the yard. They were greeted at the front door by the middle-aged woman Rasha had seen in the ombrederi. The clothes on her minute frame were worth more than all of Rasha's and Haya's worldly possessions. Her hands clasped the doorframe, as Haya had when she'd warned off the witnesses at the caravan site.

'That Vanessa asked you to come?'

'Not exactly – '

The woman went to wrench the door shut, but Rasha slammed her hand against it.

'It's your daughter, isn't it?' Rasha asked. 'Doing things she shouldn't be able to?'

The mother nodded. Her grip on the door loosened.

'I was like that not long ago. They saved me.' Rasha gestured to her friends. 'Let us help her. Please.'

The mother muttered something under her breath and pushed the door wide open. She led the witnesses inside, through three storeys of pine and slate, the aesthetic often punctuated by a bookcase or a family photo of the woman and her four identical blond children.

'You have other kids?' Trish asked.

'Three, four altogether.'

'Have they been affected?'

'No, they're perfectly normal. God, she's only twelve.'

'Kasey, any mental illnesses? Depression, bipolar?'

'I told you, perfectly normal.'

She reminded Rasha very much of Fred, and for a moment Rasha was less inclined to help the family.

The office was exactly as Rasha saw in the ombrederi, with a hectic gallery of drawings tacked to the walls. It provided an insight into the girl's poor occupied mind.

Kasey. She levitated by no physical means, the space between her body and the pine floor empty. The frequency energy around them was electric, as if Rasha's skin was pricked with hypodermic needles.

'Trish . . .' Rasha said, reaching for Trish's elbow.

'Kasey, stop it,' the mother begged.

'It's not her,' Sam said, and he crouched down. 'Kasey, can you hear me?'

The girl cocked her head.

'Kasey,' Sam continued, 'if you can hear me, tell me your last name.'

'Her last name is Nancarrow.'

Sam stepped back. Had Kasey's voice been altered a few octaves lower, what they would have heard was Will.

Sam inched toward the floating girl. Trish grabbed his arm, but he shook her off.

'Are we talking to William Reeves?' Trish asked.

The girl's body flipped through the air like a tossed coin, knocking Sam and Trish to the floor. The girl turned upright, and her toes skimmed the polished floorboards, face struck with horror.

Rasha retreated, her back pressed to the wall. Her hands grasped one of the many sheets of paper tacked to the wall. The pages weren't filled with drawings at all but streams of numbers and interlocking circles, much like the Network's symbol.

'Mummy!' Kasey cried.

'I'm here, Kase, oh god, I'm here!' Ms Nancarrow hollered. 'What are you doing?'

Trish and Sam had equipment in hand to record the event.

'We need to deduce the severity of the occupation before we can begin,' Trish said.

'And how severe is it?'

'Grade three imprint,' Trish read out, 'with a 65 percent hold of the cerebral cortex. Moderate occupation. Known imprint.'

'Known?' Ms Nancarrow spat.

'Yes,' Trish said. 'The imprint was a friend.'

'Was?'

'Until he died, which I've not forgiven you for yet, William!' Sam hollered. 'Are you there?'

A shudder, and the girl's eyes found Sam. They blinked as Will had, twice fast. Rasha watched Sam tread closer to the occupied girl. She could only fathom how conflicted he was to find his spouse in another body, and a child's at that.

'Will, you're going to have to leave Kasey,' Trish said.

Kasey's face twitched.

'I can't stay,' Kasey-Will agreed. 'What is the date?'

'May 5,' Rasha said.

Kasey-Will exhaled sharply.

'It's too soon. This is the wrong intersection.'

'The wrong intersection?' Sam asked. There was no response. 'How are you here? How are you strong enough?'

'One question at a time,' Trish warned.

'It's everything and it's nothing,' Kasey-Will said in both voices, the audio equivalent of drinking hot tea after ice cream.

'What does that mean, Will?' Sam asked.

'We all belong to the frequency.'

The ominous riddle made Rasha's heart plummet. Chills spread across her body, but not from Will's words nor the frequency energy. The paper on the walls rippled despite there being no wind. The numerous LED ceiling lights dimmed of their own accord, and colour – the garish Crayola'd numbers, the leather-bound spines on the bookcases – dulled to various grey hues. In the corner of the room, a tentacle of molten black fluid seeped up from a crack in the floorboards and unraveled itself into the gywandras.

'It's here,' Rasha whispered.

Trish and Sam were drawn to the corner. Sam lowered the spectro.

'What is the gywandras, Will?' Sam asked.

'You're asking the wrong question,' Kasey-Will said. 'You need to ask how they became the gywandras.'

'They?' Trish asked. 'Who is it?'

'An acquaintance.'

'You're working with it?' Sam asked with disbelief.

'Your notes, the archivists,' Trish said. 'The Network knows about the gywandras, right?'

'They're facilitating it,' Kasey-Will said. 'Trust no one. We have no friends left there.'

In the corner, the gywandras groaned, hollow and guttural, as if an entire continent had imploded and slid beneath the sea. Its body quavered. Frequency energy coursed from it, stronger than Rasha had ever experienced. She could understand why Vanessa and Leri spoke about it with equal parts awe and fear.

'Transcendence!' Rasha shouted. 'That's what the gywandras wants.'

'You cannot seek transcendence; it finds you,' Kasey-Will said. 'It is the ultimate death.'

Kasey's body slumped to the floor. Her eyes rolled, and her mouth frothed.

Trish fell to her knees beside the thrashing girl.

'Sam, the spectro!' she shouted. Sam didn't move. Rasha knew that if she were in his shoes, she would be paralysed with shock, especially now they knew Will's connection to the gywandras.

'Sam!' Trish called again.

Sam shook himself awake and pointed the gadget at Kasey.

'We're losing her!' Sam shrieked.

'Kasey, can you hear me?' Trish asked. She shook the girl's shoulders out of desperation.

The frequency energy tore through the pine room. Rasha's senses dulled, and her eyes grew heavy. Kasey's aura seeped from her writhing body and bloomed in the study's volatile atmosphere.

'I've found her,' Rasha said, and before the adults could intervene, she slipped into the ombrederi.

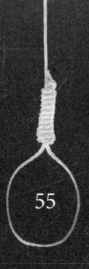

55

I WON'T LET HER DIE, Rasha thought. I can't.

Rasha's feet hit the study's floor. It was a wintry afternoon, and a gas fireplace opposite the desk threw the room into a cosy orange light. Grape-scented e-cigarette vapour wafted over a busy desk. In his leather-backed chair, a handsome man wrote a letter. Kasey, no more than seven years of age, sat on the floor by his desk and built a haphazard structure with a box of Jenga. The study in the present day still retained some sense of her father's aura, the warmth and comfort, and Rasha understood why Kasey's mind fled there. Rasha would have as well, to her pre-war apartment, if it didn't hurt so much.

The study's walls peeled away. In its place was a dense woodland of leafless trees. Rasha could not tell by the darkness whether it was early morning or late at night, but either way it wasn't an opportune time for young Kasey to adventure across the frosty ground in her nightgown and slippers. Her panicked breath left a trail of steam in her wake. She didn't flee; she ran after her father. His silhouette came and went between the barren trees.

The trees thinned, and the ground became more roots than

mud. A river sliced through the woods and babbled against the embankment. Her father stopped to shed his barber's jacket. He dropped a canvas bag to the ground, hauled stones from the water's edge, and dropped them in until it was full. He zipped the canvas bag up, tied a rope from its handles to one of his ankles, heaved the bulging bag into his arms, and crept along the river's edge toward a bridge. Mystified by his actions, Kasey continued to follow her father, and Rasha stalked after them both. She knew where this was headed. She knew how this would end.

Kasey's father stopped at the height of the bridge, climbed up onto the wall, and took the bag into his hands once again. Without a morsel of hesitation, he leapt. He plunged into the river's icy depths with a splash. Kasey raced to the bridge's wall and hopped to get a better view of the water. She yelled and cried for her father.

She never saw him again.

Back to the study, the morning before, and her father scrawled into his journal. Rasha looked over his shoulder and read the passage in his diary.

I can't do this anymore, he wrote. *Even my happiest days are bleak. It's just emptiness, day after day, and it'll never end.*

The study exploded. Walls collapsed, books burst apart, a window smashed, and Rasha knew where she was: in what remained of Will's room, just as she had seen the night the gywandras occupied her. She teetered across the bloodstained carpet, mindful of the glass, to pick up the shredded painting. Aflame in the corner of the room, strung from a beam by a weathered noose, was an imprint that Rasha recognised from witness accounts: Abidemi. The heat of Abidemi's body chilled, and the room darkened. The gywandras unravelled itself before the window. Rasha had met Trish's theories with dubiety, but now she believed them: the gywandras targeted them.

Amidst the two entities was Will, and he was not as she remembered him; his endowed nose was snapped at an angle, clawlike cuts spread across his cheeks, and his face was purple with bruises.

'I'm early,' he said.

'Will, I'm sorry. I could have saved you.'

'No. It was done, and when it is done it is written, and when it is written it has to happen.'

The walls of Will's room wavered as if they were bedsheets. The room grew darker and colder. Kasey's aura slipped away.

'Let Kasey go,' Rasha said. 'Do your business and let Kasey go. She's just a kid.'

'My business is done,' he said nonchalantly.

Will nodded, raised an arm, and flung it forward. Rasha was lifted off her feet, out of the wrecked room into the physical.

56

'EXTRACTION SUCCESSFUL,' Rasha heard Sam cry. 'She lives! She lives!'

Rasha opened her eyes to find herself on the pine floor. A surge of nausea rocked Rasha's stomach. Kasey was wide-awake, cradled in her mother's arms, much as Rasha had been in Haya's the night of her own occupation.

There were tears in Sam's eyes, and he appeared the most relieved she had ever seen him.

Frequency nausea subsided, and Rasha scrambled to her feet with Trish's help.

'Kasey Nancarrow,' Trish uttered, 'we witness you.'

The witnesses packed and ignored Ms Nancarrow's questions, not dissimilar to what Rasha had muttered after her occupation.

'But who, exactly, are you? How did you find us? Are you watching us? I demand answers!'

They ignored her. Sam stopped to survey the paper tacked to the walls. He snatched a few up and thrust them into a pocket.

The witnesses slunk from the house with equipment in

hand. Rasha was relieved to go back out into the open, under the bruised evening sky.

Sam and Trish halted, and Rasha walked into the square of Sam's back. James, Vanessa, and Leri headed through the Nancarrows' gate. A handful of witnesses were with them, people Rasha knew by face but not by name.

'What in the frequency are you doing here?' Vanessa spat. She set eyes on Rasha, and her face softened.

'Extraction successful,' Sam said simply.

A gust tore across the driveway between the witnesses.

'Need I remind you about the conditions of your disciplinary – ' James began.

'Let's not do this here,' Vanessa said, a hand on James's forearm. Her eyes hadn't left Rasha.

James nodded and gulped down spittle – an unsavoury retort, perhaps. Rasha couldn't understand why they weren't thankful for a positive extraction.

'Debrief at the collieries, now,' he commanded. 'Miss Abadi needs to go home.'

'I'll do that,' Vanessa said.

'I want Trish to do it,' Rasha blurted.

'Trish and Sam are needed at the collieries,' James retorted.

Leri stepped forward with a bag of equipment.

'I'll arrange aftercare for the family,' she told James.

He nodded and watched Leri rush into the cottage. He beckoned everyone out of the yard. Vanessa's Land Rover and James's people carrier sat aside the Reliant. Trish hugged Rasha goodbye.

'Well done, you star,' she whispered. 'I'll pop by soon.'

She and Sam departed to the Reliant, James to his people carrier. Rasha and Vanessa climbed into the Land Rover. Vanessa pulled away from Lanhydrock and didn't speak until they were bolting down the A39 toward Gorenn.

'What happened back there?' Vanessa asked. 'I want the truth, nothing less.'

'The girl, Kasey, was occupied,' Rasha recounted. 'She was grieving for her father. He ... killed himself and – '

'Who occupied her?'

Rasha froze. Vanessa knew of the gywandras and transcendence. Will warned them against it.

'I don't know.'

'You must,' Vanessa said. 'You extracted the imprint.'

Rasha thought over the stilted conversation in the Nancarrows' yard. She'd been preoccupied with images of Kasey's hovering body, her father's last moments, and Will's bludgeoned face, but she was certain that Trish and Sam hadn't said who had extracted the imprint. Yet Vanessa knew. Rasha didn't question it; she dared not fan the flames.

'It was a girl,' she lied. 'A girl I've never seen before.'

'Was she hanging by a rope?' Vanessa asked. She flicked her indicator and wrenched at the gear stick.

'Yes,' Rasha said. Vanessa spoke of Abidemi, so Rasha went with it. 'Yes, and her body was on fire.'

Silence consumed the cabin. Rasha looked out of the windscreen and noticed Vanessa's leather journal lay open on the dash. Across its pages were lines of numbers punctuated by decimals, similar to those found at the Nancarrow residence. Vanessa had either copied them from Kasey's father's study or she'd already had them. The pages were stained, bent, and torn – decades old at best.

Rasha gazed out of the window, intent to not speak either as night-soaked Gorenn unfurled before her. Kasey had levitated. It was more than human, just as Vanessa had preached the week prior. Rasha's bruised fingernails served as a painful reminder of her own occupation.

The Land Rover's lights illuminated the gates of the caravan park. Rasha gave her thanks to Vanessa and thrust the stiff passenger door open. Vanessa grabbed her injured hand.

'You may feel obligated to protect Sam and Trish,' Vanessa snarled. 'Yes, they saved you, maybe you owe them, but you're not subservient to them. All this lying. If I seem cross, it's because I am. I see so much potential in you; I know what you'll become . . .'

Vanessa turned in her seat and stared hard out the windscreen. She wasn't meant to say that.

'You want me to become a coercer,' Rasha said through gritted teeth. 'You want me to transcend.'

Rasha didn't know what either term meant, though the mention of them riled Vanessa. She still had Rasha's hand in hers, and she squeezed it tighter.

'We don't take deceit lightly at the Network,' Vanessa said. 'Trish and Sam, they're poison. Gifted people too encumbered by being alive to even consider their own talents. I won't have you turn out like them. I won't let you see them again.'

Rasha tugged her arm from Vanessa's grip and hopped down from the vehicle. She scarpered toward the caravan, ignored Mr Keats's aggravated cats, blanked the Gills' chorus of hellos from their holiday home, and barged straight into forty-five. She closed the door and dove right onto the sofa, imbedding herself amongst the cushions. Vanessa was, as were many she'd befriended, a twisted individual. Every choice word she'd used had been licked with malice, and she'd undermined Rasha at every turn, as if she knew Rasha better than she did herself. Now Rasha was forbidden to see the two most genuine people she knew.

Haya's bedroom door opened and cast a cone of light across

the dining room floor. She stepped out and watched Rasha sob into a cushion. Rasha was certain she'd retreat back to her room; after all, it was the first time they'd seen each other since she threw her cereal bowl on the floor. A week had passed, and so much had happened; Rasha barely recognised herself.

'Rasha?' Haya called in Levantine. She flicked a switch, and incandescent light swamped the caravan.

Rasha cried harder. She'd saved Kasey, only to be vilified for what she couldn't control – actions she didn't mean – by people with skewed vendettas. Everyone had their own goals, and Rasha was caught in the cross fire.

Forever helpless. Forever in a terrible situation.

'Those people are doing you no good. You're going to see the doctor in the morning.'

'I'm fine, and I'm not ever going to see them again.'

'You talk to dead people. That's not right.'

'It's not an illness; it's being a witness.'

'You've been brainwashed by people madder than you – '

'Madder than me?' Rasha growled. Tears fell. Haya stood and reached out tentatively. Haya's iron expression didn't falter. 'They helped me realise that I'm sane. They listen to me, and they understand, which is more than you ever do!'

Haya took Rasha's head in her hands; they were chapped and rough from cleaning caravans, yet retained the softness of a mother's touch.

'People lie to feel normal, Rasha.'

'You saw it with your own eyes. I climbed walls. Tonight a girl hovered, no wires, no tricks. You can't deny it because you don't want to believe it.'

'If it's all real, then where is your father? Where's Milana? Why haven't you found them? Why haven't you brought them back to me?'

How could Rasha begin to explain? To be a guide in death, a person had to have been a witness in life. And even if she could reach them in the ombrederi, searching for the dead only let someone's past corrode their future. Trish's gaunt face, the receptor in the boot of the car, Sam constantly intoxicated and withdrawn.

'Because I don't want to!' she cried. 'They're dead and gone!'

Haya shook her by the shoulders.

'How can you say that?' she said. 'How can you say that about your family?'

'They died because we never left! Aimar and his family left, and they're probably still alive.'

'We couldn't all go!'

Rasha stopped, eyes wide.

'Why, Mama? Why not?'

Haya sunk to her knees, arms wrapped around her chest.

'Your father had it all mapped out, the journey to Calais. Everything comes at a price. We only had the money for three of us.'

Rasha recollected the night her parents argued, a map of Europe between them.

'I couldn't leave him!' Haya wailed. 'I couldn't leave him, don't you understand? I couldn't leave him, I couldn't . . .'

Kasey's father in the study. Trish's father in the lighting shop. Of course Haya wouldn't let go. Rasha studied her mother's face, lined and aged with all the grief she'd bottled in. Kasey's father couldn't fight his depression any longer, and he'd tossed himself into a river with a bag full of stones. People were fragile – Haya more than most.

Rasha pulled Haya in, and she half expected her mother to pry herself away. Instead, she nestled farther into Rasha's chest. Rasha let herself cry too, head to head, together again.

'I don't want to be a monster,' Rasha breathed.

'You're not,' Haya said. 'You're Rasha.'

'You have to let me go. I have to control this.'

'Promise you'll always come back to me.'

'Promise. Unconditionally.'

'Unconditionally.'

PART EIGHT

THE RIVER
ALWAYS FINDS
THE SEA

57

'WE'RE BUGGERED,' Trish heard Sam mutter under his breath, and she couldn't disagree.

Deep within Wheal Gorenn, the duo traipsed behind James and the occupations unit toward the activity centre. Trish itched at the dielectric band strapped to her head. Despite a successful extraction, they had broken the terms of their disciplinary. Sam had been tense the whole way back from the Nancarrow residence. It had been strange for Trish to see her best friend's imprint bottled within a vulnerable body; she couldn't begin to fathom how Sam felt. An occupation broke a guide's code of conduct, which Will had known and yet still did. He had called the gywandras an acquaintance; after all, he'd worked on a report about it.

What if it was more than that? Trish thought with horror.

Who else knew of the impossible imprint that plagued them? Someone must have surely scoured the archives for past occupations and come across it. If they had, they withheld answers that she and Sam desperately sought. As Will had said, they had no friends left at the Network. They had no one to trust.

They reached the quiet activity centre. The occupations unit parted into the southern shaft toward one of the test caverns, and James beckoned Sam and Trish to his office.

'It doesn't seem like long ago,' he huffed, reclining into his desk chair, 'that we were in the boardroom discussing your disciplinary, explicitly saying no involvement with the public – '

'It's no different to the shambles at Angove Lodge,' Sam interjected.

'Yes, it is,' James growled. 'You had my permission, and it was a difficult case where your involvement was justified.'

'What does it matter?' Sam cried, slamming his palms onto the desk. 'We saved her, didn't we? We saved her, and we found Will!'

'It was Will?' James uttered. Sam nodded, unable to vocalise an answer. James was even more fired up when he said, 'The occupations unit had it under control. Kasey Nancarrow was being monitored.'

James's eyes fell to the floor, lips pursed.

'You weren't planning to extract Will from Kasey?' Trish asked. 'It was an experiment?'

'After what you saw at the care home?' Sam added. 'You saw what that poor man went through, and you still thought it was a good idea to prolong an occupation?'

'This is the fourth occupation in half as many weeks,' James said. 'Understanding why is important in stopping them from happening altogether.'

'It's the shadow,' Sam uttered.

Trish drew a deep breath and closed her eyes. She wished she could give Sam a telepathic telling off.

'The shadow?' James shuffled forward in his chair. Trish decided to take over before Sam's loose tongue complicated matters further.

'In every occupation we've witnessed, there has been a second imprint. It doesn't have a clear projection, and it offers no memory, no emotional stimulus. It's empty.'

She dared not mention that she'd found the gywandras on the night of Shauna's death or of Rose's occupation in the archives; James would hit the roof if he learnt she'd used Network equipment for private means. Neither did she use its name; she was unsure how much James knew.

James glanced between his associates. His forehead developed a sheen.

'Where was this in your notes?' he asked. 'Trish, where was this in your seminar?'

'I thought I was wrong,' Trish said, which at the time of the seminar wasn't false. 'There was a lot going on and – '

'You realise that this would have helped us?'

'You don't know anything about this?' Trish said.

'It's news to me,' James said, eyes to the floor.

Trish stared hard at him.

'James, look at me,' she said. He did, and they maintained eye contact. 'Gywandras.'

James's left eye twitched, knuckles whitening on the desk.

'You knew about it,' Trish said. 'You knew, and you lied. You vilify us, and all along – '

'Whatever you know, whatever you think you know, forget it.'

Sam stepped forward, mouth agape, hands animated.

'Will said it was the ultimate death, as if the gywandras is beyond any imprint we've encountered. It was there the night Will died, and it drove Mum to the Refinery.'

'As if it's commanding the occupations,' Trish bookended.

There was a knock on the door, and Vanessa sauntered in

without invitation, bypassing Trish and Sam as if they weren't there at all. James maintained his eye contact with Trish.

'Rasha and I had a little chat,' Vanessa said. 'She identified the imprint that occupied Miss Nancarrow.'

Trish's stomach plunged. Sam held his breath and rubbed the scar on his arm. There was no doubt in her mind that Vanessa knew about the gywandras.

'From what she described, it was definitely Abidemi,' Vanessa continued. She turned to Sam and Trish. 'Depending on whether you've been made aware.'

'Yes, they just informed me,' James said.

Trish held back a moan of confusion. It was clear everyone in the room, to varying degrees, knew of the gywandras, but James didn't want Vanessa to know that. When James had told Trish and Sam to forget about it, it hadn't been a threat but a well-intentioned warning.

'Good,' Vanessa said. 'I've already spoken to OU. They're setting up the transfer. We're going to trial Abidemi.'

This'll be interesting, Trish thought. Guiding imprints had as much mental capacity as living humans, so they were held accountable for actions that broke Network code. The transfer was the strongest piece of equipment that the Network owned, so powerful it could detain and even permanently destroy an imprint. It was never used lightly.

'We can't, the board is two short,' James said. Trish presumed he was trying to delay the trial. 'Leri is at the Nancarrows', and Will's gone.'

Vanessa turned to Trish and Sam.

'We have two right here,' Vanessa said. 'Fitting, considering they witnessed the last extraction. Retrieval and trial in thirty.'

Trish edged to the door with Sam's arm gripped in her hand.

'We were both saying on the way over how we need the toilet,' Trish said. 'We'll meet you there.'

James nodded profusely, and so Trish and Sam fled the birdcage, then meandered through the activity centre's chipboard partitions and into a winding tunnel that would take them to the collieries' only bathroom. When they were safely out of earshot, Trish pulled Sam into a dark alcove.

'I don't know about you,' Sam said, 'but I couldn't tell who the director was.'

'Vanessa must have something on James,' Trish said. 'Whatever it is, he doesn't like it. Why else would he lie for us?'

'Think about it,' Sam said. 'When we accidentally pushed Rasha into an occupation, Vanessa was pretty quick to snatch up the adolescent program and mentor Rasha.'

'She made Rasha push her abilities,' Trish agreed. 'She has plans. The report Will worked on – who signed it off?'

Sam thought a moment, his mind likely scouring the documents he'd whisked from the Reeves' cottage.

'Vanessa,' he said. 'I'm sure of it.'

Trish's blood froze at a sudden thought.

'I don't trust her,' Trish said. 'Not one bit. We agree that the gywandras is dangerous, right? Look how terrified James was when I said its name. We've just been cornered into joining a trial. We're going to have to share our memories with the rest of the board.'

'If they see what we've seen' – Sam caught Trish's train of thought – 'we might be giving her information. But can we get out of it?'

Trish looked out into the tunnel, as black as the gywandras's oily hide.

'The gywandras could still be Abidemi,' Trish said. 'If not, she'll know something. We follow through with the trial, find out either way.'

Sam nodded, and Trish continued.

'When was the last time you saw Abidemi? Your flat? Focus on that, nothing else but that, and don't give anything away.'

'And what will you focus on?'

'Vanessa,' Trish replied.

After all, to join a trial Trish would have to engage with the other board members and use the transfer machine; she would need to remove her dielectric band.

She could uncover the lies buried within the Network.

58

A DOZEN vertical beams supported cavern 3C's ceiling; it resembled an industrial nest. At the centre stood the egg of the nest itself: the transfer, a six-by-six-foot cube of glass and steel. The transfer served a dual purpose: it measured an imprint's strength and kept them contained. An expensive cage, Trish used to joke.

The fourteen witnesses circled the machine, six feet apart. Sam and Trish ensured they stood together near the cavern's exit. Trish held her hands behind her back so that no one could see them quiver, not that it mattered; the cavern was one of the most ill-lit rooms in the Network behind the Long Walk. Trish gave Vanessa her full attention. Vanessa stood at the control panel and pressed a few buttons. The transfer revved to life, and smoke pumped into its belly. Vanessa nodded at James. The machine was ready.

'Okay, witnesses,' James said, stoic. 'We've evidence that Abidemi has been active in the area recently. Think of her. Project onto the frequency. The most recent memory you have, if not, the most palpable.'

Trish removed the dielectric band. Waves of frequency

energy struck her cranium: thirteen voices, thirteen fractured images. She closed her eyes, tuned out the noise, and thought of Abidemi. The last time she had encountered the imprint was the day in Will's bedroom: the toppled wardrobe, a desk in smithereens, a bed upturned, and blood splattered across the carpet. Strung to a wooden beam, Abidemi burned with velocity and spun in an absent breeze. Trish's body grew warm, and violent flames doused her body. She'd found Abidemi first and brought her to trial.

Trish opened her eyes.

In the transfer, Abidemi's form unfurled amongst a grid of red lasers, contained within the glass. The imprint stared out with hollow eye sockets, her skin charred and her back flayed. The board members stood at one with the darkness, faces lit amber from the lights of the transfer; they seemed more inhuman than Abidemi was.

James broke the ear-throbbing silence.

'Abidemi,' he began solemnly, 'we call upon you today in the belief that you have broken many imprint protocols, most notably involvement in multiple occupations and the murder of fellow witness William Reeves. If the board finds you guilty, your punishment will be expulsion. I want to remind you that means you will cease to exist. Do you understand the parameters of today's trial?'

'As much as you understand the parameters of death, James,' Abidemi retorted. Her form shimmered as if she strained against the electricity that coursed through the transfer.

'Then enlighten me,' James spat.

'An imprint returns to the frequency once the body is wilted, as a flower might return to the soil. From that very soil another flower takes its place.'

'There are more occupations to come?' Vanessa barked from the console.

Abidemi failed to reply. Dying embers wafted from Abidemi's projection.

'The frequency recycles imprints?' Trish asked.

Abidemi turned to her, an opaque hand on the transfer's glass. 'The river always finds the sea.'

James stepped forward and continued with his preempted speech.

'Trial is in session. Abidemi, where were you the night of William Reeves's death?' He gestured to his colleagues. 'Witnesses, engage with the ombrederi.'

Trish's heart kicked inside her chest. She closed her eyes and succumbed to the ombrederi.

59

THE OMBREDERI TOOK the form of Will's tarnished bedroom.

In a hellish time-lapse, multiple versions of Will, in various states of fatigue and unkemptness, sidled into the bedroom. They sat on chairs, the bed, and the windowsill, writing or typing or hand over chin in thought. The witnesses used their own memories to draw out Abidemi's recollection of Will's murder. One version of Will sobbed and pointed an accusing finger. To her right, Sam radiated heat; the last time he saw Will alive, she guessed.

This is my chance, she thought for a moment. She searched the abstract version of Will's room and found Vanessa's imprint, except her imprint was the strangest Trish had ever seen. Muddied with a magenta haze, there were no distinguishable features on her imprint. Instead there were mismatched eyes and echoes of different noses and mouths, as if it were a loose stack of translucent portraits.

Vanessa was no ordinary witness.

'Abidemi.' James's voice wavered across the ombrederi. 'Show us your truth. Don't let us resort to manipulation. Your cooperation will fare you favourably.'

The fourteen witnesses waited with bated breath. The scene changed, but not by Abidemi. A multitude of Wills rose from the bed. Their forms bled and pulsed, and all shouted and pointed at a coffee table covered in white dust. This was Sam's memory.

Trish's worst fears were realised.

The gywandras materialised from thin air and staggered like a maimed animal. Its silhouette was more humanoid than before but still retained no sense of an identity, any life before death. It absorbed the colours of Will's bedroom as a black hole digests nearby stars.

Will became aware of the gywandras when it approached the bed from his left side. He looked from Abidemi to it and called out to them. Abidemi rocked back and forth from the beam, no answers given. The gywandras stalked closer. An oily tentacle connected its disfigured forehead to Will's. The tentacle pulsed and writhed until the shadow imprint passed into him.

Will was occupied.

The memory flickered. In each fragment of light, Abidemi was in a different part of the room, whilst Will – occupied, frantic – whirled through the space, a path of destruction in his wake, a haunted stop-motion animation. For the final act, Will leapt at the window. His body tore through the glass and became at one with the mist.

The physicality of Will's death was undeniable. Anguish tore through Trish's diaphragm.

'That's enough.' James's voice cracked. 'Witnesses, disengage.'

60

TRISH BLINKED, and test cavern 3C swam into view. The board members turned to her and Sam with sombre faces. Behind the console, Vanessa's face was underlit, her eyes just dark sockets locked intently on Sam. Without her dielectric band, Trish felt the tension build between the witnesses.

They know, many thought. *They know about the gywandras.*

Trish took Sam's hand into hers.

James stepped toward the transfer and croaked, 'Abidemi, it's clear that Will was occupied. You failed to help.'

'Guilty by association!' Vanessa hollered.

The witnesses' voices continued to echo through Trish's head. *Will must have told them. He could never be trusted. That's why he died when he did.*

Sam shook himself from Trish's grip and stepped past James to the transfer.

'Abidemi, who is the gywandras?' Sam hollered. 'Why did it kill Will?'

Trish's eyes flitted from Sam, his fists balled, to Abidemi as she writhed within the transfer, to Vanessa swooping in toward Sam.

'It killed Will, and you didn't even try to help!'

Vanessa grabbed Sam by the shoulders.

'How do you know?' She yelled. 'How do you know?'

'Transcendence!' Sam cried. 'Is that what Will died for? Abidemi, you traitor!'

James raced toward the transfer's console. The rest of the board members swarmed around Sam and Trish.

'Abidemi,' James yelled hurriedly, 'the evidence that we have witnessed in this trial, paired with your lack of contribution, leaves me no choice but to conclude you were involved in William Reeves' death.'

The electromagnetic grid burned brighter as James navigated the machine's controls.

'Abidemi,' James concluded, 'the river always finds the sea.'

'You consider yourselves superior because you have bodies,' Abidemi said. 'Encased in flesh and bone, and therefore virtuous. It will all fade, and in death it will come undone.'

The transfer's grid burned until white-hot light dominated the cavern. It faded as the unit powered down with an almighty groan, and the cavern was swallowed into darkness.

'Get off me! Don't touch me!' Sam yelled to Trish's right.

Hands gripped Trish's arms tightly and pulled her from the room.

61

TRISH AND SAM stumbled in the dark, pushed and pulled around bends and up tunnels.

A board member thrust the dielectric band back onto Trish's head. Any chance of her looking further into Vanessa's mind was scuppered. Ahead, the terminal room loomed into sight. Sam leapt, headbutting Peter – a witness twice his size. Peter clamped Sam's neck and shoved him against the rock wall.

'Stop this!' James yelled. He and Vanessa escorted Trish. She shook herself from their grip. Peter released Sam.

'You've no right to do this,' Trish exclaimed.

'As much right as you have to meddle in things you know little about,' Vanessa scoffed. 'How long have you known?'

'Long enough to know that people are suffering because of it.' A thought struck her. She turned to James. 'Did you create the gywandras?'

'Getting cold, Trish,' he huffed. 'Ice-cold.'

'You're experimenting with it,' Sam said. His nose flowed with blood. 'You don't want to stop it, you want it for something else.'

Vanessa turned to them, eyes sharp, and soaked up their dishevelled appearances.

'I'll ask again,' she said. 'How long?'

Trish didn't want to say. If they'd uncovered information the board needed, it could lead to further experiments and prolonged suffering.

'If they're not going to tell us what they know,' Vanessa said, 'the archivists will get it out of them.'

'Vanessa, that's not going to happen,' James growled. 'Not under my governance as director.'

'We're a majority verdict, are we not?' Vanessa said. 'Who opposes the idea of confession via the archives?'

Not one board member blinked, no sign of hesitation. They were all on Vanessa's side. James was powerless. As Will had said, there were no friends left in the Network.

The board members grabbed Sam and Trish and thrust them down the tunnel. Trish and Sam fought and yelled. None of Sam's punches hit hard enough, and Trish's repeated questions were met with silence. After a short steep incline up a narrow shaft, they arrived at the archives. Vanessa swiped her keycard against the sensor, and the door swung outward with a groan. Sam was pushed in first. Vanessa swiped the dielectric band from Trish's head and forced her inside. The door slammed shut before the duo could climb to their feet. All Trish saw before the door clicked shut was James's horrified grey face.

Trish gathered herself up and avoided eye contact with the six archivists. She helped Sam to his feet. His face was awash with blood. She withdrew an unused tissue from her pocket and dabbed away at his nose.

'I'm sorry,' he said. 'I lost control when I saw Will's room . . .'

'I know,' Trish said, discarding the bloodied tissue.

'They were about to exterminate Abi. It was my last chance to find out.'

'I get it,' Trish said. 'Right now we've got bigger matters.'

Around them, the six archivists – their projections in various states of decay and deformity – awakened on their pedestals. Their disfigured limbs flexed and stretched, and multiple eyes blinked from sunken sockets.

'They're not taking anything from me,' Sam declared. He edged to a nearby archivist as it thrashed against its electromagnetic cage. 'Look at them. They're just prisoners.'

Trish looked at the archivists – really looked for the first time. Before they were chained via electromagnets in the archives, they'd been stripped of all their memories. At the beginning of her witnessing career, Trish grew comfortable with imprints once she'd learnt they were just people without bodies. The archivists were less again. Without memories, they'd lost their humanity altogether.

'The transfer is better than this,' Sam muttered.

Trish only realised how much her heart thumped in her chest when he said that. Without her dielectric band, the archivists tugged at her mind as if it were strung on a six-thronged rope of tug-of-war. *What happens after they scour our minds?* Trish wondered. *Will they subject Rasha to the same?* A mind as subservient as hers would likely give more away.

'Sam, what if they go after Rasha next?' Trish said. 'She isn't safe. We're stuck down here, and after everything she's at the centre of it all.'

Sam turned to her, his hand over his pocket. He withdrew an EMP – the one used at Kasey Nancarrow's occupation, no less.

'Will always told me off for not putting equipment away,' he said with a slight smile. He switched the gadget on. 'It's at 35 percent battery, enough for a good blast.'

'You're a brilliant pain in the arse,' Trish said with a grin. The EMP would overload the archivists' pedestals and free the imprints. They'd need not give up their memories.

Sam tapped the EMP in his hand, bottom lip between his teeth.

'There'll be no more Network for us after this,' he said.

'I don't think there has been one for a very long time. It's just been the board – the board, the gywandras, and misery. Light it up.'

Sam pressed a button on the EMP and threw it onto the central dais. The duo retreated to the walls. Within the pedestals' electrical barriers, the six archivists squirmed and writhed as if they knew what was ahead.

A bright silver flash.

Frequency energy tore through the room and doused Trish's body. It was her only chance to scour the archives once more.

Her mind rode the energy surge into the ombrederi.

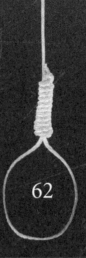

62

GYWANDRAS, Trish thought as the ombrederi whirled around her. *Transcendence, gywandras, transcendence.*

Trish was thrust into the archivists' mist-strewn version of the collieries' yard. To her right, the engine house chimney crumbled. Cracks ripped through the yard floor. The EMP tore the archives apart.

Gywandras, transcendence, gywandras.

She mulled over the occupations of Kasey, Ted, Rose, and Rasha, the gywandras's body comprised of liquid shadow.

The fog parted, and Will strode from between the curtains of mist. This wasn't his imprint but a memory of him. His skin glowed, he was clean-shaven, and there was more bulk to his lean stature than there had been in the weeks before his death. Trish supposed that this was from months ago, before Sam's addiction and the Network took its toll.

Will ambled across the yard, and as if Trish were conjoined to him, they were both whisked into the terminal room. Amongst the darkness, Will was joined by members of the board. James greeted him.

'Welcome to the board,' he said, arms out in welcome. 'I

know the answer already, but have you prepared for your initiation?'

Will smiled.

'Of course,' he said. 'Not that I entirely understand it.'

If this was Will's graduation into the board, Trish figured it would place the memory at least fourteen months into the past.

'It'll make sense soon enough,' Vanessa said, stepping forward from the ring of board members. 'And when it does, you'll never see death – or life, for that matter – the same way again.'

'Let's not get ahead of ourselves,' James chortled. Some of the other board members sniggered. The board seemed to be more like an exclusive fraternity than a network designed to protect the living from the dead.

The scene changed, and Will was now sat in the chair before the terminal. Letters lit up. Trish saw a list of numbers on the adjacent computer monitor: a range of dates and years.

'It's not enough to ask what the gywandras is,' Will uttered. His hands squeezed the arms of his chair. 'We have to ask *when* is the gywandras.'

Vanessa stepped forward. Her face seemed rotten in the sea-green light of the terminal.

'We have our latest board member,' she announced.

The terminal room faded into the front of James's people carrier. A storm lashed rain and sleet onto its windows. James argued with Will.

'It could be disastrous,' Will cried. 'No, it will be. People should never be entrusted with such power. It spells catastrophe for existence.'

James slammed his hands against the steering wheel.

'You think I don't know this?' James said. 'Why do you

269

think I'm still director?'

'You think you can stop this from getting out of hand?' Will scathed. 'You can't control Vanessa.'

'Not alone,' James said. 'You know the science inside out. If anyone can steer Vanessa away from progress, it's you.'

'I didn't ask for this,' Will said. 'If I'd known, I wouldn't have taken up the offer. Actually, no, I wouldn't still be a part of the Network. You think I can keep this from Sam and Trish –'

'You have to,' James said. 'Because whilst they're with us, the Network can still do good.'

Will sat back in his seat and wiped frustrated tears from his face.

'The ability to transcend time through emotional connectedness. It's the most dangerous weapon man could lay their hands on. The temptation to travel through time, to alter it . . .'

'Gywandras,' James stated. 'Cornish for traveller. Which is why we won't let this happen. Which is why I need you.'

White light doused James's people carrier.

63

TRISH OPENED her eyes to the empty archives.

The six archivists were gone, just frequency particles now. Sam, with the flat EMP in hand, raced back to her.

'What did you see?'

'Will was trying to stop it all along. I don't even know where to begin. They're trying to change time, Sam.'

'Time?' he repeated. Forehead creased, he reached into his pocket and pulled out the paper he'd collected from the Nancarrows' study. Sam ran a hand over the stream of numbers. 'Intersection . . . Maybe that's what Will meant?'

'Gywandras. It's Cornish for traveller. That's what the gywandras initiative is. Something beyond human, beyond death.'

Trish continued to recount Will's memories, how fanatical the board seemed.

'Madness, complete and utter madness, but why us?' Sam asked. 'Mum, Shauna, Rasha – why are we a part of it?'

'I don't know,' Trish uttered.

'I knew Will was doing good,' he said with a small smile.

A bang caused her to jump out of her skin. Further slaps

and punches rebounded off the archive door. Muffled words were shouted on the other side.

'They've overloaded the power! The door won't open.'

Sam held Trish by the shoulders. Her eyes had adjusted to the darkness and could see Sam's wide eyes.

'We've only got until the emergency generator kicks in,' he said. 'We both can't get away. One of us has to protect Rasha. I'll cause a distraction when they come in. You have to get out.'

'What about you?' Trish said.

'I'll be okay – pain in the arse, remember? This is bigger than me. Bigger than any of us.'

A buzz sounded, and lights popped on overhead. The archive door swung open, and hands grabbed at them. Leri joined them.

'Don't hurt them!' James hollered.

The rest of the board seemed to not hear, nor care. Trish and Sam were pulled into the mineshaft, and Vanessa scoured the archives. She screamed with frustration and raced out with the dead EMP in hand. She shook it beneath James's nose.

'The archivists are gone!' she yelled. 'Our research, our shared history, erased.'

The board members grumbled. Peter, the burly man whose eye was bruised thanks to Sam, screeched, 'Punish them!'

'You don't need your research,' Sam said. 'You want to know who the gywandras is? Look no further.'

'Garbage,' Peter hollered.

Leri's grip loosened on Trish's wrists. Trish was just as puzzled as the board. Unpredictable by nature was her friend.

'Think about what the gywandras is. It transcends time. I'm the only one who can withdraw his imprint from his body.'

Vanessa stepped forward. Her eyes studied the terrain of

Sam's face as if she searched for lies in the bags beneath his eyes or the grey in his stubble. She grabbed his face.

'So you're telling me,' she said, 'that you killed Will?'

Sam took a deep breath. He clearly hadn't thought that far ahead.

'I haven't yet,' he retorted. 'Transcendence, after all.'

James was to Trish's left. She looked at him with wide eyes. She heard his thoughts. *Sam, you idiot.* No one had replaced Trish's dielectric band. She thought hard, going beyond his skin, his skull, and planted into his mind, *'Blink if Rasha is in danger.'*

James went slack-jawed, regained his composure, and blinked hard.

'I need to get out. Get me alone with someone.'

James inserted himself between Sam and Trish.

'We need to test this,' James said. 'If he is the answer, then transcendence is ours. It's in our grasp.'

'Agreed,' Vanessa said. 'We have the necessary equipment at the Refinery.'

'Sam can't transcend alone,' Trish said as an idea came to her. 'He'll need the mobile receptor.'

'Where is it, Trish?' James asked.

'The Reliant.'

'Right, Leri, escort Trish to her car,' James demanded. 'Bring the receptor back at once.'

Leri stayed firm. She didn't take orders from James anymore. Vanessa looked from Trish to Leri and nodded.

Leri pulled Trish up the shaft to ground level. Trish shook herself from the nimble woman's grasp.

'I can walk by myself.'

Before they rounded the corner, Trish looked into Sam's mind, swiped away thoughts of Will and the gywandras, and projected, '*Whatever they do to you, you're stronger.*'

The activity centre was empty, so Trish placed the time in the early a.m. There were so many questions Trish still had left to answer concerning the gywandras's agenda and the rise in occupations.

'Sam wouldn't tell me what the occupations are for,' Trish said. 'He said I wouldn't understand transcendence.'

'Clearly not,' Leri scoffed, 'if you think the gywandras is causing them.'

'It's not?'

'The frequency was always going to retaliate.'

'The frequency is fighting the gywandras.' Trish mulled it over. So many of the occupations had been personal. Sam had ties to Angove Lodge, and Will had taken Kasey's body. 'The occupations are targeting the Network. You've been chasing the gywandras, and the occupied have been chasing you. That's why you wouldn't cure Kasey Nancarrow.'

Leri pushed Trish into the final shaft that would take them to the parking warehouse. They passed the Edward Penrose plaque.

'Man's greatest achievements have always come at a price,' Leri said matter-of-factly. 'If we have to defy nature to transcend, then so be it.'

Leri's cold delivery sent shivers down Trish's spine. The Network was never meant to be callous with its experiments; it should have maintained a balance between the dead and the living so that they could coexist in harmony. The obsession with the gywandras, and everything it could do and be, would spell disaster in the wrong hands.

Trish and Leri reached the parking warehouse.

'So when you have the gywandras, and it's willing to play your twisted games,' Trish said, 'what do you want with it?'

Leri pushed Trish toward the Reliant and didn't reply. She no longer wanted to talk. Trish withdrew her keys from her pocket and opened the Reliant's boot. The receptor remained on the back seat after she'd navigated the Reliant to the Nancarrows' household. The boot contained an assortment of tools Sleep had provided her for emergencies, a car jack amongst them. She detached the lever from the jack and gripped it tight. A thought bothered her: Will had been inducted into the board, and ever since he'd spent sleepless nights working on the project. When James announced Will's death that day in the birdcage, the board knew about the energy spike in Rosenannon.

'Tell me one thing,' Trish said. 'Was Will meant to have been the gywandras?'

'What does it matter?'

'Because he died for the project.'

Trish swung the jack's lever. It slammed into Leri's temple with a hollow plonk, and she collapsed to the floor. Pole still in hand, Trish raced to the warehouse doors and pushed them wide open. The cold night washed over her, the darkness incomparable to the gywandras.

She raced back to the Reliant as Leri staggered to her feet. Blood veined across her right cheek.

'You can't escape the gywandras,' Leri spat. 'The tide is strong.'

Trish stepped forward and feigned a lunge. Leri retreated, hands up in surrender.

Trish threw the pole aside and raced to the driver's door. She jumped into the Reliant, shoved her keys into the ignition, and sped out into the collieries' yard. Her headlights illuminated the gate.

The locked gate.

Trish put on the handbrake and hit the throttle. Smoke billowed from the tyres. She pushed the handbrake down. There was a moment of unsteadiness as the Reliant tried to veer sideways. *Thwack.* The gates flung open. The bonnet rippled. The Reliant threatened to roll.

Trish realigned the vehicle's course and sped on down the lane.

She wiped away the tears that fell from her eyes. She'd abandoned her one remaining friend and fled a place she'd once called home. Rasha was a target, and being in her presence only put the teenager in more danger.

What was there to do? Where was she to go? *Answers*, she thought, *the one thing that matters now*.

Only one place remained where she could find answers about the gywandras, and that was within Michael's own head, sixty miles away in Dartmoor.

64

DUSK DESCENDED as Trish rolled up to the caravan site. Steam hissed from the Reliant's bonnet. She rose from the car and paced toward Rasha's caravan.

What would she do? Knock on the door? No, Haya would be problematic. There was no way she could hide Rasha away. The Network was clever, but they weren't above the law. Rasha couldn't just disappear; neighbours would question her whereabouts, then soon Gorenn Comprehensive and the social services would be involved. The teenager was protected, to some degree, by people who governed her well-being.

Trish crept around to the right side of the caravan. Images flooded her mind: desolated Syrian streets, a bloodied hand torn apart by a saw, a teenage boy with broken arms and a twisted neck. Confident she'd located Rasha's bedroom window, she knocked lightly.

The carousel of Rasha's thoughts halted; Trish had disrupted Rasha's sleep. She knocked on the glass once more.

'Rasha!' she whispered.

Dark shapes moved beyond the glass, and a weary Rasha pushed the awning open.

'Trish?' she said. 'Vanessa said I can't see you again.'

'You might not, for a while. Listen, kiddo, things aren't great. I'm going away for a while. Sam, he won't be around – '

'What happened?' Rasha asked.

'The board, they know about the gywandras. They've been trying to create it, to use it. Will was meant to be the gywandras, but that failed, and . . . I think they're going to try and use you next. They won't just come and get you. So you have to promise me. Take the bus to and from school. Stay in school all day. Never leave the caravan park without someone. Do that, and they can't take you. Don't ever be alone.'

On the outskirts of Trish's mind, an EMP filtered the air of frequency energy.

'Trish, you're scaring me.'

'Sorry, Rasha, but I have to be quick. After you were occupied, Sam and I placed a couple of EMPs around the park to help you. There's one under that caravan there.'

Trish pointed to the caravan immediately adjacent.

'That's Mr Keats's caravan,' the teenager said.

'I want you to take that one and keep it with you. Put it in your schoolbag. As long as it's transmitting, the Network will struggle to access your mind remotely.'

'You're not part of the Network anymore?'

'I'm not,' Trish confessed.

'Do you know what the gywandras is?'

'Not exactly,' Trish said. 'But I know what it does. It transcends time.'

'Time travel?'

'Right. No matter who it is or what it wants, its origin could be at any time. God, whoever it is might not have been born yet.'

'That's impossible.'

'After everything we've seen, the goalposts for what is plausible have been moved.'

Trish noted that the sky was a lighter navy.

'I have to go,' Trish said. 'Remember, EMP with you at all times. Never be alone.'

'Never be alone,' Rasha repeated.

Trish went to walk away, then turned back to Rasha.

'You're special, Rasha. That also puts you in danger. Understood?'

Rasha went pale, swallowed a response, and nodded instead. Trish, as satisfied as she could be with the exchange, raced across the caravan site back to the Reliant and drove away.

By the time Trish drove to Princetown and caught some disturbed sleep in a lay-by, the sun had risen and a plan had formed in her mind. She squeezed the Reliant into the last available space on Tavistock Road. Moor Crescent was to her left, and right of her was an empty park. The town was just as drab and grey as the prison. Princetown had been built as barracks for HMP Dartmoor, so the houses had belonged, as some still did, to the prison staff. Beyond their rooftops, the prison walls loomed, a reminder that the law governed all.

Trish's plan was far from watertight. She needed to access Michael's memories of the night Shauna died. She was confident that, in his intoxicated state, he had sighted the gywandras and even saw what it planned to do. The problem was that she couldn't visit him again, not without a booking, and not on a Tuesday when visitors weren't allowed. So her only other choice was the receptor. The prison was riddled with imprints, so Trish was certain she could probe through memories from Michael's short spell there to pick up on conversations he might have had with inmates. His cellmates probably came together to reminisce over nights out, the drugs they'd taken, the sports they'd played, and the girls they'd pestered.

Trish couldn't walk up to the prison walls with the receptor and expect to go unnoticed. She needed a conductor to amplify the signal. Her answer lay just twenty feet from the parked Reliant: the Church of St Michael and All Angels, righteous and out of place in a prison-bound town.

Receptor in hand, Trish abandoned the Reliant and crossed the road into the church. It was a late Tuesday morning, and the church, with its stonework and narrow pews and faded stained glass windows, was desolate. Frequency energy was thick; the tapered piers and chamfered arches were made entirely of granite, a commonplace material in Princetown's construction. HMP Dartmoor's energy was palpable – eerie and acquitted, endlessly hopeless – and the frequency was intensified in a church of granite.

The brevity of her task dawned on her. She strode through the church and found an alcove behind the pulpit that would shield her from view of visitors. She sat on her trench coat and adjusted the receptor's straps. With the motor's buzz as ambience, Trish secured the receptor, closed her eyes, and fell into the ombrederi.

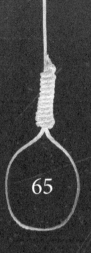

65

PRINCETOWN SHIMMERED around Trish in the
ombrederi. The many pasts of Dartmoor gathered together
in one infinite landscape: the bloodied carcasses of civil war
soldiers rotted in bogs, rudimentary Neolithic farmers herded
sheep amongst the hills, and builders mastered stone as they
were bitten by winter frost. They laboured, fought invisible
enemies, and signalled to awry cattle, unaware that blood no
longer pumped through their veins.

A trail of colour, like car lights in a time-lapse, leaked
across Moor Crescent. Trish touched it. Michael's aura came
to her, a volatile mix of anger and primal urges, a predilection
to sin: his emotional tether.

The moorland melted away into a whirl of colour, and
Trish found herself within the prison's walls. She stood on
the first floor walkway of an empty atrium, cells stacked four
storeys high. Fifty-foot safety netting was strung between
balconies from one side to the other. A lone guard strode by
to do his rounds. It was after hours and quieter than Trish
imagined, clinical too; its white walls, iron railings, and strip
lighting were immaculate and cold, just as hospitals could be.

Projections materialised across the walkways; blurred and devoid of detail, they were grade one guides. She moved toward a cluster of them on the ground floor and turned everything over in her mind: the conversations with Michael, the gywandras and its viscous black skin, Shauna found dead in Penzance with a bloated purple neck. Then a voice reverberated in the ombrederi.

'You're an idiot,' Shauna's voice chimed.

As the ink of a Polaroid blotted into being, The Puffin and Hare sprouted around Trish. A regular Saturday night, the bar brimmed with drunken punters, air so thick with alcohol fumes that the smoke on the locals' breath could ignite the place.

At the bar, Michael had a thin lad pinned to the wall. Michael's eyes danced in their sockets, too intoxicated on drink and god knows what to focus. From the blurred crowd, Shauna raced over to try and wrench Michael's grip from the boy's collar.

'He's just a kid!' she yelled. 'It's just a stupid game of darts! Get over it!'

Michael pushed Shauna away and knocked her to the grubby carpet.

People offered to help her to her feet, but Shauna did so of her own accord. The pub's bouncer hurtled over, pried Michael's fists from the lad's collar, and thrust him out onto the street. Shauna followed, apologising to the bouncer on her way out. The bouncer disappeared back into the hustle and bustle of the pub. Shauna turned to Michael and jabbed a finger into his chest.

'You're an idiot,' she growled. 'Getting high, picking on kids half your age. Some man!'

Michael staggered upright on the cobbles and looked

through her.

'I don't know what Trish sees in you. Never have, never will. Waste of the air you breathe.'

'She ain't got anyone else,' Michael said. 'She'll never leave.'

Trish's stomach sunk. She'd proved Michael right.

'Disgusting prick,' Shauna retorted. She ambled up the cobbles, taking her mobile from her jacket pocket. 'Taking coke, starting fights. Trish will want to hear about this. Maybe she'll finally see sense.'

The ombrederi grew vacuum-quiet. Unbeknownst to Shauna and Michael, dark shadows in the mouth of the butcher's shop rippled. From them came the gywandras. Colour and shape disintegrated around its edges. Trish shrunk in its aura. Its influence was boundless. A thousand answers lurked beneath its blank facade, and if it had transcended time, perhaps a thousand years of knowledge.

This is it, she thought. In the physical, her heart hammered in her chest.

The gywandras glided over the ground, its legs barely contacting the cobbles. It reached Michael. Trish half expected it to envelop him. No. It gestured to the darkest corner of the alley, from which stumbled an imprint Trish had seen before, days ago when she first tried the receptor in Penzance: the murderous woman. On the gywandras's command, the woman floundered toward Michael, pressed herself against his body, and sunk into Michael's pores.

Michael was occupied.

'No!' Trish hollered, not that anyone could hear. 'Don't you do it!'

Occupied-Michael propelled himself up the alleyway. Shauna heard his thunderous footsteps and began to jog, her stilettoed feet distrusting the ground with her drunken gait. In the moonlight, Michael's face came into focus, eyes blank. His body was there, but his mind was elsewhere.

He grabbed Shauna and turned her to face him. She slapped him. He punched her, grabbed her by the scruff of her top, and pushed her into the darkness beside the garage. All that came was Shauna's muffled gasps of air. A sliver of blue twine bit into her bloated neck.

It was done. Shauna, no more.

Trish was cemented to the cobbles. Her heart pounded in her chest – the only thing assuring her she was still alive. Her veins burned hot. Deep down she had blamed Michael for Shauna's death, and it hadn't been him at all. Not truly. It was the gywandras. She no longer feared it.

She hated it.

Occupied-Michael tottered out of the shadows and back down the alleyway. He stumbled against the doors of the butchers' and slammed to the ground. From his open mouth spilled the wild woman, and her imprint melted into shadows, never to be seen again.

The gywandras loitered in the alley. Its chest heaved. Trish forgot it was a memory and hollered, 'Why her? Why us?'

She hadn't anticipated the gywandras to turn and face her. For the first time, she saw its somewhat-eyes, without any indistinguishable shape, two burning stars absorbed into an endless void. The gywandras, unbound by time, whose present could be others' pasts.

It shook its distorted head Trish's way and dematerialised, leaving only the night and Shauna's lifeless body.

Trish's heartbeat pulsed in her fingertips. The receptor's frayed supports bruised her collar bone –

66

TRISH CAME TO on the floor by the pulpit and vomited across the granite floor. She tore the receptor from her head and cast it aside. It clanged on the stone and rolled to a stop.

Shauna had died again, and Michael had been wrongly implicated.

Michael would age in HMP Dartmoor if he were so unlucky, but it didn't matter because he wasn't the perpetrator.

Michael was innocent. The gywandras had taken everything from her: her loved ones, her friends, the Network.

Trish gathered her things and raced back to the Reliant before she was caught by a member of the public. Her life was barely worth living.

She'd do anything to stop the Network.

INTERLUDE III

EWELLA WATCHES KYAUTA raise a coconut above his head. His other clamps an invisible neck. He swings the coconut down and mimes clubbing someone over the head, as silent as possible; the cargo hold brims with captives now. His nightly visits to Ewella grow later and ever more silent. She learnt his name, one particularly chilly evening by torchlight and took to the language well; she'd shared Ebok's mind and inherited an instinct for the Zarma dialect. Ewella shakes her head to his plan: *no*. He hears that a lot. *No*. He learnt to use it.

'Can you get me more food?' she asks.

'No.'

'Tonight,' she says and pulls at the chains that shackle her to the ship's gullet. She points out, beyond the sea, to the land, to home. 'Let's escape tonight.'

'No.'

Kyauta knows the workings of the ship: the routine of the watchmen, how sea sickness deprives the crew of sleep, the wandering thieves who steal food or a girl's innocence, or both. Kyauta illustrated a steady movement with the flat of his hand: the sea must be calm. There was a full moon the last four nights; the waters were turbulent and rocked the ship so much Ewella was sick to her stomach. Kyauta ate her dates.

She points through a slit in the hull. The sea is lit by the moon, a tear drop in the oily sky. The tide laps calmly in the ballast below them. The wind is still.

'Yes,' Ewella whispers, enacting the steady sea with her hand.

Kyauta's pupils dilate with fear. Ewella can see his mind go through the motions: terror at abandoning his ship mates and a guilt from wanting to be free from them. The night before they had a fragmented conversation disrupted by the cries of a particularly disturbed girl. Ewella and Kyauta realised the ship wasn't headed back to his home. Ewella recalled Ebok's memory of the cargo being taken directly to the Arabian markets. Kyauta learnt their ship restocks there before it returned to European shores. Kyauta whispers with heartbreak:

'Ile.'

Ewella presumes it means 'home'. She points to the shoreline and to him.

'Ile,' she says.

His face softens in the moonlight. A daring smile breaks the sadness on his face.

Kyauta rushes from the deck and tiptoes up the ladder. The crew's quarters are on the floor above. Ewella looks over the other girls, who sleep lightly in the constant terror of their situation. Fifteen girls in all, at one with the straw and the dirt and their own faeces. Ewella is selfish. Her escape means little if the other girls don't come. She won't be able to live with herself.

There is barefoot pitter-patter, and Kyauta returns to the

lower deck, a warped metal key in hand. Kyauta puts it into the lock of her shackles and twists. They do not open. He wiggles it a little. The shackles come loose. She shakes herself out of them, crawls forward and stands up to her full height. Her twisted spine aches; the blood rushes to her disused limbs. Kyauta grabs her hand and pulls her towards the ladder. She digs her feet into the splintered floor and gestures at the sleeping, ill-trodden maidens.

'No,' Kyauta says. A sentence follows she cannot translate, but his gestures she can: there is not enough time.

Ewella fears what awaits the girls in the markets and beyond.

'Come back,' Ewella demands.

Ky nods.

'You promise?' Ewella asks, her usual response.

'Promise.'

They skulk up the ladder. Her joints click and her heart pounds. *My fear shall awaken them.* The sleeping quarters reek of body odour, the kind Ewella likens to her father and brother after a day of thatching. The crew sleeps in worn, filthy hammocks that sway in and out of grey moonbeams. They customised the quarters with leaves and branches from the wild country to soften the harsh reality of living at sea. The acidic undercurrent of vomit shatters the illusion. The pair push on through the deck. Ewella makes sure to keep her eyes to the ground. If she doesn't see them, they might not see her.

There is another ladder to climb. At its end is the open world. The cold salt air reinvigorates her soul. The duo manoeuvre across the top deck, between masts, nets and kegs, to the side of the ship where two wooden boats lay side by side, ready to be dropped into the water at short notice.

Kyauta mimes lowering of the boat by rope. It comfortably fits eight people. Ewella knows she is not strong enough. She shakes her head and presents her dainty arms. Kyauta mimes pushing it. She nods.

They shove the boat towards a gap in the railing. There is a ledge. Kyauta takes an oar from the boat, slots it beneath the hull and applies leverage. Under his instructions, Ewella pushes. It inches near. The underside scrapes the deck. She grows impatient and her hands tire.

The hull of the boat thwacks the ledge. Ewella and Kyauta pause, eyes wide on each other, breath held. The urgent sea babbles and they hear no footsteps or hurried voices. Ewella sighs relief, and they both turn back to their work. One more push.

There is a third shadow on the deck. Silver glints in her periphery. Kyauta throws himself at the shadow and tackles the man to the ground. A blade scuttles across the deck. In the weak moonlight Ewella recognises him: Kyauata's often rapist. Kyauta is half his size, yet punches and slaps, overcome by his urgency to escape a life he never asked for. The watchman kicks Kyauta away and jumps on top. He presses his fingers into Kyauta's throat. Kyauta's body thrashes and his eyes roll to the back of his skull.

The blade glints by Ewella's feet. She snatches it up, colder and heavier than she anticipated, and lunges it into the man's back. The knife slices through meat and tendon as if they are water. She plunges into his flesh again. A third time. The life leaves him, and he collapses aside Kyauta. The boy coughs, rolls onto his front and breathes. Ewella stabs and stabs. The watchman's blood pools across the wooden deck. She jabs, she cries. Kyauta picks her up into his arms and wrenches the blade from her grasp. He tosses it into the dingy.

Ewella comes to her senses. *Escape*. They push the boat —
one final heave of adrenaline. The boat topples over the edge,
snags the side of the ship and slaps into the water. Movement
sounds under their feet. Kyauta takes Ewella's hand and leads
her to the ship's edge. She looks down at the hungry water.

'I can't swim,' she utters.

'Down,' Kyauta commands.

'No.'

'Yes.'

He steps back from her and scuttles towards the ladder to
the lower decks.

'Come back,' he promises and lowers himself into the
darkness. He buys her time. If she does not jump his efforts
— successful or not — will be wasted. She is prized. She will
face few repercussions. For Kyauta it means death. Ewella
curls her toes over the lip of the deck. The ship bobs with the
motion of the waves. She breathes as they rise; exhales as they
fall and succumbs to the rhythm of the ocean. She drops.

Ewella takes a gulp of air before she hits the water. The sea
envelopes her, and rushes into her nostrils and ears. The water
is icy and her limbs tense with shock. She clamps her mouth
shut so it doesn't spring open and gulp down the salt water.
Her hand brushes the underside of the dingy. She cannot
kick, no matter how much her mind screams for her body to
move. The amassing weight of the water pulls her down. The
dingy is lost in blackness, more absolute than a starless night.

A body hits the water. Hands find her and wrench her up
by the armpit. She runs out of air. Giddiness overcomes her.
They have captured her again. Should she open her mouth to
a watery death and take her life into her own hands?

No, the water whispers. *Your purpose has not yet come.*

She kicks. The underside of the boat looms into view. Her

head breaks the surface. Kyauta is beside her. They are both alive. They are both free.

Ky helps her onto the boat, and after a few attempts, she clambers up onto a seat. He springs up, snatches a pair of oars and wades. They drift from the ship. The waves roll them closer and closer to the shore. The ship shrinks behind them.

They both dare to smile. But Ewella cannot revel in her delight for long.

A clap rumbles across the sea. Ewella looks over Kyauta's shoulder: the second life boat. Bodies drop into the water — one, two, three, four. Kyauta rows faster. Ewella picks up the second pair of oars and begins to wade. It is harder work than she imagined and it takes every morsel of energy to row as fast as Ky. She will. She must.

They will not go back.

PART NINE

A SLAVE
TO FLESH

67

'YOU DON'T HAVE to take me there,' Sam said for the umpteenth time from the passenger seat. The morning sky bled crimson. *Red sky in the morning, shepherd's warning.* He glared at James as he drove his people carrier down the motorway. 'Pretend you've dropped me off.'

'Don't be an idiot, Sam. People talk,' James retorted. He took a sharp turn onto the A30. 'Vanessa gets daily reports on the Refinery's work.'

Sam swallowed spittle and balled his fists, tempted to punch James if he weren't in control of a vehicle doing eighty down the motorway. He couldn't believe James had let the board go awry, for Vanessa to have tight reins over the entire operation.

That notion was quashed when Sam's phone rang within his pocket. He withdrew it to find that Margaret (caller ID complete with dragon emoji) was calling him.

'Don't answer it,' James said.

'People talk, don't they?' Sam scoffed. 'If they can't reach a junkie, they'll presume the worst.'

'Fine, make it quick.'

Sam swiped to answer and held the phone to his ear.

'Samuel,' Marge sneered. She knew he hated his full name. She loathed having hers abbreviated.

'Marge, how are you and Phil keeping?'

'So-so. Morgues don't really incite positivity. Yes, they've released the body.'

The body. Sam met the news with indifference; witnesses understood the body to be a vehicle. Margaret's detachment from Will's body made her compatible for a life in the collieries.

'It's with the funeral directors if you want to see it,' Margaret continued. 'Put it this way, Phil's in bits. It's not the last image of Will he wanted.'

'So you've got a date for the funeral?'

'June 3rd. It's soon, I know, but leave his body too long and, well . . .'

The line fell silent: Margaret had hung up. Sam had barely spoken, and Margaret had had a conversation with herself.

Will's body. *Just a flesh prison entombing the imprint,* he tried to tell himself. That was wrong. It had been an inexhaustible source of warmth when alcohol and drugs weren't enough. Strength when his depression rendered him physically weak. It would be cold and lifeless forever, and its forever would rot in a wooden coffin. He had to see it one more time. To say goodbye.

James held out a hand for Sam's phone.

'You won't need it where you're going,' he said.

Sam tossed his phone into James's hand.

'Any chance of taking a detour?' Sam said. 'The coroner's released Will's body and – '

'I sympathise, but it's in the other direction entirely, and if Vanessa catches wind –'

'All right, how's this: take me there, and I'll go to the Refinery quietly. I won't kick up a fuss. Believe me, I was planning to.'

'Fine,' James said. Sam didn't care if he was a pain in the arse; after all, James was driving him to the Refinery, so Sam didn't trust James as far as he could throw him. 'Which morgue?'

Margaret had been purposefully vague with the morgue's location, but Sam gathered that, in proximity to the Reeves' home, it could only be Tredrae Funeral Directors.

'Rosenannon,' Sam confirmed.

After forty-five minutes of hard driving and cold silence, James pulled up at the Chapel of Rest. Freshly painted and endowed with potted plants, the chapel was a monument of pride for the community. The Reeves often hosted dinners for the Tredraes, giving into the innate desire for the village people to forge good relationships with those who would bury them and their loved ones. *What we fear most*, Sam pondered, *are the people who'll see us at our worst.*

James turned the ignition off and faced Sam.

'I can only give you twenty minutes,' he said. 'The Refinery nurses will be waiting for us.'

'If Vanessa calls, tell her you treated me to a last meal at Maccies,' Sam said. He opened his door but didn't climb out. 'What does she have over you?' he asked James.

'She's a force to be reckoned with.'

'No,' Sam said. 'Something changed after Will died.'

James took a deep breath and squeezed the steering wheel between his hands.

'After Will, I was next in line for the gywandras trials.'

Sam sat back in his seat. To be at the mercy of the gywandras was a fear all its own.

'Was?' Sam asked. 'Let me guess, until Rasha came along?'

'But she's untouchable.'

'It better stay that way.'

James rubbed his forehead. 'Agreed,' he said. 'Twenty minutes.'

Sam jumped from the car and raced into the chapel. Stained windows, pointed archways – Sam half expected to be greeted by Wednesday Addams upon arrival. The reception smelt of fresh paint – the kind synonymous with stale armpits. Eddie, the undertaker, squeezed himself into a black suit inches too small and sweated profusely as a consequence. Sam knew by Margaret's incessant local gossip that he was the Tredraes' youngest son. Dealings with the dead were generally a family affair and, akin to farming or building, one had to be raised in it to find appreciation for the craft, just as Rose had introduced Sam to the Network, to his uttermost reluctance.

'You're a family member?' Eddie asked him when Sam gave Will's name. Sam paused. Margaret called him Will's –

'Partner.'

Eddie swallowed his embarrassment, face scarlet.

'I'm sorry for your loss,' he said. Sam distracted himself with various funeral care plan leaflets spread across the desk.

'Thanks, I appreciate it,' Sam said. Eddie went to get keys from the metal cabinet below the desk and steered the conversation toward the chapel's awkward location on a one-way road.

'You found us okay?'

Sam stole the moment to wipe a tear from his face. All too real.

Eddie's keys jangled in hand as he led Sam down a dated hallway. To think there were dead bodies refrigerated on the other side, chilled so their loved ones could delay their grief and abide more time in their not-so-blissful ignorance. *Still a sceptic*, Sam thought, despite the fact he sought what he vilified others for: closure.

They passed a fire exit – that'd be Sam's escape route; there was no way in the frequency he'd go to the Refinery. Eddie led Sam past a door labelled 'Morgue: Employees Only.' A light wave of frequency energy doused Sam's skin. The assortment of bodies the morgue housed, with brains in varied states of detachment from their imprints, fizzed like newly opened soda bottles. Memories popped into Sam's mind: a plane crashed in southern India, a family fought over dinner because their mother had cheated with the groundskeeper. Imprints rarely clung to happy memories. *A waste of life for people to die embittered*, Sam thought.

Eddie led Sam into a side room. The frequency energy eased with each step. Flower-printed wallpaper and discount vinyl flooring covered the walls and the floor. Will's body lay in a coffin, the lid open. His coffin.

His body.

'Take all the time you need,' Eddie said. He squeezed Sam's shoulder, departed from the room, and closed the door softly, as if careful not to wake the dead. Will's body would not wake again. It was in a suit, as his parents promised, skin grey, eyes locked closed. The undertakers tried to make it look asleep rather than dead: light makeup poorly hid the bruises acquired in his final moments. A cut embellished the forehead where surgeons had drained the fluid from a haemorrhage. The nose, once beautifully beak-like, sat crooked. A crop of red hair sprouted above the right ear. Sam leant over and rubbed the auburn strands. He expected makeup residue to come away between his fingers. It didn't. The hair wasn't curly, but flat and thin and not Will's at all.

Rasha's words from the day they had introduced her to the Network echoed in his mind.

'It's like I'm becoming someone else. Becoming them.'

The eyebrows were the same, lips unchanged, details he should know, but not for sure. He couldn't mistake the eyes. He rolled Will's eyelids up, pebble heavy. The left eye was its usual autumn hazel. The right eye was toad green.

Sam closed the eyes and raced to the reception where Eddie diligently worked at the computer.

'Hey, mate, don't suppose I could borrow your mobile? Left mine at home.'

'Of course,' Eddie said. He withdrew his smartphone and passed it to Sam.

'Won't be a sec,' Sam said. He strode back down the corridor and found signal by the fire exit. He had two minutes before James would start looking for him. Sam opened Google, searched for Gorenn Comprehensive's number, and rang it.

'Hello, Gorenn Comprehensive, Suzie speaking,' came the receptionist's sickly sweet voice.

Sam spoke with a rasp to age his voice as much as possible.

'Hi there, this is Mr Keats. I'm ringing on behalf of Mrs Abadi for one Rasha Abadi.'

'Good morning. No problem, she'll be in class now. Would you care to leave a message?'

'I would, my 'andsome, problem is there's bit of a language barrier, see. I don't quite understand what she wants to say myself. They have a delicate relationship, what with all they've been through. Seems urgent, though.'

'Ah, no problem. Hold on the line, and I'll have her come down.'

'Thank you.'

Sam checked the phone screen. His twenty minutes were

up. James would come and find him at any moment.

'Hello?' Rasha answered. 'Mr Keats?'

'Rasha, it's Sam.'

'Sam? Are you okay? I saw Trish, and she said she's not with the Network. Told me to be careful, never to be alone – '

'Promise me you'll do exactly what she says.'

'Okay.'

'I need to ask you something. When you were occupied, you said your body changes?'

'I feel their pain. Is that normal?'

'I don't even know what that word means anymore. But Rasha, does it feel like . . . your body is becoming that person?'

'Yeah,' Rasha said quietly. 'Sam, the receptionist is listening in and – '

'Right,' Sam replied. 'If a witness approaches you, don't listen to them, don't go with them.'

'Even James?'

Sam thought over the hold that Vanessa had on the director, how terrified he was of the gywandras scheme.

'Yes,' Sam retorted. 'Even James.'

The line went dead, cold silence in which his synapses seethed. There must have been a reason the ombrederi chose occupations to counteract the gywandras; and it must have been more a coincidence that a body changed allegiance to the occupying imprint. There was only one person Sam knew who'd been occupied for an extended period of time: his mother, Rose. He knew the answers he needed were where he least wanted to go.

The Refinery.

68

THE REFINERY, a double entendre all its own, was a seventeenth-century arsenic refinery that stained the view of Portreath's North Cliffs. In the turn of the twentieth century it passed into the hands of the Network under the guise of Cornish Heritage. A brand-new building was erected alongside its one remaining chimney and equipped to be a mental hospital for witnesses. From the outside, it could be mistaken for any old heritage site.

James drove his people carrier into the Refinery's courtyard. Sam broke his nervous silence that he had maintained for a good fifty minutes.

'What experiments was Vanessa talking about, exactly?' he asked. His hands gripped the seat.

'I don't think telling you would make you feel any better,' James replied.

'How the fuck did it come to this, James?' Sam growled. 'To let it get so out of hand.'

'You have to understand that I came onto the board as director thinking what you do, that the Network was there to stop hauntings and support witnesses, that any and all experiments were to benefit that purpose.'

'They were experimenting with the gywandras before you joined.'

'No, it's been occupations ever since Edward Penrose established the Network and funded it with his trust. But whatever the Network is intended to be, I know it can do good. We've proven that, haven't we?'

Sam shrugged, uncertain as to whether he could support that statement. Yes, they'd collectively spared Rasha and Kasey from occupations in recent weeks, but there was no doubting the trauma they'd induced. Sam stared at the building through the windscreen.

'If I'm doing this, then you have to swear to me that you'll protect Rasha, and Kasey too. Don't let Vanessa have them.'

'I'll do what I can.'

'When can I come out of the Refinery?'

No answer from James.

'Will's funeral is soon. I need to be out by then.'

'It'll depend on your behaviour,' James said. 'Honestly, right now your best bet will be another occupation. That's where you and Trish seem to excel, and it's the only time the board has agreed to award you some merit.'

'Let's hope it doesn't have to come to that.'

The two men climbed from the people carrier. With its barred windows, electronic doors, and flock of CCTV cameras, Sam doubted the gothic building had many attempted escapes.

The wooden double doors opened before they pressed the buzzer. Two women in clinical uniforms stepped out. The taller of the two, witchy with her hair clipped into a bun on her crown, spoke first.

'Samuel Bickle?' she asked, face stiff as if emotions did not come easily. Her name badge read, 'Mallory.'

'The one and only,' Sam retorted.

'Better late than dead,' the other, labelled 'Lilith,' said. Her eyes studied Sam's heavy eyes, wispy beard, and clenched fists. She turned to James. 'We can take it from here.'

'Remember,' Sam reminded James.

James nodded profusely. Sam followed the nurses into the Refinery's foyer. The doors closed behind them with a whine and click.

Sam realised that a majority of the Edward Penrose fund was diverted into the Refinery rather than the collieries. Despite its outward demeanour, the building's interior was immaculate: floors lined with nonslip linoleum, walls seamlessly tiled and grouted, no imperfections in sight. The foyer had five doors, all of which locked with key fob readers to the left of them. Sam was escorted through the door straight ahead into a wide luminous hallway where identical locked doors were spaced twenty feet apart. Open serving hatches offered glimpses into the madness that the Refinery kept hidden. A stick-thin man, his hair down to his knees, consulted feverishly with his own shadow. In another, a riled woman cradled a blanket in her arms then thrust it into her toilet. Sam kept close to Mallory and Lilith. *I don't belong here. I can't. I won't.*

It was only when Mallory glared at Sam that he realised they'd spoken to him.

'Come again?' he asked.

The matronlike woman breathed in deeply and said, 'The Refinery runs on mealtimes. Breakfast seven to ten, lunch at one, tea at six.'

'And in between?' Sam asked. He held his breath for the answer.

'Treatment,' Lilith said matter-of-factly, as if he should have known the answer.

'We'll have you settled in before your assessment,' Mallory explained. They turned onto a second wing and stopped before cell – room – seventy-one.

'Welcome home.' Lilith smiled, her mouth crooked, eyes empty.

As Sam entered, he wondered whether Lilith's lexicon had 'home' and 'prison' confused. He had a single metal bed frame in the corner by a barred window. In the opposite corner was a ceramic toilet and sink. The walls were padded with a yellowed impact foam, and a CCTV camera was mounted above the door. The Refinery didn't operate on trust.

'Cosy,' Sam quipped.

'Change, and we'll be with you in twenty.'

The door was locked shut behind them, and Sam, minus the CCTV camera, was alone. On the bed lay a bundle of stiff white pyjamas. He tore his shirt off. A foul stench rose from his armpits; he'd not showered in three days. He slipped the garbs over his thin frame. They had the rigidity of tarpaulin – to restrict any superfluous movement, he suspected. He slid his bare feet into cardboard-thin slippers, certain that he'd find many things in the Refinery, but comfort wouldn't be one of them.

There was a startling buzz, and his door swung outward. Mallory returned with a touch screen tablet in hand.

'Ready for the assessment?' she asked.

Sam nodded; he did not want to discover the consequences if he said no.

They traipsed down an assortment of identical hallways, forever white and forever devoid of patients, and descended a flight of stairs to a floor far colder and more industrial than its predecessors. A lack of windows made him presume they were underground. Mallory escorted Sam into a low-ceilinged room, its walls coated in ridged soundproof material, every surface black. There was no furniture, only a tripod, atop which a metal ball the size of Sam's head was erected. It reminded him of a plasma ball, except it wouldn't be a surprise to learn there was more than a Tesla coil inside.

'What's the assessment?' Sam asked. He rubbed his thumb against his palm; his hands were saturated with sweat.

'You've made some broad claims, Mr Bickle,' Mallory exclaimed. Her eyes raced across the tablet's screen. 'That you are a gywandras, no less.'

Of course the Refinery's employees know, Sam thought. *Everyone but us.*

'Claims?' Sam prompted.

'You didn't think we would take such a statement lightly, did you?' Mallory sneered. 'No, you're far from it. But you made a comment that sparked a few ideas. You can withdraw your imprint from your body, is that right?'

Sam was glued to the floor. He'd thought he was a step ahead of Vanessa, when in actual fact she was many ahead of him. He'd been double bluffed into another trap altogether, one that was potentially worse than the archives.

'With a little help,' Sam replied. He tried to remain stoic; he'd never let the fear show.

'Yes, we have that here too, dependency on ketamine,' Mallory said. 'But I'd imagine any hallucinogenic substance would do, wouldn't it? Yes, thought so. Alcohol too? Well, Mr Bickle, this isn't the collieries. Here you can't empty the stores of our opioids, and if you did, the repercussions wouldn't be worth it.'

Sam didn't want to listen to such dribble. He just wanted

answers, straight up.

'So you want me to withdraw?'

'Please,' Mallory said. She pulled a small box from her pocket, opened it up, and showed him two ketamine pills. 'We'll make it easy on you for your first day.'

Sam's stomach lurched, and his veins burned hot. He hadn't taken ketamine in a few days, and the sheer sight of it made him want to lunge forward and snatch them from Mallory's grip, to be in a state so far removed from reality that he'd have little care what was to follow. Any ounce of self-control, any morsel of retaliation, dissolved. He shot a hand out to the ketamine. Mallory retracted her hand a little.

'But note, we won't make a habit of this. An intoxicated mind is an unreliable one, and that just won't do for a gywandras.'

Sam caught the end of her sentence, a phrase he'd earlier dismissed as a figure of speech.

'A gywandras?'

Mallory didn't answer. She rattled the box for him to take the ketamine. He doubted such an uptight woman would allow him to crush and snort the pills, so he swallowed them in one.

The nurse navigated the controls on her tablet screen. A whir filled the room, as if an old generator had creaked to life after years of disuse. The plasma ball crackled with static. Sam's senses dulled, his body lightened, and the dark room burst with colour. His imprint spliced itself from his many nerves and ligaments. The frequency energy emitted by the plasma ball flowed strong, and he stepped out of his body –

A flash of light.

White-hot agony fried Sam's body, and he collapsed to the ground. His imprint was back in his body, and his muscles cramped. Mallory's face leered above him, distorted in the glare of the plasma ball.

'What . . .' he murmured. He couldn't enunciate, as if his face had been numbed before a dental procedure.

'Withdraw your imprint at will,' Mallory's voice echoed.

Sam's imprint crawled from his body once more. His heartbeat simmered.

Multiple flashes of white.

Unable to speak, he howled through his slack mouth. His limbs flailed and jerked. His imprint hadn't resealed connection with his body.

Mallory towered over him.

'See, Mr Bickle,' she said. 'To be a witness is a gift, and gifts should be cherished. If you didn't numb your body and mind with narcotics, you could have become more than you are. You wouldn't be lying here now, in pain, a slave to flesh. You'd be a gywandras already. But perhaps there is hope for you yet.'

Of course the Refinery wasn't a health centre; it conducted experiments the Network wouldn't allow within its caverns.

The Refinery, where people were degraded to lab rats and doomed to die before escape was possible.

A white-hot flash. A void of colour and a calamity of sound overwhelmed his senses. It all gave way to complete darkness, impenetrable silence, and utter agony.

69

IT WAS ONLY his third morning in the Refinery, but for Sam it could have been a lifetime.

Maddened howls, more animal than human, kept him awake. He lay on the hard mattress and listened to the drip-drip of his faulty toilet, his desolate room a prison cell designed to prevent sleep. He doubted the CCTV camera slept either. Cravings took hold of his body, not for food nor nicotine. Ketamine. His addictions had kept him in bad choices and poor company since 2013.

Poor company, indeed, he scathed. His treatment sessions – nonsensical torture for the straight talkers – were short but often. In a room painted coal black, the nurses submerged him into an ice-cold sensory deprivation tank. In a clinical room, acupuncture needles wired to a car battery caused his body to convulse with a torrent of radiating pain. Every day there was the plasma ball, and with each use his imprint returned to his body less and less. His reflexes were slower, he stammered when he spoke – which was little and rare – and he became bogged down with depression.

Beyond his own room were other rooms in which a myriad

of patients cried and screamed, rooms that only the white-clad staff could access. That's all the Refinery was: a compilation of spaces in which terrible events happened, of which the worst could not be seen.

The morning sun bled tangerine through the square window above his bed and cast shadows of the iron bars across the three other walls. He took caution when he rose from bed; sciatica spasmed across his lower back. Sam expected to wait at least another thirty minutes before being escorted to breakfast when the door to his cell – room – opened, and both Mallory and Lilith entered. He hadn't been blessed with both of their presences since the day he was admitted.

'Treatment first,' Mallory said. 'Breakfast as a reward.'

It took Sam longer to walk to the room, but when the plasma ball was lit up it took him less time to withdraw from his body. The nurses stopped supplying him with ketamine, but that no longer seemed to matter. Withdrawing had become his new escape, no longer weighed down by the pain or the cravings or the sluggishness and ineptitude of his body. He could withdraw farther now, able to walk – as his imprint – to the very corners of the black room, and as he looked back at Mallory and Lilith, with expressions that could only be accomplishment, he was still able to control his body. No longer did it fall to the ground as a lifeless sack of flesh, but it stayed upright and maintained its balance. If he could do that, his plan to find Rose might just work.

As Sam progressed with his ability to withdraw, Mallory and Lilith exercised more patience when he returned to his body. They let him recline against the wall whilst sensation returned to his hands and feet and waited as he sipped a sickly sweet tea. He did wonder when he'd be freed, for surely he had reached the extent of what withdrawing from a body could achieve. He dared not ask, not whilst they showed him some humanity.

Afterward, the nurses escorted Sam to the canteen, its walls insulated with deflectors; frequency energy couldn't penetrate in the communal areas. Sam sat at a plastic bench and watched Mallory skirt away. When he'd first arrived, he quickly concluded patients were mentally ill or permanently occupied. The tests he was subjected to confirmed it was both.

As Rose would surely be.

Two gents, well into their sixties, were escorted by a stout male nurse to the neighbouring table. The nurse was the youngest Sam saw there and the only one who cracked a smile at the patients – a genuine, toothy one at that. His name tag read, 'Nathan.'

'Henry, Dave, breakfast will start soon,' Nathan said in a light but authoritative tone. 'Sit tight here, and someone will come along. Good gents.'

Nathan waltzed back the way he'd come and left Henry and Dave in a dazed state.

'It collapsed,' Henry said. He'd lost weight fast; the skin on his forearms flapped like a deflated balloon. 'They're all trapped down there. They'll die if we don't help, they'll help if we die.'

'Mary's coming for tea,' Dave retorted. He quivered with onset Parkinson's. 'Should I tell her? That it's all gone?'

Henry itched his elbows and rocked back and forth. He stopped, sat upright, and grabbed Dave by his wrist. Sam deduced that another imprint spoke from within him as he said, 'What are you doing down here? This isn't a place for kids. Where are your parents?'

Sam didn't stare right at them in case he antagonised them. He'd never been a people person. Irregular eyebrows, mismatched eyes, hair of multiple colours and textures: the men were survivors of occupation. They experienced what Will had. The desire for answers overtook Sam's instincts to avoid them. He staggered from the bench he sat at and parked himself opposite the two men. Dave failed to notice him. He clenched his right earlobe and sucked on his left thumb. Henry swivelled on the bench to face Sam.

'She's an innocent woman,' he said. 'I know your type. What you want with her, and it's only ever one thing . . .'

Sam let them ramble on. He scoured his fractured memory for what he could remember of the strange events since he was admitted.

'Gywandras,' Sam uttered.

Henry fell silent. His irises grew a shade blacker, and his hands balled into fists.

Dave's shivering depleted. He addressed Sam in a cool tone. 'We all belong to the frequency.'

'This body won't do,' Henry uttered. 'It's all wrong.'

'How many bodies have you had?' Sam asked. Both men – or rather, the congregation of imprints inside them – grew tense.

'No right one in seven, no right one in seven,' Dave said.

'Because seven eight nine.' Henry cackled.

Sam sighed, as deflated as Henry looked. Sam was ravenous for answers, more so than he was for the Refinery's grey slop. Both men – or whatever imprints controlled their bodies – had recognised the word 'gywandras.' There'd been a flash in their mutated eyes, a quiver of their lips. He didn't know them well enough to navigate a coherent conversation, but he could find Rose. He took a fist of sugar cubes from a canister at the centre of the table, pocketed them, and stumbled into the halls.

The Refinery had one redeeming quality: patients were

allowed to roam the hallways between mealtimes if they were compliant in their tests. Sam had a short but opportune window to try and find his mum.

Few mulled through the halls, and he'd certainly recognise Rose amongst those who did. She was nowhere to be seen. Most of the cell doors were closed, as were the serving hatches. Sam glanced into a dozen of the open ones, met unfamiliar faces, and admitted defeat. A new plan of action.

Nathan strolled down the hallway with a locked medicine trolley. Sam approached him. What would he do – garner sympathy? The last thing he wanted was pity.

'Hey, mate, got anything for pain?' he asked. 'It's been a rough few days.'

Nathan didn't seem sure whether to smile at the news of Sam's discomfort. *Finally*, Sam thought, *someone around here with an ounce of morality*.

'Can I take your name, buddy?' Nathan asked.

'Bickle, Samuel.'

Nathan consulted a register on top of his medicine trolley and ran his finger across the table of names and room numbers. He paused, thinking he'd found Sam, then continued on. Sam caught the name Nathan had faltered on: Rose Bickle, room sixty-three. That was all he needed. Nathan looked back at Sam.

'No can do, I'm afraid,' he said.

'Got me down as a compulsive addict, eh? That's a hard label to shake.'

'You're here, aren't you? We'll have you cured in no time.'

Sweet summer child, Sam mused.

'We can only hope,' he said, and he walked away as briskly as possible in his cumbersome body. Room sixty-three. It was only a few doors down from his own.

Sam took a deep breath, ready to withdraw for the second time that day. He'd initially thought to withdraw in his room but knew that he'd be spotted by the CCTV camera mounted there. In the hallway, the CCTV cameras were at either end of the low-vaulted ceiling, and Sam, at its middle, would surely be just a blip on a security monitor. He stopped outside room sixty-three and closed his eyes. His imprint untangled itself from his body.

Unsure of whether he would be able to pass through solid matter, Sam – his imprint – dove toward Rose's cell door. A laminated medical record tacked beneath the serving hatch outlined how Rose's care demanded two nurses minimum. 'High risk,' it concluded in bold. He pressed on and leapt right through the door. As easy as that. Finally, after many years, there was Rose.

Except, she wasn't anything as Sam remembered.

Oh, her poor body, he thought. Rose's naked body was skeletal and brittle, and she turned as Sam's imprint crossed into her cell. She stumbled forward upon weak legs, wiping drool from her mouth. Liver spots and self-inflicted scars decorated the back of her hand in an intricate game of noughts and crosses. Her eyes, once sea blue, were now cement grey. One autumn, during the ten tours, Sam had happened across a deer, riddled with disease and starvation, slumped in a ravine on Bodmin Moor. He couldn't help but be reminded of that. Rose's arms were just bone, and the skin around her eyes was so sunken they may just pop from her skull. A sympathetic farmer had eventually shot the deer dead.

Rose's cell of fourteen years was decorated with a chaotic mural of crayon. A dozen various styles and subject matters were scrawled over the padded walls and provided an uncomfortable glance into her occupied mind. As Sam expected, a scribble of black represented the gywandras at the corner of the room. Many were streams of numbers, similar to those found in the Nancarrows' study.

Sam lurked closer to Rose, and as if her body were magnetised, his imprint was drawn to it, inviting him to fuse with flesh once more. If any part of Rose remained, buried inside within the dilapidated body, he'd be sure to find it. He started with his hands on hers. Weakness, the kind caused by malnourishment, coursed through his imprint. An arthritic ache niggled away at her knuckles, and so Sam's knuckles too. It was then he noticed a bruise on her arm – no, not a bruise, a tattoo of a cherub – that seeped up from underneath her skin.

Her arrhythmic heart skipped every fourth beat, a chill swept across her naked body, and she had a constant awareness of the caesarean scar, stretched into a hopeful smile, where Sam had been brought into their cold world.

Sam occupied Rose.

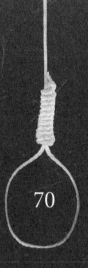

70

'WILL YOU STOP ignoring me?' Rose yelled.

Sam blinked and looked over at his mum from the passenger seat of her Beetle. He'd crossed into the ombrederi, into his own memory.

He remembered that afternoon well. He and Rose were stuck in after-school traffic. Sam had loosened his tie and unbuttoned his shirt. The unbearable summer heat left him drowsy, and he'd begun to daydream about boys – those who were certainly alive, and one who was not.

'I'm just tired,' Sam told his mother.

He had fled to the woods the previous night to find a boy he often lost to the shadows. The boy never changed clothes and didn't grow dirty, and his hair was always in a slick crew cut. In fact, over the few months since Sam had found him, he hadn't seemed to age at all.

Sam didn't know which was stranger: that the boy was most certainly a ghost, or that Sam didn't seem to mind.

'Mrs Prideaux said you've been excusing yourself to go to the toilet all day,' Rose continued.

'It's hot,' Sam lied. 'I drank a lot.'

'Don't think I can't smell cigarettes on you because I can.'

What excuse was there for that? He'd frequented the graffitied boys' bathroom every period. Tim from 10SM perched on the windowsill above the sinks and puffed his way through a pack of cigarettes.

'Skiving,' Sam had sneered that morning. Tim smiled. The next period, Tim joined Sam at the urinal and slid his hand down the waistband of Sam's trousers. Twenty minutes into fifth period, he waited for Sam by the toilet cubicle. How could he tell his mum, in the front of the stuffy Beetle with no escape? Rose was a straggler of the seventies liberal punk era, but he didn't know if she was *that* cool. A part of him screamed to tell her, to have a confidante. Surely she understood the allure boys had over him? He was also sure she understood about the dead boy in the woods — that she saw them, too.

'You talk to yourself,' Sam said. He'd caught her doing it often, usually late at night when Sam was in bed. Rose turned to him with pained eyes.

'You're mocking me. I'm not talking to you if you're going to be in one of those moods.'

'What moods?'

'That pigheaded, arrogant voice. No, you know what, you're so much like your father when you do that.'

'Well, I wouldn't know, would I?'

'You're better off for it.'

Silence. Sam and Rose both opened their mouths, decided not to speak, and closed them.

'Ghosts?' he asked.

Rose turned the ignition off and faced him. Cars bleeped their horns as they overtook her Beetle. A few blurred middle fingers passed them by.

'Sammy?' she asked. 'What have you seen?'

'People who shouldn't be there,' he croaked. 'They come out of the shadows . . .'

The summer light faded, and Sam found another room. Except, this was a room that he'd seen before, not so long ago.

A bare-bones doctor's office. A portly doctor was splayed across the wooden floor, the needle of a syringe stuck in his eye, which leaked a clear liquid. Nika stood over the lifeless body and clutched her torn hospital gown around herself. She shivered; chemotherapy had made her body thin and hairless. She hadn't felt warm since her treatment began, especially there in the presence of a dead body.

Sam circled the scene. *Impossible,* he thought. *She can't be here.*

Nika turned and looked right at Sam.

'Is it impossible?' she asked.

'How can you be here, occupying my mother? A week ago you were in Ted Lower.'

'I don't know anyone by that name,' Nika said. 'This is the first and only body I've occupied.'

She was agitated; Nika didn't want to be there at all.

'The ability to transcend time through emotional connectedness,' Will had warned James. Nika hadn't, in her own timeline, occupied Ted. It begged the question, one that Sam yearned to have answers for.

'Why are you occupying Mum?' Sam said. 'Are you trying to transcend?'

'Transcendence? No, never,' she spat. 'It's an abomination. I didn't want this. Becoming dasfurvya is a last defence.'

'Dasfurvya?'

'To be reborn into a new body. He doesn't know . . .'

'All those symbols you've drawn on the wall,' Sam said. 'They're dates, aren't they?'

'Coordinates,' Nika confirmed. 'Unreliable coordinates, frankly, but it's the best Abidemi has.'

'Abi?'

'If the dasfurvya doesn't succeed, then Abidemi has to instigate the unthinkable.'

'Which is what?'

'A gywandras of our own.'

Sam didn't like that idea. He nodded.

'Just tell me, please,' Sam said. 'Where is she now? Where's Mum's imprint?'

'I wasn't meant to be in her body this long,' Nika stammered. 'But then the Network locked her up here and –'

'Where is she?'

'She couldn't make it to the frequency. The occupation whittled her imprint down . . .'

An absolute death.

'No,' Sam said, and beyond his mother's body his own came back to him. Warm tears rolled down his face. 'But I thought . . .' He didn't understand why he confessed to Nika. Perhaps it was because she occupied the remains of his mother. 'I thought that maybe I'd see her one more time.'

'There are traces of her still circulating this brain. It might be failing, but there are memories, and every one has you in it.'

'Leave her body,' Sam begged. 'Give her dignity in death and let her go.'

Nika stared on. He worried she wouldn't comply.

'I want to, believe me,' she cried. 'But there are dampeners in these walls. If I leave this body whilst still inside the Refinery, I won't make it either.'

A jolt coursed through Rose's body, and the irregular heartbeat and lethargy was snatched from Sam's senses.

71

SAM WOKE in the Refinery's hallway, in his own body, damp with his own sweat and tears. Beside him, an EMP rotated to a standstill on the tiled floor. Mallory and Nathan towered over him, faces black against the ceiling lights. They said nothing for the longest time; Mallory twirled her tablet stylus between her fingers as if deciding which punishment to inflict upon him.

'Her body,' Sam slurred. He crawled to Rose's cell door. His arms were heavy, and his mind was slow. 'It's empty. She's gone.'

Sam reached into his pocket with an unsteady hand and ate the sugar cubes. When the sugar hit his system and the post-withdrawal fatigue subsided, Mallory asked, 'Can you walk?'

Sam used the wall to steady himself and tried to climb to his feet. His body trembled, unable to make sense of gravity in that moment. Nathan slid beside him and propped Sam up with an arm. He steered Sam toward his cell.

'No,' Mallory said. 'To the basement.'

'No!' Sam yelled. He thrashed against Nathan's grip. 'I'm staying here. Her body, her body . . .'

'Where, exactly?' Nathan asked Mallory. He ignored Sam's blows as if he didn't feel them at all.

'The cradle,' Mallory said. 'It is time to meet the dasfurvya.'

72

THE UNLIKELY TRIO was buzzed through a door at the end of the hallway and paced down an iron spiral staircase into the basement levels. By the bottom of the stairs, Sam's imprint reattached to his body enough to walk without support, so Mallory sent Nathan off to finish his meds round.

Mallory and Sam continued to subzero-two. Red brick walls, the foundation of the Refinery itself, shone in the white strobe lights. The air carried dampness, and the wind screeched from outside. They passed a cluster of mixed-sex nurses who all stared at him with the same steely expression. Another door opened, this time by a keypad, and Mallory led him into a circular chamber. At its centre stood a bulbous machine from which wires spouted out at six regular intervals. Each bundle of wires snaked outward to one of six beds. No, Sam realised as he tread closer through the dim lit room, they were not beds, but coffins: four-foot-high tin boxes with copper lids latched to mechanised hinges.

'Wait,' Mallory told Sam. She joined a straight-backed technician by the machine. They conferred amongst themselves and looked over data on tablets. The door behind them opened again; a ginger woman and a bespectacled amputee entered, each accompanied by a nurse. They were led to each of their own coffins – *beds, they're just beds*. The door opened again, and three timid female patients were escorted to the last three beds. Mallory circled around them whilst the technician consulted a panel on the central machine. It whirred to life. Sam's coffin was close enough to the screen that he could see a crawling bar measured in newtons: the machine generated an electromagnetic power source. Sam turned back to Mallory as she said, 'You will simply have to climb into your cradles and lie still. You may experience visions, emotional stimuli. Don't let it worry you.'

'What does it do?' Sam asked. The nurses' stares burned through him. Mallory raised her eyebrows as if to make a sarcastic remark. Sam was sick of finding out the effects of their equipment only once he was under their influence. 'No, what does it do? We have every right to know.'

'It measures your witnessing capabilities against others,' Mallory explained. 'A reactive process as your minds come into contact with those similar and those different to yourself. From there, we know how maladjusted you may be and what further treatment you will need here on out.'

The spiel didn't ease the patients' confusion. Mallory gestured with her hands, the way a vicar addresses their Sunday service, and invited the patients into their cradles. The other five were aided by their respective nurses. Thankfully, Mallory dared not assist Sam into his. He lifted his heavy legs into the cradle and lowered himself down. The tin was ice-cold, and only a thin yoga mat cushioned his sore spine from the metal base. Mallory's face loomed over him.

'Patients in position,' she confirmed to the technician.

The last thing Sam saw before the copper lid creaked shut

and spelled him into darkness was Mallory's thin smile and her empty black eyes.

A thin strip of yellow light puckered at the edges of the lid, lighter than the sensory deprivation tank had been. The generator's revolving sound was distant. The copper lid clattered on the lips of the coffin.

Sam's body lightened. The darkness pulled him into sleep. His sciatica eased. Cravings for alcohol and worse subsided. Instead, hunger wrenched at his gut – a sensation he'd not experienced in a very long time. His head itched. He reached out, his limbs lighter than they'd been before, and in his fist was a plume of long scraggly hair – not the short, thin mess he'd sported when he'd lain down in the coffin. It wasn't his body.

He was in someone else's.

The copper lid rattled. A riptide of fatigue. The cradle grew smaller, and the cold tin sides pressed against Sam's arms – the arms of whatever body he was in next. The electromagnet's swoop intensified. His left shin itched. He reached down to it, only for his hand to meet the gym mat beneath him. His heart detonated in his chest. The hand he used clutched at the rubber mat, and his fingers brushed over the roundness of an amputated knee.

Sam laid the foreign body back to the ground. His head hit the mat, and metal slid down his nose. He reached out. Spectacles. A wedding band sat on his right third finger. Sam ran a hand across his head: a short buzz cut. He reached out with arms far more muscular than his own and pounded on the copper lid.

'Stop this!' said a strange voice. His words, but not his voice.

The sound of the loop generator beat faster, and Sam's

senses numbed as if it were a mechanical lullaby. He wondered if he'd ever make it back to his own body.

A mechanical whine. Yellow light danced around the coffin as Sam opened his eyes. Mallory's shadow hung over him. He licked the insides of his teeth and found his chipped bottom left cuspid. Never had he been so relieved to find himself back in his own body.

He sat up. A spasm shot through his lower back, but he couldn't think on it. He pushed Mallory back and flailed from the coffin onto the brick floor. His arms and legs seemed to be connected to the wrong part of his brain, like wires in a parallel circuit.

'That wasn't a measurement,' Sam slurred.

'No?' Mallory asked as she straightened out her uniform. The technician came by, a tablet and stylus in hand. Around him, the other patients ambled from their tin boxes. The man with one leg got to his foot and found balance with his crutches. He looked up, eyes fearful, and found Sam. They understood what the other experienced.

'You're reverse engineering the dasfurvya,' Sam growled.

Mallory wrote on her tablet, eyes glued to the screen.

He had lost all that meant anything to him, and brutally too, because of the experiments the Network conducted at the hands of awry witnesses who wanted to achieve a being greater than human. He was motherless and friendless, trapped in a place worse than a prison.

Only, his captors had taught him the key to escape.

He'd learnt to occupy other bodies.

Mallory grabbed him by the arm and escorted him from the room. His eyes lay on her keycard, strapped to the lanyard around her neck. Grief made Sam think before he spoke, and with that he had become observant. He'd noticed, with himself and other compliant patients, cell doors were automatically opened between lunch and tea. It meant beyond the patients' living quarters was a security room chockablock with CCTV screens and computers that could open any door. Every nurse, Mallory included, wore a lanyard with a keycard attached. The Refinery, akin to the Network, used keycards to log witnesses into computers and grant access to software.

Sam stumbled through the basement levels alongside Mallory. His eyes never left her keycard. He was weak, body still tingling where his imprint was returning to it. Mallory was a bull of a woman, and there was no way he could overpower her to take her keycard.

There was, however, withdrawal.

Mallory had taken her time to confer with the technician. The four other patients were already upstairs. The hallway was desolate bar Sam and Mallory. He hadn't seen one CCTV camera below ground level. It was time, or never at all.

Sam stopped to clutch the wall. He rubbed his head and shook his arms. Mallory supported his elbow.

'You shouldn't have eaten all that sugar, Bickle,' she snarled. 'Take a moment.'

With her taloned hand on his arm, withdrawal was quick. He let his imprint slide from his body and propel into hers.

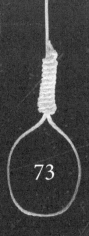

73

A DARK ROOM. He hadn't successfully fused with Mallory's body. He'd slipped into the ombrederi, a cold and desolate place.

'Did you think it would be that easy?' Mallory said, except there was more than one voice.

Sam turned. Mallory's imprint wasn't alone. Fused with others, an ensemble of many hands and faces were bound to her. It was as Trish had described Vanessa's imprint the day that Abidemi was trialled. Now Sam understood. She was dasfurvya, too. Sam would no longer be surprised if most of the board and the Refinery's nurses had all been reborn in bodies not their own.

'What number body is this?'

Mallory – if that was her original name at all – filled the space. The imprints imbedded within her writhed and struggled as they tried to break free.

'Nine, I believe. When you've come as far as I have, well, all bodies feel the same. It's all flesh, dirty and heavy.'

'All the occupations –'

'Weren't us. No matter how much you'll dislike it, you will

be dasfurvya, Bickle. The frequency will turn against us.'

Sam's heartbeat thudded in his chest, distant but there. With his mind firmly in the ombrederi, Sam raised his arms in the physical.

'That's what the Refinery is,' he continued. 'It's not treatment, and it's not experimentation. They're all here, all the ones ever occupied, hidden away so you can keep dasfurvya to yourselves.'

'Not everyone can be post-human, nor should they.'

'Being reborn isn't about living forever, then? It's to become something more.'

'A gywandras, for all of time.'

'More than one gywandras,' Sam concluded.

'So, Mr Bickle, are you going to return to your flesh cage?'

'I already have.'

Sam released himself from the ombrederi.

74

SAM THRUST himself back into his body. He tore the lanyard from Mallory's neck and stepped away. Her hand shot up and grabbed his arm. She'd returned.

'I don't think so,' she said.

With his right hand, Sam scooped the remains of the sugar in his pocket and threw the granules into Mallory's eyes. She released Sam and rubbed her eyes. Sam scarpered as fast as was possible on his jellied legs and climbed the spiral staircase. Mallory was just steps behind, hands outstretched to feel for the bannister.

'You can't escape the frequency,' Mallory cried. 'You can't deny the gywandras.'

'The fuck I can,' Sam stammered. He reached the door, swiped Mallory's keycard against the sensor, went through, swiped again, and it was locked. He knew he didn't have long. He had come out halfway down the hall, and it was vacant, but he only had until one of the nurses heard Mallory thump against the steel door or the technician came up for lunch.

Sam plunged Mallory's lanyard into his pocket and darted right to the staff quarters. He imagined that the security room would be off from the reception, if anywhere. Without hesitation or the want to check where the CCTV cameras were pointed, Sam swiped himself into the reception area. It was, as were most of the rooms in the Refinery, vacant. Who'd want to visit if they could? Sam thought.

The door Sam needed was the third along: *Security – Staff only*.

With a swipe of Mallory's keycard, he lumbered into the security room. There was one black-clad guard on duty, his hand half outstretched to the walkie-talkie on the desk. Sam's imprint fled his body and seeped into the security guard.

Sam opened his eyes – no, not his, but the security guard's. His lean arms shook as he leant toward the computer monitors and navigated through different menus. It was the same software used in the collieries for remote access: RemoteKey. The program required another scan of the keycard. Security-Sam swiped the card against the reader, and he was in. A multilayered three-dimensional map popped up. It highlighted over a hundred doors – all red. All locked. He clicked the button 'Open All.' An access window sprung up and asked for clearance from Vanessa. Plan B. Sam scoured the map and clicked multiple times to dismiss dialogue boxes. He opened each locked cell door and a string of fire exits to create the most efficient route from the wing to its closest exit.

A trail of go-green lit up the hallways of the east wing. Security-Sam stared intently at the monitor. A heat signature trailed from room twenty-one, then another from forty-three, and a flood of purple heat signatures swarmed out of their cells toward the reception. The prisoners were free.

An alarm boomed. Sam snapped from the security guard's body back into his own. He stumbled into the reception. The double doors were open, and the patients, all with varying degrees of dasfurvya transformation, bounded toward the open front doors in a bid for freedom.

It occurred to Sam – *where will they go?* There'd be no hiding from the Network. It seemed the dasfurvya had their own ideas.

Mallory, Lilith, and a band of nurses barged out of the door opposite the security room.

'Stop!' Mallory commanded. She threw herself in amongst the dasfurvya. 'There'll be consequences. Don't make it harder on yourselves.'

The horde of patients stopped in their tracks. They all turned their heads at once, as if they were all remote-controlled puppets. They leapt at the nurses – punching, kicking, and biting. The nurses were silenced one by one until all that could be heard was Mallory, and then she was quiet forever.

Good riddance, Sam thought. *Nine lifetimes too many*.

Satisfied with their revenge, the dasfurvya retreated away from the four nurses' bodies and strode for him. His post-withdrawal legs wouldn't outrun the dasfurvya. What words were there for occupied people who had spent years being tortured?

The crowd accumulated in the reception, and Dave strode forward. He'd changed so much since their conversation in the dining room: his skin smooth, hair dark, eyes blue. He was familar in a strange way. Dave, and yet not.

Not-Dave reached out a hand and said, 'No need to stand there, Sam. There's work to do before the gywandras arrives.'

INTERLUDE IV

THE BARBARY PIRATES chase Ewella and Kyauta across the choppy waters and near with tremendous pace. The duo thrust their oars into the water with all their might as the night dies around them. The wild country fills their vision, but it isn't close enough.

Ewella dares not look back at her former captors. She fears the next time she does the whites of their eyes will be plain as day. An earlier head count told her there are six of them. After the murder of Kyauta's rapist, there will be bloodlust amongst the pirates – lust for her and Ky's blood, to be precise. The very thought makes her row faster.

With an exasperated shout and nod, Kyauta directs Ewella's attention to a cove ahead in the green-orange sunrise – the very same spot where the crew docked their dingy to kidnap Ewella.

'Not far!' she shouts. Ky yells with glee.

Kyauta paddles with velocity, leant forward in his seat. Their chasers' oars are synchronised, efficient, fast.

The underside of Ewella and Kyauta's dingy snags the seabed. They throw their oars down, scramble up from their seats, and jump into the water. The surface comes to Ewella's abdomen. She does not register the cold – numb from the crisp night air or the adrenaline of the chase, she is not sure. Kyauta holds her forearm to support her in the water, and they wade onto the pebble beach and bolt inside a cave, its mouth a brutal slit on the rock face.

The darkness suffocates them. They trip and amble their way over stones and find places to hide. Ewella tries to control her breath. A nettle-like tingle scuttles across her arms and neck, and she knows she is in the company of the dead. There is a vengeful aura in the cave.

A crunch of gravel. Ewella peeks over the rock she hides behind. The pirates enter, torches in hand. The tallest shouts anxious words in his native tongue. A stone is thrown – the size of a man's head – and lands by their feet. A second strikes the tall man down. More come. The rocks rise from the ground, held by nothing but air. A second man – a toothless runt – is flung sideways. He slams to the ground and is dragged past Ewella and Kyauta into the deepest blackest pits of the cave. His screams are silenced.

The barbary pirates abandon their torches and scarper to the boats, two into each dingy.

Ewella smiles at Kyauta. He looks back at her with horror. She rises, steps over to him, and holds out a hand.

'No,' he says, trembling with fear.

'Isle,' she responds. She points upward.

She steps out into the fresh sea air, sure Ky will follow. She savours the very fact she stands on still land.

The duo climbs the cliff whilst the sun wakes. Ewella's

shins cramp and her back aches. At the top of the cliff, the path back to the village is clear. She stays a little ahead of Ky. Girls disappearing, whispers of dark men from foreign lands: the Kernewek won't welcome him.

Ewella's pace quickens as they enter a cluster of trees. Smoke hangs in the air, the way it does when the village fires are lit for winter. As they break through the very last of the branches, she stops dead in her tracks. The sky is polluted with brown smoke that billows from houses on fire. Horse-backed soldiers zigzag amongst burnt homes. Pistols gleam in their hands as they herd terrified locals toward a hanging frame. Ewella won't be welcomed back, not when it is occupied by Britons.

Fear solidifies in Kyauta's face. He steps back into the tree line. Ewella follows. Her heart thumps a hole out of her chest, and tears sting her eyes. She remembers the burning huts in Ebok's memory and understands Ky's discomfort.

Ewella takes Ky's hand and leads him farther into the woodland until the ransacking of her home is no longer seen nor heard. Concealed by overgrown thickets and the lip of a steep cliff, it is as safe a place as any.

'Who?' he manages to say and points toward the village. 'Who?'

Ewella is not confident enough to try and explain the story with words alone. She plucks a twig from the dirt and draws simplistic stick figure representations of herself and her family into the dry soil: parents larger, females with triangles of curtain hair. She points to each in turn.

'Me, Ewella. Mother. Father. Jory. Meraud. Baby Chesten.'

She scrawls what resembles a Briton soldier.

'Briton. Soldier. Bad.'

She points to a pistol in the Briton's hand. She had never

seen one herself, but she knows the story well. She knows what the pistol did to her father's body. Ewella carves a line through the drawing of her father. She can't stop and scratches out the entire picture. Kyauta grabs her wrist and pries the branch from her grasp. He takes her other hand in his.

'Kyauta. Sorry. Ewe . . .' He stumbles with the consonants. He glances at the drawing of the ruined family, the deceased father, and instead calls her, 'Abidemi.'

He is sympathetic; she does not need to be told the word means grief. She knows there is more to come – it happens now, the other side of the woods. She rubs her eyes to console her tears and evade her fatigue. They rowed and ran and climbed over the last four hours, and now as they rest Ewella is aware of how tired she's become. Kyauta's eyes are heavy and weary.

'We can sleep here,' she says. She mimes sleep with her hands and pats a flat area of moss between the tangle of tree roots. 'When we've slept we'll eat and drink.'

They lie down. The spongy soil eases her tightly coiled back, better than any straw mattress. They lie there a while, unable to sleep, but even the physical rest is enough; the fire around her hips subsides. Cormorants and blue tits chirp in the canopy above them, and apart from the occasional shout from the village and the hunger that growls within their stomachs, the coastline is silent.

'When this is over, we'll go to the village,' Ewella says. 'They'll fear you at first, but there's building work to be done, and when they see you're kind and ready to help, they'll accept you.'

Ewella knows Kyauta barely understands what she says, yet he looks at her and grins. Hope is a wonderful thing.

A rustle of leaves. Heavy stomps. Kyauta drops his smile.

Ewella rights herself and crawls through the undergrowth. Feet away, on the outskirts of the thicket, an armoured man stops by a tree, his cock out to piss on a berry bush. A sky-blue tunic juts out beneath his chest plate. He is a Parliamentarian: a group intent on stealing Kernew from the Royalists.

The worser of two British evils, Ewella thinks.

She recedes. A branch cracks beneath her knee. The Parliamentarian snaps his head in her direction. He points and shouts words she does not know. Ewella backs away and takes Ky by the hand. Footsteps rush at them from all sides. Ewella is struck on the temple. She falls to the ground. Ky is tackled by two men twice his size and pushed beside her. The soldiers shout in a queer mix of fear and fascination.

Ewella and Kyauta have their hands bound and are wrenched up onto their feet. Blood trickles from the aching wound on Ewella's forehead. She counts six men in all. They are pushed and pulled through the trees. One man with an unpleasant sharp nose snaps a branch from a fallen tree and prods Kyauta with it. Ky's eyes are wide with fear, and his cheeks flush with shame. The soldier Ewella caught pissing bears a pistol. She had never seen one up close before but learns that it was aptly described to her: it bears a phallic quality, phallic and cunning.

On the outskirts of the trees are the soldiers' horses, all strong and athletic steeds compared to those seen around the village. Oh, the village – smoke settles into opaque plumes. All that is left is stone and ash.

The soldier who found them shouts. She does not know English, only Kernewek and a little Nigerian. His words are abrupt and harsh; it must be an order.

He grabs her bound wrists, laces a rope from them to his steed's saddle, and mounts. One of his fellow soldiers does the same with Kyauta. He kicks the horse into submission and canters toward the village. She is forced to sprint. Her legs are unused and her stomach unfed; she has neither the agility nor the stamina. She trips, facedown in the sun-baked soil, and is dragged behind the horse. Stones tear her skin. Dust grates her windpipe.

The horse slows, and her short journey ends. Hands bound, legs ravaged, Ewella struggles to rise. She tries to keep her face blank of emotion – the Britons do not deserve more. A mass of kneeling villagers sharpens into view. She recognises familiar faces – neighbours, the blacksmith, a butcher – but cannot find her family. Amidst the terrorised locals is a hanging frame where three limp grey bodies sway in the breeze. Ewella's heart stops.

Soldiers sigh with disbelief at the sight of Kyauta. He failed to run and is dragged up beside Ewella. Village folk scream and recoil.

'Kyauta,' she mumbles.

A Briton untangles a whip from his belt and strikes the dirt beside Ewella.

'Be good,' she says to Ky. 'Don't fight.'

The lightning crack of a whip, but this time it strikes Ewella's thigh. Instant fire.

She watches on, defiant, and dares to catch a soldier's eye and scare them into submission with her bravery. They are too intent upon their conversation. There will be no innocence in their plans, Ewella realises, as many gesture to the empty nooses that sway alongside the dead. Some fondle the pistols strung to their belts. *The pistols*, Ewella thinks. *I beg you, a quick death for a sweet boy.*

Kyauta's fate is decided. Two broad soldiers step forward and drag Ky from the ground. They tug his rope and lead him to the hanging frame. He struggles a little. An impatient Briton strikes him with their whip.

Ewella yanks at the rope connecting her to the horse. It comes loose. She hobbles to her feet and propels forward at tremendous speed. She collides into Kyauta's back. They hit the dirt. She tenses her body around him – a flesh shield. The soldiers tug at her rags, but she is entangled around Ky. Burns ripple across her back as she is struck by the whip. The pain rattles her body. Two soldiers dive forward and pry her from him.

Ewella and Ky are thrust beneath the hanging frame and propped up onto logs by the soldiers. Nooses wrap around their necks. Villagers scream – *not a child, not a maiden!* – but it only fills the Britons with intent. A soldier steps forward and kicks the log out from under Ky. Ewella diverts her eyes to the ground, on Ky's shadow as it flails. With all the courage she can muster, she looks up and finds, and only concentrates upon, Kyauta's eyes as they dim. He manages to mutter, with his last breath, 'Abidemi.'

Life and pain and recognition fall from his face. He is still.

The world upturns as the log is kicked out from under Ewella. Her throat tightens in a tug-of-war between rope and gravity. Tendons pop and vertebrae crack. She gulps for air. It comes to her mouth, to tempt her, but no further. Pain slides away, and the heat of the summer's day dwindles. Only a tingle remains, as though she swarms with thousands of fleas, and the world around Ewella darkens with an early night.

Article: 27

In order for the Imprint Activity Network to shield the public from imprints, it is imperative that the organisation remains covert. It is strongly recommended that witnesses, practising and retired, refrain from disclosing their role within the Network; the Network's existence; and the work it undertakes. An rise in public awareness of our activity increases risks similar to the Chenoweth incident*.

*On 7th July 20023, ex-witness Patrick Chenoweth involved his wife (a non-seer) in an experiment with an imprint that led to her death.

PART TEN

DOWN AND DEEPER

75

RASHA DECIDED to fight.

It was the third evening after Trish's midnight visit. She and Haya sat at their dining room table and studied diligently, as they had every night since Trish's warning. Haya stumbled over consonants with a textbook given to Rasha by Gorenn Comprehensive. Rasha half paid attention to her homework as she watched Haya over the lip of her history textbook. Her mother made huge leaps of progress, not that Rasha was completely surprised; Haya was the sharpest person Rasha knew. Haya coughed, sipped the dregs of her tea, stretched, checked the clock – 7:15 – then returned to her work. Rasha analysed her in the meek light of their Cornish Hospice lamp, one she'd mended herself. Haya frowned as she worked, the lines on her forehead age's language: the history of a grief-stricken forty-three-year-old. The lamplight caught her gaunt cheekbones and thin hair. Why did no one discuss the horror of a mother's physical demise, made withered and brittle by age like seaworn jetsam? Joel had a mother too, did he not? She must have grown frail too once she'd learnt her son died.

Not letting her dark thoughts fester, Rasha returned to her

textbook. She read up on the siege of Troy, where ballistae were draped with soaked horse hides in protection from flaming arrows. Since then it had, by way of oral minstrelsy and numerous translated texts, become the myth of the great Trojan horse that held Greek soldiers in its wooden belly to get beyond Troy's walls. Constantly turning Kasey's occupation over in her mind, and never far away from Joel, Rasha couldn't help but draw parallels to the Trojan horse.

That night Rasha endured a disturbed sleep, dreaming of a burning car that hurtled down a tree-strewn hillside. Half awake, she rose with Haya in the morning. Her mother escorted her to the caravan park gates to greet the school bus. Haya hadn't questioned the new routine and put it down to Rasha's anxiety of taking public transport.

Haya waved at Rasha as the bus pulled away. The morning before, children had teased Rasha for having Haya walk her to the bus stop. Today the children were concerned over other matters.

'I heard he can't toss himself off now,' said a pigtailed girl from the seat in front of Rasha.

'Don't be a pillock, Shan. He still has his other hand,' her friend responded as she drew a cock in the steam on the bus window. 'His kids might come out one-handed, though. Genetics.'

Fred and his severed hand made the wildfire gossip that gripped the school, hence Fred no longer taking the bus. Rasha hadn't seen Fred herself. The whispers informed her that he'd been reduced to a gag in which old friends would scare their peers with the monstrous stump on his right hand. Girls dared not put him at the centre of their lust. All he'd once been – and still was, minus four fingers – had disappeared from public consciousness in the mishap with the saw. *Because of me*, Rasha thought. For all the bad she had put out into the world, Rasha was determined to do some good.

She had to wait for third period to be in the workshop. Her classmates were on the final stages of their wooden LED lamps. The brief was simplistic: a wooden lamp to house an LED bulb. Hers was an ode to her trip to the Lost Gardens of Heligan, and now her space within the greater ombrederi. Inspired by that day, Rasha carved the base into a myriad of engravings. It depicted Cornish flowers that she'd found in Heligan, and acacias and brugmansias and bechsonarias tapered around the base.

Her delight simmered when Cridland came over to her desk. He smiled when he saw the end product. It turned Rasha's stomach.

'Good to see that you have turned your attitude around,' he said. 'I knew you weren't so easily influenced.'

Rasha remained silent and glared at Cridland. He turned on his heel and told off a table of girls for internet shopping on their phones. Her anger got the better of her. A monster roamed amongst children two decades after he'd murdered one in cold blood, and it couldn't go on any longer.

Rasha reached beneath her desk, withdrew the EMP from her rucksack, and planted the device into her trouser pocket. She scurried to the vacant storeroom, made sure Cridland hadn't seen, and closed the door. She took out the EMP and looked over its controls; the power button was clearly labelled. She took a deep breath, readied herself for the onslaught that would follow, and turned the EMP off.

Frequency energy slapped at her full force and pricked her skin. In an instant, Joel emerged amongst the shelves – a broken doll remembered by a sadistic chant whilst his murderer walked free. She wasn't scared of Joel anymore.

The living horrified her more than the dead ever had.

Joel stumbled closer. Rasha regurgitated the anger she'd felt the last time she controlled Joel: at Fred and friends bullying their helpless peers, at Cridland as he prowled amongst a school of children.

Agony fired through her limbs, back taut as if the discs in her spine had collapsed. She had control of Joel.

Rasha raced to the door and peered into the classroom. Cridland ambled back to his desk. Sitting was best whilst Rasha forced occupation onto him.

Would the plan work? She couldn't be sure, but it was the only justice suitable that Rasha could think of which didn't end in violence. If Joel's imprint could fuse with Cridland's body long enough to run to the headmaster's office and confess the teacher's sins, then it was a decent plan.

Cridland lowered himself into his chair. Rasha had to act fast – she couldn't hold Joel's imprint for long. She imagined Joel walking toward Cridland, and Joel passed through the storeroom into the classroom as if the walls were projections, headed straight for Cridland, his broken arms outstretched. The woodworks teacher looked forward, straight at Joel. He couldn't see him, but he seemed to sense the dead boy. *Maybe*, Rasha thought, *a bond ties murderer and their victims together in life and death.*

Joel reached Cridland. Rasha thought hard. *Occupy him, occupy him.*

The imprint grabbed Cridland's head with his disjointed hands. Rasha's heart palpitated – he might've snapped the teacher's neck. He didn't. The imprint pressed his head against Cridland's brow and disappeared.

Joel occupied Cridland.

Cridland's body slumped in his seat, head bowed. He

could have slept, and the class supposed so, too. One by one, they whipped out their phones and Snapchatted and tweeted their teacher. Rasha squeezed the cupboard's doorframe. She wondered if Joel tormented Cridland from within the ombrederi. *What if Joel killed him?* Cridland was close to retirement; the odds of a heart attack were great. Death was an easy way out. It wasn't justice. Joel seemed to agree.

Cridland's body jerked in his seat. He stumbled up, legs bowed as if they were broken, arms limp at his sides. There was no way that Joel could manoeuvre the heavy body to the headmaster's office.

The class rose from their desks, utterly horrified, their phones still locked on Cridland as he waltzed amidst the desks. Rasha betted that some of them were streaming live, too. All Rasha and Joel had to do was have the teacher confess.

Cridland let out a yell and crumpled to the floor. He rolled and convulsed, kicked and shook, and then he opened his mouth and cried, 'I killed Joel Tredethy! I killed Joel Tredethy!'

At the back of the class, Gregory Dingle bolted through the fire exit. The rest of their cohort continued to record and take photos. Tens of videos probably circulated social media, and as soon as their family and friends recognised Joel's name, Rasha knew it'd spread like wildfire.

76

JOEL DEPARTED Mr Cridland's body before Gregory returned with the head of Design and Technology, Mr Pritchard. As soon as his imprint vanished into the dusty air, Cridland came to and clambered to his feet. He was pale and dared not look anyone in the eye. Police and paramedics were called.

'It was just a seizure,' Mr Pritchard told the class.

The unruly children were told to depart to lunch early. Rasha was one of the last to pack her things. Mr Pritchard escorted Cridland to a chair. As she passed, the pair locked eyes. Did he know Rasha was involved? Cridland could have looked into Joel, as Rasha had looked into Will the night of Kasey's occupation.

Her stomach was lighter, free of anxiety, when she crossed into the playground. Rasha was certain Joel would never plague her again. Sirens hurried through the air. It was out of her hands now.

Not wanting to spend her twenty extra minutes in a bathroom, Rasha found an empty IT suite. She logged on to a computer and opened her internet browser to find Sam and

Trish staring back at her from a thumbnail.

The thumbnail didn't have their faces, exactly, but warped E-FITs from a local news article that read, 'Two Suspects Wanted for South Cornwall Murder.'

Rasha pulled her chair closer to the desk and flicked through the article. It described the elderly care home, Angove Lodge, where Ted lost his life. Two people had entered with false identities and butchered the old man. That was where the details went awry. It didn't mention a third – for James had been there that night, as Rasha understood it – and of course the paper wouldn't have reported anything paranormal even if they'd been told it.

Vanessa and the board. They'd promised to conceal Trish and Sam's connection to Ted's death but had instead used it to eradicate them as threats.

Is that what happens to people who know too much? Rasha wondered.

Rasha logged out, collected her things, and raced from the IT suite. Trish was in hiding and probably didn't have internet; she wouldn't know. Rasha wasn't sure if her foresight, along with the receptor, reached Gorenn from wherever she was hidden. There was only one way to be sure.

Rasha darted back through the playground. If she detonated the EMP, she'd need to be high above any of the school's electronic equipment. Rasha had watched the boys in her year climb to the DT department's roof to retrieve their awry footballs many a time. She copied their route – onto the general waste bins, up the brackets that held the dust collection chute to the wall – and heaved herself onto the flat roof. The building was only one storey, so she hoped that would be high enough to send a message far and wide.

Rasha traipsed to the centre of the roof. She withdrew

the EMP from her bag. Her stomach sunk. The device had been off since Joel occupied Cridland. Her mind hadn't been protected for a good half an hour. Allah knows the thoughts she projected, who heard them first. She'd been so intent helping Joel get his revenge that she hadn't remembered to turn it on again.

She wasn't sure if she could reach for Trish, but it was the only thing she could think of. If the police caught up with Trish there'd be no one left to stop the Network. The gywandras would roam, and occupations would continue.

Rasha pinched the power dial on the bug-like contraption and turned it up as high as it could go. The frequency energy seethed around her, and Rasha thought of Trish's warm face and many different hairstyles. She recollected Shauna, the sister Trish desperately sought after, and envisioned the Calypso in Sleep's farmyard.

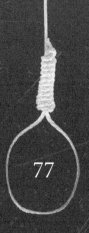

77

RASHA HIT the floor of Calypso's sky-blue saloon. Trish sat at the kitchen table in near darkness, the blinds drawn. She supposed that it was a memory until she saw the clock on the wall above Trish: quarter past twelve. It was the present.

Rasha wasn't the only one there who shouldn't have been. At first she thought the imprint was the gywandras, but it wasn't black at all – in fact, it was the furthest thing from empty. It had multiple faces and many hands and arms: at least ten entities conjoined as one. One face shone stronger than the others: Vanessa.

She must have locked onto Rasha's signal. She'd revealed Trish's hiding place.

'Run!' Rasha screamed. Trish jumped to her feet and looked square at Rasha. 'They know where you are! Run!'

Trish bolted from the Calypso, and the scene was lost in a whirl of colour, as was Rasha. An immense panic stirred Rasha's gut, as if she was the sea and tides lapped at her intestines.

The rugged Cornish countryside flashed before her, on top of which staggered a mass of misshapen people and –

'Sam!' she cried out. Sam conferred with the contorted people. They all wore white uniforms, some dirtied, some bloodied.

The world lifted from under her feet, and a cliff top towered above her, where a horde of people surrounded a lighthouse. They had mismatched eyes, patchwork hair – Frankenstein's monsters with knitted facial features.

'Dasfurvya!' a hundred voices cried out.

They eroded to a heap of ash, and Rasha sunk into the ombrederi's inky space, down and deeper.

78

THE NIGHT'S cold wind startled Rasha. The sky was a fierce pink, the rooftop dewy around her.

Her father impaled by a steel girder.

No, this wasn't Syria. It was very much Cornwall, and as she remembered more, she realised, *I've put Trish in danger.*

She raised herself from the ground and felt in the near dark for the EMP. The dial was on, the analogue screen dead; she'd run the battery dry. Trish had once said witnesses projected in their sleep as their subconsciousness came to the forefront. She'd been without an EMP for at least nine hours. She needed to move.

I must get home.

Flashlights swept across the playground. Four, maybe five. She dove back onto the roof and strained her ears for scraps of conversation. Due to the lateness of the hour, the people below were either a friendly search party or the Network, but there was no way to know for certain. Rasha thought of Joel, and he materialised by her side. She closed her eyes and connected to him.

Joel leapt from the roof. Flashes of faces came to Rasha as

Joel coursed through the strangers: a brute of a man and a bug-eyed woman, all whom Rasha did not recognise. But the third face she did: Leri. The Network knew she was alone. She'd projected after all. Trish would be in trouble too. She needed to get home before she could attempt to make contact. Haya would be worried.

Rasha thought over the school's layout and concocted a plan. All the flashlights were grouped at the eastern side: the playground, tennis courts, and gymnasium. If Rasha climbed down from the roof on the western side and stayed away from the lit car park, she could cut through the alleyway between the English and history buildings under the cover of night. There was a taxi rank two minutes away in town – maybe one at a sprint. It was as good a plan as any.

As silently as Rasha could, she gathered up the EMP and her rucksack and shuffled along the roof on all fours to its western edge, then lowered herself onto a windowsill. The gutter broke with a snap, and Rasha slammed into the bushes below. She froze, ears turned toward the awry witnesses.

A barrage of footsteps echoed across the playground.

'Over there!' a witness cried.

Rasha sprung up, untangled herself from the bushes, and hobbled down the alley with a bruised ankle. Her stalkers' flashlights thrust the many windowsills and awnings she passed into cones of light and shadows. The footsteps grew louder. Hands grabbed her shoulders. Rasha was wrenched to the ground.

She was flipped over and came face-to-face with Leri.

'I've got her!' Leri cried, eyes manic.

Rasha thought of Joel, and the twisted boy slid from the shadows. He clamped Leri's neck with a gnarled hand, hauled her into the air, and slammed her against the wall.

Rasha didn't need to see the outcome. She scrambled to her feet and raced toward the end of the alleyway. The bus bay was in view, and the town's lights glimmered beyond that.

Out in the open, Rasha sprinted along the pavement. An engine roared. Headlights swamped her. A vehicle screeched to a halt beside her.

'Rasha!' Trish yelled.

It was the Reliant – its bonnet twisted – and Trish was in the driver's seat, the receptor strapped to her head.

'Get in!' Trish said. 'Hurry.'

Rasha vaulted over the bonnet and into the passenger's side. Trish sped away onto the main road. Behind the Reliant, board members flooded out from the alleyway. Trish turned the corner, and they were out of view.

'I led them to you,' Rasha cried. 'I'm sorry.'

'I know.'

'I didn't mean to project, I just saw the news article . . .'

'I know.'

Rasha realised Trish wasn't disgruntled – she had the receptor on. It must have fed her information. The woman blinked and came back to herself.

'Can you take the receptor off for me, kiddo?'

Rasha nodded and did as Trish asked. She threw it onto the back seat. Trish thanked her and relaxed into her seat.

'You controlled the imprint back there?'

'Like I did the day I hurt Fred,' Rasha exclaimed. 'Is it right that I can do that?'

'A coercer,' Trish said. 'It was often theorised, but no witness ever achieved it. But two weeks ago I didn't know about the gywandras, or imprints living between bodies.'

Rasha threw Trish a quizzical look.

'Right,' Trish said. 'Vanessa isn't, well, Vanessa. At some

point she was occupied by an imprint.'

'I saw her when I reached for you. Loads of different faces.'

'Vanessa's had many bodies,' Trish mused. 'Whoever she used to be was gone a long time ago.'

Occupations were one thing – and a scary one at that – but for imprints to change bodies like a fresh set of clothes set Rasha's hairs on end. Outside the Reliant's windows, the town's lights shrunk away.

'Where are we going?' Rasha asked.

'I was following Sam with the receptor,' Trish explained. 'He was taken to the Refinery, but now he's escaped. He's running to Pendeen.'

'Pendeen . . .' Rasha thought, trying to put a place to the name. 'Is there a lighthouse there?'

'Yeah.'

'When I was lost in the ombrederi, I saw a lighthouse. There were people watching from the cliffs. They shouted a word. Dasfurvya.'

'Then there we go.'

'But what is it all for?'

'The board wants to achieve gywandras. To transcend time. The occupations weren't random. The ombrederi tried to stop them. Everyone died because the board meddled with something they shouldn't have, and we got caught up in it all.'

That all made sense to Rasha. She recalled Vanessa and Leri's conversation outside the Long Walk, Vanessa's spiel about becoming post-human. It only led to one further question.

'Then who is the gywandras?'

Trish didn't reply. Rasha couldn't tell whether Trish didn't know or, worse yet, she had an inkling but didn't want to voice it.

Rasha thought over the way the gywandras controlled occupations. They willed imprints onto innocent victims, as Rasha had forced Joel onto Fred and Cridland. An old fear niggled away in Rasha's mind.

What if it's me?

79

TRISH BOMBED the Reliant down the A3071 toward Pendeen. Beyond the flatlands, the lighthouse was a hazy nub on the horizon. They'd arrive in a matter of minutes. Rasha's stomach writhed as frequency energy condensed.

'What do we do when we get there?' she asked. She hoped Trish's foresight conjured a series of potential outcomes.

'It all depends on what we find.'

'You can't see what's ahead?'

'Not through this frequency energy, no.'

Rasha noted Trish's white knuckles and her bitten bottom lip.

The gates to the lighthouse were open on their arrival. Trish slowed the Reliant and rolled into the yard. The headlights illuminated a congregation of people, all dressed in white. They turned to the Reliant with welcome.

'Who are they?' Rasha asked.

Trish peered through the Reliant's cracked windscreen. Rasha looked too and saw the mismatched faces.

'I think they're from the Refinery,' Trish deduced.

The crowd parted, and Sam raced toward the Reliant.

Trish unclipped her seat belt, jumped from the car, and hugged him. Rasha got out into the yard and sidled around the Reliant. She avoided the countless ill-sorted eyes fixed upon her.

'Hey, kid,' Sam said and squeezed her shoulder. He slurred when he spoke, and his actions were slow, as if he was drunk or worse.

'They're from the Refinery?' Rasha asked.

Another man broke through the crowd. He somehow looked sixty and thirty respectively as his blond hair turned black, his nose and mouth sharply defined – the body adhered to a new imprint. It could have happened to Rasha's body that night in the caravan had the Network not saved her. 'Dave' was sewn onto his Refinery garb.

Rasha understood Sam's random phone call at school, how Vanessa and the board occupied their present bodies.

'Sam, set us free,' Not-Dave said.

'I'm good at being a pain in the arse,' Sam retorted. He didn't seem entirely comfortable in the presence of dasfurvya either. *Who could be*, Rasha noted, *when they could have your body next?*

'You shouldn't be in those bodies,' Rasha snapped. Her father and sister only had one chance at life, whilst other imprints snatched bodies and lived forever.

'Well, Rasha,' Not-Dave said. 'Do you believe you have the right to your body because you were born into it, you and it as one?'

'Of course.'

'Was your mind born then?' Not-Dave continued. 'Or was it just your body?'

'Birth, rebirth, they're one and the same thing?' Trish asked over her shoulder.

'Let's walk and talk. In bodies, we are bound by time. There isn't much of that left at all.'

Sam escorted Trish and Rasha toward the lighthouse.

'It was already opened when we arrived,' he explained. 'We think the board got here first.'

'More will come,' Trish said. 'They were after us. They won't be far behind.'

Not-Dave muttered commands to his people. They raced to the yard gates and yanked them closed. He led Sam, Trish, and Rasha inside the lighthouse. The hallway was white. Pipes and wires snaked across each wall and the ceiling with Kubrick perfection. Above them, the sound of the beacon rotating was distinguishable – for all Rasha knew, a body was being hauled across the landing. The hallway was short and ended at the bottom of a spiral staircase that looped up to the beacon. A hatch was built into the atrium floor. Trish looked back at Rasha. Her nerves must have showed. Trish took her sweaty hand in her own.

'The mineshafts here go out under the sea,' Trish explained to Rasha. 'They've collapsed, and whatever is left is waterlogged, so there's no way into them. The lighthouse's engineer, Thomas Matthews, was a witness, and he built a tunnel underground, where activity was heightened. Little did he know it was directly above a ley line, a vault of frequency energy.'

The hatch was open, and in turn they climbed down. Four of the dasfurvya took the rear. Rasha could only have faith that her two friends knew what they were doing. Each rung down into the warmth of the tunnel brought on a denser frequency energy. It wasn't until they were in the sloped tunnel that the conversation started again, and it was led by Trish.

'The ombrederi is causing the occupations, is that right? Is the ombrederi itself conscious?'

'Some might call it a collective consciousness, others the source,' Not-Dave said. 'A little of it lives inside everyone. There is a primal instinct in us all to survive when we are threatened, and the ombrederi is no different. Becoming a gywandras with the ability to rewrite time would rip apart all of existence.'

'Which is why Will died,' Trish said. Rasha saw Sam flinch. The wound that was grief was still tender. 'To stall transcendence.'

'He wanted to achieve it first,' the man said. 'If he knew how it worked, he would've been able to deter them from discovering it.'

'But he didn't have to die,' Sam said. 'There must have been another way.'

'Once he died it was written,' Not-Dave retorted. The tunnel expanded once more. 'To change that would tear reality apart.'

Not-Dave raised his hand to stop the convoy. Voices echoed up ahead. With their backs to the wall, the trio and the five dasfurvya tiptoed closer, concealed by the darkness. The frequency's static fizzed warmly, a dry spring rain. Up ahead the shaft was lit. Vanessa and a handful of the board were stationed around James. The Network's director knelt on the tunnel floor, a receptor latched to his head. A wire ran from the contraption to a machine mounted to the granite wall.

Vanessa crouched beside James.

'It's okay to be in pain,' she said.

'They might come back,' he croaked. 'My girls might be imprints.'

Sam whispered, 'They've killed his girls.'

Trish gripped Rasha's shoulders tightly.

'Better yet,' Vanessa continued up ahead. 'They needn't die at all. To hurt is to be human, but what does pain become when you're superhuman? Transcend.'

'I can't,' he said, drained.

'Find them,' Vanessa urged. 'Home in on their voices.'

The machine on the wall was a generator, and it whirred louder. Girlish laughter rose from the shadows.

'What's the matter?' she asked.

'I can't . . . I can't maintain the connection,' James uttered.

'You have everything,' Vanessa growled.

'It won't be long,' James said. 'They know about transcendence. They'll know what we've done. The dasfurvya are free.'

'By then it'll be too late.'

'To hell it is!' Sam yelled.

He raced toward Vanessa, and the five dasfurvya followed. Trish stayed back, arms wrapped around Rasha.

'Get it off him!' Sam yelled. 'Stop it now. It's over.'

Vanessa and company turned, barely surprised and even less concerned about Sam and the dasfurvya.

James's eyes rolled, and his body slumped to the tunnel floor.

'It's too late,' Vanessa informed them. 'Take the receptor off him and his imprint will be lost forever.'

'This is madness,' Sam growled. 'You can't kill people to force them into your experiments. Experiments that will change reality.'

'That is where you're wrong,' Vanessa declared proudly. She flexed her shoulders and stood to her full height. 'The gywandras won't change reality. It will fulfil it.'

Rasha stared at the back of the dasfurvya's heads. She hoped they'd prove Vanessa wrong. Trish stepped forward.

'The gywandras is written,' she said.

Sam turned sideways and stared between Trish, Vanessa, and Not-Dave.

'She's right.' Not-Dave sighed. 'The gywandras has happened, so it must happen again.'

'It only happened because of what you were doing! Will died because of you! Mum too!'

Sam hurled himself at the board members. He threw a right hook and broke an obese man's nose. Two female board members tackled a dasfurvya to the ground. Trish stepped back and pulled Rasha with her.

Amidst the fight, Vanessa knelt beside James. She checked his pulse. Satisfied, she turned and spotted Rasha for the first time. She rose, a gruesome smile stretching over her face as if she'd forgotten about the carnage around her.

'As it should be,' she uttered.

'Go!' Trish yelled. She took Rasha by the hand, and they raced down the tunnel. Behind them, Vanessa's footsteps slapped against the rock, her breath heavy but calculated.

'You can't deny the frequency!' Vanessa cried after them. 'It has happened and it will happen, it has happened and it will happen.'

Rasha stumbled, regained her balance, and raced on, Trish's hand supporting the square of her back. The tunnel's darkness swallowed them up. Rasha reached out and used the walls of the tunnel to guide her. She couldn't fault Vanessa's fanatical shouts. If time was as delicate as the dasfurvya said, then everyone who had died would. They couldn't be saved.

Rasha and Trish reached the ladder and climbed two rungs at a time, clambered through the hatch, and raced through the pipe-lined hallway. All the while, a thought niggled away at Rasha. Vanessa had many bodies. A slew of dates were written in her journal. The plaque that greeted witnesses at the entrance to the Network with Edward Penrose's death – 1837 – was also Vanessa's passcode.

'I think I know who Vanessa is,' Rasha panted. 'She has a journal full of dates, like the ones at Kasey's house. She used to be Edward Penrose.'

Trish didn't slow but took Rasha by the hand, eyes fearful; she didn't doubt it. They bounded into the yard and froze at the scene before them. The yard was littered with the lifeless bodies of the dasfurvya – eighty, ninety, too many for Rasha to count.

'My god!' Trish exclaimed.

'They've left their bodies.'

Rasha recognised a couple of members from the board, both lifeless, who had chased her through the school earlier that evening. Ahead of them, the gates were opened.

'They must have fulfilled their purpose,' Trish said. She looked to the Reliant. The passenger door was open, the back seat empty. 'They've taken the receptor.'

There were footsteps, and arms wrapped around Rasha from behind.

'Trish!' she exclaimed.

Rasha was thrust to the ground. She kicked and screamed, but to no avail. Above her, Vanessa leered. Another of her board members – the burly man with a black eye – raced over and thrust a cold object over her head: Trish's receptor. Its generator buzzed. Frequency energy scalded her skin. A switch was flipped. The lighthouse's yard and Trish's terrified face were snatched from sight.

There was only the black void of the ombrederi.

Rasha fell, and the fall was forever.

INTERLUDE V

IT IS THE thirty-sixth thousandth day since Abidemi died and assumed her name.

She wakes before dawn and exits the workman's cottage to the left of Pendeen Lighthouse. The sun – yolk orange and warm – leaks across the crisp teal sky. Flowers bloom along Pendeen's hilltops, and the waves chorus from the shore. A morning in the ombrederi eases the heartache of being dead.

Between folds of leaves, nooks of rock, and thrashing tides come glimpses of those spaces in other times.

Vehicles mill through concrete towns.

A future ravaged by an abomination: the gywandras.

The council of the dasfurvya stalk across the lighthouse yard to meet her: sweet Kyauta, Nika, and Will. They have all existed long enough in the ombrederi for the frequency energy to nourish their imprints, their forms no longer scarred by their physical deaths.

'In defence of the ombrederi,' the four say in greeting.

'We were displaced,' Nika informs Abidemi. 'I became dasfurvya in a place and a time only vaguely connected to the three.'

'And I was too early in the sequence,' Will states. 'Days before Sam is incarcerated.'

'Time is running out,' Kyauta says. 'Abi, we've exhausted most intersections between here and the physical world. There aren't many options left.'

Abidemi looks out at the sea. The ombrederi chose her as the origin to lead the revolt against the gywandras. After her death, she woke with the ombrederi's voice in her mind, as though it had conjoined with her very imprint, and it nurtured her until she became the leader of the defence party. She was thrust from a perilous childhood in the physical into a permanent adulthood in the ombrederi, only to be burdened with a war led by fanatics who tried to defy nature itself.

'If we're the first to create the gywandras, then they have won,' Abidemi says. 'We've played straight into their hands. We made the abomination.'

Ky steps forward and takes her hands in his.

'It's not about creating the gywandras,' Ky says, voice gentle. 'That is already out of our control. It existed in Will's timeline, and so it will, and it must happen.'

'It's our intentions that matter,' Will chimes in. 'If it brings peace back to the ombrederi, with little damage to the physical-ombrederi balance, then that is good.'

Abidemi turns back to the cliffside. The rebels' experiments with the gywandras damaged the ombrederi. Intersections – portals between the two worlds – opened where they shouldn't, and excess frequency energy flows through them, causing the cliffs to crumble and wildlife to wilt.

The gywandras's very existence will kill all life in time if they don't act. *The irony*, Abidemi thinks bitterly, *for the enemy we're fighting is the very weapon we need*.

'Then we must begin the flaying,' Abidemi commands.

'Will, Nika, we'll have to send you back to an earlier intersection. You must integrate with bodies that aren't your own. It will be hard. It will defy everything the council believes in. But we have to guide the three to the right moment, and you can only do that as the dasfurvya.'

From his pocket, Ky produces two slips of parchment with intersection coordinates written on them. He passes one each to Will and Nika.

The four descend the steep footpath to the rock pools below. Will and Nika race ahead toward separate rock pools. They dive beneath the water. The surfaces bubble and glow, and then they still, and Will and Nika have gone.

Abidemi and Ky walk on until they are surrounded by moss-laden pools.

'Will there be pain?' Abidemi asks Ky. The ombrederi, as per its name, reflects the physical and at times can be just as cruel. The flaying will certainly live up to its name.

'The pennsers say it'll be quick,' Kyauta reassures her. The architects of this world, the pennsers had an abundance of wisdom and were never wrong about the ombrederi.

They reach the centre of the rock pools. A flurry of birds – storm petrels, gulls, shags, and cormorants – erupt from the sky. They dart at Abidemi, plant their talons into her skin, and gnaw at the flesh on her back. There is pain, but not one of torture, like being unshackled from heavy chains. Yes, unshackled. The birds gouge at the flesh around her spine. With the bones of her skeleton clamped in their beaks, they kick with their wings and pull her bent vertebrae from her body. They plunge into her eye sockets and mouth. They rip away her eyes and all the death they have seen. They dismantle her tongue and all the words she has used to calm and support. They flap to the pond and drop the organs in the water. Trish breaks the surface with a splash.

The emerged water pools at Abidemi's feet and courses across her body and into her bloody mouth. It swashes, cool and tender, over her mutilated tongue and fills up her lungs. She experiences a heavy drowning sensation, the very same feeling when she learnt of her father's death, or when she saw the Britons destroying the village: alone and displaced. Abidemi regurgitates the water, and it slithers to the pool. Rasha floats to the surface, her hand in Trish's.

A rumble of upturned earth. Roots burrow and leap from the tree line. They puncture her skin and crawl into her veins, her arteries, her nerves. They course up through her gut and wrap around her heart, and they take all of her inadequacy and indifference, her inability to trust. They writhe to the pond and drop her organs into the water; she is purified. Sam's body erupts to the surface.

The three, all of which are bound to the gywandras, are collected. It will be up to them to fight, there in the ombrederi, and out in the physical world.

'It begins,' Kyauta says.

An arm splashes from the pond, followed by a head of ever-changing hair. Trish is awake and ambles through the pool water. The ombrederi reaches into Abidemi once more.

Oh, she thinks, *what a task indeed.*

Article: 71

All witnessing practices, including the use
of I.A.N technology, must first be cleared
by the Network's board. There are only three
instances where these should ever be used:
device testing*, Network regulated projects,
and public incidents leading to civilian harm.
Beyond that, witnessing practices and Network
technology is prohibited. Witnesses cannot
use it for personal gain, nor lend expertise/
devices to the public. Any activity that
directly contradicts the I.A.N's principles
will lead to instant dismissal.

*Please note: all device testing must be
undertaken on-site, to minimise risk of harm
to the public.

PART ELEVEN

SHE TAKES YOU
WHERE YOU NEED
TO GO

80

TRISH PINNED Vanessa to the concrete and punched at the woman's face. She wouldn't let the board take someone else from her. Vanessa took the punches as though she couldn't feel them at all. After so many bodies, perhaps the imprint had learnt to disassociate itself with pain.

'Was it worth it?' Trish cried. 'All this death? Is transcendence worth it?'

'Transcendence is everything,' Vanessa spluttered.

Trish punched and slapped. Her knuckles became bloodied, Vanessa's face no longer recognisable. Beyond them, Paul slung Rasha's limp body up over his shoulder and stumbled back into the lighthouse. There was nothing she could do for Rasha now; the teenager was lost in the ombrederi.

'It's for the dead,' Trish cried. 'Bodies are for the living, and transcendence is for the dead.'

'Do you think that's true for Rasha?'

'You're forcing her to transcend.'

'No. Her occupation wasn't ordinary. It was a gywandras that occupied her.'

'So James made her.'

'You don't know, do you?'

Vanessa cackled. Trish shook her shoulders.

'What don't I know, what don't I know?' she screamed.

'A gywandras creates itself. They are the ultimate paradox. An imprint shouldn't come into contact with itself. It goes against nature – against the frequency. So when it does, it becomes a different kind of imprint entirely – a gywandras.'

Trish climbed from Vanessa onto the cold hard ground. Rasha had first presumed it was her sister, Milana, and later Rasha wondered whether it could be a manifestation of her own imprint. The teenager had every right to find the gywandras familiar.

'A gywandras, as a paradox, isn't bound to chronological time,' Vanessa hollered, too enthusiastic – fanatic – for Trish's liking. 'Don't you understand? No matter what you do, it's always going to happen.'

Trish didn't want to admit that Vanessa was right. A paradox. Rasha would become a gywandras. The teenager would occupy herself, sixteen days ago in her mother's caravan, and in doing so give her the abilities of a coercer. She'd predicted Will's death and envisioned Michael killing Shauna. She was the gywandras, that stormy evening in caravan forty-five.

A gywandras. Rasha wasn't alone. It was more than one person – James had transcended. A gywandras appeared when terrible things happened but also made itself known when the trio discovered new information. Trish rose to her feet.

'Even when James and Rasha transcend, they're helping us,' Trish cried. 'They've guided us to what we know now. Your project has gone rogue.'

Vanessa roared and tackled Trish to the ground. Vanessa

punched her cheekbone, her nose. Warm blood trickled across her face. Pain spasmed across her body. The frequency energy swelled. She became too weak to retaliate –

'Edward!'

Vanessa — or rather, Edward — froze.

'Answer me this,' Trish spat. 'Before you lost track of all your bodies, was the Network meant for good, or had it always been about the gywandras?'

Vanessa-Edward opened her mouth as if to speak, then looked up to the lighthouse door.

'Get off her, you crazy cunt!' Sam yelled.

A metal rod smacked Vanessa-Edward. They slumped sideways onto the gravel. Sam lowered the rod and limped to Trish. His face was bruised, eyes bloodshot, but he was alive. *Thank the ombrederi.*

'Rasha's under,' Sam said and helped Trish to her feet. 'She's in the ombrederi.'

'I know.'

'We need to perform an extraction,' Sam said.

'We haven't got the technology,' Trish said. 'No EMPs. They took the receptor from my car, used it on Rasha.'

Not-Dave appeared by Sam's side.

'To reach her, you'll have to be detached from your body,' Not-Dave said. 'To become a gywandras too.'

Sam rounded on him.

'So you do something,' Sam said. 'You died once. Die again.'

'There's more to this than just saving Rasha,' Trish interrupted. 'A series of events has to unfold. Will still has to die.'

Sam turned to her, his fists in balls.

'What do you mean? He's already dead?'

'Time, Sam,' she said. 'Will joked, but I think he knew. Before he died he was plagued by someone familiar.'

'Abidemi,' Sam said.

'No,' Trish said. 'No, it wasn't. It was the shadow imprint. A gywandras.'

'So James, then. Rasha.'

'Anyone can take its form,' Trish and Not-Dave said together.

'So if it isn't James?' Sam asked.

Trish stepped toward the Reliant. Tears burned her eyes. Rasha had plunged into the ombrederi's depths alone. Trish had abandoned Shauna in her time of need, and she wouldn't repeat that same mistake with Rasha.

'Trish?' Sam asked.

'I can't let her be alone, Sam,' she uttered. 'Rasha will be lost, and she'll be scared. She won't . . .' Trish faltered. 'She won't be able to do what needs to be done by herself.'

'What needs to be done?' Sam questioned.

'There has to be a reason I have foresight. The gywandras was there the night Shauna died.'

Trish turned and raced to the beaten Reliant.

'What? No, no, Trish!' Sam yelled.

Trish jumped into the Reliant. Not-Dave – still eerily familiar – restrained Sam.

Trish sped onto the road, throwing chippings and dust into the air. The lighthouse's heavy beam shrunk to a blip in the mirrors. The Reliant's steering wheel juddered under her grip. The jagged tree line crept closer. She couldn't stop the tears. She wasn't a murderer. *Not yet,* her mind whispered. *But it is written.*

Frequency energy surged around her. Trish didn't dare entertain her fears over a physical death. The tears on her face chilled, and her hands on the cold leather steering wheel numbed; her imprint began to withdraw. The Reliant pulled to the right.

She takes you where you need to go.

So Trish let it.

I'll never breathe again.

The car veered from the road, slammed into a tree trunk, spun onto its side, and tumbled down the hill.

Sam will be fine without me.

The windscreen's glass disintegrated. Beyond it was a whirl of muted colour. Terrible mechanical sounds bombarded the interior.

The Reliant hit a second tree. Its steel frame compressed around Trish's brittle body.

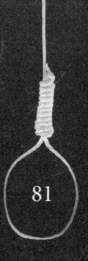

81

DARKNESS.

Trish cannot feel her body. The Reliant, the woodland, and Pendeen are a million light-years away. Salt water envelopes her, and she swims upward. Her head breaks the surface, and she clambers out from a rock pool.

A sun floods the sky, but it is no day on Earth. Gold rays shine over Pendeen's cliff tops as they move – no. They erode into the sea as it thrashes faster than is physically possible. Atop the cliffs, huts of wood and stone rise and collapse. Across the hills, trees unfurl. Brick by brick, Pendeen's lighthouse erects anew.

Then it all collapses once again, and the woodland diminishes and the fragments of rock rise from the water to rejoin the cliff. A settlement of stone and wooden huts spreads across the hills, and it is on fire. Abidemi is there, and she watches on with much sadness.

Abidemi turns to greet Trish. Her back is flayed, her sockets are empty, and roots throb beneath her skin where veins should be. Trish does wonder, by a miracle, whether her own body is still alive and if she is still connected to it.

'Lovely Trish, where life is infinite, death is absent,' Abidemi says.

'We all belong to the frequency,' Trish returns.

'You'll know this place is the ombrederi.'

'The afterlife.'

'Of sorts. Each and every human who has ever been or will be joins us here after death,' Abidemi explains. 'All of humanity, from all of time, all at once.'

The skyline torrents, and the wind carries a billion voices. Her knees buckle. Even her imprint cannot fathom the ombrederi's scale.

'We were never meant to know about transcendence,' Trish ponders.

Abidemi beckons her across the rock pools, and she follows.

'That is true, but equally, I think you knew,' Abidemi says. She invites Trish closer to a pool strewn with sea urchins. 'Your mind finds the future before it finds the past, does it not?'

Just as she suspected.

'I can become a gywandras too?'

'Yes. I'm afraid Rasha and James are lost, stuck too firmly to their pasts,' Abidemi says. 'My telling you all that you'll come to learn from exposure of the ombrederi is a waste of physical time. You have a task.'

'I have to . . . my god, I have to kill Will.' Although it already happened in her past, it still hurts her deeply to know it in the ombrederi, to know his blood was on her hands and will be again.

'You have to ensure he dies,' Abidemi agrees. 'I'm afraid it is much more than that. Every moment that led you here is still in limbo. It still might not happen.'

'And if it doesn't?'

'The physical, the ombrederi, they all depend on cause and

effect,' Abidemi says. 'After all, emotion and experience are what tie us all together. Undo that, and existence falls.'

'The occupations. The hauntings. The dasfurvya.'

'The river always finds the sea.'

'Why me?' Trish asks. 'Any witness, from any place, from any time.'

'To answer that, let me tell you why the ombrederi chose me. There was a threat to the balance. I am tied to you and to others. We have tread similar paths at different times.'

'We're emotionally tied to the core events. It's chance.'

'Tied, yes. Chance, no. It is choice. You chose to protect Rasha, and that is why you're here. Now that it has happened, it was already written. You must transcend.'

The pool beside them bubbles and writhes and becomes molten black. It has an allure to it. Trish longs to be with it, the way she searched for Shauna with the receptor.

'The ombrederi can only send you back to certain points in time.'

'Intersections,' Trish says. 'Will told us.'

'As if it was always written, there is an intersection that takes you to your past.'

'A gywandras creates itself,' Trish quotes Vanessa-Edward.

'From there, you will have agency,' Abidemi says. 'The ombrederi will guide you. Descend if you consent to transcendence.'

What can Trish do but accept? She walks to the pool and submerges into the black water. Her mind fills with information: an empty library whose shelves are inundated with volumes, access to all information if she desires. The water is all around her. It laps, gentle and warm, around her imprint, an amniotic fluid to birth the bringer of misery.

She dives down into the blackness.

82

FIRST THERE IS DARKNESS. Then a voice, without gender or age, like a flat piano chord, whispers, 'The river always finds the sea.'

The pond water bubbles with bright light. It rises, swirls, and forms a tunnel of colour, one solid enough for Trish to walk upon, and she does to find herself in a room she never thought she'd see again.

Trewin's Halfway House has a bedroom just for teen girls. Four singles and three bunk beds are crammed between walls tacked with posters of pop stars. Trish, at the age of thirteen, and Shauna, fifteen, are forced to share a single bed by the window. On the cusp of winter, cold air seeps through the single glazing, so the sisters have to spoon beneath a heap of thin blankets to keep warm. It is at this time that Trish comes into her witnessing capabilities and learns that the dead do not remain so. It is a period of life where she can't tell reality from memory, life from death. She faints often and sleepwalks just as much. Many times she thrashes at the air whilst she sleeps, and Shauna wakes her, often to the taunts of the girls they share the room with.

Trish walks to the bed. Young Shauna, aged by tragedy, and stranger still, her thirteen-year-old self, are wrapped up together, safe in the idea they'll always be together.

Trish is not welcome. Her skin pinches as if fishing hooks are strung across her body to wrench her from a place and time she has no business being in, from a space that her own imprint already inhabited. She reaches out to her younger self. The frequency energy intensifies. Trish struggles to reach herself; they repel each other as if she is one of two positive magnets being forced together. With all her might, she touches young Trish's forehead.

Her imprint splices apart as if she is shoved through a sieve. Her teenage self thrashes and rolls in the bed. Shauna wakes.

Adult Trish surveys her hands; they are space black, glass yet liquid. She is burdened with an armour, one linked to so many catastrophic events in recent weeks.

When her young body calms, Trish knows that she is done. On the bed, Shauna cradles teenage Trish, and around them the girls crowd – some are horrified, but most snicker and point. Teenage Trish wakes, and her eyes look straight ahead, alert and terrified, locked on the Trish that is now before.

At the gywandras she has now become.

And Shauna. What Trish would give to be in her sister's arms just one more time, to see her as she was, in her early thirties with a happy married life ahead of her.

That is it, her next destination as a gywandras.

It is time for Shauna to die.

83

IF TRISH is to describe what it is like to be a gywandras, it is an inferno of contradiction: indestructible to the point of fragility, hollow of emotion yet brimming with vehemence. The pool water tunnel churns and snatches the halfway house away. Within its currents come images from hundreds of moments, and in each of them the faces of Sam, Will, Rasha, James, and Trish are reflected.

Of course, the gywandras festered into Trish's life long before they met Rasha. It was there when Shauna died – or dies. It forces an imprint to occupy Michael and kill Shauna.

I'm ready, she thinks to the ombrederi.

The Puffin and Hare amalgamates from the water, its sticky tables and far stickier patrons crammed between its bloodred walls, as she remembers it. Raucous laughter rings crisply. It is not abstract in the way a memory obtained through the receptor would be. It is real. It happens now.

Oh, her freckly face full of love and life. Shauna laughs amongst her friends, all decorated in a variety of pink bridesmaid accessories.

A man carries a round of drinks and trips before her:

Michael. The contents shatter to the floor. He looks around as patrons jeer. Only Trish could have tripped him. Michael, who is long from sober himself, pauses. He doesn't look through Trish, but rather right at her. He blinks, considers what he sees as a drunken illusion, and sulks back toward the bar.

Trish is frozen, petrified to move. This has happened before, but it happens now. She is not merely a spectator: she is an active participant.

The memory shifts again. Shauna stumbles up the cobbled high street, phone in hand. Trish races after her.

'Disgusting prick!' Shauna yells. Michael hobbles behind her on Market Jew Street, intoxicated to the heavens. 'Maybe she'll finally see sense.'

'I'm here,' Trish calls, but Shauna cannot hear her.

In fact, Trish realises the ombrederi brought her to the wrong spot. She saw this moment the day in Princetown, nestled deep within Michael's subconscious. A gywandras materialised from the butcher's doorway. And it does now.

It just isn't Trish.

The second gywandras is mostly a waxen chest on deerlike legs. It skitters toward Michael.

'No!' Trish cries out. 'Please, no!'

The second gywandras falters. There is still a shred of hope – a fine sliver – that perhaps Shauna won't die.

The gywandras's skin warbles and retracts to reveal a face: Rasha. She cries, and her bottom lip quivers.

'It has to happen, Trish,' Rasha utters. 'I've seen what will happen if it doesn't. War everywhere. War like Syria.'

'Then I will do it,' Trish says, and she waltzes forward. If it has to be – if the ombrederi requires it of them. 'Let it be me.'

'What kind of friend would I be if I did?' Rasha asks.

'There's a darkness in me. I've become a coercer. How can any of that be for good?'

What can Trish say when she doesn't have the answers, when this world is as new to her as it is Rasha?

The gywandras armour envelops Rasha. With a long disjointed arm, she beckons an imprint from the shadows of Market Jew Street: the knife-wielding woman. Trish freezes. Her own gywandras skin roots to the cobbles as Shauna's death unfolds before her once again.

Occupied-Michael lumbers at Shauna, grabs her by the wrist, and forces her to turn around. She fights back to no avail, and he thrusts her into the shadows beside the garage.

Shauna is gone, and Trish burns with rage.

Shauna's body drops to the cobbles. Her imprint – faint and flickering – materialises beside her. Her eyes find Trish, and for a moment she seems to smile. Then she dissipates into the frequency energy.

Michael's body hits the ground. It shudders and rolls, and the imprint pools out of him onto the cobbles and slinks into the darkness once more.

'I'm sorry,' Rasha says beneath her gywandras armour, and she too disappears from the scene.

With a sharp intake of breath, Michael comes back to himself and rolls onto his stomach. He hurls, and vomit showers onto the ground. He wipes his mouth, rises on unsteady legs, sees Shauna's limp body, and bounds forward.

'No, no, no!' he cries.

He grabs Shauna by the armpits and pulls her into the streetlight. Michael presses on Shauna's chest, then puts his mouth to hers and puffs air into it. He performs CPR again. Pump, pump, breath, breath. He howls every time he fails, then pumps harder the more desperate he becomes to revive her.

But he cannot, and he never will.

The alleyway melts away from Trish, with the sound of Michael's cries in her ears, and Shauna's blank blue face etched into her mind.

The rage inside her intensifies.

Rasha, she thinks. *I must find Rasha.*

84

THE WHIRLPOOL tunnel dispels Trish into a patch of dense shrubbery.

She rises without her gywandras armour and scans the horizon – a riot of subtropical plants – to know that it is the Lost Gardens of Heligan: Rasha's neutral place.

Rasha's sobs echo across the warped landscape. Trish races down an intimate footpath between a bamboo plant and a man-made waterfall toward the voice.

'What have I done?' Rasha cries. 'What have I done?'

Trish scrambles up a hill and finds Rasha facedown on the earth. She sobs and pounds the dirt with her fists. Behind her lies The Mud Maiden, a sculpture of a sleeping woman shrouded in moss and ivy. Trish traipses forward, hesitant to calm her friend.

Yes, still her friend. Trish can't hold the teenager to Shauna's death, not when she was influenced by Edward Penrose to become a coercer of imprints. After all, they both have the weight of the ombrederi and humanity's existence slung on their shoulders.

Because if Rasha hadn't, in the end, Trish would have had

to. Better a gywandras of their own. It was The Network's fault.

Trish crouches beside Rasha and lays a hand on her shoulder. Rasha jumps up, startled.

'You found me,' she says. 'You came here.'

'We're gywandras now,' Trish says. 'I think we can travel anywhere.'

'I'm sorry, I'm so. . .'

'You listen to me,' Trish says. 'None of us asked for this, and if it hadn't been you, it would have been someone else.'

It would have been me, Trish thinks.

'I thought it was the right thing,' Rasha stammers. 'I don't even know what that is anymore.'

Trish can't disagree. Murder is wrong, and she grieved for her elder sister for sixteen months. She knows how much it hurts, that it aches in every organ and darkens every thought. Yet, the ombrederi flows through her subconscious and helps Trish understand it is a drop in a turbulent sea of events; existence is still at stake.

'I said I'd never be like them,' the teenager continues. She sits down, eyes fixed on the canopy where birds swarm and chirp. 'I swore I would be better than the rebels in Syria, than Cridland. I'm not. I'm worse!'

'We're the sum of our pasts,' Trish says. 'As much as we want to believe otherwise. If Shauna hadn't . . . then I would never have found out about the gywandras or what the Network was doing.'

'We wouldn't be here now! If none of that had happened, we wouldn't be gywandras now.'

Trish mulls over Not-Dave's speech outside the lighthouse, the words that led her to crash the Reliant, how Vanessa-Edward said the gywandras came to be.

'It's a paradox,' Trish says. 'If the gywandras wasn't us, it would have been one of the Network.'

Rasha wipes her eyes. Trish notes how they aren't the only victims of the Network. If they don't act soon, there will be more.

'Rasha, listen to me,' Trish says, grabbing Rasha's shoulders. 'We'll find some good in this, together. Listen, we're not the only ones down here. James is held here against his will.'

'He was bad, wasn't he?'

'He made some mistakes,' Trish admits. 'He meant well. He tried to stop Edward Penrose. You can find him. Bring him home. One fewer victim for the Network, yeah? One fewer death.'

'One fewer death,' Rasha repeats.

Trish rises to her feet. The gywandras armour swells around her once more.

'What are you going to do?'

Even though she is concealed in the gywandras armour, Trish cannot turn back to face Rasha.

'The last piece of the puzzle,' she says. 'Will.'

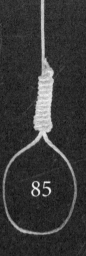

85

COLOUR, SOUND, EMOTION – it is all one chaotic vortex.

Trish struggles to find the mental strength to navigate the tunnel to her next destination, and when she finally does it isn't one place but a series of interconnected rooms. In each one is a version of Will, sat in his untidy bedroom or a dim pocket of the collieries or a quiet quayside cafe. Prepubescent Will, teenage Will, thirtysomething Will. He mostly hunches over a notebook or tablet and writes away. The words on his pages and screens are venomous; his disgust for transcendence stains the ink and pixels of his work.

Will met the gywandras, and unless Rasha is to return, Trish will have to kill him. Trish stalks through the various scenes where the ombrederi's might is strongest: the activity centre. Will turns in his seat when she enters. He shakes his head; he probably thinks it was a shadow.

A trickle. The activity centre becomes water, and the water becomes the laboratories. The ombrederi's grasp is strongest where there are no dampeners. Will jumps up from his stool. Even though he cannot see Trish, he stares directly at her.

'Abidemi?' he calls out. He waits for a response with bated breath.

Trish decides to lurk closer, toward the contents of the desk. To his right are printed copies of his report outlining the sonar program. To his left are his notes on transcendence. They continue to cause misery. How could Will have been so careless in his attempts to dissolve the project? Had he entrusted her, he may never have needed to die. Instead, so many unforgivable events occurred. She thrusts forward and swipes the sheets of paper to the floor in a flurry of secrets.

Will recedes from the desk. He takes out his smartphone and speaks into the dictation app.

'April 22, 2016,' he begins. 'Location: laboratory offices, the Network. Time is 19:43. I've been engaging with a grade three imprint for several weeks. Moments ago, it displayed physical strength. I can sense that it's highly aggravated, angry perhaps. It doesn't respond to Abidemi . . .'

The room grows darker as the ombrederi leads Trish to the next in a swirl of colour: Will's bedroom at his parents' cottage. It is the dead of night, and the double bed has been pushed into the far right corner to give way to the mass of notes sprawled across the floor and walls.

Will senses Trish's presence and leaps from his bed. He reaches for the EMP that lies on his side table. Trish is not sure what the EMP will do to a gywandras, but if it reacts in the same way as it does with imprints, then she cannot take the risk. Everything that led her to this very moment pivoted on Will's death. He stalled the gywandras project and led them to multiple clues. Trish would never discover the gywandras at the scene of Shauna's murder, and Sam wouldn't go to the Refinery and uncover the truth about the dasfurvya.

She smacks the device from Will's hand. It clatters across

the floor. She cannot bring herself to do it.

A sliver of flame bursts from a ceiling beam. Abidemi rocks back and forth in the air. She urges Trish on. Trish soaks Will up as he adjusts the EMP. He is bleary-eyed; he cries over Sam and the state of their relationship, no doubt. His crooked nose, his untameable hair. It isn't fair that he won't grow old, that his eyes will not bear smile lines and his hair won't grow grey and wispy. She planned her own future, how she, Sam, and Will would spend their retirement walking coastal paths, taking picnics to St Ives and coach trips to Brighton. Whether or not such a future will come to pass lies in her tar-like hands.

I can't do it, Trish thinks.

'You don't have to,' Abidemi responds.

The wall to Will's left ripples into an archway of light. Another gywandras enters their midst. Rasha has come again. Abidemi must know Trish's weaknesses; she sees all of time, after all. She brought Rasha here.

Rasha's gywandras armour fades and returns. Through flickers of the viscous skin, Rasha's face is seen. She wails, and tears cascade across her face. She fought to be good for so long, only for it to not matter in the end.

Gywandras-Rasha glides around Will in a circle, the way a seagull inspects a carton of chips. Trish follows in case Rasha springs toward Will.

'Rasha!' Trish cries.

The girl stops. Her molten face turns to the painting mounted on Will's wall.

'The Vincent will fall,' Rasha responds. 'There's a reason for everything. I don't have a choice.'

'That's where you're wrong; time is still in flux,' Trish says. 'We are still able to make decisions.'

'But it has already happened.'

'That's right. It's happened. It has to happen. But . . .'

Trish thinks over the hours after they learnt of Will's demise, and Sam initially suspected that Will had committed suicide. Sam might have been frivolous with his emotions, but he always had a good instinct. Perhaps Sam was right after all. Abidemi's instructions weren't to kill Will but to ensure that he died.

'We're not murderers,' Trish continues. 'It doesn't mean it has to be us.'

Rasha seems to think a moment. 'Will's choice?' she asks.

'Will's choice.'

Trish takes two deep breaths despite knowing full well she has no lungs to take in air. She walks into Will's body. Their minds overlap, and their synapses fuse as one.

The lighting shop shines with millions of bulbs. Trish no longer has the gywandras armour; she's her pre-crash self. Will's projection is transparent. The lights in the distance shine through him.

'Trish? Are you dead?' he asks, alarmed.

Trish expected him to become at one with the ombrederi and have all the answers he needs; this version of his imprint is still bound to his body, bound to the physical world, and so doesn't know what his future holds.

'Not quite,' Trish replies. 'I've transcended.'

His eyes flicker.

'Is it you? Have you been haunting me all these months?' he asks. 'All these years?'

How can she tell him he is going to die? How can she make it painless?

'Yes. You're going to transcend, Will.'

'I don't want to,' Will explains. 'I'm trying to find a way to end it. The board, they want it for terrible things.'

'Show me,' Trish says.

The darkness swirls into James's incandescent office. Trish watches from the doorway as Will and Vanessa argue.

'It could be disastrous,' Will cries. He slams a paper report onto the desk. 'It could be catastrophic. A weapon which, in the wrong hands – '

'I disagree,' Vanessa says. Her voice is low and firm. 'Human evolution lies within the mind. All we have done from the dawn of time is expand our horizons. It's more than flying a plane or exploring space. True transcendence, unhindered by a physical body, is the ultimate achievement.'

'We cannot begin to understand it,' Will retorts. 'If people die – '

Trish is pulled from the birdcage and back into the lighting shop. Will greets her.

'I saw into you,' he says. 'I'm not going to transcend, am I?'

'Reality is threatened, Will,' Trish says. 'Just as you predicted. Your death is one of a series of events that will stop the board. It has to happen. It is written.'

'You've been chosen to do it,' Will says. He's caught between disappointment and disgust. He has never spoken to Trish in this way, and it hurts like hell. 'I'll fight for my life.'

A blur of light. Shauna strolls amongst the lights of their parents' shop, not her imprint, though; vague, blurred, it is a memory of someone who knew her little. Will's memory. This is how he chooses to fight.

Trish delves into his mind. It takes the Network's form. Thousands of cave openings and labyrinthine tunnels shine through the magnetic darkness. She lets her instincts lead her to a cavern – but no, it is Phil and Margaret's farmhouse kitchen. Will sits at the table, head cradled in his hands. Margaret hunches over her sink and scrubs a sparkling tray.

'This changes things, you know that?' Margaret mutters over the squeak of a Brillo Pad on glass. 'How could it not?'

'I'm the same person as I was before,' Will stammers.

'No,' Margaret replies. She shakes the Brillo Pad in her hand. 'In my eyes you've changed because I've realised how much of a liar you were.'

'I didn't lie, I just didn't know how . . . Sam gave me the confidence, he showed me it's okay – '

Margaret throws the Brillo Pad to the counter.

'But it's not okay!' she screeches. 'You're a stranger now. I don't know who you are. I don't know if you're Will anymore . . .'

The memory spins, tyres in a dark woodland. Will and Sam sit in Will's car. They hold hands as lightning strikes the valley below. It spins again, doused in blue and red, and on the floor of Teagues' Lighting Shop, Trish's parents lie still, plastic bags over their heads, taped around their necks, faces frozen in one last gasp of breath.

Trish stands on the spot, numb to it all. The anger outlives the victims twofold, aches in her chest for the parents who left her by their own admission. She could have stopped it. The GP should have offered support, the world shouldn't be so callous. Her parents should have held out for one more day, for one more business loan –

She takes the anger and fills herself up with it. Cold envelopes her as the gywandras skin seeps through her pores. She races away from the lighting shop, through the mineshafts. Life hangs in the balance, she tells herself. She finds the cave entrance and dives through.

Sam's living room. He lies on the sofa, eyes rolled to the back of his head. White powder marks the black coffee table. Will stands before him and cries. It's as though Sam cannot see him and instead looks right through him.

'He doesn't know.' Sam strings each word together.

'Know what?' Will cries.

Sam looks through Will, the wall behind him, and the world beyond that. A glimmer of fire. A flurry of priests. Sam is more focused on the dead than the living. Will snatches up the clear packet of pills, climbs over the couch, and thrusts it in Sam's face. He wants Sam to see the packet, to see his disappointment, to feel his hurt.

'He doesn't see,' Sam groans.

'See what? See what?'

'That I don't love him – '

Will sinks back onto the other end of the sofa, defeated.

' – the way he wants me to,' Sam finishes.

Will radiates an all too familiar anguish. To learn a spouse's love isn't as deep as yours is a grief all its own. Outside of the ombrederi, of this version of Will's memory, his imprint recedes.

Trish takes the chance.

She recounts all she has seen, and it unfurls around her in the ombrederi: fire engulfs buildings; the occupations of Rasha, Ted, and Kasey; Vanessa as she forces James to transcend; the disfigured dasfurvya.

Your death saves mankind. Your death saves mankind, she thinks over and over, hoping that Will's imprint will hear it.

Trish's synapses weld with Will's in an intense surge of energy. The bruises on Will's arms register with her, along with the ache at his fingertips. She opens Will's eyes to find the bedroom destroyed: bed upturned, wardrobe in smithereens, shelving and copious amounts of plaster ripped from the walls. Their fight has been physical as well as of the mind. Amidst the catastrophe, Will is transfixed on the window before him.

He blinks twice fast. His senses slip from her, and when she opens her eyes she stands aside Will and watches on as –

Will sprints as fast as he can on unsteady legs. He lunges, slices through the glass, and is gone.

He dies for the first time, again.

Trish chokes upon a scream, a roar, a cry to a god that can't exist for such needless cruelty. She screams, and she hurls. The gywandras armour extends and roots itself into Will's bedroom floor. The room dissolves and returns many times, each with a different aged Will.

A four-year-old in dungarees and a Postman Pat jumper drops a toy train at the sound of her roars.

A prepubescent Will turns his CD player up full blast to drown out her shrieks with The Cure.

Eighteen-year-old Will in a tie-dye T-shirt screams and curses back at the invisible woman.

A bearded and tired thirty-one-year-old sits with his back against his wardrobe and whispers softly, 'He tries to disappear. Wherever he goes will never be distant enough. It's me he's running from. Whoever you are, I know your pain. Whoever you are, I'm not scared of you. I feel for you, you hear me?'

Will's voice eases Trish's pain. She crawls forward and slumps against the wall beside his wardrobe. Will looks vaguely in her direction; he can sense her but can't see her.

'What has caused you so much pain?' he asks.

Trish falters. If only Will, in that time, sensed the gywandras, knew that it was Trish beneath the armour. The conversations they could have, the tenderness she could show him. After all, there is only one answer, one Will can understand entirely, imbedded in every fibre of both of their beings.

'Love,' she says.

Trish smiles and for one very brief moment is sure that Will smiles too.

86

THE OMBREDERI LIFTS Trish into the water tunnel. She thought her work was done, that she would be returned to whatever remained of her physical body.

She is thrust onto a hillside beneath a starlit night. Upon the brow of the hill, a tent ruffles in a polite wind, and a campfire simmers before it. Sat there, staring into the flames, are James and Rasha, a glimmer of gywandras armour upon their skin.

'You can't transcend much longer,' Trish cries. 'Close the connection. Go home.'

Rasha rises. James, however, remains seated. Rasha takes in Trish's appearance.

'I was waiting for you,' she says. 'Is it done?'

Trish can only nod.

Rasha hugs her. Over the teenager's head, Trish locks eyes with James.

'I'm sorry, Trish,' he says. 'I can't go back.'

Behind them, the giggle of young girls sounds from the tent.

'It's not real, James. All this time, I've been searching for

Shauna – for the truth. It's not – '

'It is real,' James says, 'in the sense that it is all I have. The girls weren't witnesses, their imprints won't survive in the physical. That has to be enough.'

The ombrederi attempts to tug Trish away from the campsite. Her efforts are in vain.

'I know I should have been stronger,' James continues. 'I should have fought Vanessa harder.'

'We all belong to the frequency, even if we don't want to,' Trish replies. 'In the end it didn't matter.'

Rasha pulls away from Trish.

'We made choices, didn't we?' she asks.

'Yes,' Trish says. 'And they were written.'

Trish looks at the Network's director, sad that he won't come with them.

'The river always finds the sea,' she says.

'It's been an honour and a pleasure,' James retorts.

The campsite dissolves, and the women are left in darkness. Trish gestures to go on. Rasha's projection fades.

The darkness has the heaviness of water. Trish swims and kicks. Her head breaks the surface of the rock pool, and the gywandras armour slides from her body. Trish climbs out onto the rock pools, stands upright, and takes in the ombrederi's landscape. Beneath the cliffs, Trish feels as though she has accomplished little.

The landscape stills, the lighthouse stands, and an array of cords flow out from its aerie as if it is a maypole. They glimmer, and beads of light flow across the landscape. Voices ring from them.

'They are tethers,' the ombrederi whispers. 'Connecting us all.'

'We all belong to the frequency,' Trish mutters.

She runs to the lighthouse, dashes inside, sprints up the spiral stairwell, and bounds into the aerie. Trish steps out onto the balcony that wraps around the base of the lighthouse's diagonal windows. The cords are joined to the railing. They swell and beat and dim and brighten. She knows the voices and can put a face and name to all; the tethers belong to each member of the Network. She grasps the bundle of cords, squeezes them tightly, and closes her eyes. She recalls her brief stint in the ombrederi and the knowledge she recently acquired, the danger the world faces if the gywandras is used for unnatural purposes. She compresses the images down from her mind and along her arm into the cords. She opens her eyes. The cords shine with a pure golden light: truth. The Network is enlightened.

The cliff tops settle to resemble present day – Trish's now, anyhow. There is peace.

Trish descends the stairwell and into the yard. Abidemi greets her there. She is whole and youthful and springs forward like the sprightly fourteen-year-old she was when she died.

'Everything is done,' Trish says. 'There are other organisations, aren't there? The Edward Penrose trust doesn't just fund the Network and the Refinery. People I couldn't reach who need to be warned.'

'I can only agree.' Abidemi gestures outward, and Will and James materialise beside her. Their projections are as strong and pure as Abidemi's; they have been in the ombrederi longer than their physical bodies have been dead. Time, a subjective measurement. 'We are three, and we can bring you back to your body.'

'You can repair it?'

'We can try. Only a fighting chance at best.'

'Thank you.'

'The whole of existence thanks you.'

Abidemi and company walk over to Trish and right into her.

Darkness.

A tingling sensation spasms across her body. The hiss of the Reliant's engine fills her ears. White-hot pain sears through every inch of bone and tissue. And life. Sweet, glorious, hopeful, physical life.

PART TWELVE

I WILL ALWAYS
PULL TO YOU

87

BRAKES SCREECHED in the distance. Sam couldn't tear his eyes from the wooded hillside. Metal thunked against solid bark. Brake lights flickered through the trees as the Reliant toppled and crunched down the hillside with Trish still inside.

Inside, but most certainly not alive.

Will, Rose, James, Rasha, and now Trish – Sam had never been more alone.

'No!' he roared. He thrashed against Not-Dave's grip. 'Let me go, you bastard!'

'It had to be done, Sam,' Not-Dave said.

Sam fought out of Not-Dave's grip. He stared hard at the man's face. He wanted to scream at him, punch, kick. But becoming lost in his eyes, he found he couldn't.

'You don't know – you couldn't possibly know . . .'

Not-Dave edged closer to him.

'I do, Sammy,' he said.

Sam stood upright and wiped the tears from his eyes. The lighthouse's beam caught the side of Not-Dave's face. The blond hair turned dark and curly, eyes blue, nose sharp.

'Will?'

'Do not get attached to this body, Sam,' Will said. 'It's not permanent.'

Sam reached out. He traced Will's face, his pronounced cheekbones, his heavy brow.

'She's going to kill you,' Sam uttered. His face was wet with tears.

'I'm already dead, but yes, she will, and Trish has to, Sam. For the good of, well, for the good of existence.'

'And there is no other way?'

'Not that can be written,' Will said. He took Sam's hand.

'Trish is going to die,' Sam said. 'You, now her, and I'm just here. I can't help.'

Someone stirred on the ground. Vanessa wobbled to her feet. Sam went to step toward her, but Will held out an arm.

'Let me go! I'll kill her!'

'That isn't Vanessa,' Will said. 'It hasn't been for a very long time.'

Vanessa staggered forward and found their faces. She hesitated.

'You've worn that body thin,' Will stated. 'Wouldn't you say, Edward?'

Vanessa, Edward – whatever imprint was within the body – blinked hard.

'Edward, yes, I haven't used that name in a long time,' Vanessa-Edward said. 'The river always finds the sea.'

Vanessa-Edward's eyes found the cliff edge, and she bolted from the yard and leapt into the hungry sea. Shock coursed through Sam's body.

'She just went, just like that.'

'Edward will be in the ombrederi now,' Will said. 'He won't be able to escape Abidemi.'

'Edward . . .' Sam uttered.

'Edward Penrose, yes. See, Sam, this all goes far deeper and has gone on for far longer than you and me, which is why we need to stop it.' Will turned Sam around to face him, more Will-ish with every second. 'We still have our small part to play. This is the strongest ley line in the county. We fight here, in the physical.'

88

SAM RACED through the tunnels with Will and the last four dasfurvya.

The dasfurvya uncovered TNT left deep beneath the lighthouse by the witnesses who'd dug the tunnels. Somehow they knew it'd be there. With Will's knowledge of Pendeen and Sam's tendency for destruction, they plotted TNT into various positions throughout the mineshafts against frequency-rich tin ore. The entire plan was just mad to Sam, of course –

'No more spikes,' Will exclaimed. 'No more power for a gywandras to exist.'

Dynamite planted, they scarpered back toward ground level. In the main cavern, Rasha and James lay comatose, both still strapped to the receptors, their imprints in the ombrederi. Sam lifted Rasha's limp body over his shoulder. He gestured for Will to tend to James.

'He isn't coming back, Sam,' Will said. 'He's with his girls.'

Sam nodded, certain there were more casualties to come. He stumbled through the network of tunnels with Rasha's body, climbed the ladder with her on his shoulder, and fled the lighthouse into the new morning.

Will ushered Sam and the dasfurvya on, beyond the lighthouse yard, up the road away from Pendeen. Half a mile from the lighthouse, Will stopped, closed his eyes, and nodded.

The ground shook as if a giant heart palpitated beneath them. Dislodged stone and gravel rustled around them. Fissures splintered the tarmac. Cracks veined the side of the lighthouse.

The frequency energy surged. A whirl of images and emotions penetrated Sam's mind. Thousands of people and lives overloaded his senses. As quickly as it had come, it went. There was calm, and the world settled once more.

'Sam . . .' came Will's voice.

Sam turned. Will didn't look well: eyes bloodshot, skin clammy. A few of the dasfurvya collapsed, lifeless. Sam rushed to him.

'Didn't it work?' he said, panicked.

Will smiled through his discomfort.

'It did,' he said. 'Without the frequency energy, we cannot sustain life within these forms. We've run our course.'

The remainder of the dasfurvya slumped to the ground. Will's knees buckled out from under him. Sam caught him and lowered his body to the split tarmac.

'I've just got you back,' Sam said.

'I'm always closer than you think.'

'I tried,' Sam wailed. 'I didn't know how to love you, but I tried.'

'I know,' Will said. The body had his eyes now, deep and wondrous and sad. 'In your own way. Your sharp edges were a consequence of feeling too much.'

'Come back,' Sam said. 'Another body.'

'This is my time,' Will said. 'It's written. Sam, don't be sad. Two are returning to you. You're not alone. Learn to see the people around you.'

Will fell limp in Sam's arms. Sam howled. Tears flowed; his cynicism and pride didn't put a stopper to them. Seagulls filled the brisk wind with the tune of their despair.

A sharp intake of breath broke the moment. Amongst the lifeless bodies in the yard, Rasha sat up and gulped down air. She caught eye of the first body, staggered to her feet, spun in a circle, and absorbed the scene. Her eyes found Sam.

'It's done,' she said sadly. 'James . . .'

Sam staggered to his feet and gave Rasha a hug. 'There were meant to be two of you?'

Rasha thought a moment and mumbled, 'Trish.'

Sam didn't hesitate. He let Rasha go and sprinted up the road, his injuries pushed to the back of his mind.

'Ring for help!' he yelled back to Rasha. 'There's a phone in the lighthouse. Ambulance, coast guard, all of it!'

His lungs burned from exertion, and his right hip seared with pain. Up ahead, crushed steel glinted amongst the trees.

'Trish!' he yelled.

Into the woods he scarpered, tripping over roots like some sort of cheap horror. The Reliant lay in a clearing, twisted and bent in half. Glass littered the ground. Petrol seeped from the tank. A fire threatened to burst out from beneath what was left of the bonnet. Trish hung upside down, still in the driver's seat. The Reliant's warped innards kept her in place where the seat belt failed. Dark blood trickled from her mouth and ears. Her shoulders were off-kilter; her chest bone had punctured her skin. Her right arm was twisted, and her hand faced the wrong way.

'There's no fucking way . . .' Sam breathed. He failed to

conclude the sentence out loud: that she's still alive.

He put a cold hand to her forehead. Frequency energy fizzed beneath her skin. He closed his eyes, and the ombrederi came to him, though not quite as strongly as it had before the destruction of Pendeen. Trish's imprint was there: Teagues' Lighting Shop. She had not detached from her body entirely. There were other imprints within her. They kept her body alive.

Relief washed over him. His body shook, his stomach heaved. Rasha appeared by his side and yelled things that he could not make sense of. Alarms reverberated in his eardrums. Red and blue lights reflected off tree bark. He was wrapped in tin foil and escorted to an ambulance, then later a hospital, a private room in which police asked him questions he could not hear because the only sound in his head was the roar of explosions and the belt of sirens, and all his mind could conjure was Will's face.

89

'YOU WERE HELPING me with my English,' Rasha said. She and Sam sat on the fence outside the caravan park, looking out over the sea, cups of tea in hand. 'We decided an early morning stroll across the beach would be a good time to go over all things nautical. Trish just dropped us off. Then the explosion happened, the landslide, the bodies outside the lighthouse. They think Trish crashed as the result of the mines collapsing.'

Sam gave a little smile. He'd grown fond of Rasha over the six days since the events of Pendeen. He'd been wary of her, for she had transcended to kill Will and succeeded in ending Shauna's life. But he'd learnt of Will's sacrifice and heard of the nightmares she'd had of the ombrederi ever since. He knew there was little to forgive. She was just a pawn whose two choices were to move between two evils. Trish was no different. He'd realised that the odd green eye and tuft of red hair found on Will's body the day in Tredraes' Funeral Directors had been Trish's. They'd been remnants of her imprint after she'd occupied Will the night of his death. Wherever Edward Penrose's imprint resided – the ombrederi or otherwise – he had a lot to answer for.

After a tumultuous row with Haya, Rasha got permission for Sam to stay in caravan forty-five for a little while. Of course, Haya didn't give him accommodation for free; soon he had taken on most of the housework and tutored her English – to the best of his ability – so Haya prolonged his stay by days at a time. He'd been there six days.

'I can barely feel it now,' Rasha said and offered him a bourbon. She clucked as he took two. 'The frequency energy, like it's not there.'

'It's how it was before the spikes happened.' Sam munched his way through the first biscuit. 'This is only the southwest. Who knows what else is out there.'

'We know so much, and we can do so little.' Rasha pocketed the rest of the bourbons , away from Sam's prying hands.

'Then little we do. If we've learnt anything, the ombrederi is not to be interfered with. We do all we can here. Trust Abidemi and Will to look after that side of things.'

'You haven't had contact, have you? From either of them.'

'No,' Sam said, 'but it's fine.'

That was the truth.

Rasha checked her watch.

'You'd better head out,' she said.

The moped broke down twice on the way over: the first on the dual carriage way and the second at Morrison's petrol station. Sam arrived at the collieries. The witnesses had gathered outside the engine house. Sam walked over, helmet under arm. The group was smaller without the board.

Whilst Trish was in the ombrederi, she had, by ways

TERRY KITTO

unknown to Sam, infiltrated the witnesses' minds with a warning. Fire, destruction, and bloodied horizons: the outcome if transcendence was utilised. Individuals had contacted Sam privately, and in the days spent maintaining the Abadis' caravan and visiting Trish in hospital, he'd contacted each and every last witness with one text: a time and a date. They should all be there at the end of the Network.

Sam looked out over them – the chubby guy who always finished the communal milk first, the woman with a nervous stutter. He had learnt them by trait but had never cared to know them by name. What could have been if he'd tried?

'This site never existed,' he bellowed over the wind. 'You've never heard of it, you never came here. We didn't work together; we don't even know one another. We never have, and never will, practice anything beyond engagement.'

The witnesses nodded. They were grave and sombre: Trish's warning still plagued them.

'Good,' Sam said. 'Please open Anascribe.'

His soon-to-be-ex-colleagues rifled through pockets and satchels for their smartphones and tablets. Sam, who'd never recovered his own phone from James, had taken Trish's over for the time being. He opened the app on her phone, screen cracked and pixelated in places from the events in Pendeen. He scrolled through the settings menu and located the option, 'End Network.' It required majority member verdict to activate, so when Sam tapped the option, a notification jingle rang sixty-seven times across the collieries' yard. On their screens, details of the function were briefly outlined, and it asked them either to agree or to abort. On Sam's screen, the question, 'Are you sure?' popped up, to which he clicked yes. A counter appeared with the number one in red: his vote.

Witnesses either jabbed at their chosen answer or idled

414

their index finger over their screen as they worked through internal debates behind pasty faces. The counter climbed, hit thirty-five, and turned green – majority vote. All sixty-eight agreed. The Anascribe app went blank.

The witnesses looked amongst themselves. The ground quivered underfoot. The application set off fail-safes and burst waterlogged caverns. Research, equipment, and any trace the Network had existed was sent into a watery grave to rust and rot.

No one said goodbye. One by one, the witnesses pocketed their devices and went in their own directions, not one handshake or glance back. The yard emptied as cars and bikes sped through the gate. Only Sam was left. He deleted the Anascribe app from Trish's phone. When the last brake lights were out of sight, he climbed back onto his moped and drove from the collieries' yard.

He was as carefree as he'd ever been.

90

WHEN HE returned to the caravan site to collect his clothes, Haya bribed him to stay with rose cake – a tempting offer – but he politely declined at least a dozen times before he set back off on the moped.

For tomorrow was Will's funeral.

He thought of Will, as was often the case. Will still stole the quiet moments, but Sam was no longer resentful of it; memories brought him more happiness than grief. It only registered he was home when he unlocked the front door and the putrid smell of the unkept flat filled his nostrils. He dropped the bag of Network equipment onto the sofa and got to work in the kitchen. He washed the dishes and vacuumed the carpets and mopped the lino and scrubbed the bathroom tiles and emptied the bins, and as the sun wilted for the day, the flat was the most pristine it had been in months.

While stripping the sheets from his bed he kicked a shoebox. He upturned it, and out flooded photographs of him and Will: a bonfire night surrounded by Trish, James, and Network colleagues, an ill-focused selfie before the Parthenon temple, a sweaty hike in the Lake District one foggy weekend.

Sam always questioned Will's need to have photographs printed. 'It's a waste of money, and we've got that electronic frame now,' Sam would say. Will had said they should be treated for the precious commodity they were. All along, he had been right.

Now the funeral would be another memory.

When Sam arrived at the church – on time, a rare achievement – he didn't dare join in on the procession with Will's close friends and family. He hung back by an arthritic tree that parted the church path from the graveyard. Phil carried the oak coffin, even thinner than the last time Sam saw him. With sharp noses, thick eyebrows, and wild hair, the rest of the pallbearers were Will's cousins and uncles. The ladies of the family followed and outwardly showed their distress as if they compensated for their bearing partners. Margaret was the only one with a dry face. Eyes wide, mouth pursed, she reminded Sam of the shock Rose had endured after his grandfather passed. The poor woman; grief still riddled her.

After a few minutes, Sam slipped through the doors and was directed by Eddie, the funeral director (as red and sweaty as ever) to a pew at the back. The bearers settled the coffin onto its stand with a creak. The group took their rightful places on the front pews. The organ music – a rather tone-deaf performance of 'Amazing Grace' – ended abruptly. In the front pew, Marge turned in her seat and glared at Sam. He went to wave, but she rose to her feet and strode up the aisle.

Not here, Sam thought. *Not here on his day*.

Sam was surprised to see her offer him a hand.

'What are you doing, sitting back here?' she hissed. She

pulled him from the pew and stormed him down the aisle. All the Reeves squeezed themselves up on the front bench, and Margaret sat Sam between herself and Phil. Phil squeezed Sam's hand with his signature wink and smile. A fresh-faced bishop sprung up to the altar.

'You join us here today to mourn the death of William Reeves.' Her tone a tad cheerful, she corrected to a sombre one and continued. 'But most importantly, to celebrate a life well lived. Born on February 1, 1980, to parents Margaret and Phil at the height of a blizzard, Will's birth set the standard for the rest of his life: always early but always welcome. The loving boyfriend of Sam, Will was also a grandson, cousin, friend, and colleague, and he was loved by all. A gifted man, wise beyond his years . . .'

Sam's tears rolled. His stomach writhed with bittersweet happiness. He hadn't thought he'd be mentioned – in fact, he had planned to slink away at the end of the service, no more than an imprint, unseen by all there. Instead, Sam sat between Margaret and Phil, and he couldn't take his eyes off of them. Their heads were bowed to read the order of service. Sam had spent so much of his adulthood longing for a complete family, and he'd had one all along, right underneath his own nose, if only he hadn't been so bitter to not accept it.

'Margaret and Phil have given me a poem which reminds them very much of Will.' The bishop rearranged the papers on her altar and began to read.

> 'I riptide, I surge,
> Never sit long enough,
> For fathomless depths of mystery
> await,
> We must lose ourselves to be found,

Bermuda sunsets fill the horizon,
Every view has you in it,
You were my moon,
And I will always pull to you.'

Sam lost himself in thoughts of Will, the rugged face perfectly asymmetrical, his double blink, the way his laugh was a silent wheeze. He'd have those memories forever, and when he departed this life too and crossed into the ombrederi, they'd be eternal.

When the funeral ended and the procession milled outside, Marge hung back, and Sam decided to as well. She withdrew a cigarette from her handbag, lit it with cumbersome hands, and took a drag.

'Didn't know you smoked,' Sam said.

'From fourteen until I was pregnant with Will. Didn't want him to set out on the wrong foot. Now he's not here. Some sort of rite of passage in and out of motherhood.'

'You're still a mother,' Sam said.

'Collecting flowers, pruning a grave. It's gardening now.'

'It's remembering him, and that's good.'

'Look at you, being the sentimental type. What changed?'

'Will.'

Margaret tutted in disbelief.

'And I regret it, not being sentimental,' Sam continued. 'After we got together, he spoke about you and Phil all the time. "Wait until you meet my mum, you'll love her, her pasties – best in the southwest, that's a guarantee." He adored you both. I liked you before I even met you.'

'A fairy tale if there ever was one,' Marge muttered.

Sam tapped the church wall with his heel. The end of Margaret's cigarette burned to a slug of ash, but she didn't notice. Her eyes wavered all over Sam's face and never blinked.

'I'm an addict, Margaret,' Sam said. 'Self-destruction, it's in my DNA. Flay me and you'll see it tattooed all over my organs. It was easier and less painful if I destroyed something good before I could believe it'd last.'

'Four years. Four years of a relationship, three weeks of him being dead . . .'

Clearly she thought it was too little, too late. Sam rubbed the carrot-shaped scar on his arm.

'I just want you to understand,' Sam said. 'Through all the shit I put him through, he never stopped believing in me. That's the man he was. A testament to how you raised him. That's why you'll never stop being a mother. You can't. You were too good at it.'

Margaret's lips wrapped tighter around the filter of her cigarette. The sliver of ash fell to the ground. She stood rigidly, a mountain unmoving, yes, but one less imposing.

'I don't think I can do the wake,' Sam said. 'That's a lot of people. But could I come over tonight?'

Marge flicked her cigarette to the ground, stomped it out with her heel, wrapped her arm around Sam's, and walked him toward the graveyard.

Phil opened their front door that evening. Bleary-eyed and with a ruffled comb-over, Sam must have disturbed one of his post-dinner naps. His face split with joy, and he beckoned Sam into the kitchen. The kettle boiled when Marge came through from the hall. She saw Sam, wrapped the drapes of her cardigan around herself, and joined them at the table.

'I didn't even ask how Trish is doing,' she said. She pushed the empty fruit bowl to the side. 'I was so preoccupied. What's the latest?'

'Brain activity is through the roof,' Sam said. 'She'll wake up. Just a matter of when.'

Phil handed out tea and biscuits and sat down between them.

'But I said, and I always have,' Marge said after a sip of tea, 'those mines, all those tunnels underground, all the equipment that was abandoned down there when it closed. Well, an explosion was going to happen sooner or later.'

'Poor Trish, though. What are the chances of getting caught up in it all?' Phil said. He rubbed his bad hip. 'Always happens to good people, too.'

'Seems to be that way,' Sam said. He reached for his satchel, took the shoebox out, and laid it on the table. 'Brought you this. Thought you might want to have a look through.'

He opened the box, took out the wad of photos, and put them at the centre of the table. Margaret spotted Will's face amongst them. She dragged her chair closer to Phil's. Sam did the same, and all three sat at one side of the table to pore over the photos. Infectious laughter ensued; many photos were accompanied by a story. Sam pointed at a collection of photos taken on Bodmin Moor. They were of Will, and as if they were pages of a flip-book, a blip grew larger in the background of each photo as Margaret trawled through them.

'See that there, coming up over the hill? That's only a bull,' he said.

'Never,' Marge squeaked.

'We didn't know it was breeding season. There were three bulls in this pasture. This one bolted straight for us. Never ran so fast in my life. Will lost a welly.'

'So that's why he wanted a new pair that Christmas!' Phil

chuckled.

'Yeah, and afterward we bolted over the fence and straight into a pen of geese. Oh, how they bite! Talk about jumping from the frying pan into the fire!'

Will's parents laughed. Marge delved into a stack of Polaroids from a Halloween two years ago, where their son's attempt at a raunchy pumpkin had left him resembling a deflated carrot.

'With those skinny legs of his!' Phil laughed.

Sam excused himself for the toilet. As he walked along the hallway, he looked back at Margaret's and Phil's faces lit up over the pieces of Will they'd never known. Sam smiled; he hadn't done that in their house for a long time.

Sam didn't go to the toilet. He went to Will's bedroom. The police tape was long since removed. The broken furniture was gone, the carpet taken up altogether, a new window installed. He feared the Reeves had thrown Will's possessions away, but the largest wall was decorated with school photos and university degrees and childhood drawings. A celebration of his life. Beyond the smell of fresh paint, the chorus of birds outside the open window, and the dry heat from the radiator, was frequency energy. An imprint signature. Sam closed his eyes to the ombrederi.

There was laughter, Will's memories of baking in the downstairs kitchen with Marge, Phil teaching him to drive, lightning in Lanhydrock.

He hadn't forgotten the ones he'd left behind.

91

RAIN AND LIGHTNING lashed at the train windows. After multiple delays, Sam was relieved to finally head to Plymouth. He was Trish's next of kin – her only option – so visits to Derriford were paramount. He got the rush hour train from St Austell, complete with a bus replacement service from Bodmin Parkway to Saltash. By the time the 4:49 Great Western arrived in Plymouth, he had been kneed in the thigh by one of seven excitable pensioner shoppers and the automatic toilet door had sprung open on him midpiss. *I need a semi-decent car.* He passed a few chain pubs and bars in the taxi to the hospital. Teeth clenched, fists tight, he pushed himself back into his seat. He craved a bitter, a lager shandy – even the fumes from a shot of Pernod. His resolve was absolute. He fondled the scar on his arm for the remainder of the journey.

Derriford's intensive care unit swam into view. A cluster of white tower blocks and tall chimneys, it was a building Wonka would create whimsical treats from and not a ward where Trish lingered in the balance of physical life and death.

Trish had been transferred to a private room painted

duck-egg blue, with a window that caught the brunt of the storm. Her skin was Rorschach-ed with bruises. Synced up to multiple machines, wires and tubes pierced her skin; Sam pretended she was using a gadget in a Network cavern instead. He kissed her on the forehead. The heat her body gave off was incredible. Static pinched at Sam's skin; frequency energy was rife within her. It leeched outward, and tendrils of light flooded the room. Sam closed his eyes and engaged with the ombrederi.

Trish and Shauna paddled in the sea at the height of summer. A look of complete desperation on Michael's face in HMP Dartmoor's visitation room.

Sam came back to the physical. Above Trish's bed was Abidemi. She swayed from the noose bound to her neck, her body rotten and back flayed. Maggots wriggled from her eye sockets, and vomit and blood oozed from her crooked smile. Fire erupted all over the imprint's projection. Sam sprung back from his chair and gripped the window blind for support. The fire blew out, and Abidemi was whole: a hopeful smile, eyes of joy. No noose. She had died younger than Sam thought: a young woman of no more than fourteen. A change had occurred in him the past month. He was a little less bitter and a little more optimistic. She wanted Sam to know that she was too: forever his guiding imprint.

In a swath of light, she receded into Trish's body. Her face glinted. Sam looked closer – tears pooled above her cheeks and meandered to the end of her round chin.

The monitors bleeped.

Article: 62

Whilst we stress the importance of developing and maintaining stable relations with imprints, specifically guides*, the Network urges that all communication is strictly work-related and that the periodicity of interactions is kept minimal. Once detatched from their original bodies, imprints can be volatile in nature, and so it is in a witness' best interests to ensure that no emotional connections develop between themselves and imprints. The Network strictly prohibits the contact of deceased loved ones.

*Guides are the only grade of imprint cleared for work with a receptor or terminal.

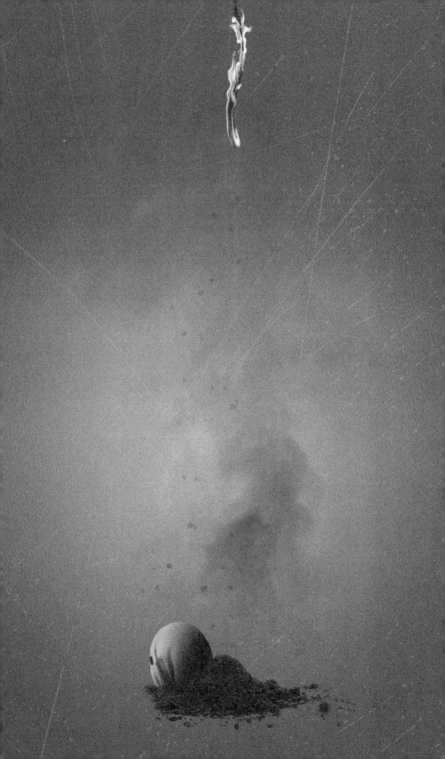

PART THIRTEEN

BODY OF
THE CRIME

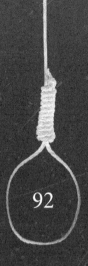

92

RASHA TOWERS over her younger self.

It is just as she remembers the seventh night of her haunting to be. The moonlight splices the contents of her room into ghostly shapes. Her former self hugs her bedsheets tightly and shivers in the presence of a gywandras. Except, the transformation isn't yet complete.

The gywandras pincer erupts from her stomach and punctures her younger self. Younger self – it had been just sixteen days, and yet so much has changed.

The only thing that hasn't: remembering Syria.

The acrid smoke swarms across rabid fires, and singed flesh smothers her nostrils. Helicopter rotors beat as quickly and as loudly as her thumping heart.

That is it. Rasha is the gywandras.

She knows what is next.

The ombrederi whispers in her head, 'Kill Shauna.'

93

HAYA WAS HOLDING Rasha tight when she awoke from her nightmare.

It had become a regular occurrence since that night in Pendeen. Rasha couldn't tell Haya anything, so she lay there in her mother's arms, the warmth of her breath on the back of her neck a small comfort in such troubled times. She lied to herself, convinced that the ombrederi was far too complex for Haya to fathom, or that the concept of the dasfurvya may scare her. In reality, Rasha didn't tell her because she'd only just got her mother back.

She didn't want Haya to know she'd killed Shauna Teagues.

As Haya sorted out her school stuff, Rasha showered and thought over Sam's words. It had been the second day of his stay with the Abadis. He'd tried to quell Rasha's worries and justified her actions because they were written – that Shauna's death, no matter how tragic, was necessary.

'There are actions,' he had said. 'And then there are reasons for them. You did it for the greater good. If you were truly a horrible person, you would sleep easy.'

Before Rasha left for school, Haya handed her a note. That was their routine now. Rasha unfurled the scrap of copy paper to examine the word she read every day in various degrees of legibility.

Unconditionally.

She surveyed her mother's handwriting, amazed at how far Haya had come in language and in life.

'Nice,' Rasha said in Levantine with rare glee. 'Consistent lowercases. Just mind how you join the t's.'

Rasha hugged Haya.

'Haya improves because of your dedication,' Sam had said before he'd left. 'She's doing it for you, you know.'

Rasha pocketed her mother's note, as she did every day. Just like the note, her mother would never be far. Whilst she kept it on her person, Rasha could remind herself of what good she could accomplish.

94

IT WASN'T the same now that Cridland had taken an early retirement.

In his place was a chirpy, fresh-faced graduate by the name of Mr Roskelley. He was young enough to play cool with the boys in Rasha's class whilst most of the girls seemed to swoon over his golden hair and bright blue eyes.

He didn't bother Rasha. Despite Cridland's absence, she named herself a failure.

Cridland's case never made it to court on rule of 'corpus delicti,' as the local newspaper put it. Haya told her it meant the confession alone was not enough. Because Cridland had confessed midfit in front of class that often sung about Joel, his confession was deemed unreliable. Cridland banked on the judicial faux pas and never confessed when in better health. There was a silver lining, however: whether spooked by Joel or embarrassed by what he had done, Cridland gave in his notice and never set foot in Gorenn Comprehensive again.

Her efforts seemed to have appeased Joel, for she never saw the imprint. She hoped that he'd found peace and left for the ombrederi. The small victories would have to do.

In her usual spot on the back bench, Rasha sat and pulled out her homework for Mr Roskelley to look over. Two seats over, Fred joined the class late and awkwardly emptied supplies from his rucksack onto the bench with his only good hand. The other was still kept bandaged.

He sat down, pulled a notepad toward himself, and quickly scrawled a design to fit their next brief: a puzzle box. He'd clearly not gotten around to his homework. Rasha watched on as the lead in his pencil snapped. He unzipped his pencil case with a struggle and rummaged around for a sharpener. His attempt to sharpen the pencil, with the sharpener wedged between his elbow and the desk, was feeble at best. Rasha couldn't bear it. She reached across the table, snatched up the pencil and sharpener, wrung them a few times, and handed them back. She gathered a new piece of drafting paper and continued with her work, ignoring how Fred's gaze lingered on her a moment too long before he turned to his render.

95

'YOU REALLY don't have to come,' Trish called from the back of the converted van. 'I don't want to trigger any memories.'

'After everything, it's the least I can do,' Rasha persisted. She shivered in the cold. 'Please.'

Trish nodded, and Rasha jumped into the front of the cab where Sam was sat. He kick-started the engine and pulled away from the caravan park. They were only meant to say hello as they passed through. Rasha had only seen Trish once since she'd woken from her coma six months ago. She knew that the duo kept her at an arm's length. They were still processing the events in Pendeen. It only made Rasha keener to make amends. The thought of prison was far from enticing, but she reminded herself, *Trish protected me in the ombrederi. She's in a wheelchair because of me.*

Trish was in the back, the wheels of her chair strapped to the van floor. She reached out as far as she could. Rasha offered her hand, and Trish squeezed it.

As Sam drove on to Dartmoor, Trish filled Rasha in on her rehabilitation. Despite weekly physio appointments, she'd reached the extent of her recovery and would never regain the use of her legs. Rasha thought it strange how nonplussed Trish was about the situation. After a little talk, Trish reclined in her wheelchair and went silent, eyes closed. Rasha hoped they'd talk about their time in the ombrederi; she wanted to know where she stood after killing Shauna. That being said, Rasha doubted Trish slept when her eyes were closed, which Sam confirmed when he whispered, 'She spends more time in the ombrederi than she does with the living.'

Rasha hoped that Trish had found Shauna in the ombrederi, at the very least.

Sam told her how he had become Trish's full-time carer. The council had found them a ground floor flat in Camelford – in a unit of pensioners, no less – which meant that Sam could give up his slew of part-time kitchen work. He was the healthiest Rasha had ever seen him; his frame had filled out, and colour had returned to his cheeks.

HMP Dartmoor was even more dismal in person than the photos that Rasha had Googled. Weather-stained and dull, she thought it was the best place for those inside. Everyone but Michael, at least.

Michael, the innocent man found guilty of Rasha's crimes.

Sam dared not enter the building.

'It's too much like the Refinery, if I'm honest,' he muttered.

Sam pushed Trish's wheelchair to the entrance, then skulked back to the van. Rasha pushed Trish inside through the various sign-in procedures and into the visitation room. They were given the far left table closest to the vending machines, and Michael was already seated when they crossed over. Rasha's stomach writhed. She kept her composure and pulled the brakes on the wheelchair. Michael cast his eyes over Trish and her wilted legs. He buried his face in his hands.

'Oh, Trish!' he exclaimed.

Trish looked at Rasha and nodded. Rasha half smiled and crossed to the vending machines. She pretended to make a decision between fizzy and chocolate. She folded her arms and clamped her eyes shut, then focused on her breathing, trying to stop the anxiety that flooded through her chest.

Rasha suspected that she'd always be haunted – if not by the dead, then by the acts she'd committed in the ombrederi.

She caught fragments of Trish and Michael's conversation behind her.

'When Sam told me,' Michael whined. 'When he rang me, I didn't think it was as bad as . . .'

'I'm still here,' Trish said. 'Which these days is a blessing, all things considered.'

'I didn't think you'd come back, not after last time.'

'I've been doing a lot of thinking,' Trish said. Rasha saw their table reflected in the glass of the vending machine. Michael reached across the table, his hands in Trish's. 'I believe you. I know you didn't do it. I know you're innocent.'

Michael sobbed loudly, head in Trish's hands, and muttered over and over, 'Thank you, thank you.'

'You have to be good now, you hear me? You have to try. Don't give them any reason to extend your sentence.'

There was no evidence to be procured that the courts could use to free Michael from his sentence, but that didn't seem to matter as much as someone believing in him.

Rasha couldn't bear his sobs any longer. She approached a guard for directions to the nearest toilet. The visitation room's doors were unlocked for her, and she scarpered to the woman's bathroom and bolted into a cubicle, where she remained until the visitation was up.

No matter her reasons for taking Shauna's life, Rasha knew she should be in prison, in Michael's place. If she'd learnt anything at all in the ombrederi, people made themselves monsters, and she was the making of herself.

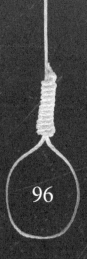

96

DEEP IN THE OMBREDERI, Rasha skulks across Pendeen's hillside. Shauna's death cycles through her mind. She tries to focus on the task at hand.

Ahead of her is a four-man tent with its door unzipped, and a Tilley lamp shines a triangular path to Rasha's feet. Inside, James sits alongside his wife, Jane, and their three daughters. Jane nods at him and ushers the girls outside. Rasha and James are alone.

A wind rustles through the tent. James looks around.

'The happiest memory I have. It's amusing, really, how we wish our time away for holidays and adventure, always looking forward to the next best thing, rarely content. But then your world turns upside down, and what you crave most are the mundane and ordinary moments.'

'That's true happiness,' Rasha says. 'That's when you know you've had a good life.'

'I can look into you,' James says. 'I see so much darkness.'

'It finds me. It defines my reality.'

'Interesting. I used to think we defined our own reality. We choose what we believe. It's ignorance, really, and we're

437

all pretending. In this world, you have to do it just to remain sane.'

Beyond the tent flaps, James's girls laugh and skip in a game of tag.

'What you're doing isn't sane,' Rasha says. 'It's unhealthy to hold on.'

'I know that, yet I cannot let go. Do you understand?'

Rasha nods. Even though she tells herself that she's moved on, really she holds on to the past tighter than most. Perhaps, in the end, that was what truly made someone a gywandras: so tied to the past that they never left it behind.

'You're a gywandras?' Rasha asks.

'You and me both, it seems.'

'Then you created me.'

'That is not how a gywandras comes to be. Trish told me what you said to her the day after you were occupied.'

Rasha thinks a moment. So much had been said.

'I thought the gywandras was me . . .' She pauses, eyes wide. James looks at her, and it was clear they had the same thought. 'I will create myself.'

'Fitting, don't you think?'

The tent flaps flutter, inviting Rasha forward. She looks out – at herself, in her bed at night in caravan forty-five. The night of her occupation.

'And if I don't,' Rasha says. 'If I don't right now, it'll never happen.'

'There's a phrase slung around here an awful lot, but it does what it says on the tin: it is written.'

Perhaps that was why she didn't sense the gywandras was her for definite. She'd no longer recognise herself, after everything she had done, and everything she was yet to do.

Rasha steps out of the tent and into caravan forty-five.

97

THE BONFIRE of the memorial service cast Pendeen's cliff tops into an amber hue so that the spectators looked like insects preserved in resin. The heat sliced through the summer evening chill and took Rasha's breath away. She, Trish, Sam, and perhaps the entirety of the town were nestled on the cliff tops, the repaired lighthouse a candlewick on the horizon. One by one, the vicar of the local church, a nervous town counsellor, and a suited Conservative MP – campaign badge and all – gave speeches in turn. The story that officials pulled together was frighteningly far removed from the truth and fed many political agendas: Europeans without ID had been trafficked to Cornwall and were caught up in an environmental disaster by mere coincidence. As James had told Rasha in the ombrederi, 'Reality is what you choose to believe.'

A volunteer offered them mulled cider. The three kindly refused. Sam watched the embers that were spat out by amber tongues. She knew he thirsted for narcotics, but his sobriety conquered. He admitted that he often thought of Will. It was how he healed, he said, and it was how he had found strength.

To think of her family, with Haya's notes on her person, helped Rasha in her dark moments as well. Trish sat in her wheelchair, her lap blanketed, and looked into space as if numb to the fury of the bonfire. Rasha wondered whether a little of her still remained in the ombrederi – if she hadn't fully returned to her body.

Between both women, Sam took their hands in his. They looked amongst one another with harmonious expressions. That night was their last together before the adults moved north. Trish and Sam had picked up a lead – multiple, in fact – of the Hive in Greater Manchester, an organisation whose activity threatened the ombrederi-physical balance. After much internet research, they'd discovered it was funded by the Edward Penrose Trust. They had asked Rasha to go, and she really wanted to, but she and Haya had been granted full citizenship that month, and Cornwall had become home – 'Thanks to you guys!' she'd made sure to add. So that winter was their last together. Rasha would finish her GCSEs, go to college, and work part-time at the computer repair shop, a pound above minimum wage.

Yes, for she'd learnt that being present was the best she could do. That night was theirs, and when she woke in the morning she would face that day, and the next day, and the next. They were moments, after all – many joyous, some tough. She had Haya's daily notes, and Sam, and Trish.

Rasha had her tomorrow, and a chance to do better, and be kinder, and love furiously.

She'd make herself a home.

THE STORY CONTINUES IN

THE IMPRINT QUINTET: II

THE
CONVERGENCE

EXCLUSIVE PREVIEW

EXCERPT SUBJECT TO CHANGE

THE FIRST SNOW slurry of the Winter of 1891 brought a visitor to Pendeen.

Construction of the lighthouse was arduous; before the workers could lay its foundations, the headland had to be dug out and flattened. During that process, they discovered a grave, and all work ground to a halt. Hushed gossip ripped through the labourers and traveled to the barmaids and shopkeepers in an afternoon. They reported that the site manager, Arthur Carkeek of Redruth, had discontinued work until further notice. Strangely, Carkeek's first telegraph was not to the local Parish nor the undertaker. Instead, he sent one urgently to Manchester for an investor named Edward Penrose.

Two days later, Penrose arrived by horse and carriage, one bitter day in November when the air chewed people's ears. Despite the site being closed, it was busier than ever: the workers wanted to understand the importance of the grave — after all, without work, they would not be getting paid. Many wives and mothers perfectly timed the delivery of pasties and sandwiches, only to ogle at the northerner with the Cornish surname.

Edward Penrose moved like a man who had struggled in the north. He'd ambled precariously down the carriage steps and walked with a stoop, leaning heavily on a cane. Penrose's wild, black eyebrows were permanently arched as if bracing torrential rain, and his skin was as leathery as the suitcase he carried in his left hand. As he walked by, children bickered about how large his mansion might be; the men bet on whether he was in the trade of cotton or steel; the women pondered over how many mistresses he might have. Regardless, Edward hobbled past them as if they weren't there.

Carkeek greeted Penrose at the graveside. They shared a short, stiff handshake and muttered stern words that the locals couldn't catch over the howling winds.

Despite the snow and sleet turning the mud to sludge, Penrose handed his briefcase to Carkeek and descended a rickety ladder eight feet down into the grave. Carkeek handed the suitcase over.

Most didn't see what Penrose did next. He turned his back to the locals and hunched over the grave. All accounts later agreed that he had opened his briefcase and withdrew some contraptions from within. Beyond that, stories quickly turned to fiction. Some reported that the skeletons were no larger than that of children. Some say the remains were charred. One older woman — who had certainly been too frail to be out on the cliffs in November — claimed there was a local legend about a Cornish maiden and a Nigerian pirate who were tortured by British invaders three hundred years prior. The Britons discarded their burnt bodies for local villagers to deal with. Perturbed by a boy with a complexion so dark, the locals decided that they would bury him on the headland, away from their graveyard. They buried the girl with him so he wouldn't be alone.

By the time the wizened lady finished recounting her fable, Penrose had completed his work and ascended the ladder. He stiffly thanked Carkeek and made his way back to the rental carriage. Ten feet from his transport, he stopped and turned. Rumour has it he looked straight at the baker's daughter, who had brought a basket of loaves to the workers. She was a troubled girl locked up inside for most of her life. Penrose and the baker's girl stared at each other like there were decades of bad blood between them. After a minute, Penrose carried on, hobbled into the carriage, and drove away. The locals say Penrose never returned to Cornwall — for a good reason. When the undertakers arrived that night, something was missing from the grave.

Edward Penrose had taken the skull of the smallest child.

Save to Goodreads and pre-order now:

WITNESSING GLOSSARY

Anascribe
Computing software for witnesses.

Anchor Points
Frequency-rich geological areas that attract imprints (formerly ley lines).

Amplifier
A gadget that condenses frequency energy and allows the user to withdraw their imprint from their body.

Archivists
Hollow imprints used to store memories in place of hard drives or clouds.

Coercer
A witness that can assume control of imprints that are not their own.

Dasfurvya
An imprint that has occupied a body that is not their own, for a long period of time. (Cornish for reborn).

Dielectric Band
A copper headpiece that dampens the frequency signal, for young or inexperienced witnesses. Echo A grade one imprint that cannot sustain an existence beyond the body.

EMP (Electromagnetic Pulse)
A device that can emit frequency energy to attract, detain, or destroy an imprint. Can also be paired with beacons to measure frequency energy.

Engagement
The process in which a witness connects to an imprint or the ombrederi.

Expulsion
A measure of punishment whereby an imprint is cast into the frequency; an infinite death.

Extraction
A process whereby an occupying imprint is removed from another's body (formerly possession).

Frequency
The energy source that connects witnesses with imprints and the ombrederi.

Guide
An autonomous, free-thinking imprint also known as a grade three imprint.

Gywandras
An imprint that can travel time freely between its past and present self. (Cornish for traveller)

Imprint
The residue of the human soul and consciousness after death.
- Grade One: No autonomy, wilt after death of the body (also known as echoes)
- Grade Two: Little autonomy, able to absorb memories (also known as shells)
- Grade Three: Full autonomy, able to think independently (also known as guides)

Imprint Activity Network (I.A.N.; The Network)
A covert group of witnesses intent on protecting the living from the dead.

Long Walk
A trial where new witnesses walk amongst guides, in order to assess one's mental capacity before enrolling in the Network.

Occupation
The action in which an imprint occupies another's body (formerly possession).

Ombrederi
An astral plane or after life, in the image of the physical world. (Cornish for re!ection)

Pennser
An architect of the ombrederi. (Cornish for architect)

Projection
An imprint's chosen appearance, not always tied to their physical body.

Receptor
A device that enhances a witnesses connection to the ombrederi and weaker imprints.

Seer
A witness with telepathic abilities.

Shell
An imprint with little autonomy or will, also known as a grade two imprint.

Sonar
A process in which a witness can use memories from grade two imprints to recreate a moment in time.

Spectrophotometer
A machine used to measure the signal of an imprint.

Taken
A term for an imprint whose body has been occupied by das-furvya.

Terminal
A device used to help weak imprints communicate with witnesses. A mechanised version of an Ouija board.

Transcendence
The act in which a person or imprint becomes a gywandras.

Transfer
A machine to capture and destroy imprints.

Withdraw
The ability in which a witness can withdraw their imprint from their body (formerly astral projection).

Witness
A person with a heightened sensitivity to frequency energy, who can interact with imprints and enter the ombrederi.

Acknowledgments

It takes a village to raise a child, but an army to make a book. I would not be where I am today, writing this acknowledgement for my debut, without the effort and support of some fantastic people.

Firstly, a massive thank you to my beta readers: Holly Challinor, Deborah Challinor, Beth Kitto, Jackie Burnard, Adam Hammond, Katherine Mycock, Emily Palmieri, Charlotte Johnson and Natalie Lukes. Without you, the story wouldn't be what it is today.

A very special mention to Dr Ken George, author of Gerlyver Kernewek Kemmyn, for keeping the Cornish language alive.

To Nathan Beasley Joseph, for a kick ass author photo and your wisdom concerning tin mining.

And finally to you, the reader, who took a chance on me, an indie author, and this book, an unconventional ghost story.

I witness you all.

ABOUT THE AUTHOR

Cornishman Terry Kitto was never found without reading a book or penning one of his own. He took his creativity to Film School at Falmouth University, earning a First Class with Honours and later a PGDiP with the University of Salford.

Noteworthy accolades include Best Writer at the New York 100 Hour Film Contest with Can You See Me? and making the BBC's Writers Room 2016 shortlist with Brunswick House. The Frequency is Terry's debut novel.

www.terrykitto.com

instagram.com/terrykittoauthor

tiktok.com/@terrykittoauthor

facebook.com/terrykittoauthor

twitter.com/terry_kitto